The Dutchman 2: Test of Character

Written and Illustrated by Susan Eddy

The Dutchman 2: Test of Character

Written and Illustrated by Susan Eddy

Robin Van der Kellen

Adam Hudson

Chapter One: The Arrival

"Robin! Robin Van der Kellen!"

Robin waved his top hat to alert the carriage and dodged through a row of carriages, halting just before being run over, and then leaped onto the footboard of a brougham. He yelled into the open window, "We must pick up Marie. Round that way driver. Back around and up to the curb. See the woman in green?"

Through the window of the carriage, a butler called out. "Sir, you haven't changed a bit. Still the dare devil. Get inside!"

He held on outside, standing on the footboard. "Driver, the woman in green. Circle round and pick her up."

"You left with one wife and return with another. She looks nothing like your first." The butler reached through the carriage window, getting a grip on Robin's arm. "And you have a child!"

The carriage stopped where Marie was waiting with their luggage, baby on her hip, and a young man standing close beside her. Robin hopped off and took Marie and the baby into his arms. "Quickly into the carriage. It's dangerous to stand here in this traffic. Adam, get in right after Marie."

Porters began loading their bags and three chests onto the boot of the carriage, and up top.

The door to the carriage was opened by the butler and he held out a hand.

"Up you go, darling. Hand the baby to Simon," Robin told her.

"Oh my. It's insane here." Marie looked up at the man who now held out two hands. Marie handed her baby up and then took Robin's hand to climb up inside. Adam clambered in after her. Luggage was loaded onto the boot of the carriage, piled up and strapped on.

Robin was soon in as well and called to the driver in Dutch, "Move on!"

Inside the carriage as it jostled and bumped into traffic, the butler shouted over the noise of wheels on cobbles. "The house is in chaos, sir. Thank God you are home. We must rush you there immediately."

"What has happened?" Robin said in Dutch.

"They must give you all the details there. All I know is they arrested Tess's husband last night. He's in jail and we don't know what to do," Simon, the butler, declared. "Don't even know if you can help, sir."

"There's everything I can do. My law license has only just expired. I can take care of that quickly. I must stop home, change suits, and hurry to the courthouse immediately," Robin said in Dutch. Then he changed to English as he checked the time on his pocket watch. "Adam, my all black suit and best white shirt, white neck tie. I need them readied immediately. I must go to the courthouse as soon as possible. Marie, Tess's husband, the banker, has just been arrested. I must run to his aid."

"Can you help him, Robin? Can you still practice law in this country?" Marie asked.

"My license expired five years without a case. I must petition the court for an extension. With any luck, the judge will be one of my professors. I must hurry before the court closes for the weekend and he's stuck there for days."

Fields of tulips, blooming in purples, reds, and yellows lined both sides of the drive into the estate of Robin's childhood. Marie looked out the carriage window in amazement. Beyond the tulips were green hay fields and windmills. Adam blurted out, "Didn't realize Robin stepped out of a fairy tale."

"And we just stepped into one," Marie told him.

The estate unfolded before them, a beautiful stone mansion fronted by a pond and moat, three bridges, many fountains and gardens.

The carriage pulled in around to the main entrance beneath the archway and into a barrel-vaulted tunnel beneath the entry porch of the mansion and carriage house beyond.

Six staff members lined up to take the luggage. A valet named Noud met them.

Robin stepped down from the carriage and reached up for the baby. Then he held one hand up for Marie.

Marie climbed down.

Adam climbed down after her, glancing about to look after their luggage. He began sorting each piece as his was set beside the carriage. Then he pointed them out to the staff as Robin's, Marie's, or his own.

Robin held Marie's hand as he carried his baby daughter up the stairs and into his childhood home.

"We have prepared your old room, Sir Robin. And beside that your wife's room," Simon said. "Is this your valet? He will have a room upstairs with us. Does he speak any Dutch or French?"

"No. Only English. He'll be fine. Where is Lynn?"

"Resting sir. She sends her regrets. I am happy to make you feel at home here, sir. Welcome back," Simon said. "Your sisters are awaiting you."

"I'll need a carriage ready. I'm going straight to the courthouse after I change clothes." Robin passed the baby to Marie.

Adam carried Robin's briefcase along, glancing about at salons as they passed them, possibly a music room.

Two women came toward them in the hall, both dressed in fancy gowns. One was blonde and Marie's age. One was brunette and closer to Robin's age.

Mila called out in Dutch, "Robin, you're home."

"Oh, Robin have you heard about Wout?" Tess begged, hugging Robin about the neck. Tess was the blonde.

He hugged her and kissed her cheek. "Yes. I'll go straight to the courthouse and see to him. I'm only here for a moment. This is Marie and baby Frida. They speak English and French. Well, Marie does anyway." Robin switched to English. "Marie, my sisters Tess and Mila. Sisters, this is also Adam Hudson, my valet. Please look after them. I must hurry. Adam."

"Good day, ladies." Adam chased after Robin toward the stairs.

Tess and Mila each took a turn holding the baby. "What a delight this little angel is. How she looks like Robin. Welcome Marie. What can we do to make you feel at home?"

"I'm thrilled to meet both of you," Marie said. "So sorry this is happening."

"Lynn's nanny will care for Frida as much as you wish," Mila said. "Lynn is very much with child. She had to go lay down. With all the excitement about Wout, she is resting. Wout is Tess's husband."

"I can't wait for Frida to meet her cousins. You both have children?" Marie asked.

"I have three, two girls and a boy. Tess has one, a boy," Mila said.

"I'm so worried about Wout I could get sick," Tess admitted. "I'm so sorry this is happening."

Marie held hands with both sisters. "Nothing to be sorry for. Robin will help, I'm certain. I'm still so dizzy from being on the boat."

"You're certain you are not with child again? Come and sit on the terrace. We'll get you something to eat."

"Oh, I'm certain I'm not." Marie went with them.

Tess carried Frida.

"You're not sleeping with your husband yet? You will be. I'm surprised he's being patient," Mila said.

"Really?" Marie asked. "He's very patient."

"That's a first," Mila said. "Robin and his appetite for everything."

May 10, 1840, Canterbury, Connecticut

"They're not up yet?" Adam questioned, entering the kitchen, looking about.

June pointed at the ceiling. "I'm thinking his wound has healed. They're newlyweds again."

"I saw them kissing in the library yesterday. It was…" Adam blushed.

"It was what? I haven't had a man in years. I could use all the details you've got," June said.

Marta burst out laughing.

Adam turned red and shook his head. "It was passionate. I was so envious."

"Yeah, but of whom?"

June 12, 1840. Canterbury, Connecticut.

June rushed to Marie and took her by the arm. "Come in out of the heat, Marie. Let's get some cold water into you."

"I'm all right. I've just been so queasy lately. I don't know why."

June held her up and steadied her as they walked through the row of tomatoes on one side and carrots on the other. "Marie, how long have you been married?"

"Four months now."

June smiled.

"You don't think?" Marie urged.

"Darling, you're with child."

Marie slipped from her arm and passed out in the aisle.

"Robin! Robin, get over here now, dammit!" June called out.

From near the barn, Robin had to run and vault over the stone wall into the garden. He hurried up the row to see June getting Marie into a seated position.

Robin skidded down before them. "What has happened? Marie, darling?"

"Let's get her into the house," June said.

"Marie, get your arm about my neck." Robin scooped her knees up and then took her arm around his neck. "Hold onto me. You okay, love?"

"I'm okay. I was just dizzy."

June followed them as Robin carried her toward the house. "I'll get the gate and the door. Hold on, Robin. You have her?"

"I've got her." Robin let June past into the front.

June got the kitchen door open, and Robin carried Marie through to the parlor and laid her on the sofa. He let out a breath and stooped beside her. "What is it, darling?"

"I'll get her some water." June left the room.

Marie looked up at Robin.

He smoothed her hair back from her eyes. "You're not feeling well?"

"Robin..." Marie sat up and wrapped her arms around his neck again, hugging him tight.

"What is it, darling?" Robin asked softly, embracing her.

June paused in the doorway and then backed up, pulling Marta away with her.

"Robin, I think we are going to have a baby."

Into the jail and down the row of cells, Robin waited, with papers in his hands.

"Says he won't see you. Doesn't want another court appointed moron." The guard shrugged. "His words."

"He'll see this one. I'm appointed by a *higher authority*," Robin called out loudly.

"What authority?" the prisoner called from down the row of cells.

"Your wife's. My sister, Tess," Robin called.

"Robin Van der Kellen?" the prisoner called.

"He'll see me now," Robin said. "And keep an eye out for a runner from the courthouse. He's to be released into my custody tonight."

"You got to be joking." The guard unlocked the gate to the cell block. "It's almost five o'clock on a Friday for Christ's sake."

Robin entered quickly and made his way down to a cell where a young man had two hands held out through the bars. Robin stopped before him, briefcase and top hat in hands. "Wouter Van de Berg?"

"Robin Van der Kellen? You look exactly like the painting in Robert's house." The young man still reached out to him. "Are you still a lawyer? Is there anything you can do to get me out of here? I can't spend another night in this filth."

Robin took his hand firmly into more than a handshake, and something of a lifeline. "The judge is sending an order over here shortly. You'll be released into my custody while I solve this problem of yours. You'll tell me everything, but not in here."

"Oh, thank God." Wout gripped onto Robin with both hands. "Did you just arrive from America?"

"Just arrived. Haven't yet eaten or bathed."

"That makes two of us. Is Tess all right?" Wout asked.

"Worried sick about you, but better now that I'm here."

"You don't actually think I did it, do you?" Wout asked.

"We're all innocent in here," the next prisoner said to much laughter.

"Shut up. Mind your own interests," Robin scolded.

"She said you were cocky," Wout said. "Good. That's just what I need. As long as you're as smart as she says you are."

"Tess? I'm far more intelligent than she says I am." Robin stood back and examined his brother-in-law through the bars. "So, my father married her off to a bank robber, I see. I'm getting the last laugh more every day."

In just a matter of an hour, Robin was escorting his brother-in-law up the stairs and to the street where Robin had a magnificent Phaeton waiting, pulled by a Friesian horse and minded by a young courthouse porter. Robin slipped him a few more coins and then assisted Wout up into the carriage. "You're injured?"

"Roughed me up in the arrest," Wout said.

"They what? I can't wait to hear the story in entirety. This is enraging." Robin climbed up to the driver's seat. "Lopen up. Not only am I going to get you off because I will prove you didn't commit bank fraud, but I'll also get you off for not being arrested proper."

"Climb up there with you but my rib hurts too much. I wouldn't suppose you'd be willing to stop at a pub, would you?"

Robin looked back at him. "Actually, oh my God, I'm starving. You know a good pub between here and Robert's place?"

"Oh God yes. You got any guilders on you? They took all of mine."

"They robbed you as well?" Robin turned in his seat to look back at him. "Don't tell me anymore until I've eaten. I'm just crazy enough to go back there and kick some ass."

Wout laughed in the back of the open top Phaeton. "I knew it! If only half the stories of the famous Robin Van der Kellen were true, I knew it."

Robin assisted Wout up the entry stairs of his family estate, quite late that night, after dark, and into the parlor where young sister Tess ran into her husband's arms.

Robin looked over her to Marie and the rest of his family in the room.

Tess moved to hug the stuffings out of Robin then, even making him cry out. He lifted her off the floor in his embrace. "Tess, I will take care of everything. I'll begin on the case at first light."

"Thank God you're home, Robin." Tess returned to her husband's arms.

Robin entered the room and handed his hat and briefcase to the butler. Robert came to him first, to shake hands. "Welcome home, brother. We were about to hire an attorney for Wout, Mr. Landsberg."

"Sem Landsberg? You don't want him. You want me. He barely passed half of his courses," Robin said.

"And you haven't tried a case in Dutch courts in over five years. Laws change," Robert said.

"So, I'll brush up." Robin shrugged. "In all my cases in America I only lost two, and those because I was defending the guilty. You want me."

"Of course, we want Robin," Tess declared.

Mila moved into Robin's arms and hugged him hard about the neck. "I just love your wife and daughter. Love them. Thank you for bringing them to us."

"Thank you for welcoming them home. And where is Adam? You have to look after Adam. He doesn't speak any Dutch. Where is he?" Robin asked.

"He's with the maids in the kitchen. I will fetch him at once, sir," Simon, the butler, said. "Creating quite a stir in there, no pun intended. And can't even speak Dutch."

Robin took that in with raised eyebrows. "Ha? Waat?"

Wout managed to sit down, holding his ribs.

"Robert, they beat him when they arrested him. Be a doctor, would you?" Robin indicated Wout.

Robert went to him quickly. "You are injured?"

"Cup of tea, Robin?" Robert's wife Lynn reached for his hands and kissed his cheek.

Robin returned the kiss to the very pregnant wife of his brother. "Something stronger would be in order."

"This is an alcohol-free house," Robert spoke up, starting to examine Wout.

"You mean I traveled six weeks at sea, and you can't even offer me a drink?" Robin said. "Thank God Wout and I cleaned out that tavern on the way here, then. That's ridiculous Robert. You used to drink Father under the table. You should at least have a brandy and some wine on hand to offer your guests."

"When have you ever been a guest here, Robin?" Robert said. "There's no alcohol in this house."

"There will be tomorrow," Robin said.

"Brothers, it is very late for an age-old argument," Lynn scolded.

Robin kissed her cheek again and moved past her to take Marie into his arms. "How are you, darling? Settled in?"

"Yes. My room is wonderful. Right next to yours," Marie said.

"We put you in your childhood room, Robin," Lynn said. "Redecorated, of course."

Adam entered the room then, relieved to see Robin had arrived. He slipped in behind Robin and laid a hand on his shoulder. "I prepped your room for you, for the night."

"Meaning?"

"You know very well what I mean," Adam said under his breath.

"Oh. Thank you. Thank you." Robin turned and patted Adam on the arm. "I would like Adam to dine with us, if you don't mind. He doesn't speak any Dutch or French."

"He's your valet, isn't he? He can dine with the help in the kitchen," Robert said.

"We're not like that in Connecticut. We're friends with those who work in our household," Robin said. "Adam will dine with us."

"I'm fine in the kitchen. They are very kind to me there. They just can't talk to me," Adam said. "Lots of pretty girls working here."

Robin looked at him and then looked again at him.

"Robin, you always have a way of upending the household every time you come home," Robert said. "Next you'll be throwing a ball and inviting us in our own home."

"I might," Robin said. "I have reason to celebrate being home again. I've brought my two girls home to see where I grew up. And my friend Adam. And I'm grateful to be here in time to help Wout."

"Robin, may I take Wout home to rest?" Tess asked.

"No, you may not. He must stay with me, I'm afraid. He's under my custody until the trial date. I need to prepare his defense. I need to find out what happened," Robin said. "When I'm in the courthouse tomorrow, he must stay right here in the family house. He's not to even go outside."

"You took him into a tavern," Tess reminded. "He smells of brandy."

"He's a bit drunk, and I'm armed," Robin explained. "I'm his protector as well as his guard. If anything happens to him, I go to jail. Do you understand?"

"I won't go anywhere," Wout insisted. "I'll tell you everything I know and stay right where you put me, good sir, the honorable barrister Van der Kellen. Should have seen the looks on the guard's faces when the judge came down himself to free me to your custody. Knew him well, did you?"

"He was my mentor all through law school," Robin said. "And he'll be my mentor through your case, my brother."

They climbed the stairs, rounded corners, walked hallways. Both Robin's and Marie's rooms were elegant, with fireplaces back-to-back on the wall they shared, and with large canopy beds. Marie's room had a crib for the baby. The nanny took the baby to get her ready for the night. The valet, Noud, busied himself in Robin's room to see that Robin had everything he needed, saying, "Your valet has already brought many of your things down to laundry and he's ironed the rest. Though, where he is now, I have no idea. With the maids I expect. Where did you find him?"

"What?" Robin froze in the doorway to his room. "There is nothing in here I recognize. Where did it all go?"

"Remodeled soon after you left for America. However, there is a trunk with many of your boyhood possessions inside. We moved it from the attic to the foot of your bed. Can I draw you a bath, sir?" Noud said.

"Please. I've been on a boat for six weeks. I'm sure the entire family would thank you to put me in a proper bath." Robin left his room for Marie's.

Marie saw that the baby's diaper was being changed. She went to Robin.

"Don't worry. I am sleeping with you tonight and every night, unless you throw me out. This is just a formality," Robin said.

A young boy appeared in the doorway. Two young boys appeared.

Robin said in Dutch. "You must be Robert's sons."

"You must be Uncle Robin," the older one said.

Robin went to the hallway with them.

"I am Lucas. This is Ruben," the eight-year-old said. "You're the cavalry officer, aren't you?" the boy asked. "You just arrived from America."

"I served for six years in the Dutch cavalry. I am also a barrister like your grandfather was," Robin said. "You are not in bed?"

"We stayed up to meet you, sir," Ruben the six-year-old, said. "Do you have to fight wild Indians in America?"

"No. I have met some Indians. I like them very much. I'll tell you about them sometime. Now run along to bed before you get me in more trouble."

The nanny put Frida to bed in the crib. A maid was tending to Marie.

Robin entered Marie's room. "You're tired. Of course, darling." Robin kissed Marie. "Get some rest. I'm going to have a bath next door."

Robin had just sunk down into his hot bath, drenched his hair, and reclined back in the steamy water when the door behind him from his bedroom opened. "I thought you were resting, darling."

"I brought you a drink, sweetheart."

Robin jolted, splashing water out onto the floor.

Adam burst out laughing and set a brandy snifter down on the silver tray at his bath side. "Heard you had returned. What do you need, Robin?"

"Jesus, you scared the shit out of me. I was expecting Marie," Robin said. "Do you want a room across the hall? Or are you okay upstairs with the butler and maids?"

"Upstairs with them is fine. They gave me a small room of my own. Don't worry about me." Adam paced with his back to Robin in the darkness of a room lit by only an oil lamp. "I remember how to eat in the kitchen."

"Strangely, I am not worried about you, even if you can't speak with them. But you come to me if you have any issues or needs. All right? Get over here and sit down on the stool," Robin said. "I won't be talking over my shoulder and you've become the subject of some discussion."

"What?" Adam held a hand over his eyes until he was seated down on the stool, sitting too low to see into Robin's bathing tub. Then he looked at him. Robin's wet hair was flat to his head and dripped onto his shiny wet shoulders.

"What's this I hear about you spending time with the maids?"

Adam laughed. "What? I just got here. Subject of gossip already? I still do my job, right?"

"Of course you do. But get some rest or whatever it is you need right now. I do apologize about the formality of this place, and especially the stations. I'd still rather you dined with us. I told them I want you there with me."

Adam revealed a second glass of brandy in his hand and took a sip. "Apparently you get whatever you want in this house."

Adam Hudson awoke in a small bed, in a small room, on the third floor of a Dutch manor. The sounds of maids and the butler moving about awoke him. Then the knock on his door. "Coming." Adam swung back the covers and hurried to the door. He opened it to find Robert Van der Kellen's valet Noud, in the hall.

The older man offered him boot blacking and shaving cream.

"Thank you." Adam accepted them.

"Bedankt," Noud said.

"Bedankt?" Adam asked.

The man nodded and repeated it.

"Bedankt," Adam said. "Give me five minutes." He held up a hand with five fingers spread.

Noud nodded and left.

Adam closed the door and quickly got himself dressed and shaved. He glanced out the window at the Dutch dawn over the red tulip fields as far as he could see into the mists.

Again, came the knock at the door.

Adam finished buttoning his jacket, stepped into short black boots, rubbed some blacking on the toes, and hurried out the door.

The valet Noud led him to the back servant's stairs and down. Down, down what seemed like several floors, out into the kitchen hall below the house. Inside the kitchen, while cooks and bakers hurried about, pretty maids were seated at a table having breakfast. The valet pulled out a chair, indicating it was for Adam, and then he sat beside him pouring coffee for them both.

Adam sat with a smile for the young maids surrounding him. Some of them giggled and said, "Goedemorgen," to him. He said the same back to them. A black haired one across from him caught his eye. She was fair skinned with pink lips. Her fingers were delicate on her teacup.

The plate before him was quickly filled with eggs, pastries, cheese, sausages, breads and jams. He happily placed his napkin over his lap and sampled everything on his plate, trying hard to eat neatly while being observed by so many.

After they had eaten, Noud led Adam up two flights of stairs and into a hallway he finally recognized. He was brought to Robin's room. The valet knocked on it. No response. Knocked again.

"He's with his wife," Adam said in English. He opened the door and entered.

"Do you need anything?" the valet said in Dutch.

Adam shook his head and began to lay out Robin's suit for the day. The door was closed gently, and it was safe to assume the valet went down to Robert's room to tend to him. Adam opened the wardrobe and selected out one of the black suits and white shirts that he had ironed tediously yesterday while Robin was away. Underclothing, stockings, silk ascot were all arranged on the bed. Then he checked on the bath and found pails of hot water ready for him to pour into the grand porcelain tub. Towels were folded ready and even a pot of hot coffee was waiting on a silver tray with cups and cream. Biscuits were there as well.

Adam went to the hall and knocked on Marie's door. It was opened by Robin in his wool robe.

"Ready for you, sir," Adam said.

"Shhh." Robin joined him in the hall and closed the door silently. He followed Adam to his own room. "Frida is sleeping so Marie is finally getting some rest. Wow. Well done, Adam." He surveyed the suit on the bed.

"I want to get you new white shirts. I can't get these any whiter after the salt air at sea. You won't have time to go to the tailor. What do you think if I get fitted in your stead?" Adam followed him into the room.

"You think you are the same size?" Robin looked at him.

"I am. I tried on your shirt before," Adam said. "You know, to see if I had all the wrinkles out."

"Oh. Well. Take money from my purse, all you need." Robin started untying his robe. "You have no idea how much you need. Take one hundred Dutch guilders. Get whatever you like and get for the house a case of good red wine and a case of that brand of brandy." He pointed at the bottle on his night table. "Don't let me leave today without my pistol."

"You won't. You don't need to wash your hair and there's coffee in there for your bath."

"You want a cup?" Robin handed him the robe and entered the vanity room in his undershorts.

"Already flying on several, sir."

Robin sat down at the breakfast table beside his older brother, across from Lynn, beside Marie. Tess and Wout were next at the table and then Robert's two boys.

"What are your plans today, Robin?" Robert asked.

"Going to Wout's bank first, to go over every record I can find. Lunch with Judge Janssen. He will be tutoring me in recent changes to Dutch law and advising me on this case. And very likely I will be called into court today or tomorrow for my request of postponement to the court date. I need time to prepare the defense. They are sure to grant it." Robin unfolded a napkin onto his lap, over crisply ironed black trousers.

"You can ride into town with me then," Robert said.

"You're not going into the hospital, are you?" Robin looked at him.

"I have two surgeries today."

Robin met eyes with Lynn across the table. He mouthed a word to her. "Waat?"

She shook her head. "I'm fine Robin. This baby is not expected for another two weeks."

"Frida came two weeks early," Robin said. "You don't think you should stay home with your wife? Maybe you miscalculated."

"Are you also a surgeon, Robin? You're an expert at everything," Robert snapped. "I'm glad you are getting some local help on this case. You hardly practiced law at all before leaving for America. Your brother-in-law's life depends on this."

"I passed the exam with one of the highest scores they ever had. You don't think I remember Dutch law? What do you think American law is built on? The same French and English law ours was. I remember you were only 15th in your graduating class," Robin said. "I don't think I'm hungry. Can we get going?"

"I have not yet finished eating," Robert said. "And it was 15 out of 65."

Robin stood up, gave a kiss to his wife. "I'm taking one of your carriages then. I'll see you for supper, if I am not tied up in town. Wout, stay put."

"But I should help you with the bank records." Wout stood up.

"No. You would be seen as manipulating records. I'll get the exact charges against you, who brought them, and see the records for myself. I'll talk to you later tonight, Wout. Hide out here." Robin met Adam in the hallway where the briefcase with pistol was pushed into his hand, with a top hat. "Thank you, Adam."

"Be careful, Robin." Adam handed him a biscuit with sausage in it.

"At last, I've found a way of communicating." Adam set his hands on his hips.

The children's tutor, Eva de Goede, translated the English into Dutch for the butler Simon and valet Noud. "He is pleased to be able to communicate with you. He has need to go into town to a tailor's shop. He needs new shirts for Mr. Van der Kellen."

"Tailor's shop? Well, all right then. I suppose they can do it by measuring another shirt. Isn't he bringing one?"

Eva translated.

"I am the same size. The tailor will measure me," Adam said.

"What? Robin is not hardly the size of this adolescent boy valet. He will need room for expansion," Noud said.

After the translation, Adam laughed. "I know how he likes his shirts. They are not needed to expand. Trust me. He's not about to get old and fat on my watch."

She translated exactly.

Noud said to Simon. "Where did he get this little peacock? The nerve of him."

"Americans. Crude, aren't they? Ask him if Mr. Van der Kellen left him money for shirts and we will bring him."

Adam demonstrated the money in his pocketbook. "I also need to purchase wine and brandy while we are out."

Eva did the translation and told Adam, "There is to be no alcohol in this house."

"I have my orders. Does he expect me to disobey Mr. Van der Kellen?" Adam said firmly.

That prompted quite a discussion between the three of them in Dutch.

Adam just put away his pocketbook to the inside pocket of his jacket and donned his hat.

When they finished squabbling, Eva told him. "I am to accompany you for your translation. They are too busy. The children will have to miss out on an English lesson today then, yet another disruption caused by the younger Mr. Van der Kellen."

"Very well then. Let us complete my business."

"How much money did he give you?" Eva asked.

"100 guilders."

Her mouth fell open.

"They're not too busy, are they?" Adam said. "Let's go. We'll have more fun without them. I will buy you lunch."

"Judge Janssen, this is my great pleasure." Robin rose and reached across the table to shake hands with a man maybe ten years his elder.

"Robin Van der Kellen. I am pleased to see you back in country. I hear you have been in America, making headlines, apparently. Famous for getting shot catching bank robbers. How are you?" Janssen sat down across from him.

"I'm fine. Thank you so much for consenting to be a consultant on this case."

"Not that you'll need one. But I will lend a second set of eyes, if you wish. Is it true you were shot in America?" Janssen asked.

Robin's left hand went to his right shoulder. "I'm fine. It just bothers me with the weather, sometimes."

"Did you catch the fellow?"

"Killed him."

"Calvary experience did not go to waste on you," the judge said. "Mr. Van der Kellen, your brother-in-law is in very serious trouble. I have read the charges against him. What does he have to say about it?"

"It's a set up. Someone in his bank is the real criminal and set it up to make Van de Berg take the fall. I have the ledgers on me. I've got to say, even the handwriting does not look the same. Two of the managers were very suspicious of me. I'd like to dig into the background of these men. The secretaries would not really speak with me, not freely anyway. There is something going on in there," Robin said.

They paused as coffee was poured for them and the first of three courses of lunch was laid before them.

"What is your gut instinct?" Janssen asked.

"One or both of those managers set up their owner to take the fall. One of those secretaries knows something. I need to get her to tell me. I'll study these and be back there tomorrow," Robin said.

"Did we ever discuss the art of witness interrogation, without the witness knowing?" Janssen asked.

"Oh, you mean flirt with the girl?" Robin asked.

Janssen laughed. "That will probably work for you. Never worked for me. The trick is to get your answers without ever asking the question. Can you do that?"

"I've become an expert at omission," Robin said.

"Eliminate your brother in law's motive."

"Easy. He's wealthy as hell. Why would he cheat the books to bring home a bit more?" Robin said.

"42,000 guilders are just a bit more?"

"To Van de Berg, it is. His family owns half the banks in Brussels. He alone takes home over 200,000 a year," Robin explained. "And he's the eldest brother. He stands to inherit half of Belgium."

"Well. Then find out which of those managers needs money badly enough to steal it. Look at their bank accounts. Follow them home."

"Are you suggesting I must find the guilty party just to clear Wouter Van de Berg?" Robin asked.

"Suggesting? I'm flat out telling you to. It's a cut and dried case against him, save for some handwriting differences. He's bound for jail if you do not."

"Damn." Robin sat back and looked down at his meal.

"Eat something. Do you remember Niels De Vries? He graduated a year after you perhaps. Specialized in criminal law. Red hair."

"Yes. I remember him. Is he any good?"

"Terrible. He became a detective. Come by my office after and I'll give to you, his address. Put him to work digging into their financial situations." Janssen sampled his food. "This is delicious. Eat up, Robin. You are no good to your brother-in-law if you are not thinking clearly."

"Quite right." Robin picked up his spoon.

"And how is your personal life? Melissa sends her affections, of course." Janssen ate more. "We have two children now. They don't look like you."

"Glad to hear it. I have a wife and child. They're with me, staying at my brother's estate," Robin said.

"We shall expect you for dinner then, when you have time."

"That would be delightful, your honor. Thank you very much, for everything."

"Do not tell your client how grave the situation. Keep him out of sight, out of his banks. Who stands to take over the banks with him out of the way? There's a motive. Hire the detective. Dig deeply through those books. Match the handwriting. Interrogate those secretaries. That is your mission for now."

"The bank would go to Van de Berg's brother should anything happen to him. Suppose the manager expected to stay on and with a remote owner he could get away with anything," Robin said. "What law has he broken, whoever is the guilty party?"

"As you know, much of our financial law comes from the brief period of French occupation. It was the Dutch who pioneered stock exchange capitalism back in the 1600's. The French put a lid on speculation on VOC stock. The VOC did not heavily invest in steam power, something Germany and England especially, did. As such, our economy has been failing and dropping ever since 1830. The laws public limited company or naamloze vennootschap, a precedent set by English law, regarding the setting up of companies whose primary purpose was private profit rather than public good. It is this law Van de Bergis accused of breaking.

His is a private bank for profit. But he took public funds that were invested in his bank and reinvested it in steam power engines. The law says all profits must be returned to the public accounts. He kept them. Or so it appears."

"It seems to me that investing in steam engines is a guaranteed money maker. Seems very smart to invest in that," Robin said.

"Smarter than the Dutch government, yes. But where did the profits go? The city wants their profits back. And the mayor is up for reappointment. It is very important to him to claim he found this money."

"Oh my God. That's why Wout is in jail for this. Of course. I'll have to meet with the King's Commissioner. This is political," Robin realized.

"Don't you dare. This is too close to the Crown. It will be much better for a Judge to discuss this matter with the Commissioner of the province who appoints the mayor. And you have a tendency to be rather...how shall I put this? Proud."

"Do you not think humility has moderated my pride?" Robin asked.

"Have you acquired humility?"

Robin looked down at his coffee cup as the server refilled it. "In America, I had to fire all but one maid. I tended my own livestock. I chopped wood or would have frozen to death that winter. Lived off vegetable soup and bread. I nearly died of sickness if not for the maid and neighbors helping me. Pride is utterly gone when it is your maid keeping you alive, your neighbor's son tending your horses, you can't get hired by law firms you once trammeled in court, you don't know how you will get the hay fields harvested."

"I thought there was a seasoning about you that was not there as a student," the judge said. "Poverty taught you what war could not, it seems. I shall enjoy getting to know you, as a human and friend."

Chapter Two Frida

March 4, 1841. Canterbury, Connecticut.

"Robin, get out! The baby is coming. She can't do it if she's worried about you." Alice Poole turned Robin in the doorway, pushed him into the hall and shut the door.

Michael Poole took him by the arm. "Come this way. It can still be a while."

"I can't just listen to her scream," Robin declared.

They passed Marta in the hall, carrying an armful of Robin's clothing and a bowl full of his shaving supplies and hairbrush.

"Where is that going?" Robin asked.

Poole pulled him into the room at the far end of the hall, the room he and Alice were sharing.

"June told me to bring some of your things to the bedroom on the end," Marta explained.

"Waat?" Robin declared.

Adam escaped to the room across the hall and began to set up Robin's things in there.

Michael sat down by the fireplace in one of the wooden chairs. "Robin, that's the practice. You won't be getting any sleep in there with a baby crying every two hours. Bad enough down the hall."

Robin paced by the hearth and folded his arms. His brow was furrowed. His mouth pursed shut. He unbuttoned his suit coat and fanned himself with the sides. "I'm sweating like some sort of farm animal."

Marta emerged from the room across the hall, met eyes with Robin and went down the stairs.

Poole reached forward to a small table containing whiskey and two glasses. He poured two and picked up one of them. This he put into Robin's hand. "Drink this. And if you don't calm down, I'll have to take you outside to wait this out."

"I...."

"Shut up. The more drunk you are the easier this will go."

Robin finally nodded and drank a little bit.

Poole returned to his chair and picked up his glass. "Do you have names picked out?"

"Waat?"

"If you have a boy or girl? What will you name it?" Poole asked.

"Oh. Frida if a girl. Liam if a boy," Robin said. "Liam after my childhood friend."

Adam entered the room with the men, and lowered his chin as he watched Robin. He folded his arms. The three men looked at each other in their uselessness.

Marta returned, a tray of sandwiches in her hands. She met eyes with Robin again and set the tray down on the table with the whiskey.

"Robin, you haven't eaten anything all day. I was hoping you might have a little something."

Robin returned to pacing and downed his whiskey. Then he picked up the bottle.

The second evening in Robert's home, Robin escorted Adam Hudson into the dining room. Robin said in English, "Adam will be joining us for dinner tonight, as my guest." Then he pulled out the chair for Marie. Adam took the chair beside Marie. Robin sat beside his brother and set a very expensive bottle of brandy on the table.

Robert looked up at him. "I will not have that on my table."

"This is mother's table. Mother's porcelain. Dutch East India Company. Wonder where she got that from? Mother's crystal," Robin said. "And she enjoyed a nice glass of brandy on special occasions. She had no religious reasons for not drinking wine."

Simon began distributing crystal glasses to the table and serving a bottle of Bordeaux intended for the ladies.

"I've come a long way to see my family and I wish to celebrate," Robin said. "You don't have to drink it if you don't like it."

Robert silently watched his butler and the staff serving wine to the ladies and brandy to the gentlemen before dinner was even served. "Well, I see, it didn't take you long to turn everyone. Your special talent, little brother. You've put on quite a show here, arriving from America dressed in finery. Your wife is in Mother's jewelry. Expensive wine and brandy on the table. Clearly, you've come here to beg me for money."

"Robert!" Lynn blurted out.

"We know about father's debt. You sold the practice to settle it. Have you now lost the estate in Connecticut as well?" Robert asked. "Needing to be taken in with your wife and infant in tow? And your valet."

Robin picked up his brandy and made eye contact with each of his siblings. "To family. We can't choose who we get, now can we?"

Adam ducked his chin down and closed his eyes.

"Robert, why would you say such a thing?" Mila urged.

"Robert, he is your brother. My brothers died in the war," Jonas spoke up. "Robin is a decorated war hero."

"Yes, yes he is," Robert said. "I'm only surprised with his vanity that he isn't wearing medals all the time."

"I haven't had everything handed to me," Robin said. "I earned my medals by not dying when everyone around me did."

"Please." Marie spoke up. She put a hand on Robin's arm. "I have no family. My father ran out on us, and my mother died. I was so looking forward to meeting Robin's family."

"I'm so sorry, my love." Robin ducked his chin down.

"And we do welcome you, Marie," Mila urged. "There is tremendous love between Robert and Robin. They have just never been able to say so. They're so very different men. As eldest daughter in this family I urge everyone to calm down and enjoy this time together. Wout is in terrible trouble. Tess is worried. How much we could all use a distraction. I want to hear all about Boston and Connecticut. I want to hear how Robin met Marie. And I want to congratulate Robin and Marie on their lovely daughter Frida, named after our grandmother, I assume."

"Thank you, Mila." Robin looked to Robert.

Robert smoothed his hands down his suitcoat.

"And you don't mind if we imbibe, even if we cannot tempt you?" Robin questioned.

"With my compliments." Robert succumbed.

Dinner was finally served.

Robin kissed Marie on the temple. They tapped her wine glass to his brandy snifter and sat back quietly to take their meals.

"So, tell us Robin, how did you and Marie meet?" Tess asked conversationally.

Robin inhaled deeply. He looked at Marie.

Marie set down her fork beside her plate. She would say nothing except look at Robin and nod.

"Is it that difficult to say? I thought it a quick answer," Tess said. "I apologize."

"It is a long story and I do wish to share it. It will make you come to understand what an incredible woman Marie is and how I lost my heart to her." Robin paused to sip his brandy. "A little over a year ago I became terribly ill. The doctor came and said I was on the verge of consumption and that it was going around in every farm in the territory. Marie took care for me. It was only her and I in the house. My fever went so high that I did not know where I was. I could not speak English. She could not understand me. And she saved my life. In the days and weeks of my recovery, we fell in love. I...I had hired a man to work the estate then. Two days later I would have to kill him. I came in one day and found him attacking her. I threw him off. I walked him off at gunpoint. I later learned that he was part of a bank robbery ring that our father was working to prosecute, one by one. Since one of the robbers was in jail and about to die, he told our father where all the money was. The word was out. The remaining robbers knew our father had the money. Marie and I married, and I took her with me to New York to investigate the bank robberies." Robin wet his lips.

Marie took up the story. "In New York, Robin was attacked by one of the robbers. Got him arrested. And then the following day Robin was shot down in the street by another right in front of me. I handed Robin his pistol and he shot and killed the man."

The women gasped.

"Robin had to endure surgery and then a recovery in New York. There were still more of that bank robbery ring on the loose. We didn't know that until we got back home in Connecticut, and they came looking for the money. One of them kidnapped me on horseback," Marie said. "Robin rode after us. I never saw such a hero as my Robin. He leaped from the saddle and fought the man on the ground."

After several moments of silence, finally Wout asked, "What became of the bank money?"

"Father had it. Two banks were burned to the ground with the owners and all records inside. A third bank, the owner was in on the robberies and stole from his own bank and burnt it down. Also, French traders were robbed by these men. I found our father was investigating all of this. I was walking in his path. He wrote it all out in his journals. I brought one with me," Robin said. "All record of the rightful owners of the money burned in the fires."

"That's why I keep my records at home," Wout said. "Copies anyway. The money is yours."

"Good heavens." Robert blurted out. "That just figures."

"What? I just told you. Father and I both tried all we could to find who to give it back to," Robin said.

"How much money are we talking about?" Wout asked.

"Five hundred and three thousand US dollars. Fifty thousand in French francs. Bonds worth twenty thousand US," Robin said.

Wout's eyebrows rose. He smiled and sat back. "Jesus."

"You just walked into a fortune," Robert stammered.

"I wouldn't say I walked into it. I did get shot," Robin said. "Father walked into it."

"You're bloody rich," Mila blurted out.

"And father said I may share it with my sisters and brother as I see fit," Robin said. "I've come to bring your American inheritance."

"You are not to split it four ways. You got shot for it, Robin. You did all the investigation. Marie could have been killed," Tess spoke up. "I insist that you do not."

"As I see fit," Robin said. "When I produce Father's journal you can read it in his own hand. My intention was to share with the three of you, three portions."

"Is this money legal? Didn't you swear an oath to uphold the law? Shouldn't you give it back to the banks?" Robert asked.

Wout spoke up, "He tried to. He just said the bankers and records were all burned in the fires. What is he supposed to do? Put an advertisement in the New York papers asking who wants it? In America, banks issue their own currency backed up by their own vaults. These robbers emptied the vaults."

Some at the table laughed.

Wout laughed. "You're bloody rich, man. Well done."

"You did not get shot. You'd be dead by now," Robert insisted. "I've seen men shot."

"Not like I have. I've been shot three times. This is the first time it stuck. Very well then." Robin began undoing his ascot and made a show of unbuttoning his vest.

Mila and Tess burst out laughing.

"You're not actually going to..." Marie gasped.

"Looks like he is from here, I dare say." Jonas laughed.

Adam laughed and sat back.

Robin unbuttoned his shirt enough to pull it back off his upper right chest. He revealed the nasty scar he had and looked at Robert. "I do not speak of being shot and nearly dying lightly. I know war and combat and dying up closer than anyone here. Don't call me a liar, brother."

Lynn sat forward, across the table from Robin. "Well. I haven't seen that much of a man in months."

The women and Adam laughed.

"And that much of Robin since he was seventeen," Lynn added.

Marie turned and reached for Robin's buttons. "Let me help you, darling."

"I...I can dress myself now." Robin rebuttoned his shirt. "Now anyway."

"Do you suffer much from that wound?" Jonas asked.

"Some," Robin said.

"Marvelous distraction, Robin," Jonas said, grinning. "Was that a lucky bullet wound to your medical eyes, Robert?"

"Damn lucky one. Didn't hit anything vital and only inches away from certain death." Robert sat back in his chair at the head of the table. "Robin has more lives than a cat. Always has."

"Robin." Mila stepped up beside Robin at the balcony railing, looking out with him over the gardens in the moonlight. "Robin, do you wish me to talk to Marie?"

"What about?" Robin asked.

"When our baby was only a few months old, Jonas had the same look in his eyes. You've waited many months. You're ready to resume...intimacy with your wife. But she is afraid to. I know my brother. He likes to be with a woman. And now that I'm married with three children, I don't wonder why, or how for that matter."

Robin looked at her. "Really?"

"She's afraid it will hurt. She's afraid you don't want her anymore. She might be a little afraid of getting pregnant again. But while she's nursing, I heard it won't happen," Mila said. "Let me work on her. And you be patient."

Robin let out a long slow breath. "I look that frustrated?"

"Look like it's about to come out your ears." Mila turned to look out at the gardens again. "You are so in love with her. I'm happy for you. You never did say how you two met. Cleverly avoided that."

Robin also looked out at the gardens.

"Secret then?" Mila said.

"Yes."

"Need it be?"

"Yes. For now."

"What's important is that you love her. I'll talk to her tomorrow. You have to get through tonight. I'll tell the nanny to take Frida for you. After I talk to her in the morning, you must court her. Take her to see Amsterdam. Take her on a boat. Take her to dinner."

"I have to work on Wout's case. I have no time for that now."

"When you can, take her on a gondola in the canals. Fill her arms with tulips. Float with her beneath the bridges and windmills."

On the ship:

Robin sat on their bunk legs folded, elbows on his knees, and glass of whiskey in his hand, as the brandy had run out.

Marie held up the knitted little baby dress. "Robin. Did you hear me? Natasha made this. Isn't it wonderful?"

"Yes. I actually saw her making that yesterday. She said nothing about making it for Frida. How nice."

"It will look so adorable on her." Marie laid it over the baby's chest in the cradle. "You're still troubled about that privateer, aren't you?"

"Yes. I'm sorry. It's hard to put war behind me sometimes." Robin sipped his whiskey. "Marie, I've been such an ass lately. I would tell you something."

Marie went to sit with him and take his hand. "You've been a hero again. I don't know what you are talking about."

"About us, in this bed," Robin said. "Is it best that I stop pressuring you? And let you...let me know when you're ready? I can guarantee you that I will not try again the rest of this voyage. That will give you time to heal. We'll get to dry land. You'll enjoy nice hot bath and new clothes from Amsterdam. And then perhaps I can court you again."

Marie smiled warmly. "Court me again? You're my husband. I think if you keep trying, I might just surprise both of us."

Robin lowered his chin and smiled just a little. "May I ask one favor? Reject me a little sooner than you have been. It's getting harder to stop. Not that I won't stop. It's just that...."

Marie squeezed his hand in both of hers. "Robin darling, it is just that hard to resist you."

"I won't hurt you," Robin whispered. "Was I that bad the first time?"

Marie laughed. "No. Of course not."

Robin smiled.

One of the maids, a young brunette, observed Adam's hands as he walked by. She stopped him. She took his hand and held it for him to see that his finger was bleeding.

"Oh. I stuck myself with a needle. I guess it won't stop now," Adam said.

He followed her into the kitchen where she gave him a bowl of water and a towel. She went to retrieve some bandaging and scissors. Two other maids looked on. They began talking about him in Dutch.

"Put some alcohol on it. Hopefully that was a clean needle he did that with. Looks rather deep. He's got hands like he's never done any work besides ironing and folding."

"And can't say he's done much ironing. No burns at all on his left hand."

"I'm glad he can't speak the language. Look at those blue eyes on him. Have you ever seen prettier?"

"Has eye lashes like a girl."

Adam sunk his hand in the water.

Zoey brought the bandaging and cut the right length for him. She cut another piece to tie it with. She pulled out a chair at the table.

Another set a bottle of gin beside her.

Adam sat down in the chair and dried his hand in the towel.

Zoey reached for the gin and opened the cork.

"Wait a minute." Adam gestured for the bottle. He accepted it from her and gave it a sniff. "Oh. I get it." He poured some over his finger and the towel. Then he winced.

"Bet he makes the same face in the bedroom," one maid swooned.

"Not if he's doing it right. It's not supposed to hurt," the other said. They all laughed.

Zoey fixed the bandage about his finger.

"I do wonder what you are saying about me," Adam said in English. "How I'm a stupid American, in love with someone I can never have? How I'm just a valet? How stupid I am for trying to make alterations to clothing on my own?" He lowered his chin sadly. "I guess I'm not much of a tailor after all."

One of the other maids brought him a piece of cake on a plate with a spoon. She set it before him with a smile.

Another brought him a cup of tea.

Adam observed a slip of paper beneath the plate. He slid it out to find a note written in English.

My dear Mr. Hudson,

I wish very much that I could speak English with you. I do apologize that I cannot. You must be terribly lonely so far from home. I wish there was some way to make you feel welcome here. You're very brave for coming.

Sincerely,

Zoey

Adam looked up at the three women. "Ah, which...which one of you is Zoey?"

The two others pointed at the girl who had bandaged his finger.

Adam smiled at her then. "Zoey. Thank you. Bedankt."

Robin met the nanny in the hallway upstairs. "One moment. Please." He knocked a special knock of his and entered Marie's room. Marie was in her nightgown, tucking the baby into her crib beside the bed. "Marie, darling. I would like you to let the nanny watch Frida tonight in her room."

"What? No." Marie stood up.

"Marie, you haven't slept much in days. Neither have I. Frida liked the applesauce. The nanny can give her some of that during the night when she fusses," Robin said.

"Robin, no. I'm her mother," Marie said.

Robin touched her cheek and smoothed her long dark hair back. "I just want you to get some sleep tonight. Six hours. She can go six hours without nursing. She can have some applesauce. Right?"

Marie held onto Robin by his vest. "I'm so tired I can't think straight."

"Of course, you are. You're a wonderful mother. Just take some rest tonight. It's not a bad thing," Robin encouraged. "I'll let her in."

"Are you certain? It's not evil of me?" Marie asked.

"Totally acceptable to do this. All right? And we will get a nanny back home too, to help look after her." Robin kissed her forehead and then opened the bedroom door. Looking at the woman in the hall he said, "If you could just take Frida for the night, please? Marie hasn't slept in many nights because Frida wakes up so often."

"Of course, sir, and ma'am. That is perfectly normal for a baby of four months. I'll sit up with her tonight, if need be, in the rocking chair. Look at the darling little girl." She picked Frida up from the crib and brought her stuffed bunny with her. "Come knock on my door when you're ready to nurse her in the morning. Just come right in and get her."

"Thank you so much," Marie said.

The woman left with baby Frida. "So wonderful to have a baby girl in the house with all these boys."

Robin closed the door.

Marie wiped her eyes and walked to the bed. "I feel so guilty."

"All young mothers do. But you know you need some sleep to stay healthy for Frida. You're doing a wonderful job." Robin began unbuttoning his shirt and vest.

"You really did a number on Robert showing off that scar at dinner," Marie said. "And your beautiful chest in the process. Shocking nudity in the dining room. I think ten maids peeked through the kitchen door."

Robin smiled. "You can appreciate my flair in the courtroom then."

Marie laughed. "Shut up and get some sleep while we can."

"May I stay with you?" Robin asked.

"Well, I can't sleep without you," Marie said.

On Sunday, banks and courthouses were closed. Robin had spent all morning studying the bank books in the library of the estate. Maids kept bringing him tea. Finally, Adam followed them there. He found them giggling in the hall after serving tea and biscuits. He met eyes with Zoey and smiled at her. Adam entered the library then.

Robin looked up from the books. "Well, if it isn't the star of the kitchen."

Adam entered and approached the desk, his hands held together and close to his stomach. "Why do you say that?"

Robin set out a blank sheet of paper. "Sit." Then he passed forward the inkwell and a pen. "You've got three women giggling in the hallway."

"Oh, that's for you, no doubt." Adam sat facing him, across the desk. "Is there something I can do for you?"

"Yes. Write this down for me."

"In English?" Adam picked up the pen.

"Only you and I and Marie can read it fluently. Robert a little bit," Robin said. "I need you to take notes for me. I can't think and write at the same time." Robin stood up and rubbed at his eyes and his bangs. "I'm thinking too fast. Safe combination changed Tuesday at 5 PM. Three of them knew. Six PM, Wout left the bank. The ink was not dry yet. If the ledger was dabbed with cloth, the entry could be rewritten."

Adam wrote quickly. "This isn't very neat."

"That's fine if you can read it," Robin said. "The ink was a different color. Oh my God." Robin paced and held his hand to his forehead. "Where did the ink come from?"

Adam wrote that and looked up at him.

Robin paced toward the window. "I want you to go to town with me tomorrow to Wout's bank. You will sample ink jars from every desk. Keep record of where they came from. You draw out samples of each...and smudge them."

"Smudge them?"

Robin rushed forward to the desk and opened a ledger. He flipped pages to one in particular and opened it before Adam. "Like this. Make it look as if you are taking notes. Don't show it to anyone. Show it to me tomorrow night."

"All right," Adam said. "Your new shirts will be ready tomorrow."

"Get those too. I'm wearing Robert's. He's fat as a cow," Robin complained.

Adam burst out laughing.

Robin showed how he had the shirt doubled over on his sides beneath his vest.

"Do you wish me to stitch that in place temporarily?" Adam asked.

Robin shook his head. "No. I'll be giving them back to him soon as I get the new shirts. It is just hot in the court room with the extra layers. I'll survive."

Adam found that no one spoke English in the bank, and so he simply sat down at an empty desk and used the inkwell and pen to make some notes. He observed the secretaries moving about. One set some letters down on the desk where he sat. He rose and moved to the desk beside it. When he smudged the ink with his finger, the secretary brought him a cloth for the ink on his hand. "Bedankt," he told her with a smile and blush to his cheeks.

"Adam, that secretary likes you." Robin leaned over him.

"What?"

"You must flirt with her."

"She doesn't speak any English," Adam reminded.

"Befriend her. Wink. Smile. Stand near to her," Robin suggested. "Touch her hair a bit."

"What? Why?"

"She knows something. Maybe she'll tell you if not me," Robin suggested. "You're going to lunch with her."

"I'm what?" Adam panicked.

"I'm telling her you like her. Charm her, Adam. You're the right age for her. Here's five guilders. Take her to the cafe on the corner."

"What if she...you know?"

"In a cafe? I think your virginity is quite safe." Robin put his purse away. "There will be at least one person there to translate for you. Just ask if she is happy in her job. That's a good opener."

"Mr. De Vries, may I come in?"

"Please do, sir. To whom do I owe the pleasure?" The man stepped back from his door and watched the gentleman in top hat and fine suit enter, along with a younger man dressed rather plainly carrying a briefcase.

Robin removed his hat and extended his right hand. "I am Robin Van der Kellen, Barrister at law. This is my assistant, Mr. Hudson."

De Vries shook both their hands. "Van der Kellen? Yes. I remember you. You graduated law school a year ahead of me."

"That is correct, sir. I am told you are now a detective. I wish to hire you," Robin said.

"Well do have a seat. Both of you, of course." De Vries moved behind his desk and opened a ledger to begin taking some notes.

Robin held out a hand. "If you would, this is confidential. I prefer you didn't write anything more than absolutely necessary."

"Shall I write in code or memorize?"

"Yes," Robin replied.

De Vries sat back away from his ledger and pen. He nodded. "I know what case you are on. Wout Van de Berg is a relation of yours, is he not?"

"The little you know the better." Robin laid a small packet of money on the desk.

"Who am I to investigate?"

Robin told him the names of the two managers. "I need to know who is in debt, who is in trouble, who had motive to steal from the bank, and where is the money. Both of these men have been purchasing houses, carriages, women."

DeVries pushed the money back toward Robin. "Write your own fiction."

"See for yourself," Robin said. "The man makes 1000 guilders a year. He is not married. He just bought a 2,000-guilder town home in the New Market area. He has been dropping a lot of money in the red-light district. Has a fancy new Phaeton and new team of Belgians. I'm just asking you to find out if he had a wealthy uncle who just passed, a frigid female benefactor with a huge dowry, or perhaps he has forty-two thousand guilders from the bank tucked into his mattress, well thirty-two thousand after the purchases."

DeVries burst out laughing. He reached forward and began counting the money. "You had me with frigid female benefactor. How do you know he's been across the canal to the red side?"

"Parked that garish red Phaeton at the same livery every night this week, a fellow named Verstappen said. Tips him well, too, not as well as my brother-in-law Jonas did," Robin said.

"Your brother-in-law, not you, were questioning around that livery?" DeVries asked.

"I can't be seen down there," Robin said.

"No, you cannot. You stay out of there. Let me do my work without interference," DeVries said. "And this is only a down payment."

"Of course," Robin agreed.

"Get out of here and in the future, you just send Mr. Hudson for my reports."

"Mr. Hudson only speaks English."

DeVries switched to English, met eyes with Adam and pointed down the street. "Meet me at the tavern on the corner at 4:00 Friday. Give me a couple days to collect information."

"Yes, sir," Adam said.

"Very well then." Robin rose from his chair.

DeVries jingled the packet of coins. "And double this."

Adam and the young blonde secretary entered the cafe on the corner. A waitress who spoke English was assigned to their table, and she showed them to a small one in the windows. A quick look over this young couple revealed to her a secretary with ink-stained fingertips, and a young man not quite a gentleman as his suit was plain and overly mended. "Here you are sir and lady. The special today is fried herring served with a side of peas and potatoes."

"Naturally," Adam said. "I do not think I could stand yet another meal of herring today. What do you recommend for an American palette?"

"Ah...the sausage and potatoes are very popular, sir," she said.

"Would you ask Miss Van Voorden what she would like?" Adam asked.

The woman changed to Dutch to ask the secretary for her order. Then she changed to English to say, "The sausage and potatoes for you?"

"Yes, please."

"All right then. You brought her to dine with you, but you can't speak any Dutch? And she can't speak any English."

"Hoping you will tell her how much I appreciated her help today in the bank," Adam said with a smile and shine of his blue eyes at them both.

The two women spoke and giggled.

Adam did his best imitation of Robin, wet his lips and sat back with legs crossed, head tilted. He tried to exude confidence but probably only showed youth and nervousness.

Then the waitress laid a hand on Adam's shoulder. "She fancies you, sir. Watch yourself. Are you old enough to have an occupation?"

"I am a legal assistant," Adam said. "I assure you I have an occupation."

"Well, carry on then, young man. Mind it that you don't have a proper chaperone." The waitress laughed.

"You'll do just fine, love."

The secretary took out some papers from a desk, looking for a blank one as Adam stood over her shoulder. The top paper had indentations from writing on the page above it. She set that aside to look for a clean neat one.

Adam spotted a word in those indentations. He grabbed up the paper and dropped it into the waste basket beside the desk.

The secretary found clean paper and set these out for Adam. Then she got up and offered the chair to him.

Adam sat, picked up the quill.

Behind him the girl stroked a hand into his curls.

He smiled shyly, lowering his chin until the girl walked away. He made eye contact with her and then she was taken by another secretary to handle some banking customers. Surprisingly, his heart raced.

Adam kept watching her and the others as his left hand retrieved that paper from the basket. He slipped it into his notebook. Then he wrote some notes.

Miss Van Voorden has worked at the bank for two years. About a year ago, she expected a proposal from Mr. Mahoric, but he married a woman worth 500 guilders a year instead. She noticed he has new suits, new carriages. And yet he has not inherited from anyone that she is aware of. She took my hand when we left the café. I set it on my arm as I've seen others do. It was like lightning through my body. I could hardly walk calmly. All these pretty girls in Amsterdam. I don't think I ever noticed how easy it is to flirt with them.

"Robin, you need to see this." Adam drew Van der Kellen into Robert's office. Then he took out one of his own pieces of charcoal for drawing and unfolded that paper out on the desk. "You see that word, there, it says combination."

"So?"

Adam gently dragged the charcoal across the paper. As the dark color could not get into the indentations, whatever was written on the sheet above this one appeared as if in white lettering. "Someone with a heavy hand wrote in English. 'ames combination 22-14-11-80'. Right-handed person. Probably wrote with lead graphite to make impressions in the paper beneath it. Not that little secretary. But I'm guessing she knows who did. And get this, I could not find any lead graphite in the desks in the bank, and I sneaked a look into every drawer."

"Combination it looks like. What do you suppose is ames combination?" Robin said.

"I can't make out what came before it. I don't know. Is it Dutch? What about French?" Adam looked up at Robin. "Generally, if I continue to muck with these, they get worse."

"Leave it as is. We must show this to Wout." Robin patted Adam on the back. "Well done, Mr. Hudson. The way you are thinking is the way we are going to solve this case. Where did you learn that charcoal trick?"

Adam stood up, looking at the charcoal on his fingertips. "Seriously?"

"I'll take you on a tour." Robin held Marie's hand and walked her along the hallway until they turned a corner. "On the end there the master suite, Robert's room on the right and Lynn's on the left. Probably the two boys have rooms along this hall as well. Upstairs would be staff quarters. There is also a roof garden up there."

"Roof garden?" Marie questioned.

"Unless he changed it, part is open air and part is a green house. Flowers and herbs are grown there, for use in the house and kitchen," Robin explained. "I'll take you up there later. It's a nice place to sit and read on a winter's day. Let's go down and look about."

Marie held up her skirt a bit to walk down the grand central marble stairway. Her eyes were drawn above to the domed glass ceiling and to the massive paintings on the walls. "This place is so formal. Where did you play and have fun?"

"Outside, mostly. Had to behave ourselves indoors. I remember being yelled at for tossing a ball around in the hallway, with Mila."

Marie stopped, looking up at an oil painting obviously of Robin many years younger, in the dress uniform of a Cavalry officer. "Oh, I love this." He was holding his hat in his left arm and standing beside a fine horse.

Robin stood before it and waited. "Thought he'd move that to the basement. Or the barn."

"Robin, you look the same. You haven't aged any. You looked so arrogant standing beside that horse," Marie said. "Did you have to stand long for the portrait?"

"Not long. He had the uniform painted already, and the horse. He had come to see me, so he knew I was quite thin. He just had to paint in my head and hands. Mother commissioned it. There's Robert's. Mila and young Tess are together here." Robin pointed up at the paintings in the stairway.

They toured through the library, the music hall, the formal parlor, the family parlor, Robert's home office. They wandered down another stairway from the dining room to the kitchen below where a number of staff members were thoroughly startled. Cooks and maids scrambled to stop what they were doing and gather themselves up into a line between the doorway and the worktables.

Robin explained to them in Dutch, "Hello. This is my wife, Marie. I am just showing her around."

"Good afternoon, sir. Is there anything I can do for you?" The head chef hurried right up to him, almost as if to block entrance to the room.

"Not at all. Carry on," Robin said. "There is something. How many cooks and maids are there?"

"Three cooks, one baker, and myself, sir. The household has 12 maids."

Robin translated for Marie into English.

"That is a massive kitchen," Marie commented.

"Thank you so much." Robin led Marie out the other door of the kitchen, letting her get a look toward the laundry rooms. They climbed the stairs upwards.

Robin brought her to the balcony of the dining room, an outdoor seating area beneath the roof and overlooking the gardens below. An ornate wrought iron table beckoned them to sit at it, both facing the gardens.

"This is beautiful. What else is out there? Those buildings?" Marie pointed.

"Carriage barn and then several horse barns beyond that," Robin said. "It's too bad it's gone now but Robert and I had a fort right about down there. I suppose that's where I began playing soldier."

Marie smiled.

"And Robert began playing physician when I fell down."

Two maids hurried out to them. "Sir, is there anything we can get you?"

"Tea, if you would please," Robin said in Dutch.

The maids would not make eye contact with Robin, ducking their eyes away and giving him a curtsey before they left for the kitchen.

Alone together again, Marie remarked, "You must have thought me very informal when you got to Connecticut."

"Thought you were so gorgeous." Robin sat back. "I nearly shook to stand beside you. Still do."

Adam followed the pretty brunette maid into Robin's bedroom. He made the excuse of straightening things inside Robin's wardrobe.

Zoey set down a basket of linens and started to peel back the covers from the bed.

Adam went to the other side of the bed and pulled that side down.

They met eyes across the bed, and he smiled. He helped her unsheet the bed, remove pillowcases, and then place fresh clean ones on. Adam helped tuck in his side of the bed.

Zoey collected the used linens into her basket. She gestured for Adam to follow her.

Curiously, he followed her down the hall and up the stairs. They were now on the servant's level, where his room was at one end and hers at the other. She set the laundry basket down on the floor. She pulled him toward her room by the hand and the touch of young fingers intertwined was thrilling to him.

Inside her small room was her small bed, a dresser, and her mouth met his.

Adam was surprised. The girl in his arms was soft. Her kiss affected him emotionally and he found himself entranced. That corset was hard about her waist. But other than that, the girl was soft in his arms, and she smelled like lavender. Stunned, he pulled back.

Zoey looked up at him, her mouth wet from his.

When his blue eyes met her dark ones, she teared up.

Adam grabbed hands with her. "Oh no. Don't be sad. If only you knew. I think you are fantastic." Adam then stroked her cheek and a lock of her dark hair that had fallen loose from the bun at the back of her head. He gave her a smile that instantly set her at ease.

The girl smoothed her hands up his vest and shirt. And then she delved a hand into his stylish curly hair that came down to his collar but was about five inches long on the top.

She pressed into his arms again. "Oh, I just want to pull you down on this bed. You are so exotic and beautiful."

Adam kissed her again. And he withdrew his hips from hers. "Please I...Mr. Van der Kellen will kill me."

"Oh, you are worried about Mr. Van der Kellen. We must find a time when he is not expecting you. Don't you worry. I know what to do. Do you like me?" Zoey looked up at him.

Adam kissed the pretty girl again.

Chapter three: Pressures Mount

March 10, 1841 Canterbury, Connecticut.

Robin sat down at the kitchen table, beside Marie and leaned over to kiss her. "Good morning, darling." Then he wrapped his arms about the baby's basket on the table and pulled her up close to him.

"He lights up when he looks on her," June commented from behind the kitchen worktable.

Robin slid fingers in to touch tiny baby fingers.

Marie put her hand on Robin's back. "You finally got some sleep last night. Lucky man."

"Well, I can't do anything about feeding her, now can I?" Robin smiled. "When will she be able to see me?"

"Not for about two months," Alice said, from across the table. "But as you have the only male voice in the house, she knows you're her pa."

"That's right. In America I'm her pa. In the Netherlands I'll be her father," Robin said, without looking away from the baby. "What about Adam?"

"Adam's voice is higher than mine," June said. "It's good to see a man happy about having a daughter for a change." She brought Robin a cup of coffee and plate of biscuits and eggs.

"Thank you. I'm starving." Robin accepted his coffee first. "Why wouldn't I be delighted to have a daughter? What good are boys anyway? Or men for that matter?"

"Only good for one thing," Alice commented, making all the ladies laugh.

"Alice, I'm shocked." Robin looked at her. "Actually, I'm not so shocked."

"Making the money, of course," Alice said.

"I thought it was making love." Robin turned to kiss Marie again.

"When do the workmen get here?" Marie asked him.

"Ah. What day is this?" Robin looked to June.

That made them all laugh again.

"I've been out of it for a few days," Robin shrugged. "I wanted to get down the stairs so fast, I barely remembered to put on trousers this morning."

"Today is the tenth, Robin. And don't bother with trousers for our benefit," June said. "Your workmen don't come until the fifteenth."

After he laughed, Robin said, "The Mohegans are coming too. They're excellent workmen."

"With all those men to feed, we'll be needing that cow from the Lee's. Need that for milk for the baby too," June reminded. "I can make cheese finally."

"Yes. I'll go fetch him today," Robin said.

The women laughed.

"What?"

Marie combed through Robin's hair and said, "You'll never make a farmer, darling."

"Adam, are you all right?" June asked.

Adam was washing his face in a bowl in the back of the kitchen. "Yes. Sorry. Just tolerating the heat or trying to."

"That's not what I meant." June moved closer to him. "Marta likes you a bit. She's about your age. Have you no interest in her that way?"

"I beg you." Adam shook his head.

"No. I won't tell anyone. I just thought, it might be easier for you."

"Easier how?" Adam asked, toweling his face.

"If you were like everyone else and took a wife," June asked. "Or at least, made the appearance of it."

"How did marriage work out for you?" Adam walked out.

March 12, 1841. Canterbury, Connecticut.

Marta entered the master bedroom and stopped in the doorway.

Robin was lying on the bed with Marie and the baby. He was fully dressed and on top of the blankets. His back was to the doorway and his arm around Marie's waist.

Marie looked over and whispered, "It's okay. Come and take Frida."

Marta walked in quietly and rounded the bed, trying not to look but unable to avoid seeing Robin sleeping behind Marie .

Marie unwrapped Frida from the blanket. "Let him sleep."

"Yes, ma'am." Marta gently scooped up the baby into her arms. "I'll take her across the hall and get her changed."

Master of the household was beautiful, lying there sleeping, but a shocking sight when Marta realized that he'd been with Marie for the nursing. Perhaps things were different growing up overseas, but this was not to be seen by staff in this country and Marta hurried across the hall with the baby.

Marie went back to sleep with Robin's arm around her.

Later, when Robin woke up, he let Marie continue to sleep while he pulled on his suit jacket and went down to the kitchen.

"Good morning, Robin." June was cooking.

Marta was eating lunch at the table with Frida in her basket. She started to scramble to remove her plate.

"Stay. Relax." Robin cautioned her. "Good morning. Finish your meal." He leaned into the baby basket and kissed the baby's forehead.

Marta looked away from him, finishing her biscuit.

With Robin's eyes on the baby, he was oblivious to all else.

June brought over a plate of breakfast for Robin. "I can watch Frida for now. Why don't you go finish with the laundry?"

"Okay, sure." Marta took her plate and cup away and then disappeared down the hall.

"Thank you." Robin glanced up at June, picking up his fork.

"May I have a word with you, Robin?" June sat down across from him.

That made him sit back and look at her. "What is it?"

"Marta is still very young and impressionable," June said. "She had younger baby sisters, so she is excellent at tending to the baby. Grew up doing that."

"Am I in trouble for something? What did I do?" Robin asked quietly. "I never laid a hand on Marta."

"No. Of course not," June said. "I think we all realize I am older and...though not exactly married, I am far from a virgin. And I understand certain things."

"None of my business." Robin sat back further. The baby made a sound and he glanced into the basket but then back to June. "Just be blunt, June. I prefer it. What did I do wrong, so I won't do it?"

"You are supposed to be sleeping in the other bedroom as long as Marta has to go in there to tend to the baby," June said. "Nannies see a lot of things that maids typically do not. Marta is so upset..."

Robin's eyebrows rose. "Oh. I'm terribly sorry. I fell asleep."

"You are falling asleep all over the house. I understand. Your baby cries every two hours. We all hear her. I understand." June laughed. "But Marta can't even look at you."

Robin's chin lowered.

"Comforting your wife is admirable. But being in bed with her gives the impression you are pressuring her to resume relations."

Robin dropped his forehead into his hand.

"I know you're not. I know you don't want to miss out on any of the new father experiences. And you just fell asleep." June smiled warmly at him. "Robin, we all just want to support Marie and Frida as much as possible. We support you as well."

"I just fell asleep there. It won't happen again." Robin looked at June across the table. His cheeks had blushed.

"I didn't mean to embarrass you," June said. "It's your bed. It's your house. But it's best if you sleep in the other bedroom until Frida can sleep apart from Marie. Right now, she needs to nurse every couple hours. That won't go on forever."

"I do apologize."

"I am sorry, Robin. Just a while longer. We so appreciate that you let us take rooms upstairs this winter. It is us who are imposing on your privacy."

"What...What...How do I mend this with Marta?" Robin asked.

"Don't say anything. I'll let her know we had this talk and you'll be sleeping in the other room until we have another talk. All right?"

"Yes, June. And please just bluntly tell me these things going forward. Or tell her to tell Marie, if that is easier for her. Marie will yell at me." Robin let out a breath.

"Eat your breakfast before it gets cold," June told him.

"I couldn't possibly eat now. I've been so rude and ungentlemanly," Robin said sadly.

"No, you haven't. You've been a new father. That's all. Go ahead and eat, Robin. It's not as bad as I made it sound." June looked into the baby's basket. "She's overreacting. I'll talk to her. You'd think she walked in on you and Marie making the next baby."

Robin almost laughed and June laughed outright.

"It's just...I was raised to be a gentleman. I had a nanny myself. My parents always had separate rooms. I just wasn't thinking. I must apologize to Marta," Robin declared. "It never occurred to me that once we had a baby, we would not have the same bedroom together anymore."

"You can have whatever you want in your house. Only wealthy people can afford two bedrooms. Let me talk to her. You just have to sleep in the other room for a few months probably. Eat your breakfast. Watch your baby for a few moments." June stood up. "I'll just be down the hall."

"What? No! What do I do if she cries?" Robin looked up in a panic.

"Comfort her. If she smells like she filled her diaper, come and get me, unless you want to learn diapering the hard way," June said. "If you pick her up remember to support her head. Babies can't lift their own head yet when only a week old."

Robin nodded. "Do return soon. I'm so terrified at this moment."

Baby Frida

When June returned to the kitchen, Robin had the baby up in his arms, lying with her little head against his neck. She was still swaddled in her little blanket.

"Well...look at the happy baby," June said, ducking to see Frida's face. "You're learning."

Robin smiled. "She said to me she wanted her pa to hold her."

"Said all that, did she?" June grinned. "Marta, get in here."

Robin looked up in horror then.

Marta skulked in from the hallway to stand beside June. "I'm so sorry, Robin."

"Marta, I do apologize. It won't happen again."

"I'm so sorry. She shouldn't have told you," Marta said.

"Yes, she should. I have been falling asleep all over the house. It's a wonder I haven't fallen asleep in the barn yet. I have my room. I will sleep in my room from now on," Robin insisted. "You have been doing a wonderful job as nanny. June has been doing some excellent cooking. I fear I'm the only one not working two jobs here."

"You're working way more than two jobs," June said. "Landowner, stable hand, wood chopper, town lawyer, town judge, Indian agent, architect for your new wing, and now father. Marta, go check on Marie. See if she needs help getting dressed."

"I'll bring that basket of clothes up when I go."

Adam handed letters to Simon, the butler, and said in English, "Would you post these for Robin?"

Eva de Goede explained, "He has correspondence to post for Mr. Van der Kellen."

The butler took them and looked through the addresses. "I'll see that they get posted today."

Adam then walked outside to await Robin's carriage. Today it was the yellow Phaeton, a sporty flashy carriage with one Friesian pulling it.

"Get in. This is Friday," Robin said from driver's seat.

Adam climbed up into the seat with him. He tucked Robin's briefcase down at their feet. "How do I handle this? We don't even know yet what De Vries is going to tell me."

"Can you remember a lot? Must you take notes?" Robin asked.

"I can jot down very little and still be able to translate it later. It will be quite cryptic to anyone else, even if they do read English. That and my penmanship is messy when I write fast."

"He may have something. He may need more time. This is what we will find out. And while you are there, I should be able to get my new court date. I should have the postponement approved by five o clock this evening as it is Friday. Are you all right getting from the courthouse to that tavern on your own? I can draw you a map. It's only a few blocks," Robin said.

"Draw me a map and I'll manage. Enough folk do speak English in town. I can ask around if I get lost," Adam said.

Robin patted him on the forearm. "You're really adapting well here, to life in another country. I'll try to meet you for lunch, but I may be in court awaiting my case postponement."

"I'll manage fine. I did it before," Adam said. "I have the money you gave me. I'll watch De Vries's office for a while before I go in."

"Good."

"I used to be quite unseen in alleys of New York. I can do the same here," Adam said.

"I have no doubt."

Adam entered the café where he was to meet Robin for lunch, at one of several restaurants and taverns surrounding the courthouse and law firms.

A host spoke to him in Dutch.

"Excuse me, would you happen to speak English?" Adam asked, hat in hand.

The host indicated that he should wait there. He ducked back to speak to one of the waitresses. Then she came forward to the host's booth. "Good day, sir. Will you be needing a table for lunch?"

"Yes please. I should be joined by my employer as well." Adam followed her to a table near the windows.

"What does he look like? I'll be happy to send him your way," she said.

"He's very handsome. Black dotted ascot today. The only barrister in all of Amsterdam with the guts to wear anything but a plain white ascot," Adam said. "Looks to be about thirty in age."

"Well. He's not married, is he?" she teased.

"Maybe." Adam smiled.

"I'll watch for him. How handsome?"

"Beautiful."

She smiled and set the menu on Adam's table. "I don't have an English one. I can tell you what we have that's good though."

"Let me guess, herring?"

The girl escorted Robin to Adam's table. "Your description did not do him justice at all. Not at all."

Robin took a seat and looked up at her. "Pardon?"

Adam laughed. "The pea soup is excellent."

"Oh? Bring me that and bitterballen," Robin said. "On a plate of noodles."

"Yes, sir."

"No brandy?" Adam asked.

"No. Problems," Robin said. "They have chosen the prosecutor and he's a politically ambitious son of a bitch. I've got to head him off somehow. It just could not have been worse." Robin shook his head as he unfolded the napkin into his lap. And then he raised his head and his gaze became fixated.

Adam casually turned to look where Robin was looking. It was a blonde woman with a man just entering the restaurant.

Robin's eyes followed her across the room to a table where her gentleman pulled out the chair for her and the young lady sat down in a shimmering gown of poppy yellow and black velvet.

"You know her?" Adam said.

Robin broke off eye contact with the woman, and shook his head. "Looks like my wife. First wife."

"I'm sorry," Adam said.

"Chased her down this very street once, just to get her name," Robin said. "Adrianna, that is."

"I'm sorry," Adam said again.

"I must pay a call to her parents. I've just been putting that off since I got here," Robin said. "I planned to give them some money. Least I could do for killing their daughter."

"Robin, you certainly did not," Adam said. "Don't talk that way."

Robin looked down at the napkin in his lap and his cheeks flushed.

"I followed Mr. De Vries today," Adam said.

"You did what?"

"He never saw me. He was following Mr. Mahoric most of the day, to and from the bank. To his home on the canal. One of the five thousand canals. Then De Vries went to the registry building," Adam said.

"What registry building?"

"Around the corner from here. That way. Registreren."

"That's a newspaper office!" Robin said.

"Oh shit."

"Was he buying a paper?"

Adam shook his head. "Didn't come out with one."

"Don't let on that you saw him there. But we must find out what his business was." Robin signaled to their server. "This day is becoming perfectly awful. If he's sold my pathetic story to the paper, the judge and jury will certainly not look well on me or my case. A carafe of brandy, if you would please."

January 13, 1841. Canterbury, Connecticut.

"Robin! Robin, there are Indians in the courtyard." Marta skidded to a stop in the kitchen.

Robin got up from the table and went to look out the window. "Mohegans."

"Is there trouble?" Marie asked, very pregnant as she sat at the kitchen table.

"Maybe they have a problem." Robin glanced at the rifle on the mantel, but he did not take it with him. He grabbed his coat and walked out the back door.

June went to look out the window. "Four Indians. One is dismounting. Rifle, Robin?"

"No." Robin pulled on his coat as he walked out through the snow into the courtyard.

The one on foot walked toward Robin and met him part way. "Mister Van der Kellen?"

"Yes. Yes. I remember you. What brings you all the way out here?" Robin asked.

"We have no money to pay you. Do not know if you will help," the Indian said.

"You helped me at harvest time. If I can help you, I certainly will. What is the trouble?" Robin asked.

"We are being pushed off our land. White landowner next to us say we are on his land. But we have had this land many many fathers. My grandfather's father lived on this land. It is winter. Our children cannot live out in the cold."

"A land dispute. Have you any money on you? Any money at all?" Robin asked.

"Only two dollars. It is to buy food," he said.

"Give me the smallest coin you have." Robin held out his hand.

"I...cannot pay for a law help."

"By giving me something, even a penny, I am your lawyer. I can legally help you," Robin explained.

The Indian handed Robin a penny. "Two will stay and chop wood for you. All that wood there. Will that pay you?"

"Yes. Let me saddle a horse and I'll come with you. I will also need to go to the Norwich land office for a map of the reservation land. Just wait a moment. Tell your friends I can help." Robin returned into his house. Inside the kitchen he collected that rifle and reloading kit. "Marie, some of the Mohegans are being forced off their land by a white neighbor. I'm going into Norwich to see what I can do for them. I shall be gone over night."

"Don't you need Michael Poole?" Marie asked.

"It's a simple land dispute. I can handle this," Robin said. "June and Marta, look after Marie. Michael will know where to find me if you need me. I'll be back as soon as I can." He kissed Marie, put on his hat, and held onto the door with his rifle in hand.

"Robin, bring your pistol," Marie insisted.

"I can fetch it for you," Marta offered.

"Would you please?" Robin asked.

She hurried upstairs.

"Be careful, Robin," Marie said.

"I will, darling. Don't be surprised if I stay over the night," Robin said.

"Where will you stay?" Marie asked.

"Norwich somewhere. I'll find a place. It's too long a ride there and back yet today." Robin accepted his pistol and holster from Marta. "Thank you."

"You didn't need a change of clothes?" June asked.

"I'll be fine." Robin strapped on the holster. He walked out to the barn and the Indians waited on their horses. Once Robin had Jumper saddled, he rode out with the Indians, while two remained behind and started to work on the wood pile.

"What can I do for you, sir?" the man in the land office asked.

"I am Robin Van der Kellen of Canterbury. I am a lawyer representing the Mohegans. I would like to see what properties they are deeded," Robin said.

The man stood up behind his desk. "You're not serious."

"I'm quite serious."

"The state sold their land off years ago. Keeps selling off more of it every year. They know they're to stay on the reservation land west side of the Thames, south of the Yantic River."

"They are. This is the land I'm speaking of. Show me the deed to a Mr. Jones, north of the Trading Cove Brook," Robin said.

"Jones? Let me look." The man moved back to his file cabinets.

Robin took out his pocket watch. It was three PM. He watched the snow come down through the window.

"Here. Here it is." The man brought out the deed with map drawn on it. He laid it on the desk.

Robin leaned over it to study the map.

"Angus Jones bought the land two years ago."

"He didn't buy any other land since then or before?"

"No, sir. That's the only deed to Angus Jones."

"His land ends at Fitch Hill Road. He's trying to throw the Indians off the land on the other side of Trading Cove Brook. His land does not extend that far." Robin pointed on the map.

"Yes, sir. I would agree with that," the man said.

"You'll testify to that in court," Robin said. "Come with me. The courthouse is still open."

"I don't close until five."

"You closed early because of the snow. Grab your coat, sir. Mr. Jones is trying to throw women and children out into the snow tonight," Robin said. "Move your ass, sir, or I will move it for you."

The man pulled on his coat. "I don't want town people to know I sided with the Indians."

"You're bringing that deed to show the judge. That's all you're doing, and it is your job, need I remind you." Robin watched the man fold up the deed, put it back in the envelope and then into an inside pocket of his coat.

"I have to return this to the file right after," the man said.

"Of course. Come along."

"I ask to petition the court." Robin stood up in the courthouse when the judge asked if there were any other business. He held hat in hand.

"State your name. On what matter, sir?"

"Robin Van der Kellen, barrister at law, State of Massachusetts, and The Netherlands. On the matter of Mohegan Indians vs Angus Jones in a dispute of property," Robin said.

"Where is Jones then? You're his lawyer?" the judge asked.

"No, your honor. I am representing the Mohegans," Robin said. "I believe you were acquainted with my father, Willem Van der Kellen."

The judge sat forward. "Approach my bench and explain."

Robin looked at the Land office clerk. "Don't you move." Then he walked up to the bench, standing formally. "Your honor, Mr. Angus Jones is evicting a group of three Mohegan families off their land, reservation land, north of Trading Cove Brook. Three families in the dead of January. It's their land."

"The Mohegans have no deed to their land. All of eastern Connecticut was once their land, including your farm in Canterbury. They are to stay on their reservation now," the judge said.

"I therefore offer into evidence the deed to Angus Jones' land."

"Let's see this deed."

Robin looked back to the clerk who removed the envelope from his pocket, unfolded it, and brought it forward to Robin. "Your honor, this is the land office clerk, a mister Joseph Miner."

"I know Mr. Miner. Let's see the deed."

Robin passed the deed to the judge who studied it.

"Mr. Van der Kellen, where on this map do these Mohegans live, and Angus Jones is claiming the land?"

"Forgive me for pointing, your honor." Robin leaned in and pointed on the paper. "They live here."

The judge pulled out a piece of paper and began writing on it. "Give him back the deed and let him return it to the land office."

Robin took back the deed, looked at it again and handed it to Miner.

"You may go, Miner." The judge continued writing.

The clerk took the deed and quickly exited.

Robin waited, standing as if at attention, in his fine suit, though somewhat wet with snow.

The judge finished writing and said, "Let this dry before you deliver this cease eviction order to Mr. Jones. Or do you require a police escort with you?"

"I shall attempt to deliver it myself tonight."

"Van der Kellen, approach my bench please."

Robin did so.

"This would have put you on less than speaking terms with your father, Mr. Van der Kellen." The judge gave Robin the court order.

"Thank you, your honor," Robin said.

"Why did you do it? They couldn't have paid you."

"That land is all they have left. It is the right thing to do. As is your court order, sir," Robin said. "My father's estate was once Mohegan land?"

"All of Eastern Connecticut. Watch your back. Get that order out of here before I change my mind, for your own good."

"May I inquire…."

"No. You get a reputation for siding with Indians over the whites around here and you'll never find work."

"I couldn't care less."

Chapter 4: Fine Foreign Species

Adam hurried down the street, moving from alley to alley, avoiding carriages in the twilight that lingered endlessly on summer days in Amsterdam. It would not be dark yet for another two hours as it was only seven o-clock. He saw Robin's carriage parked still at the livery near the courthouse. Adam decided to look into the nearest pub. Through the window, Adam could see him deep in conversation with several other lawyers and tipping back a brandy. The men were sitting round a table near the front of the pub, all of them similar in age to Robin, all of them in black suits with white ascots. About Robin's collar was an ascot of pale blue silk. The men were laughing heartily.

The host brought a note to Robin's table. "Someone's driver is out front. He gave me this note. Any of you Mr. Van der Kellen?"

Robin held out a hand for the note. Then he looked at the door, seeing Adam. "Thank you, sir." Robin unfolded the note and waved him to enter. "Please show him in. He's my assistant, not a driver."

I have good news.

A

The host then escorted Adam to the table of finely dressed barristers. A chair was pulled up for him. Brandy was poured. And it was then that Adam joined the gentleman's gathering, much like the observer of a fine but foreign species.

Robin leaned in toward him as the pub was loud. He leaned his mouth almost to Adam's ear to say, "What did you find?"

Adam then turned his mouth into Robin's hair. "Too much to say here. He's still working. But he went to the paper to view last week's land transfers. Mahoric bought more than one house with cash."

"Really?" Robin let out a relieved breath. "Thought he was selling me out. He's been doing his duty."

"Wants more money for it next week when I meet with him again," Adam said.

"I'll pay. Drink up. Are you hungry?"

"Starving. Many thanks," Adam said.

The other lawyers asked in Dutch, "Has he American legal expertise? Does he aspire to become a barrister?"

Robin explained also in Dutch, "Exploring possibilities for his career at present. I thought a trip to Europe would be beneficial to his decisions. Perhaps I can persuade him of the benefits of law school. He has unique observational expertise."

They nodded as if they understood.

"I have found him very useful in interrogations for example. Because he cannot understand the language he focuses on mannerisms. Told me the other day that a man was lying to me. And you know what? He was right," Robin explained.

Adam was served the meal of the day, deep fried herring, fried potatoes, cheeses, and rye bread rolls.

Robin put a hand on Adam's shoulder. "Need anything? Here, rather have a beer? Try this. I was in law school with these men. Know them well."

"Wonderful. Do apologize for my lack of Dutch. I only know the curses." Adam glanced around at the men and tasted from a glass of beer set before him.

Robin laughed. "He says to tell you he's sorry, all the Dutch he knows are the curses. I believe that reflects poorly on me."

The men all laughed.

Adam observed that often Robin said something that broke the men up laughing. And then the man on the other side of him wrapped an arm around Adam's shoulders to lean forward and say something to Robin.

"Says I should warn you to keep your women away from me," Robin translated.

"My women?" Adam raised his eyebrows. "I'm usually the woman in my relationships."

Robin smiled. "Is that the way of it? Hey, Albert here married one of the women I turned down. He's wealthy now with three children." Robin said something to Albert in Dutch, who then spread his hands out wide. The men all laughed again.

Adam laughed too. "That was very inappropriate."

The man beside him took his arm away and patted Adam on the back. "This young man needs educating. Did you take him across the canals yet?"

Robin shook his head. "Too shy. He won't go."

The man pushed another brandy in front of Adam. "Get him drunk. He'll do it. Get it done right the first time."

"Adam, he says I need to take you to the red-light district for your education."

Adam said to Robin, "You know, I'm not a complete virgin."

Robin shook his head. "I don't care how many you've been with. If not a woman, you're still a virgin."

Adam smiled as he ate his herring and drank from the brandy or the beer.

The conversation returned to their law cases and Robin's. The gentlemen smoked some tobacco after their dinner, drank brandy, laughed about old times. Listening to Robin speaking his natural language was fascinating. Clearly, he had to translate in his head to speak English, because he was more fluent with these old friends and the words just rolled off his tongue in a beautiful way. Adam found himself just watching Robin's mouth.

Later they walked in the street lantern light, back to the livery.

"How will you find your way home in the dark?" Adam asked.

"I know these roads very well. Grew up here, you know?" Robin said.

"Thank you for that, sir. In the tavern. You did not tell them I'm only a valet," Adam said.

"You are absolutely more than a valet," Robin said. "Wait until we get on the road home before telling me anything of the case. By the way, how are you getting about the city so easily on your own?"

Adam shrugged. "Grew up in a big city. Is this so different than New York? Canals, I'll give you. Half the languages in New York, I could not speak either. I still got about, didn't I?"

Robin laughed too. "I have underestimated you, Mr. Hudson. I won't make that mistake again."

Marie entered Robin's room that night, hearing him arrive. "You're so late. It is midnight, Robin."

Robin was untying his blue ascot as he walked toward her. He kissed her mouth. "You needn't wait up for me on these late nights."

She clung to his vest pockets. "I was afraid you took a room in town. I never see you anymore, Robin. I'm so bored with nothing but domestic details."

"I'm sorry, darling. I had Adam with me. We were working on the case quite late tonight. This is going to happen quite a lot until the trial," Robin said.

Marie frowned and unbuttoned his vest for him. "I know you are saving your brother-in-law. I'm just being selfish. This the life you were missing, when you arrived in Canterbury that November."

"Yes, that is quite right. I am sorry, Marie. I have a family now. I should not work to such late hours," Robin said.

"The tailor dropped off more suits and shirts for you there," Marie said.

"That's wonderful. What about you, dear? Did you go with Tess or Mila to buy dresses?" Robin pulled off his jacket and vest. He unbuttoned his white shirt.

"I will tomorrow. You'll be working again?"

"Yes."

"Adam is helping you? What is he doing for you in town?" Marie asked.

Robin turned, his shirt open all the way down, and poured himself a glass of brandy. "Adam is turning out to be an excellent investigator. Even if he cannot speak Dutch, he makes very clever observations. He has a talent for reading people, it seems."

"Really? I'm so jealous of Adam now. He's with you all day."

"Darling, you are my beautiful wife. You're a mother now. Frida needs you."

Mila took Frida from Marie's arms before breakfast. "Here is my little niece."

Robert appeared with medical bag in hand. "Give Robin my regrets. I have to get to the hospital early today." Robert left.

"Where is Robin?" Mila asked.

"Getting dressed," Marie said. "Got in late last night."

"Make use of that nanny. She's wonderful. You two should go into town. Let Robin show you around," Mila said. "You know, Marie, after my first was born were some of the best times with Jonas. And my brother looks at you with his heart on fire. I have never seen him so in love."

Marie smiled, tucking little Frida's shirt into her jumper. "He's wonderful."

Mila said very quietly, "It goes right back to the way it was, in the bedroom. You'll see."

"It does?" Marie asked.

Mila nodded. "They talk about men having needs. Women do too. Once in a while, let the nanny take Frida for the night."

"I'm so exhausted by the time he returns at night."

"Then let her take Frida in the afternoon." Mila smiled.

Marie giggled.

"Tell Robin you...need help with something upstairs."

"How could I be so bold?" Marie laughed.

"I doubt that's a problem for you."

Robin entered the dining room, looking about. Wout and Jonas followed him.

Marie took Frida back into her arms giggling.

Mila smiled at Robin.

"Where's Robert?" Robin asked.

"Off to work," Mila said.

The butler burst into the room. "Lynn is in trouble. We need someone to fetch Robert back."

"In trouble?" Robin asked.

"With the baby," the butler said.

"How long ago did Robert leave?" Robin latched a hand onto Wout's arm.

"God, nearly a half hour ago," Mila said.

"Wout, stay put. Jonas, help me saddle a horse quick." Robin and Jonas ran out the back of the house, toward the carriage barn.

Mila and Marie hurried up the stairs with the butler.

In a few moments Robin shot past the house, on a horse that was stretching to top speed and hardly touching the ground. Jonas followed moments later, riding another horse at a more reasonable pace.

At the front entrance to the hospital, Jonas recognized Robin's horse at the top of the stairs. A police officer was holding the reins.

Jonas drew to a stop beneath the stairs. "How did you come to be holding that horse?"

"Chased him down after he jumped some fences and rode straight down the walk to get in here. Rode it up the stairway and jumped the damn fountain. That fountain," the officer said. "Most incredible riding I ever saw in my life. Said it was a medical emergency. I must arrest him if that's not the case."

"Oh, it is, officer. He's fetching his brother the doctor whose wife is in labor or something back home."

"I see. Here he is."

Robin and Robert dashed out the door of the hospital.

Jonas dismounted his horse and offered it to Robert. "This one is fresher. He ran the shit out of that one."

"Take the one Jonas has. Go as quickly as you can. We'll bring your carriage," Robin said.

Robert hurried down the stairs and mounted Jonas's horse. He took off.

"So, I believe there is still the matter of your arrest, sir. I didn't get your name," the policeman said.

A crowd was gathering about them, looking at the horse at the top of the grand stairway.

"Captain Robin Van der Kellen. Dutch Cavalry, retired."

"Cavalry?" The policemen looked him up and down. "Saving an expecting woman?"

"My sister-in-law," Robin said. "She's giving birth presently."

The policeman offered a handshake. "Buy you a drink if I wasn't on duty. Incredible display of horsemanship."

Robin shook his hand. "Thank you, sir. Can we be on our way back home?"

"You drive the carriage home. This one can ride the horse." The officer indicated Jonas with the horse and Robin to the carriage. "If you can get it down the stairs."

Robin smiled. "As you wish."

January 15, 1841. Canterbury, Connecticut.

Robin arrived home and strolled across the courtyard carrying his things inside and into the kitchen.

Marie met him with a kiss at the door. "Are you all right, darling? You were gone almost two days."

"I'm fine. I'm just fine. I have some gifts for you from the Mohegans." Robin set the bundle and his rifle on the table. He removed his hat and Marta took it and his coat from him.

Marta hung those behind the door. "Do tell us about your adventure."

"First, I'm pretty curious what's in here. When the Mohegan women found out we were expecting, they made me take this home." Robin untied a cloth bundle to find inside baby blankets, baby clothes, and a gourd rattle. He gave the rattle a shake and laughed.

Marie picked up some of the baby clothes, hand stitched little Indian baby clothes, even a tunic of deerskin. "How adorable." She held up tiny moccasins on her fingers.

Robin also pulled out of it a ceramic container. "Butter. They make and sell this for a living."

"Indian butter? Is it safe to eat?" June asked.

"Sure. Their corn and muskrat stew was," Robin said.

"Muskrat?" Marie said.

"I won't hear you complain about my chicken after this," June said.

Robin laughed. "I'm starving. What have you got? Might have been possum. I'm no connoisseur."

Robin waited outside the master suite with Jonas, pacing. Finally, Mila and a nurse came out.

"She's resting. She'll have to stay in bed now until the baby comes." Mila put a hand on Robin's arm. "Marie is assisting Robert. I'm taking her to lay down." Mila helped the nurse down the hall to one of the guest rooms.

Jonas turned to watch them leaving. "Marie is assisting while the nurse passes out?"

"Doesn't surprise me." Robin rolled his eyes. "Though I don't imagine this is going to help my nights any."

"What do you mean?" Jonas asked.

"You know what I mean. You have three children," Robin said. "How did you ever manage to make the second or third?"

"That's your sister we're talking about," Jonas said.

"Right. She probably knocked *you* down." Robin folded his arms.

Several moments later Marie came out and shut the door. "She's resting. Robert is sitting with her."

"The baby all right?" Robin asked.

"Felt it moving." Marie nodded. "She will have to remain in bed until the baby comes. As long as she can. Where is Mila?"

"Took the nurse to lay down before she fainted," Robin said, nodding toward the hallway.

"Passed out in there once already," Marie said. "Wasn't even much blood. I just held Lynn's hand and told her she'd be okay."

Robin took Marie into his arms. "Well done, my love."

"Marie, would you mind sitting with Lynn. She is asking for you." Robert said the next morning.

"I have her," Mila said, holding Frida in her lap.

"I would be happy to, very much." Marie rose and left the dining room.

Robert sat down at the head of the table. He was served coffee, biscuits, and preserves.

Robin sipped coffee.

Wout was across from Robin but not in Lynn's chair, one over from it.

"Going to work?" Robin questioned.

Robert looked at him.

"It's just, I want to know if I must keep a horse saddled and risk jail time again." Robin sipped his coffee and set the cup down to the left of his place setting.

"Staying home today. My partner is covering. I don't know if he can keep it up until this baby comes," Robert said.

"Bring in a midwife, Robert," Mila said. "You've been there for only two births before. A midwife has done all sorts."

"A midwife never went to medical school," Robert said. "I delivered plenty in medical school."

"Can't hurt. Can sit with her for the few hours a day that you might go to the hospital," Robin suggested.

Robert said nothing. "People dying there. It is hard to sit at home...and wait."

"You can't schedule a baby," Mila outraged. "Robert, there are other surgeons at the hospital. You only have one wife."

"Of course." Robert sunk his head. "Robin, where did you find that woman?"

"By that woman do you mean my wife?"

Robert looked at him.

"Why?" Robin reached to refill his coffee cup when a maid did so over his shoulder.

"She is so calm and steady. She is exactly what Lynn needs in there. Remembers all instructions. Delivers them firmly but with care. Mixes laudanum very well. If she was a man, would have made a fine physician."

"You'd best tell her that," Robin said. "Or face my wrath."

"I would be happy to. Where did you meet a lady of such strength?"

"America," Robin said.

"Robin, oh my brother Robin, when your first wife died in childbirth, I regret so much that I did not write you." Robert sunk his head down.

"Write me? I had no one in that country. I just got there. Could have used any gesture," Robin said. "And received none. I desperately hope Lynn and the baby are all right and I will stay to see it through. But comfort you I will not do. The only reason I am staying here is for Marie to comfort Lynn. Otherwise, I'd be in Wout's house."

March 12, 1841 After Frida was born

June walked into the master bedroom to find only Marie sleeping in the bed. She'd heard Robin in the hall that night and now found him asleep on the couch by the fire. He lay on his back in sleep shirt and trousers. He held the baby on his chest between his chin and the back of the couch. Frida was only beginning to fuss, lying on her back on top of her father, his hand on her belly.

June reached over the back of the couch to remove Robin's hand from the baby and lift her up into her arms.

Robin awoke, looking up at June.

June carried the baby over toward Marie in bed.

Robin sat up on the couch, ran his hand through his hair, and then he walked out, retreating to his other bedroom.

Sometime later, Robin strolled into the kitchen and came abruptly to a stop, taking in Marie at the table and June with Marta at the kitchen worktable. Adam was sitting at the table with coffee. Robin stood up straight in one of his grey suits, with vest and necktie on. He set one hand on his hip and said, "I broke the rules last night. I mean no disrespect to all three of you who have been doing an excellent job caring for the baby. But this is half my child too and there is no reason that I should be excused from doing my share if I am capable. And evidenced by the fact that last night was the first time all week any of us, including Frida, have had half a nights' sleep, I will make no apologies for my actions." He raised his chin and looked at Marie, waiting.

"Bravo, Barrister Van der Kellen. Case won," Marie said.

June burst out laughing and then Marta and Adam did too.

Robin smirked and now put both hands on his hips.

"How many times did you rehearse that upstairs?" Marie asked.

"Several. I'm quite outnumbered by females here," Robin admitted.

"I beg your pardon," Adam said.

"We are both outnumbered by females," Robin corrected.

"Well to hell with the rules," June said. "If you can get your baby to stop screaming even for half a night."

"Do you notice it's my baby when she's screaming and she's yours when she's cuddly this way?" Robin said, walking to Marie and leaning over to see Frida in her basket on the table. "Look at the little Indian baby in the moccasins. This is the first time you put her in these."

"She stays nice and warm in that tunic," Marie said. "Now leave her be. She's content."

"I'm...I'm content myself." Robin sat down.

"Coffee, Robin?" Adam asked. "I'll get you some."

"Are you going somewhere?" Marie asked him.

"I must go to town for a bit, yes," Robin said. "Taking Adam to Norwich for a few things. Need any supplies?"

June put a plate of breakfast before him, and Adam brought a cup of coffee.

"I can put together a list. How did you do it?" June questioned. "Get her to sleep last night?"

"I have been known to have a way with females," Robin said.

"Well, you'll have to answer me for that, for your past," Marie said. "Skirt chaser."

March 17, 1841 Canterbury Connecticut0

"June, may I speak with you please?" Robin then turned and walked to the office and took a seat behind the desk.

June followed him in and stood in front of the desk, folding a dish towel in her hands. "Did I speak my mind one too many times, Robin?"

"Not at all. Have a seat please."

"Do you wish me to close the door? What am I in trouble for?"

"Leave it open. Please, have a seat," Robin said.

June sat down across the desk from him.

"A few questions first, before I tell you what this is about. Have you ever been married? I know nothing about you before you came to work here," Robin said. "Have you always been a housekeeper?"

"Oh. I was married twice, actually. As you can see, neither one worked out very well. The first one fell off a horse. Died at the age of nineteen. Second one was a drunk. I guess technically I'm still married to that idiot, if he's still living that is," June said. "Yes. I've always been a housekeeper. Yes, always looking for the next ex-husband."

Robin sat forward then, both elbows on the desk. "Good heavens. Why did you not tell me about this?"

"What are you going to do? Make the bastard come home and support me?"

"Exactly. Or serve him with divorce papers and sue him for support payments. What do you think I do for a living?" Robin took out a piece of paper and opened his ink bottle. "What is his name and where did he last live? Where did you last see him?"

"Anthony Jones. Bridgeport, Connecticut. Haven't seen him in ten years. There's no telling where he is," June said. "He'd be about 40 years old by now and…four thousand pounds."

Robin raised an eyebrow and made some notes. "Are you going to let me look into this?"

"Just don't let him know where to find me. Unless you want to see me grab that rifle off the mantel and make a giant hole in him," June said.

"Well, what kind of man would leave an intelligent, forceful, whimsical woman such as yourself?" Robin sat back.

June laughed. "All of them. All men on earth, to be exact."

Robin laughed. "At the very least let me get you free of him so you can remarry and be happy ever after."

"Is that what you called me in here for? Unless you brought a genie in a bottle back from India, I can't see that happening," June said.

"June Jones is your real name?" Robin asked.

"Juniper Allison Jones," she said. "Maiden name was Stockton."

"It's not what I called you in here for. I want to promote you to manager of the estate. Your salary will be twenty dollars each month. You're going to be in charge of everything while we are in Europe," Robin said. "It won't be easy. You'll have the construction workers finishing up. You must keep them on track and pay them. You'll be in charge of Marta, and the stockmen. You'll keep the house running. You should probably hire another cook if you can. You'll keep the books. You're good with numbers. You'll post me a letter every few weeks to report on how things are progressing. Do you want this job?"

"I'm in shock. You would give me all that responsibility?"

"Let's face it. You've already been doing it while Marie was giving birth and whenever I was away on business. I'll be leaving you some money to handle all of that. You do realize, with responsibility and control of the money comes this." Robin set a pistol on the desktop, pointed away toward the fireplace. "Before I leave, I will give you the key to the cash box and teach you how to reload this pistol. You'll keep the pistol handy. Skirt pocket or something. Bedside drawer. You can handle yourself."

"I can load a musket and shoot coyotes just fine," June admitted.

"Shooting an attacker is no different. Just a little more mess to clean away," Robin said. "I'll teach you how to shoot the pistol. And show you where the cash box is. Do you want this job?"

"One question. Do I go back to being maid when you return?"

"Of course not. You continue on as manager. Adam continues as Valet and Butler, maybe Legal Assistant."

June looked down and then back at Robin. "I'm very excited, sir, to be your manager."

"You know, June, the head stockman at the Johnson farm is…quite available, I hear," Robin said.

"He's a hundred years old!"

Robin walked out laughing. "Available."

Robin stood in the center of his bedroom, arms extended out, chin up. He wore trousers and a shirt only. The tailor moved round him with a measuring tape. He called off numbers to a secretary who jotted them down.

Marie looked on from the sitting area of the room, pacing and glancing out the window until it came time to measure around Robin's waist, hips, and down his inseam. Robin held the top of the tape himself of course.

Marie smiled and looked out the window. "Robin what do you make of this?"

"Excuse me," Robin said in Dutch. He drew alongside Marie to look out.

In the gardens, far out along the hedges, there was a tall round rock. On top of the rock were the two boys sitting on a blanket. They had ropes coming from a tree in front of them and the older boy held the ropes in his hand like reins.

Robin burst out laughing.

"What on earth are they doing?" Marie questioned.

"Riding an elephant, of course."

Marie laughed. "Robert will kill you, with all the influence you've had on his sons."

"Can't wait to see where they find a tiger out there."

"A tiger?" the tailor asked in Dutch. "In the back yard?"

Robin returned to standing where the tailor needed him. "Carry on, sir."

"How many buttons do you like on your vest, sir?"

"Fifteen."

"Well then the vest will go all the way up to your nose, sir."

"Humor. Mr. Van Eykk. Put as many buttons on the vest as you see best. It's your expertise. Not mine," Robin said.

The man stood up in front of Robin, meeting his eyes. "Black silk lining or dark blue?"

"I like both. Would it be easier for you if I told you to make one suit of each?" Robin asked. "Here is the deal, Mr. Van Eykk. You do the best tailoring in Amsterdam. I have two suits of yours that I absolutely adore but they're so old they're falling apart. Make me four new suits. Two black. Two of your choice. I'm not fond of brown unless it is quite dark. Make shirts. Neck ties. Top hats. Deliver them to me one by one as I have much work to do in court. Make me your best."

"Sir... I do not know what to say. I've never been given such freedom to attire a gentleman as I imagine him. Four suits. You will be delighted. I am certain." The tailor almost shook with delight.

Robin patted him on the shoulder. "Breathe. And go back to your shop to make suits. Hold on a moment." Robin picked up his old jacket off the sofa and retrieved his pocketbook from inside.

"I see you like the inside pockets then," Van Eykk said.

Robin counted out some bills and placed them in the tailor's hand. "This is for the first two."

"My, that is one of my old style of suits. Do you like the tails?"

"No. They almost got me shot in New York once, mistaking me for an Englishman," Robin then added more bills to the man's hand. "The latest style then."

"I cannot wait to get back to my shop, Mr. Van der Kellen. You shall have four of the finest and latest fashions of Paris and Amsterdam. Thank you, sir."

"Thank you, sir."

"Do you know a good dress maker? Surprise my wife with some dresses, if you would."

"Sir, Robin, a letter for you." Simon offered a silver tray containing a folded letter with a seal.

Robin accepted it. "Thank you."

That night, Robin slid into the bed with Marie and wrapped his arm around her. He kissed her shoulder.

Marie did not respond.

Robin aligned his body with hers, behind her, all the way down. Even his foot cradled hers. His hand slid up beneath her nightgown. And he kissed her neck. "Darling? I heard something that might help."

"What is that?"

"It seems that you cannot become with child while you are still nursing, just after having a baby."

"Robert told you that?"

"I thought you might, understandably, been reluctant to...so soon after."

"I am, certainly." Marie leaned back against him.

Robin folded around her. "I won't hurt you."

"I know. Of course," Marie whispered.

"Darling, forgive me. I desire you so," Robin sighed. "God, you smell so lovely."

Robin made a few more advances and found Marie only to stiffen.

"I'm so disappointing to you."

Robin caught his breath. "I...love you so. I am just a man. And I... my needs are secondary to all that you have to do. I'm sorry. Just lying beside you makes my blood burn. I can't help it."

"Robin, I love you so."

"Oh Marie, my darlin."

"But you do have needs and I'm not living up to your expectations at all."

Robin took her into his arms as he calmed down. "What is it then? Are you tired? Are you afraid I will hurt you?"

"I'm always tired. And yes. Won't it be like the first time again?" Marie whispered.

"No of course not."

"I still can't get into my favorite dresses. My waistline is so…. I'm sorry, Robin."

"Darlin, you just had our baby. And you are beautiful." Robin kissed her.

Robin came in for lunch and as he was about to pick Frida up from her baby carriage, the butler removed something from the back of Robin's jacket. He showed Robin the leaves he had collected off Robin's coat.

"Oh. Oh oh." Robin looked out toward the rock.

Marie laughed. "Nice performance."

"You didn't see all that, did you?" Robin asked her.

"Sir, you'll get grass stains all over if you wear these fine suits out on the lawn," the butler said. "Actually, lying on the lawn."

"I couldn't help it. They killed me eight times," Robin said. "My sword broke in half."

The butler walked away grinning.

Robin picked up and cuddled Frida as he sat down with Marie at the table. "How are my two ladies this afternoon?"

"We were wondering if you saw any tigers out there today?" Marie said.

"Not today. Not at high noon. They said the tigers would all be sleeping since that's what the barn cats do." Robin kissed the baby's forehead. "Therefore, it was safe to practice our fencing."

"That's a relief."

"When we go into town I have to remember to look about for some Indian souvenirs for the boys. Trinkets of some kind. They won't know I bought them in Amsterdam."

"You are the best uncle," Marie told him.

Robin said with his Indian imitation, "The elephant must take his bath now and eat his wagon of hay."

She burst out laughing.

The two boys, Lucas and Ruben, came running onto the balcony and skidded to a stop at the table, hearing the butler yell at them for running indoors.

Robin looked at them. "Are we under attack?"

"Yes sir. We came to inform you, the British are attacking," Lucas said.

"Can they attack after lunch?" Robin asked.

"Depends on what we are having for lunch, sir," Lucas said.

Robin nodded. "Well, do some reconnaissance. Find out what is for lunch and report back to me."

"Yes, sir." The boys ran off again.

Robin sat back and drank his lemonade.

"Robert is going to kill you."

Chapter 5: Save the Rabbits

"Robin! Look at you. You haven't aged a day."

Robin gave a hug to an old friend, and they kissed on both cheeks. "Your vision has gone, Albert. I've aged ten years since I've seen you last. I received your letter. Thank you."

"Have a seat, my good friend."

Robin joined the man at a table in a café near the canals.

He offered Robin a cigarette.

Robin waved it off.

"Still the puritan. Tell me you imbibe at least."

"Like a fish," Robin said.

They both laughed and Albert poured. "Robin, where have you been all these years?"

"I relocated to America. You were there at my wedding. My first wife, Adrianna, died soon after arriving in Boston."

"Robin, I'm so sorry. She was so young."

"Albert, thank you. I worked in Boston as a barrister. I took over my father's law firm and then his estate when he passed. I remarried and I've brought Marie and my daughter home to meet my family," Robin said.

"Incredible. I do hope to meet your new wife and child. I myself have wife and three," he said.

"I'm so happy for you. From law school to running an inn. How did this happen?"

"Wife inherited the inn. Still do some representation on the side. But the inn keeps me busy," he said. "Your letter tells me you have a maid for me?"

"If I may explain," Robin said.

"Have a drink. Relax. And do speak plainly, Robin. We stayed up together 'til dawn studying in law school. I know you well. Why does this maid need your special attention?"

Robin lowered his eyes. "This woman was our maid and nanny on the voyage from Boston. She was very good at those things. And she finds herself in circumstances here, no job, no place to live. I am putting her up in a hostel. I believe she will be a good fit for your inn with special circumstances."

The man drank his brandy. "Robin, you slept with her?"

"Oh God no!" Robin shot back.

The man laughed. "Intend to sleep with her? Women still falling all over you? Look at you. Of course, they are. I know you, Robin Van der Kellen. With your child, is she?"

"Albert! Are you insane? I am faithful to my wife."

"Then spill it out. Robin, you're married with a child. What is going on with this maid?"

"This is a twenty-five-year-old woman. Attractive. Poor. No prospects. Her employment ended when we made port, and she received 20 guilders. No family. She speaks Dutch and Polish. She was a very good maid and nanny to my infant. She needs a job," Robin said.

"Oh Robin. Have you ever done anything but pro bono work? Always defending the unfortunate."

"Try it once in a while. It's good for the soul," Robin said.

"Speak plainly, Robin. Special circumstances?"

"I fear without assistance this woman is on the brink of prostitution or crime for survival."

"Good Lord, Robin."

"Albert, we were taught that if given little opportunity, the desperate are left with desperate choices. Don't leave her to it. The red-light district is just across the canal. I believe that with a job as maid and nanny to your patrons, and with my backing in a trust, that she can be steered toward the correct choices in life," Robin said.

"What was her crime? She was losing her job. You're not taking her on in your home. Verge of prostitution? How am I to trust her with my patrons?" Albert tapped off a tobacco cigarette into an ash tray.

"Albert, we were taught everyone deserves a second chance and that is why we must defend the guilty when called to," Robin said.

"Guilty of what? Did she rob you?"

"Extortion."

The man sat back and looked away. He puffed on his cigarette.

Robin drank his brandy and poured himself another. "The girl tried to get me to sleep with her. She'd done it before sometimes for money. Enough men had complained that she would not be asked back on the next voyage. I refused and she asked for a hundred to keep quiet. My wife and I confronted her."

"Your wife knows?"

Robin smiled. "Hard to keep Marie from throwing her overboard. Yes. Albert, a basically good woman in desperate circumstances can make the right choices given the chance."

"A basically good woman? She slept with enough men for money to get herself fired. What are you proposing? What is to keep her from robbing or committing prostitution in my inn? I can't have that behavior in my inn, no matter what I owe you."

"You owe me nothing. You will tell her, you have this employment as maid and nanny and if you do well, you Albert, are in charge of a trust I have put in place. One hundred guilders. If she does well, she has that in the pocketbook. If she commits a crime or quits her job, she gets nothing. This will give her the security in the background to make the right choices in life."

"You're giving her 100 guilders?"

"If she does well and needs it as you see fit, you release the funds. Maybe she marries and needs it for a home. Maybe she works very well for you, but you must let her go. You can release it. But if she robs, fucks a patron, extorts another man, she receives nothing and goes the hell away," Robin said. "Trust dissolved. You keep the money for your troubles."

"Good lord, Robin. You've thought this through well."

"I don't have to swear to her good behavior, as I can't. But I can swear to you this. She wants those 100 guilders. That was her fee for me to keep quiet and not send her to jail."

"100 guilders? I just bought a carriage for that."

"I know but to a poor woman who worked for 6 weeks for room and board and 20 guilders, a small fortune," Robin said. "In a hostel she could live for three or four months on that. I believe she just wanted that tiny security, when there is nothing else in life."

Albert sat back and drank his brandy. "Never lost a case, have you? Dammit. She's going to know you set up the trust."

"She'll have no way to find me, if you keep our bargain. And I'll be back in America soon."

"I will send for her at the hostel then and have her moved to my staff quarters," Albert said.

Robin handed him a paper folded into an envelope. "Thank you, Albert. Please be sure her bill at the hostel is sent to me at my brother's house. They've already been instructed to do that."

Albert looked at the packet of paper before pocketing it inside his jacket. "If I didn't need a nanny right now so critically, and the fact that she can speak to the Polish travelers."

Adam sat down at the table in the kitchen and lowered his chin onto his fist, his elbow on the table. The cooks went about their business. The bakers were making pastries and set one on a plate. They handed the plate to the young dark-haired maid, Zoey, who carried it toward the kitchen table.

Adam was staring down at the tablecloth when a plate with the frosted pastry was set before him. He looked up over his right shoulder to see Zoey, and he brightened.

Zoey smiled. She set her hand lightly on his shoulder as she moved around him.

Adam turned to see her over his left shoulder.

She walked around the table to sit across from him with her own cup of tea and a pastry.

The pastry chef said in Dutch, "Sweets for the sweet, Zoey?"

The cooks laughed.

Adam looked over at them.

"I'll bet he never had one of those. Wait 'til he tastes the currants," Zoey said.

"And you wouldn't want to taste them on his pretty mouth?" One of the maids asked.

"I don't like to see him sad. Why do you suppose he is sad today?" Zoey asked. "Does anyone know?"

"Van der Kellen went to town alone today, without him."

"Oh. He wanted to go," Zoey said.

Adam picked up the warm pastry and took a bite, finding warm berries inside. He had to pull out his handkerchief quickly to catch a drip from his mouth. "Oh my God, this is so good."

Zoey giggled and told the chef, "I think he likes it."

"Of course, he likes it. Everyone likes it," the chef declared, making everyone laugh. "I made the thing, didn't I?"

Robin and Jonas left the courthouse where Wout had to sign some papers. They walked Wout from a restaurant toward their waiting carriage.

"Robin, would there be any interest in the red-light district tonight?" Jonas asked.

"No, of course not," Robin said. "You frequent there?"

"Never been. I just thought I'd offer you every hospitality of Amsterdam," Jonas said.

Wout doubled over laughing.

Robin laughed. "No. Do I look as if I need a prostitute?"

"Yes! It has been months for you, right? Many months? I know what that's like," Jonas said. "You're a new father."

"Ahm, we're close. I don't think I'll be waiting much longer," Robin said.

"He never offered me a prostitute," Wout lamented.

Robin grabbed them both by their collars and shook them. "Be good to my sisters. I'm only six weeks away by boat, plus six weeks for them to send for me. In any *three months* I can be right back here *immediately* and throttle the both of you."

Wout and Jonas were laughing so hard as they entered the pub together.

They went up to the bar to order beers.

"You never had a prostitute in the service?" Wout questioned.

"Never paid for it," Robin said. "Always had women willing for free, in those days."

"You were in India for two years," Wout said.

"Yes."

"How did you go so long without women?"

"You think they don't have women in India?" Robin said. "How did it get so populated?"

"You...you had these women? Are they different?"

"Ahm, they're very exotic. Very beautiful. What it was...well in the barracks you know there was talk. And we had heard that British officers had their own harem. You know? Of these beautiful Indian women." Robin sipped his beer. His two brothers-in-law leaned in, riveted. "And you must realize syphilis is a real problem there. You catch that from a woman, and you can die from it and if you don't, go mad. And give it to any other women you are with. Probably plenty of that in the red-light district. So, what we did, there were some young girls, never been with anyone else."

"How did you know that?" Wout asked.

"Well, well you know. It's obvious. These girls were only had by us in the Dutch officer's quarters. Most of them didn't speak any Dutch. We picked up a few words in Hindi, the language that they spoke," Robin explained. "Now don't tell anyone this. I wasn't married then."

"You actually slept with these women?" Wout asked.

"Well, you're young and here they are in nothing but a veil. This veil over their face and half their body. You can see through this thing. And they dance. Are you going to turn them down? You have greater constitution than I do." Robin made them laugh again. "They would smell so lovely. I had two of them in my bed one night."

Wout put his head down on the bar with a thud.

"Wouter? You'll damage your brain." Robin put an arm around him. "We must get him another drink. Something stronger to nurse his concussion."

"Bartender, a round of drinks for everyone at this bar in honor of our brother-in-law, the war hero," Jonas called out.

Wout lifted his head. "I don't know about war hero but he's my hero all right."

The butler offered a letter on a silver tray to Robin following breakfast the next day. The letter had no address for the sender but was signed, "Albert".

Robin took the letter and quickly read. Then he folded and pocketed it.

Adam met him in the hall. "You're going to town?"

"Not straight away. Why?"

"Surely there are more errands I can run for you in town," Adam said.

"Yes. As a matter of fact, there are, the next time I go to town," Robin said.

"You're not having Jonas take care of things for you. He has his own business to run, doesn't he?" Adam asked.

"Jonas has nothing between his ears. You think I'd ask him instead of you?"

Adam laughed.

"You're in a hurry to go to town?" Robin asked.

Adam shrugged. "Well, sure. I like walking about town, a few guilders in my pocket. It's enjoyable."

"You're bored here," Robin concluded. "I get it. Let us challenge you."

Robert approached Robin in the parlor, finding Robin sitting with a cup of tea and a book on his knee. "You've been in the library, then?"

Robin set his tea down with his left hand on the table in front of him. He looked up and closed the book. "Yes. Very extensive, I must say. You've added to it."

Robert took a seat across from him. "Lynn and I have worked very hard on that. Lynn loves to read as well."

"Must be what you have in common," Robin suggested. "How is she?"

"Stable for now. She needs to rest as long as possible, so this baby does not come too early," Robert said. "I wanted to ask you something."

Robin looked at him quietly.

"You are right-handed. Always have been. Observing you these past few days, I cannot help but notice that you take your tea now with your left hand. You will cut your steak with your left hand. You will use the right with a fork but not a spoon."

Robin raised his eyebrows. "I did not know you were also a detective."

Robert nodded. "How bad is that gunshot wound?"

Robin wet his lips and thought a moment.

"Can you raise a rifle?"

"Yes. But it was months before I could do it without too much pain," Robin said. "I lost some control in my hand. That's why I can't lift a cup of tea without spilling it."

"Can you write?"

"Yes. Not as quickly."

"Back pain?"

"Whenever it rains," Robin said. "Right before it does. I can predict the weather now. Lovely new talent I have picked up."

"Tell me about the surgery."

"First, they did not give me enough laudanum. I was told later that I woke up during surgery and they had to give me more. I then did not wake up for a full day. I lost a lot of blood. I woke up very weak and dehydrated. The ball got stuck in my shoulder blade. I was fortunate that it missed vital arteries and the bones of my shoulder. Missed my lung and heart," Robin said. "I was fortunate to be at the end of that pistol's range. The ball did not have enough energy to blow out my shoulder blade and exit."

"You are fortunate for all of those as well as that you did not get infected. That scar is from cauterization, is it not?"

"I insisted. Yes."

Robert nodded. "All your years in the cavalry and you had to go to New York to take a critical gunshot wound. Ironic, isn't it? That it happened while performing the profession father wanted you to go into, in the first place."

"You could say that."

"You said when you met your wife that you were terribly ill, and she was the only one to care for you. Where were the servants? I thought our father had four or five," Robert said.

"He originally had three indentured servants, but they served their time and were gone. He then hired two stockmen and three maids. I had to let all of them go. Couldn't afford them," Robin explained.

"Even after selling off your Boston home and practice?"

"Yes."

"I did not realize times were so difficult for you. Could have sold off Mother's jewelry and gotten by. Father's watch."

"Would never let those go," Robin said.

"Admirable. How did you survive with no help?"

"I chopped wood, shoveled stalls, gathered eggs, slaughtered my own pig," Robin listed a few things. "Picked up a great many survival skills in the cavalry."

Robert sat back shaking his head. "Incredible. Incredible, brother. You have changed. You are no longer an arrogant war hero. Are you?"

"I am still the arrogant barrister, though."

That made Robert laugh.

"Robert, I am giving each of you, Mila, Tess, and yourself ten thousand dollars, US. I confess, I do not know what the exchange is for guilders. I've lost track."

"Robin, that is too much. You inherited nothing but debt from our father. Have you paid yourself back for that yet?"

"Yes. That is taking that into account and subtracting that right off the top. And then I kept my share. Do you believe that Jonas and Wout will look after our sisters for the rest of their lives? Is there need to withhold this money separately for them and not let their husbands have it?"

"I see no reason at all. Both Jonas and Wout are reputable men. Wout owns four banks. Has a long family history in banking. Jonas is a gentleman. His family is very wealthy. He stands to inherit more than you and me together," Robert said. "I will always be looking after our sisters. I'm certain you can give this money to them, if you feel strongly about it."

Robin sat back and crossed his legs.

"That must be something, going from fending for yourself in an empty country estate to suddenly being very wealthy. If I estimate your likely share of this bank robbery fortune. Are you pleased?"

"I am pleased that it does allow for a comfortable life for Marie and our children. I also shared a portion with a constable who worked with me on the cases. He was shot himself in the process, in the arm. And he proved himself to be a loyal and honest friend to me."

"Seems reasonable," Robert said. "Admirable what you are doing for Wout. Robin, I know you gave Marie a tour of the kitchen."

"I gave her a tour of the whole property, even the horse barns," Robin said.

"You got your friend to hire the maid from your ship at his Inn. You were alone in father's house and ill with no one to care for you but Marie. Tour of the kitchen." Robert watched his younger brother. "Still trying to save the rabbits by shooting all the foxes?"

Robin nodded.

"Hawks can still get the rabbits. It's all right. I won't tell anyone you married your beautiful maid."

Robin met his eyes a bit angrily.

"She's a strong-minded woman. Good luck with that. I know from experience it makes for an interesting marriage. I highly recommend it though," Robert said.

Robin calmed down.

"You can't cook, Robin. I know that for a fact," Robert said. "You had to have one maid there who could cook. You can learn to chop wood. You know all there is to know about horses, growing up here and joining the cavalry. You can learn to eat soup with your left hand holding the spoon. You can become fluent in English."

"I have never set my mind to learning to cook or perhaps I would master that as well," Robin said, with eventually a bit of a smirk.

"I am certain you would."

"Robert, you are finally softening a bit."

"My sons speak of nothing but Uncle Robin. You bastard."

Robin burst out laughing and Robert did too.

"Robin, will you ever tell me what happened in India that made you quit the cavalry?" Robert questioned. "I would like to understand what changed you so."

"High level summary," Robin began. "I began training camp in a group of 30 cadets, including Liam Andresen. You remember him?"

"Yes. I do. What ever became of him?"

"Died in my arms. I am the only survivor of all thirty boys. Liam was brutally attacked by a tiger and lies now in the Dutch section of a British cemetery in India. I was able to bring home to his mother a few of his personal belongings," Robin said.

"Robin, in a British cemetery? I know it went bad for us but...."

"Went bad for us? Hearing the colony was revolting, the British attacked us. We were fighting on two fronts. We lost 78% of Dutch troops. The casualties were countless every day. I was in combat 26 days out of every month for nearly seven months in a row. I have killed well over a hundred British troops and officers. I would estimate it to be closer to 300. I lost count," Robin said. "I assumed command of my regiment when my captain and major were killed. We retreated and pulled out of India. I was sent on assassination runs into Italy and Germany. British diplomats or high-ranking military. On return to Amsterdam, I was asked to ship out to the colony in Africa where I would be promoted to major. I retired instead. Married Adrianna."

"You personally have killed 300 men?" Robert almost whispered.

"At least," Robin said. "I'm a guaranteed shot from the saddle. I'm cursed, with a gun in my hand."

Robert turned his head up toward the coffered ceiling, thinking. "You grew up in the saddle. You rode much more than I ever did. Do those killings bother you?"

"Haunt me? Yes. Do I regret them? No. A few of them I see their faces. I think of the Colonel I took a pistol from. He wasn't much older than you are, perhaps. I had fired both my weapons so had to use my bayonet."

"When I am doing surgery and I cut into a patient or remove an arm or leg, I sometimes wonder how I ever became capable of such a thing. Now I wonder how my gentle brother became capable of taking life. You were always bringing kittens and rabbits into the house."

Robin smiled a bit. "Remember the raccoons? Took us forever to get them out of the house. Had the maids shrieking for weeks."

"Do you still like horses?"

"Love them. One in particular. I have a four-year-old gelding at home who reads my mind. He's an incredible jumper. He even tells me in his shoulders and neck that he's going to make a jump. I can feel it coming and how intense it will be, to lean forward and hold on."

"You speak of Connecticut as home then?"

Robin looked at him. "I guess I do."

"I wish you would consider staying in Amsterdam. You could work in your profession here just as much as in America. What are you going to do if they go to war again with England?"

"I have friends there I care about now. I'm the town judge. I'm the Indian agent. I have been offered a position as Colonel if they go to war again. I told them I would consider joining in that case and defending the new American states. With my knowledge of the British.... Somehow defending the land where I am living, makes a lot more sense than defending Dutch colonial interests in a far-off land." Robin finished his cup of tea. "Anyway, as a Colonel it would not be likely I would see close combat."

"Have you a fascination with America that I do not understand?"

"I suppose I do. It is a young country, very exciting. They very much hate the British. I kept getting mistaken for one."

"You're not serious? How could that be?" Robert asked.

"Yes. Especially since I carry British guns. Many of them were born there. They never went to Europe and don't know the different accents," Robin explained. "My suits set me apart. Most of what I had came from Amsterdam. I did get some nice ones in Boston but not as fine as in Europe. They care nothing about aristocracy or royalty there. It's just, do you have money, are you respectable, do you keep your word?"

"You do not need to work anymore."

"No but I'm thirty-six now. Am I to do nothing the rest of my life? Make no contribution to society? I'd like to defend the poor in America, influence the turn of the law. Help make it a better country," Robin said. "I want to help the native Americans."

"Admirable. Admirable, brother."

"Do you ever do surgery for free?"

"What do you mean?"

"Do you only operate on people who can pay?" Robin asked. "Once in a while, Robert, help someone who can't pay. It's tremendously good for your soul."

On the boat

Robin knocked on Adam's cabin door. "It's me. I'm sorry to wake you."

"Come in. What is it?" Adam stepped back in just his sleeping shirt and bare legs.

"May I sleep in your cabin tonight? I just...Frida just can't stop...."

"Come in. Of course. Frida's a baby. She can't help it. Take my bed." Adam invited Robin into his cabin and closed the door.

"I'll take the couch. I don't mean to displace you." Robin sat down on the couch in exhaustion, wrapping his robe closed about himself. "I'm just losing my mind with no sleep."

"Don't be ridiculous. I'll take the couch. Here. Have a drink." Adam opened a bottle of brandy hidden in his parlor and got out two glasses.

Robin accepted his drink. "You're a life saver."

"Not at all. I've been saving this for just such an occasion. Marie knows you are here?" Adam asked.

"Yes, of course." Robin sat back and downed his drink. Then he held out the glass for a refill.

Adam poured. "She won't think you're with Paula?"

"Paula?"

"You have not noticed?" Adam said.

"She is becoming a problem." Robin sulked into a corner of the couch and drank the brandy.

"Slut is what she's becoming."

"Just…ah, I'll deal with her. Just let me get some sleep tonight. I swear I haven't been this long without sleep since the war," Robin said.

"You will take my bed then. Get some sleep. I will be on guard out here. Just pretend I'm Constable Poole or something," Adam said.

Robin looked at him.

Adam deepened his voice and gestured as if he had a gun in his hand. "Go on now. I'm in charge out here."

Robin spit brandy. "That's very good. You've got to do that for him some time."

"Oh no way in hell."

Adam held out a piece of paper to a man who pointed toward an inn across the street. "Leidsestraat? Herberg Leidsestraat?"

The man nodded and pointed again.

"Bedankt." Adam nodded to him. He observed the inn across the street for a while, wondering why Robin was corresponding with someone at this location, and yet he never spoke about it. He watched the front entry for a while, as a carriage with guests arrived and unloaded.

Adam crossed the street and wandered around to the rear of the building. There he saw a dairy wagon delivering to a back door. Adam entered this door, finding himself inside a dimly lit kitchen. The smell of wood fire and bread filled his nose. And it was hot in there. He began unbuttoning his jacket as his eyes adjusted to four women sitting at a simple wooden table. A man walked through, putting away the delivery of milk and cream.

A blonde woman in an apron suddenly stood up at the table and said in English, "Adam! What are you doing here?"

"Paula? What are you doing here?" Adam said.

Paula said something in Dutch to the other women, to the effect of, "He was valet to the man I served on the boat." The table was set with pancakes and tea. "Are you hungry?"

"No. No I had my breakfast. Thank you. Why are you here?" Adam removed his top hat and stood against the kitchen wall with hat in hands.

"I'm lounging here on holiday. Are you following me?" Paula asked. "What for? You don't even like women."

"Oh, I like women well enough. Just not you," Adam replied.

"You will have just as much luck with the magnificent Mr. Van der Kellen as I do, and I don't have any idea where to find him," Paula said. "How did you get to this address? Why are you here?"

"May we speak outside for a moment?" Adam asked.

"Why? None of them speak any English," Paula said. "Have a cup of tea. Sit down. I won't eat you alive or anything."

"Very well then." Adam sat at the table.

The women said something and laughed.

Adam met their eyes.

Paula sat and poured tea for him. "Cream and sugar there."

"Bedankt," Adam said.

"They said you are handsome. I said you like men," Paula told him.

Adam sat back with a nod. "Well at least I know I'll get out of here with my dignity."

"And your virginity," Paula shot back.

"Well, that's one of us," Adam said. "Are you corresponding with Mr. Van der Kellen?"

"Of course not. I have no idea where to post him a letter. Why?" Paula went back to eating her pancakes.

"He received a letter from this address."

"Oh, so that's it." Paula sat back in her chair. "That explains it."

"Explains what?"

"How I got this job with a 100-guilder trust for me if I behave myself." Paula spooned pancake into her mouth and then said with her mouth full, "Van der Kellen's 100 guilders."

"He got you this job?" Then Adam nodded. "Well, I suggest you behave yourself. It will be a new habit for you."

"Shut up. You little fluff," Paula told him. "Still working as his valet? Get aroused when you run your hands through that hair of his, do you?"

"Not enough to get myself sent away with 100 bucks over my head." Adam sipped his tea and then added cream to it. "I'm running errands for him. Thought I'd stop by."

"In Amsterdam by yourself? You can't do that. What errands?" Paula then translated a bit for the other maids.

"I am meeting with some business associates of his. I am his legal assistant. I find someone who speaks English when I need to. Otherwise, I show an address to a boat tender and climb aboard. I get around on the canals," Adam said. "Amsterdam is wonderful."

"Lucky thing you can pass for a man, and a gentleman at that. He put you in new suits, did he?" Paula said. "Don't you look pretty now."

"Charming as ever, Paula. He gave you a chance at a new start. Aspire to be worthy." Adam put his teacup down on the saucer. "Give anything for a decent cup of coffee."

"I can get you one, if you give me where he lives."

"That's all right. I'll have a nice cup of coffee with him tomorrow morning, just like I did this morning. Shoulder to shoulder with him. Every morning." Adam slid his chair back and rose. "Tell the rest of these ladies that I wish them a good day."

"You been doing it wrong all these years. One good woman is what you need," Paula said. "One day Robin Van der Kellen will send you away too. You'll see. Tell him I said hello."

"He won't even know I saw you."

Robin made his way down the grand staircase and out onto the balcony where he found Wout and Jonas. "Jonas, you are here every day now."

"You are bored with us?" Wout asked. "It's not as if I can leave."

"No of course not." Robin sat down with them and Zoey, the maid, immediately poured coffee for him. "Thank you."

Zoey quietly stepped back.

"How was last night?" Jonas questioned, waggling his eyebrows.

"Oh, shut up," Robin snapped.

Jonas and Wout laughed.

"Well, where is she? Why are you not romancing your wife?" Jonas asked.

"She's tending to Lynn," Robin said. "She has the baby up there with her."

"Poor Robin. Everyone gets looked after but you," Wout teased.

"You especially shut up," Robin said.

"Me? I didn't offer you a prostitute." Wout drank his coffee. "Send someone shopping for more brandy. You're going to run out."

"Because you're opening another bottle every night," Robin said.

The butler approached the table then. "A letter has come for you, sir." He offered it on a silver plate to Robin.

"For me?" Robin accepted it. He broke the wax seal and unfolded it open. Inside brown paper was another white paper folded up. "It's from New York. From Elizabeth Miller. Oh." His eyes read on.

"Another woman is writing you?" Jonas said. "Impertinent."

Robin frowned. "A friend has died. Her husband Edward Miller. I shall have to tell Marie. This will be very sad news indeed." He refolded the letter. "An interesting couple, the Millers. He was a banker like you, Wout. Befriended us on the train and invited us to stay with them in New York. He was in his sixties, I'd say. Drank quite a lot. Don't know if that was the cause of his death. His wife and Marie became very good friends as they are the same age."

"A twenty-year-old and a sixty-year-old man. No doubt what killed him," Wout said.

Jonas shot him a look.

"My apologies, Robin," Wout said.

"No. It's all right. Had the same thought myself once or twice," Robin said. "She was always upset not to have children. Well, perhaps her next husband will be closer to her own age. She's a bit wild."

"Do go on, Robin," Wout said. "How do you know this woman is a bit wild?"

Robin lowered his chin. "Don't laugh. He's dead. It's not polite."

"Nobody's laughing. In what way is the twenty-year-old married woman wild?" Wout questioned.

"She asked Marie and myself if she could have a child with me," Robin whispered. "Married for years with Edward and no children."

Jonas and Wout met eyes across the table. Wout had his hand over his mouth tightly.

Jonas sat back.

Wout laid his hands on the table and looked out onto the gardens. "Do tell, Robin Van der Kellen, what the hell is it like to have women, and men for that matter, offering themselves to you all the time?"

Jonas burst out laughing.

"What are you talking about? I can't get my own wife to have me," Robin said.

"You can have everyone else's wife," Wout said. "And have a history of it, apparently."

"Maybe you should stop trying so hard," Jonas suddenly realized. "Play indifferent. She'll be all over you. How did you know your valet had affections for you?"

"Indifferent?" Robin's eyebrows rose. "When has indifference ever gotten you bedded?"

"Did you actually sleep with somebody else's bride on their wedding night?" Wout questioned.

"Not on their wedding night." Robin sat back like a peacock. "The night before, of course. Deflowered her first, you could say. Couldn't let her be curious about me for the rest of her life. Did you bring your riding clothes? Let's take some horses out for some exercise."

"Frustrated, Robin?" Jonas teased. "Needing to work off some energy?"

"But see that's another means for Mrs. Miller to stay in contact with me. And if she turns up pregnant now that her husband is dead...well." Robin rolled his eyes.

"Everyone will know it wasn't the valet," Wout said.

Marie was standing behind Robin as he sat at the dinner table, her hands on his shoulders and she let his curls wrap around her fingers.

"Darling, that feels wonderful," Robin said softly.

"How is your shoulder after the riding this afternoon?" Marie asked him.

"Sore, of course, but pleased to have your hands on it," Robin said.

"Your shoulder hurts from riding a horse?" Robert questioned, taking his seat at the head of the table. "I thought the horse did the work."

"Not the way he rides. He jumped every hedge out there," Jonas said.

"Jumped? With a horse?" Robert asked. "Which horse?"

Marie took her seat on the other side of Robin.

Robin smiled at her. Then he answered Robert, "The grey stallion. Grijs."

"The stallion? What are you doing riding a stallion? That one has been throwing the trainers off. We're just keeping him until he's old enough to breed," Robert said. "Of course I have to keep setting all the broken bones."

"Oh, definitely breed him. But don't get rid of him. He's a fine ride if you can hold on," Robin said. "Yes, your trainers tried to talk me out of it. He only bucks for a few moments. Once he realized he wasn't getting rid of me he decided to see what I had for him. I'll confess, riding him straight toward the first hedge gave me second thoughts. But then as soon as I felt him preparing to spring, I knew I could read him. And of course, once we landed and I was still on board he realized he could read me as well."

"Robin, isn't that dangerous? You'll worry Marie," Mila scolded.

"It might be crazy, but I don't worry about Robin on a horse. He's holding on like a spider with a gentle but unshakeable grip," Marie said.

"And eight legs," Robert said.

Robin met Marie in her bedroom for a passionate kiss. After it, she looked at the crib.

Robin embraced her. "She's sleeping. Don't worry."

"Shhh," Marie cautioned. She pulled back from him and began undressing.

Robin moved in and opened some of the buttons on her dress.

Marie stepped back again.

Robin remained where he was and began undoing his tie, but watching her.

She removed her gown. Her corset was tied in the back. "Can you help me with this?"

With the invitation Robin stepped in to untie her stays and leaned to kiss her throat warmly. He embraced her and slipped his hands beneath what he'd loosened on her.

Marie blocked his hands.

At that Robin stopped his advances and lowered his chin sadly. "Have I misunderstood?"

"Misunderstood what?"

"I thought your signals were encouragement," Robin said sadly.

"I didn't send any signals. All I did was touch your shoulders," Marie whispered.

Robin let out a breath. He lowered his eyes to the carpet. "And my knee and hand and..."

Marie went to him and held onto Robin's arms. "I'm sorry."

Frida began fussing and Mare went to the baby.

That left Robin to take a long breath and walk around to the other side of the bed. He unbuttoned his vest, his shirt, and removed them. He opened his belt and his trousers. He stepped out of the trousers and laid all of it on the chair beside the bed. Robin folded back the covers and climbed into bed.

Chapter 6: The Dutch Hero

May 6, 1842 On the ship toward Amsterdam

"Sir, you're looking very tired this morning."

Robin met eyes with the young blond Polish maid in the small sitting room of their shipboard cabin. He could barely stand up straight without hitting his head on the low ceiling, as he stood near the doorway of the small cabin.

The maid squeezed past him to the bedroom of the cabin.

Robin was still buttoning his shirt and tucking it in. "It was a long night."

"Let me take the baby for the coming night then. She can sleep with me and let you two get some time alone," the maid said as she fluffed the pillows and pulled up the sheets.

"That is up to my wife." Robin exited the cabin to the small dining area in the center of the first-class cabins. Marie was sitting at the table, holding the baby and chatting with two of the other wives.

One of the husbands was standing beside him, holding onto the wall, and gave him a look over.

"I do apologize. She is just two months old," Robin said.

The man nodded. "And last night was two months long. Sleeping now, isn't she? Figures."

"Charles, that's rude. You make your apologies," the man's wife snapped. "The baby is seasick."

Marie glared at the man as well.

Robin moved past the man and took a seat across from Marie. He poured himself a cup of coffee from the pot in the center of the table. "Sit down, Charles, before you fall on me."

"Try just a little brandy on your finger tonight. She may be teething as well," the other wife suggested.

"Is that safe for a baby?" Marie asked.

"Oh yes. Did that for my babes," she said.

"Van der Kellen, what do you do on deck every day?" Charles finally did take the seat beside Robin. The benches and table were bolted to the floor. The edges of the table had a wooden trim piece surrounding it, keeping dishware from sliding off at the ship's angle.

"You know what I'm doing," Robin said.

"Thought maybe you take a nap in one of the row boats," Charles said. "A rather good idea, actually."

One of the crewmen suddenly entered. "Mr. Van der Kellen? Captain needs you on deck sir."

Robin set down his coffee and stood up. He quickly exited with the sailor.

Charles mocked him, "Captain needs you on deck. He's a cavalryman. Did somebody see a horse? A sea horse?"

"A lot you know," Marie said. "We're in the shipping corridor with England right now."

"And what's he going to do about it?" Charles asked.

They suddenly heard a distant cannon firing.

Charles sat up rigid then.

Everyone listened intently.

Footsteps were coming.

Another crewman came down to the dining room. "I was sent to collect Mr. Van der Kellen's coat and hat. It's raining."

Marie indicated the cabin, and the maid opened the door. She handed the coat and leather hat out.

"What was that sound?" Charles grabbed the sailor's arm.

"Two ships on the horizon. We believe one fired on the other."

"Is one English?" Marie asked.

"That's what we need your husband for, ma'am, and his eagle eyes."

"Marie, we need to talk, darling." Robin sat across from her at the table on the terrace.

Marie looked at him. "What about, dear?"

Robin set an envelope on the table between their two place settings. "Elizabeth Miller wrote to me. She wrote in English."

"English? Why wouldn't she write in French to me? Nothing in French for me in there?" Marie said.

Robin shook his head. "She felt it better that you hear this from me. Edward has died."

"Edward? What happened? Are you sure you read her right? Edward is dead?" Marie sniffled.

Robin took her hand beneath the table. "His heart. Much like my father. Edward went peacefully, dying in his sleep. He was found by Jonas one morning. Elizabeth is now a young widow."

"I must write her immediately," Marie said. "Unless."

"Unless what?"

"She didn't...in that letter...request you again?" Marie asked.

"I'll read it all to you. You can have anyone in the house translate it for you. It was all very appropriate," Robin said. "Her mother is staying with her. Edward left everything to her. The manager at his bank is appointed as her trustee. The fortune is all hers. As trustee, he can't have any of it, he just advises her so that she does not spend it all foolishly. Edward trusted the man."

"I will write a long letter to her today," Marie said. "Have you heard from June?"

"Not yet. The next post will probably have letters from home, June, Michael Poole, and such," Robin said.

"I will write to June and Alice Poole too." Marie kissed Robin on the mouth. "I will get Adam to write English for me, if you can loan him to me for an hour."

Marie entered the giant kitchen in the lower level of Robert's house and immediately staff members came to her. The head chef spoke in Dutch to her.

"I beg your pardon. Do any of you speak French or English?" Marie asked.

The head chef changed over to French then, "Yes, madam. What may we do for you, please?"

"As you know my husband is Robin Van der Kellen. I would like to learn recipes for some of his favorite foods that you prepare here. I want to bring them back to my chef in America to make for him."

The chef translated for some around him. Then he said, "Of course Madam Van der Kellen. I can only write them in French or Dutch for you."

"French will be fine," Marie said. "May I also observe how some dishes are prepared? I love to cook myself."

"Observe yourself? Certainly. I must insist that we give you an apron just to project your lovely gown in the kitchen. We will get you one immediately."

"A letter for you, sir." The butler held out a silver platter toward Robin. "And a messenger awaiting a response."

Robin collected it and stared for a moment at the seal.

"What is it?" Robert asked across the dinner table. "Is it about the case?"

"What is it, Robin?" Wout questioned.

"Excuse me, a moment." Robin rose from the table and set his hand on Marie's shoulder. "I shall return momentarily." Robin followed the butler out to the hall and then to the far side of the hall. "Did a royal messenger bring this?"

"Yes, sir. Just moments ago," the butler said. "I am told he is awaiting some answer from you, Sir Robin."

Robin looked down at the letter and broke the seal to open it. Gold foil stationary unfolded in his hand, and he quickly read it twice. He looked at the butler.

"Shall I provide paper and ink to write a reply?"

"No. Tell him immediately that my answer is yes," Robin told him.

The butler nodded and walked off toward the barrel-vaulted entry of the house.

Robin returned to the dining room and refolded his letter to hide the golden interior of it. He reclaimed his seat and said to Marie, "I must away for a few days. I do apologize for this. But it is most urgent that I go pack and leave at once. There is a carriage waiting for me." He went to the kitchen door and looked inside to see the staff sitting about the kitchen table. "Adam, I need you."

Adam rose and moved around the table of maids and cooks.

Marie stood up at the family dining table. "What is it, Robin?"

"The king asks that I explain to him at once, Wout's case," Robin said. Then he directed at Mr. Van de Berg. "It has come to his attention, and he sent for me with a carriage to Soestdijk Palace. I must away at once. I'll bring Adam with me. I need those new suits packed quickly." He kissed Marie on the mouth and hurried off.

May 7, 1841 Robin returns to the ship

"Fetch his wife. The boat is returning," Second mate of the ship ordered.

Marie left Frida with Paula in their cabin and Adam helped her up on deck. "Where?" The fog was milky white around them.

"Prepare to weigh anchor and make sails as soon as we get the boat on board."

Marie stared over the rail in the direction the other men were watching. She could barely make out a dark shape rolling up with the swells and disappearing as it rolled down between them. She held her hand to her throat watching. And Adam held onto her.

A Jacob's ladder of crisscrossing ropes was lowered over the side as well as the ropes on swing arms extended over the rail to pull the rowboat back up.

As the rowboat came closer Marie and Adam could see just how hard the sea was tossing the little boat. Each upswell put them into a wind that splashed the icy water onto the men inside the boat. Four men were rowing. Two in the middle were not. Eventually she could make out Robin's wide brimmed leather hat. He couldn't see her until she stepped up onto the bottom rail and waved in her white blouse to him. Robin waved back briefly, having to quickly hold on again as they rolled over another swell. Adam was gripping onto Marie to keep her from falling down.

Now the wind and waves nearly pounded the boat up against the hull. Marie heard it hit.

"Stand back, mum." A sailor moved Marie to an inner wall. "Stay here and hold on tight. Boy, hold her right here."

Adam held her to the doorway, imagining Robin grabbing that ladder and climbing between swells. They both willed him to hold on tight in the slimy sea foam.

Men on board were pulling the ladder up even as others waited on lines for the rowboat.

Robin's hand reached up over the deck and was grabbed by one of the seamen. Another man grabbed his other hand and Robin was pulled on deck, dragged back from the edge on his belly and pulled onto his feet.

Robin saw Marie and Adam. He turned to see the first mate get pulled in just as he had been. They both went directly to the captain. "We make heading east northeast and go as fast as we can. We'll slip past the bow of the Vengeance. They'll remain where they are for another half day, seeking the privateer out. This should let us get away."

"They won't escort us all the way?" the captain asked.

"They're going after the privateer. With any luck we'll hear the explosions as we escape." Robin was shaking hard from the cold water and offered the Dutch Navy sword to the captain. "Present for you, from their captain."

The captain looked down at the sword. "Did you have any trouble there?"

"They were about to hang Robin over the side by his boots. He talked his way out of it and got us everything we need," the first mate said.

The captain handed the sword back to Robin. "I sent the right man. Your wife is over there. Get below and into dry clothes. Let's make sail. Quietly now. Get that boat aboard. You men, get below and get changed. You have work to do."

Robin made his way in the rolling swells across the deck to where Marie and Adam held onto the handrail at the top of the first-class stairway.

"Oh Robin…. I didn't know you were in such danger." Marie reached a hand up to his cheek and kissed his mouth. "You must be wet right through. Did you have anything to eat?"

"Let's get him to the cabin quickly." Adam grabbed onto him by the arms.

"We were treated very well. Fed. Allowed to dry up near a stove. Warm bunk to sleep in. How is Frida?" Robin was shaking, holding that sword up tight. "Start down. Hold the rail, darling."

Adam got Marie started down the steep steps, and then he pulled Robin's arm about his neck. Robin moaned in pain as he struggled to find footing with limbs too cold to take instruction. Adam took more of his weight, keeping him from falling and keeping him moving downward. Finally, below deck, Robin slipped down to his knees on the wooden floor.

Adam's forceful voice rang out in the salon. "Charles, take his arm. I'll get the other. Now! He's freezing, can't you see?"

The man came to his aid immediately. Others scrambled out of the way and got the door to Robin's cabin open. Marie hurried ahead.

Paula stood up and put the baby in her cradle on the wall. She stood back flat to the wall for Adam and Charles to bring Van der Kellen past her, into the bedroom.

"Get his clothes off now. All of it. It's just like falling through the ice. We need to get him warm quickly," Adam ordered.

Charles held Robin up while Marie and Adam both opened buttons of coat, jacket, vest and trousers. Marie grabbed the blanket off the bed to wrap around him. Adam peeled his trousers down and undergarment. Charles pulled the shirt, vest, and jacket back off his shoulders.

"Marie, get into bed with him. Paula, get the brandy. Don't just stand there!" Adam ordered.

Charles helped Robin onto the bed, wrapped in that blanket, and reached for more blankets.

Marie laid down with Robin folded around behind her, clinging to her and violently shaking.

Charles and Adam layered more blankets on top of them.

Paula squeezed around Charles to offer a glass of brandy to Robin. Adam took it from her and held it over Marie, for Robin to gulp from it.

"What now can we do?" Charles asked. "Will he be all right?"

"We need hot water to rinse the salt out of his hair. We need Paula to mind Frida. And I need to refill this," Adam indicated the empty glass.

"I will see to the water and some towels," Charles's wife said from the doorway.

"Are we safe now from the English?" Charles asked.

"Yes. We're slipping away into the fog while the French ship stays here, blocking for us," Adam said. "I heard Robin tell the captain."

Charles brought the brandy bottle from the sitting room and refilled the glass in Adam's hand.

Adam fed brandy to Robin again.

"You sure you're just a valet?" Charles asked him.

"Prince Adam?" Paula spoke up. "He's no valet."

"Robin, are you all right?" Marie asked.

Robin was still shaking against her, shivering but warmed inside by the brandy, and outside by Marie's own body heat. "Not quite yet."

Adam pulled the blankets up higher over Robin and Marie's heads. He patted Marie on the shoulder. And he turned to glare at Paula. "Take the baby into my cabin and mind her. Give them some privacy."

"Very well, your highness," Paula whispered to him harshly. She gathered Frida up and cuddled her as she left the cabin.

Charles and Adam left and closed the door.

"We're boiling plenty of water so he can clean up and get warm," Charles's wife said. Maids were busying with pots and firewood.

"Thank you," Adam told her. "He'll need hot food inside him as well." He followed Paula into his own cabin and stood in the doorway.

She sat with the baby in her lap, rocking her gently. She looked about Adam's sitting parlor, his books, his inks, some of Robin's clothing hanging to dry.

Adam said under his breath, "What is it you have so against me? You've been rude to me this entire voyage. And I don't get it. I've done nothing to you. I do my job, looking after Mr. Van der Kellen. Or is that your problem?"

"Your kind has no use for women at all, do they?" Paula asked.

"My kind?" Adam's brow furrowed.

"Does he know what you are?" she said.

Adam entered the cabin and moved Robin's shirts to a hook on the wall inside his bedroom, making room for him to sit down across from the woman.

"Do you even know what you are?" Paula looked at him. "Not a man. Not a woman." She picked up a small book from the side table. "I feel sorry for you."

"Don't touch that." Adam stood up quickly.

Paula was holding the book. She could open it a bit with one hand, the other hand holding Frida on her lap. There was handwriting inside it, drawings, and blank pages. Drawings of Robin. All were drawings of Robin.

"Give it here." Adam held out his hand for it.

"Is this where you keep your secrets? What if I give it to him? And he learns all your filthy desirings?"

Adam snatched it from her. He held it close against his chest.

"You'll never have him, don't you know?"

Adam put his book into his bedroom and shut the door. "You look after that baby, or I swear...." Adam walked out and back to Robin's cabin. He knocked on their bedroom door and then opened it.

"Oh Adam, he's not getting better. His hands and feet hurt so much," Marie called.

Adam entered and shut their door. He grabbed up a towel. "Then forgive me. This is what must be done." He crawled onto the bed with them and imposed himself behind Robin, between his body and the wall of the ship. He slid beneath the blankets, with only the one blanket between himself and an unclothed Robin. He wrapped the towel around Robin's wet head. And then he wrapped his arms around Robin and Marie, holding Robin's back against his chest. "Where's his hands? Put them in mine. God they're cold. Marie, get his hands against your throat or chest. Get them warm."

"He's shivering so," Marie nearly cried.

"It's all right. You know how he feels about survival situations," Adam said.

"One must forego silly conventions," Marie said.

Adam laid his warm hand on Robin's cheek and temple. "Take it easy. You will warm up. Easy. I've got you."

And in a few moments, pressed between Adam and Marie, Robin's shivering eased. His hands went from white to red to normal color again.

"How are your feet? Pins and needles?" Adam asked.

"Yes."

"That's good. It will pass. You're getting better," Adam soothed.

"Adam how do you know so much about this?" Marie questioned.

"Fell in the river once."

"Your river?" Robin managed to ask.

"Yes." Adam raised his head and looked to pad that towel on Robin's head and hair. "They're boiling water for you to wash off the salt, when you are ready. And we'll get some hot tea and soup into you. Warm clothes. Do you want me to get up?"

"No. No. How do you generate so much heat, Mr. Hudson?" Robin shivered.

"Nothing better to do, I suppose."

Upstairs, Adam and Robin hurriedly packed Robin's new suits and shirts, with his new shoes. Robin paused and had a good look at Adam. "Grab those two suits there, the black one and the grey. Remove your jacket. You are going to wear mine and I'll wear the new ones." Robin stripped off his own jacket at the same time that Adam also started unbuttoning.

"You wish me to go with you?" Adam stammered.

"You shall be my legal assistant. You are not a valet for the next few days. I hired you in America and you only speak English." Robin stripped off his trousers and tossed them to Adam. "Put these on." He pulled on the new ones.

Adam picked up those trousers, still warm from Robin's body. "But I was hired in America, *and I do only speak English.*"

"That is the key to this masquerade. Omit everything you must and keep what you can." Robin buttoned up his new pants and then stripped off his jacket and vest. Their hands met in the passing of the clothing.

"Where are we going?" Adam then pulled on Robin's vest and jacket. "Your pocket watch is in here."

"Keep it on you. You'll look silly without one." Robin grabbed another watch off his dresser and money out of the drawer. "Besides, it's my father's and I despise it. I was only wearing it to piss off Robert. Hurry up and fill that bag with the new suits for me and that other bag with my black and grey suits for you."

Adam rushed about doing as he was told.

"As a valet you would not be allowed into places where I need you." Robin buttoned on his new vest and pulled on his brand-new pin stripped suit. Then he dropped his pistol into one suitcase and a Colt revolver into the other.

"Expecting trouble, are we?" Adam started to reach for toiletries.

"Don't bother with those. They will be provided. There are rumors about where we are going. That is why I cannot bring Marie with me. I need your particular expertise and I need you at my side." Robin stuffed underthings and stockings into his bag. "Grab those papers, seal up that ink bottle, and bring the pens also. Put them in your case. Be sure that ink is closed, or it shall ruin everything you have."

"Sealed very well, I say. Where are we going, Robin?"

"You know what? Forget the ink. Leave it here. I will ask for some at the palace," Robin said. "Not worth the risk."

With both of them suited up properly and the suitcases closed, they looked at each other. Robin was in his new tailored suit and Adam in his older black one.

"Fits you well. Run upstairs and grab underclothing and stockings for yourself. Sleep shirt. Meet me downstairs," Robin told him. "Carry yourself with airs. Look down to no one. And when you meet the king, you must bow very low just as I do."

"Meet the king?"

Robin patted Adam on the shoulder. "I must persuade the king to save Wout. And I need your help."

"What particular expertise have I?" Adam stammered.

"How do I look?"

"Resplendent," Adam said.

Robin reached into his pocket and handed several guilders to him. "For tipping. One of those for whoever provides a service to you. No blushing. Try to look serious. If in doubt, look bored."

Robin ran down the stairs and found the family waiting to see them off. Marie gave Robin a kiss and hug goodbye. "Kiss Frida for me. I'll be back just as soon as I can. And Wout, stay here out of sight. I'll get the king to help us."

Adam joined him and stuffed his things into one of the bags. "Ready."

Adam followed Robin down to the awaiting royal carriage with its gilded trim and team of four horses. The royal messenger stood beside it. He opened the carriage door. "Mr. Van der Kellen?"

"Yes, sir. And this is my legal assistant, Adam Hudson. I need him for the case," Robin said.

"Of course, sir. It is a two-hour journey to the palace. Did you have supper, sir?"

"We did, yes." Robin boarded the carriage and urged Adam to hurry in beside him.

The messenger spoke to the drivers and then climbed in, closing the door. He sat facing them with a table between them. On the table were glasses and a bottle of brandy. An oil lamp was lit, mounted on the opposite side wall. The carriage began to move. The messenger poured three glasses of brandy, saying, "It's a chilly night, I'm afraid. My name is Luuk Klaussen. Since I have gathered you aboard, I am to school you in royal protocol."

"My assistant Adam Hudson. He only speaks English. May I translate for him?"

"I can do English," Klaussen switched languages. He opened a picnic basket and unwrapped a plate of sandwiches. "I did not get the luxury of supper. I have plenty here. Help yourselves."

"If you don't mind." Adam chose a sandwich. He munched on it.

Klaussen handed him a napkin. Then he pushed one toward Robin and guzzled a bit of brandy. "You will spend the night, and in the morning, meet the king. When you meet the king, you must bow at the waist as low as you possibly can. And you do not rise until he releases you. Usually, it is only for a moment. You will meet the queen. You do not kiss her hand or touch her in any way. Again, you will bow. Though it is customary for gentlemen to kiss on each cheek upon meeting, you will not do this to the king. Is that clear?"

"Yes, Klaussen." Robin picked up his brandy and had a sip. "I cannot meet the king tonight?"

"He is not there yet. He will be arriving from another palace in the morning. If you had refused, I would have driven on through to save him the trip," Klaussen said. "As it is, I drop you off and continue on to let him know you are awaiting him."

"Yes of course."

"Now, let me instruct you about the dining procedures. You do not eat until the king eats. When the king is finished dining, you are also finished dining."

Adam and Robin looked at each other.

"Getting all this?" Robin asked.

"Eat only when the king eats," Adam summarized. "Top hats at the table?"

"Absolutely not," Luuk reprimanded him. "Mr. Van der Kellen will sit on the king's right. You will sit beside him. Are you armed, at all?"

"Ah, I have a pistol," Robin stammered.

"Leave it in your room in your case. You will be observed for weapons before entering a room where the king shall be." Klaussen gobbled down a sandwich and started on another one. "You begin with silverware on the outside and work your way in toward the plate. There will be ten courses. If you do not wish to eat one of the courses, lay the appropriate silverware across the top of the plate and it will be removed for you. There will be other guests of course. Treat them all with the utmost of respect and honor."

Robin downed his whole brandy then and poured another. "Will I have a chance to speak with his majesty in private?"

"I would expect that is why he has summoned you. Do as he instructs."

"Of course."

"Go easy with liquor in the palace. Do not be seen behaving drunkenly. You will be expelled."

"We would not dishonor the palace," Robin insisted. "Does he wish to reprimand me?"

"I did not get that impression. Merely that your legal case interested him," Klaussen said. "You will speak of it freely with him. He is the head of all manners legal."

The carriage arrived inside the white arching structure of Soestdijk Palace, around a circle drive, and up to the front steps. "Good luck, Mr. Van der Kellen."

"Thank you, Mr. Klaussen."

They were met by several servants who gathered Robin and Adam's bags and ushered them up the stairs. They entered a grand entrance hall with marble statues and gold framed portrait paintings. Robin and Adam had little time to glance around as they were soon led down a hall, up another gilded grand staircase, and down another very long hallway. They saw many servants moving about, cleaning or delivering various items throughout the palace.

Finally, they arrived at a set of double doors. Gastenkamer Blauw. This opened to a parlor of blue silk furniture and a huge marble fireplace.

"You will have these adjoining rooms, Mr. Van der Kellen and Mr. Hudson," the servant said in Dutch. "You should find anything that you will need in your rooms but do ring the bell if anything is amiss. A late supper is provided for you on the table. We will come round in the morning to get you up in time for breakfast."

"Bedankt," Robin said.

Adam and Robin were left alone. Adam wandered inside the parlor and into one bedroom on one side, and another bedroom on the other. Both rooms were spacious with their own fireplaces lit. One room was dark blue and gold, the other was a lighter blue and gold. Oil lamps and candles were lit throughout. Both rooms had two tall windows each. The coffered ceilings were high, and each room had a golden chandelier.

Adam immediately got Robin's new suits unpacked and hanging in the armoire of his room.

Robin had a look at the muffins, cakes, meats and cheeses that were available on the table. There were four chairs at the table and a blue sofa along the other wall. Robin moved a piece of white cake with frosting onto a plate and sat down at the table.

When Adam returned, Robin had the cake almost eaten. "You're eating again? You're going to get as fat as your brother."

"I am not," Robin insisted. "You're in my pants. You should know I'm not!"

Adam burst out laughing. He pulled out a chair across from Robin and selected a muffin. "Am I doing all right, so far?"

"So far."

Adam smiled and poured himself a glass of wine. "What is this?" He indicated the carafe of green liquid and the hookah beside it.

"Don't touch those. Absinthe and opium."

There was a knock at the door.

"Drugs?" Adam burst out of the chair and stepped back.

They looked at each other. Robin got up and answered the door to find two young women in the hall.

"Good evening, Mr. Van der Kellen. May we enter?"

Robin stepped back allowing the two women to come into the room with them. He looked over at Adam. "What can we do for you?"

One began unbuttoning her gown. "It is what can we do for you, gentlemen."

"How may we entertain you?" the other said coyly, pulling up her skirt a bit too much.

Adam stood behind the table, gripping the back of a chair.

Robin stepped toward the door again. "No thank you, darling. I have a lovely wife at home."

One of the women went to Robin and stroked her hand down his chest, and onto his belt. "Are you certain, handsome?" She slipped fingertips into the top of his trousers, reaching for his top button.

"I'm quite certain." Robin stepped back and looked over his shoulder. "Adam?"

Adam backed away toward the fireplace. "What?"

"Want company for the night?" Robin asked him in English.

"Not those. Whatever those are," Adam said.

Robin laughed. "Sorry ladies. Appreciate the offer, however. Good night."

"Oh, good night, handsome. I shall be dreaming of you. Ring the bell if you change your mind."

The women left and Robin closed the door.

"Were those prostitutes?" Adam whispered. "Is that what you call them?"

Robin, laughing, returned to the table and poured himself some wine. "House entertainment."

"What if Marie had been here?" Adam made his way back to the table.

"Probably still would have offered." Robin sat and sipped his wine. "I don't think Marie would have accepted."

"Marie almost threw Paula off the ship," Adam blurted out.

"I know." Robin laughed. "Sit down. Nobody's forcing you to have sex with anybody."

"I'm not supposed to tell Marie that happened, am I?" Adam held a hand to his throat. "Or that there are drugs on the table."

Robin pointed at him. "You know? It was only an offer of sex and drugs. Not a beheading. Sit down."

Chapter 7: Test of Character

On the boat, Following the French ship mission:

That night in their cabin, with lights out and child sleeping peacefully, Robin held back the covers for Marie to join him in the bunk. He kissed her hungrily. And Marie, with an infant only a few months old, wanted very much to kiss Robin but as he pursued more, she resisted. She blocked his hand. She stiffened.

Robin stopped. "What is it?"

"Oh, I want to give you everything. I want to kiss you. Want to please you."

"I'm no stranger, darling. You know me better than anyone. I won't hurt you," Robin whispered. "I thought you were ready."

"I wanted to be ready."

"What can I do? Take it slower?"

"I feel like a virgin again," Marie whispered.

"I can fix that again," Robin whispered and kissed her passionately.

But Marie stiffened. She blocked his hand.

And when Robin stopped his advances, she cried.

Robin kissed and soothed her. "Shhh, darlin. It's alright. Wait 'til you're ready. Don't wake the baby."

Marie clung to him.

Robin wrapped around her in their small bunk. He stroked her hair and whispered to her. And with so little sleep the previous nights, with the pressure that had been on him, with his command of that whole situation, the rebuff in his bedroom was of little notice to him. He was soon sleeping.

Paula peeked into the cabin the next morning as Marie opened the door for her. Robin lay sleeping in their bunk, his back against the hull of the ship, and he was shirtless with blankets up to his waist. His head lay on one of their two pillows. His bare chest had a fascinating scar on the upper right, but the rest of his exposed body was beautiful.

Marie handed the baby to Paula. "Do you mind changing her while I get dressed?"

"I can do that, mum. Do you need help with your stays?"

"I might. I'll try to get them myself."

"I'll change Frida in the sitting room right here." Paula took another glance at Robin before exiting.

Marie dressed on her own and quietly slipped from the bedroom, closing the door.

"How is Mr. Van der Kellen? Did the French hurt him?" Paula sat on the built-in couch, holding Frida in her lap.

Marie sat beside her. "He's very tired. I think it was more dire than he lets on."

In the morning, Adam got up from his enormous bed, pulled on a fur collared robe, and wandered across the parlor to peer into Robin's room.

Van der Kellen was yet asleep in his giant bed. His arms were around one pillow and his head on two others. His hair fanned out on the pillow and his bare back was smooth and fair. Adam could see him breathing.

Adam moved closer to the bed and held onto the footpost a moment. He reached in and tapped Robin's foot through the blankets. "Robin? I don't know what time they will come round to wake us up. It is seven o-clock."

Robin opened his dark eyes and moved a bit. "Okay. Wake me when they come by."

"Yes sir." Adam went back to his room and his vanity closet to find a male servant filling a bathtub with hot water. Adam handed him a tip. Back in the parlor, two maids set up coffee, tea, and elaborate breakfast on the table. Adam gave them each a guilder as well. Adam returned to Robin's room and checked Robin's vanity closet to find the same man filling that tub now. He returned to Robin. "They have delivered coffee and filled the bathing tubs."

"Really?" Robin let out a breath. He got up on one elbow. "I guess I'll have to get up. It's just so heavenly without the screaming every two hours. Is that evil of me?"

"Not at all. I think we all prefer a night lacking screaming. Would you like a cup of coffee for your bath?"

"Please."

"With or without absinthe?"

Robin sat down at the parlor table for another cup of coffee when Adam came out with shaving supplies. He placed a towel around Robin's neck, covering his white collar and went to work to give Robin a nice shave as he did every morning. Lathered him up and shaved him, then wiped the remaining lather away.

"Thank you, Adam."

Then Adam returned to his bedroom to do his own shaving, not that he needed much. He finished dressing and returned to the table. "I still can't believe they sent you women."

"Sent us women," Robin corrected. "Bet you never had that happen before."

"Can we expect that again tonight?" Adam pulled up a chair and sat down to have his own coffee.

"After last night, probably will send us two teenage boys," Robin said.

Adam shot him a look.

Robin drank some coffee. "All yours. Welcome to Amsterdam."

"Holy." Adam let out a sigh. "It is a test of character then?"

"It is a decadent offer of hospitality from a king rumored to be quite libertine."

"Libertine?" Adam asked.

Robin looked at him. "Immoral. Decadent. Freethinker. Unnatural."

"A king? Never heard of such a thing."

"Really? Most European royalty are married to each other, whether they are cousins or not. The queen is his cousin from Russia," Robin explained. "This is why I need you here."

"What? Why?"

Robin rose from the table and paced in front of the fireplace. "How do I say this?"

Adam got up also and walked closer to Robin. He looked at him.

Robin took Adam by the arm and said confidentially to him. "There are rumors the king has male lovers, his close servants. I'm afraid he may have asked me here to...."

Adam leaned closer to whisper seriously, "Sleep with him? Well, you know, for Wout's case, you will just have to give in."

Robin shot him a look, nose to nose with him.

Adam could hold back a smile no longer and Robin shoved him away.

Adam hopped backwards, laughing. "You really think everybody on earth just falls madly in love with you? That this king has heard of how handsome you are? That it made the papers? Well, actually it did make the papers, didn't it? Wout Van de Berg being defended by the famously handsome barrister Van der Kellen, the Dutch war hero."

Robin put his hands on his hips, frowning.

"All right, I made up the famous part," Adam said. "Did we put aftershave on you? What do you smell like? Come over here."

Soestdijk Palace Dining Room that evening.

Robin and Adam stood at the king's dining table, awaiting the entrance of King Willem II and Queen Anna Pavlovna of Russia, when they entered with a uniformed officer. Robin bristled. His hand felt down his right hip and found no holster there, no weapon. He could not help but glance at the steak knife on the table before him.

"I present to you my special guest, an envoy from London. Please welcome Naval Commander James Collins," the king said.

The full-dress uniform of British Navy was navy blue with white lapels, white vest, white ruffled shirt, white trousers, and a gold sash across his chest. He took the seat directly across from Robin.

"Commander Collins and I have been in negotiations over islands between the Netherlands and England. We served together when he was only a lieutenant. I trust you will all welcome him as your King's guest, especially you, Captain Van der Kellen." The king turned to the British officer to explain, "Retired Captain Van der Kellen served in the Dutch cavalry in India. He is now a barrister on that case, I am told, interested you. Please do be seated, gentlemen."

Torn incredibly, Robin was the last to take his seat, and only with tugging by Adam.

The king looked to Robin on his right and Collins on his left. "There is a truce at this table, officers. You understand that?"

"Yes, your highness." Collins took in Robin with a serious, unrevealing expression.

"Of course, your highness. I just...wish I had been forewarned," Robin admitted.

"How could I assess your character, sir, if you had been forewarned," the king said. He changed to English then. "I understand Mr. Hudson speaks only English. We are the only five at the table who do. We may converse at this end of the table in English then."

"I was told you have been living in America, Captain Van der Kellen," Collins said. "I was offshore of Boston, for a time."

That made Robin's eyebrows rise. He began to move a plate aside to make room for his wine glass and water glass on the left side of his place setting.

"It was over ten years ago," Collins said.

"I thought perhaps I was in your gunsight," Robin said cautiously. "But I was in India over ten years ago.

The king spoke up, "Did you know, Captain Van der Kellen, that I was raised in England? As Prince I entered the British army as major-general. I was a Captain when I defeated Napoleon at Waterloo. And the Dutch people gave me this palace."

"Of course, I am aware of your accomplishments, your highness. I know that your family relocated to England to avoid the French invasion, when you were only two years of age," Robin said. "You were forced to exile in England."

"How many British did you engage in India, sir?" Collins asked.

Robin turned eyes to the king. "All of them, under orders by your father, King William the First. I was sent to India to fight for our colony. How many American ships did you sink, Commander?"

"Touché," Collins said.

"Don't you dare use a French expression. Not you," Robin said.

"His mother was French. His wife is of French descent," a man beside Collins explained. "Mixed race with American."

"This is my associate, Mitchel Evans. How does it feel now to return to your own country and find yourself an outsider?" Collins asked. "As your country has now a British officer as her king, you must feel quite antiquated."

"I feel America made the...right alliances," Robin said cautiously. "With the French and the Dutch."

"Captain Van der Kellen, is there something wrong with my table setting?" The king was puzzled.

Robin set down his water glass where he had made room for it and sat back, stunned. "No, your highness. Of course not. It is for that very reason, that the table is so lovely, that I moved my glass. I had the misfortune of being shot in the right shoulder about a year ago. I am still terribly likely to spill things with my right hand."

The king made lengthy eye contact with Robin. "Who shot you? Did you have to endure surgery?"

Robin then looked at the British Commander. "Do not worry. I can still shoot straight."

The king leaned forward. "Mr. Hudson. Were you there?"

"I was, your highness," Adam said softly. Then he swallowed and spoke more confidently after. "Mr. Van der Kellen was prosecuting some bank robbers in New York. One shot him in the street, right in front of his wife."

"And what happened to the robber?" the king asked, riveted to Robin and the young handsome American assistant.

"Robin blew his head off," Adam said proudly.

Robin held up a finger to Adam as a signal.

Adam sat back, satisfied. Briefly his brow raised as he registered the reprimand.

Collins picked up his own wine glass and sipped, silently observing.

The king gestured to the butler behind Robin then, drawing him forward. He said in Dutch, "Captain Van der Kellen is to be served his wine on his left side from now on."

The butler nodded and backed off.

The king then continued studying Robin. "You have picked up a bit of an American accent in the way you say certain words. I was hoping you would tell us something of the American savages."

"I did not realize I would be dining with the English savages," Robin said. "Why do you have an interest in my case?"

The king followed Robin's eyes to Collins. "You do not like the term savages. Indians then? Why does it offend you?"

"I was treated with great honor by Sachem of the Mohegan tribe one icy January night. He even asked to examine my British New Land Pattern Cavalry pistol," Robin said. "Then he wanted me to demonstrate how quickly I could fire it and reload. I smoked a pipe with him."

"British Cavalry pistol?" Collins almost rose from his chair. The man beside him, held him down.

"You smoked a pipe with an Indian chief, was it?" the king asked, leaning closer to Robin's side of the table. "Did you dine with him? What was their clothing like? Why were you there?"

"Sachem was a magnificent fellow, in deer skins and feathers and many beads. He had an American dress shirt on. Had a gold pocket watch around his neck. He was educated and spoke fluent English," Robin said. "I settled a land dispute between the Mohegans and a white man trying to claim reservation land. He would have thrown out women and children into the snow that January, if not for me."

"Do you have this pistol?" Collins asked.

"I did not bring it to dinner," Robin said. He added for the king, "The one you want to see is my Colt revolver."

"You have a Colt revolver?" The king reached out and grabbed Robin by the arm. "You must show this magnificent invention to me."

"The Land Pattern is ancient," Collins said. "After being shot, he probably needs the extra rounds a revolver affords."

"The Land Pattern still provides a longer spark than any other pistol on earth. It never misfired on me," Robin said. "Unlike the revolver, with only one shot, one must make good his aim. But I have learned, with the six shooter, one can make good his aim with six adversaries."

The king was riveted, still gripping Robin's arm. "After dinner you and I will discuss your brother-in-law's case. What is it I may do to help you?"

Collins slammed back in his seat with a scowl.

"I have proof the manager of his bank framed him and kept the public funds. I know who has the money. I can see it returned and your appointment saves his good name, your highness," Robin said. "And so does my brother-in-law."

"I'll see this proof," Collins said.

"What do you know of Dutch or French law?" Robin shot back.

"I do find your banter stimulating. You may continue it so long as you do no harm to each other," the king said. "Do tell us more about the Mohegans, would you?"

Robin met eyes with Collins. Then he turned to look at the king and said, "The Mohegan Indians have lost all their lands to the white men. They are reduced to living on small plots of land called reservations. As such, they cannot farm enough to support their families. They hire out then as farmers, builders, factory workers. They also fish. That night I spent in their small lodge with the family of the one who could speak English, I was provided a woven blanket and a meal beside a campfire. The children peeked out at me from the back room. They wanted me to stay on, but I informed them that I had to return at dawn to my wife who was expecting our first child immediately. And given how little they had to eat, how cold their lodge was, how few possessions they actually had, they sent home to my wife and child a lovely basket of baby clothes, a gourd rattle, and baby blankets. My daughter was adorable dressed up in deerskin tunic and moccasins."

"He wants to know about the warriors, weapons, and customs, not domestic details," Collins snapped.

"James let him speak. Were you terrified, spending the night among the Indians? You as the only white man?" the King asked.

"Cautious, perhaps. But I had just saved their lands in court that day. I was treated with great respect, interest, and curiosity." Robin added a dig for the Brit. "It wasn't the only time in my life I was the only white man."

"Curiosity? How so?" the king asked.

"The Sachem knew where the Netherlands are. He knew I was not English or American. He was, I feel, understandably curious. I tried to set a good example for my country," Robin said.

"Hmmpf," Collins commented.

The king held up a hand to him. "Remember I am Dutch, James. Do tell me more, Van der Kellen. The five of us will speak alone after dinner. And I certainly will enjoy your young assistant accompanying us, as long as he continues to disobey you and speak his mind. He speaks English quite differently than you do, James."

"He does not speak the King's English," James said. "It is a poor American dialect."

"Still upset that we ran you out of our country?" Adam blurted out.

Robin shot him a look.

The king laughed out right. "Oh continue. Continue. This is wonderful."

They rose from the table after dinner, and everyone bowed as the queen made her exit. Many of the ladies left with her.

The king exited as well, speaking with some men further down the table before he did.

"Gentlemen, if you will, the king requests that you wait for him in his private parlor. Should any of you need to smoke, do it now before his majesty arrives. There is no smoking in that parlor," the butler told them.

James Collins and Robin Van der Kellen rose and studied each other.

"Better not have any weapons on you," James said to him harshly and so quietly that only their companions heard.

"I am a gentleman," Robin replied. "What are you?"

146   The Dutchman 2 Test of Character   By Susan Eddy

"The Commander is British aristocracy, sir," Mitchel Evans sniped. "You were born to a barrister on a horse farm."

Robin let out a breath. "And just why is it you are so well versed in mine and my wife's lineage?"

"To assess your character," Collins said. "Do you think we would allow you a private audience with the king without knowing anything about you?"

"What else do you know?" Robin said. "Spill it."

"You served in India. Pulicat. The Dutch had to escape to sea on whatever floated it seems. There you acquired a reputation as a marksman, a sharpshooter, a Dutch assassin of some special rank."

"A limey would say that," Robin said.

James Collins met Robin's eyes coldly the entire time he spoke. "You killed a very important British diplomat in Germany after that, on a special mission to assassinate him. You traveled swiftly with a small team so as not to be tracked. You did the same in Italy twice. Or was three times?"

"It was three times in Germany. Twice in Italy. By my king's orders," Robin set him straight. "You know, I know quite a lot about the British Navy. How many American passenger vessels did you sink off the coast of Boston? How many Dutch? Are you familiar with the Erasmus?"

Collins stepped back from him in horror.

Robin's tone was tempered anger. He wet his lips and continued the story. "I was on the Erasmus, with my wife and infant. One of your admirable British Navy vessels fired on us until we could escape into the fog off the shore of Portugal with a French vessel."

"*That was you*?" Collins was stunned.

"What?" Evans assistant asked.

"Dutch passenger vessel, the Erasmus, believed to be carrying munitions from America, came under fire. A Dutch officer was able to persuade a nearby Frenchy to intervene. Jesus Christ. That was you?" Collins was still stunned. "Holy shit. I had no idea what we were dealing with here."

"Just what do you mean by that?" Adam blurted out.

Robin held Adam back. "Mr. Hudson."

"The famous Dutch hero," James told his friend. "Almost brought us to war again with France."

"Am I famous in England then? For saving a ship of women and children you were firing on?" Robin preened. "There were no munitions on that boat. You think the Dutch want American weapons? We like yours, thank you very much."

The king entered and everyone went silent. They bowed.

Then Collins took the king aside and presumably told him about Robin and the French ship.

Robin was breathing so hard that Adam patted him on the chest. Robin immediately smoothed his vest down and let out a long slow breath.

Adam whispered to him, "The king liked your stories of Mohegans and the Colt. His eyes go to you. Use that. Slide your hair behind your ear. Open your jacket."

"Waat?" Robin said.

"Keep his attention on you," Adam said. "His eyes like you a lot better than Collins."

"Do you think Collins is one of his..." Robin whispered.

Adam shook his head and stepped back. "Huh uh."

The king turned from Collins to look at Van der Kellen. To his butlers he gave instructions for a round of special scotch. Then he seemed to reprimand the British officer a bit. He entered the room further, walking around Robin, to take him in from all sides.

Robin stood there with fist on his hip, his jacket open, allowing the scrutiny, avoiding eye contact with his assistant. Adam was just looking at Robin rather proudly, as he had dressed him that morning in suiting that enhanced every attribute of the Dutchman.

"James, come here," the king said.

Collins moved closer, near them both.

"Shake hands with this man, your equal in war, your better in character," The king said to Collins. "Shake the man's hand. He has passed the test. And you must admit, he is a most worthy and entertaining guest."

James held out his right hand to Robin.

"James rescued women and children from a train wreck on his way here, just days ago," The king said. "You are both heros. You will respect each other, even if you despise each other."

"I have found British officers to be honorable," Robin said.

"Before or after you shot them?" James asked.

"Shake his hand or remove yourself," the king said.

"Your highness, I do apologize. Do not send me from your party," James said.

"Shake his hand gently. The man was shot there," the king said.

The British Commander and Dutch Captain shook hands.

And then the king so kindly patted Robin on the right shoulder. "A drink to new friends, I believe, two men so alike, two men on the opposite sides of diplomacy, two men I admire so very much."

Robin drank scotch with his left hand and strolled aside to whisper to Adam, "He's done everything but call me out. Difficult to endure this man."

"I know but you must. This is a test of your character. You have to be a gentleman," Adam said. "There's something else you need to use."

"Not now," Robin said.

"Now," Adam insisted. "The king is like me. You're not using it."

"Are you certain? How do you know this?" Robin whispered.

"I know. How high in rank is a Commander?" Adam whispered back.

"One notch below a ship's captain," Robin replied. "Sometimes put in charge of a smaller vessel."

"Do join us, Van der Kellen. Tell me about your case," the king said to them from the other side of the room. He was sitting down on a plush silk sofa, in front of the fireplace.

Collins sat down on the far end of the king's sofa. Evans sat in an armchair to his left.

Robin and Adam joined them, taking seats on the sofa across from them. Robin sipped his scotch first.

"I brought that special from Edinburgh." Collins indicated the scotch. "Possibly crafted by some distant relative of yours."

"Given its quality, quite likely." Robin sat back and crossed his legs. "Your highness, as much as I have enjoyed this friendly banter, I have come on behalf of an innocent and honest banker who has been framed by his bank manager for the crime of stealing public profits. It is the manager who altered the ledger, bought himself two homes and a Swedish yacht he could never afford on his salary."

There were no questions, but the king indicated he should continue.

"Your highness, Wout Van de Berg invested public funds in steam engine production. It made 42,000 guilders in profit. When he deposited the money, he entered it into his ledger and left the bank. You see, his mother had died. He left for Brussels right away. He is Belgian. That very night, the bank manager, Mr. Mahoric, altered the entry in the ledger and took the money home. He bought a house, and a foreign yacht. He went to see his mistress in the red-light district. Brought her diamonds. And you have Mr. Van de Berg in jail when all he did was make you 42,000 guilders, your highness."

"Well, public funds must be returned to us. I have spoken to my appointed commissioner. He is determined to prosecute whoever is responsible. Can you prove what you just said in court?"

"I will do my best. I can prove it was not his handwriting. I can prove he was in Brussels when the money went missing from the vault. I can show that Mr. Mahoric had motive as he had received a poor performance review and was denied a promotion." Robin sipped the scotch thoughtfully. He glanced at Adam.

"That is good but not overwhelmingly convincing."

"I realize that." Robin lowered his chin sadly.

"That won't convince the judge and jury," Collins said. "You have someone directly responsible and only a motive for another."

Robin frowned. "I am not done with my investigation. There is a piece missing, a mastermind of the whole thing. An English speaker. Someone who knew about the London steam engine investment. Someone who knew when the profits were coming. An insider, most likely."

"Have you spoken with my appointed commissioner?" the king asked.

"I have not personally. I am consulting with Judge Janssen and he felt it better that he meets with the Commissioner of the Province, instead of me," Robin said. "They met."

"You must meet with him yourself," the king said.

Robin raised his eyebrows.

"What an expression," the king remarked. "Why did the judge not want you to speak to my commissioner?"

"The judge knew me when I was in law school." Robin squirmed. "I was an arrogant, skirt chasing, prick in those days. I slept with his fiancée the night before their wedding. Deflowered her first, you might say. Never forgave me for that."

That made all of the men laugh.

"You shall meet with the Commissioner. I order it," the king said. "I find you convincing. He will also. I do find you to be arrogant. Not that I mind. A man with your talents and experience is entitled to be."

"Can't argue with that," Robin said, making the king laugh.

"A man with a reputation as a marksman and a successful barrister should be arrogant." The king held out his empty glass and his butler refilled it. "Skirt chaser? You did not like the women last night?"

Robin drew in a breath.

"Not pretty enough?" James remarked. "Wrong type? Wrong gender? Wrong color?"

Robin ignored him.

"Mr. Hudson, you did not find the women desirable?" the king questioned.

"My heart is taken," Adam said. "Though I appreciate the offer."

"What legal assistance do you provide for Mr. Van der Kellen?" Collins questioned then.

"I take notes. I meet with people for him. I...." Adam struggled to think of another.

Robin set a hand on Adam's knee then, briefly but with an over obvious affectionate slide just enough above Adam's knee to draw some attention. "Actually, Mr. Hudson, I haven't told you what a great help you were when you told me that man was lying to me. He was, you know? When people are speaking in Dutch and he cannot listen to what they are saying, he makes very clever observations about their mannerisms. It was very enlightening."

"Thank you, sir." Adam's heart raced.

"You are very welcome." Robin withdrew his hand and sat back.

"What do you read in me then?" The king looked to young Adam.

"Ahhh, it takes time, your majesty." Adam smoothed his hand onto his thigh where Robin's had just been.

Robin had to look away and bite his lip.

"How did you come to work for Mr. Van der Kellen?" the king asked.

Adam looked at Robin. "I met him in New York. I was working for a friend of his when Robin got shot. I helped get him in the house and up the stairs when he was released from the hospital. I had already sent him an inquiry of employment before that. I suppose I have been taking care of him ever since."

"Tell me about New York, young man," the king said. "I enjoy your American tongue."

Another clear beverage was served on a silver tray to each of the men.

As Adam began to talk about the buzzing American city in comparison to Amsterdam and her lazy canals, Robin and James lifted their drinks and drank together as it if was a dare, neither wanting to put it down first.

"Have another," James encouraged, again taking another drink with Robin.

Van der Kellen set his glass down with his left hand.

"How do you like your drink, Mr. Hudson?" James asked.

As Adam reached for his glass, Robin suddenly intercepted and knocked the glass out of his hand. "Don't drink that." The clear liquid spilled out across the tapestry rug.

The butler hurried to pick up the unbroken crystal glass as it bounced on the rug.

Adam looked at Robin in shock.

James too watched Robin.

Adam grabbed his arm. "Robin? What is wrong? Have you been poisoned?"

Robin let out a breath. Then a few more breaths as he said nothing.

James sat back with a smirk. "No, he has not, boy."

"What have you done to him?" Adam urged, deepening his voice.

Robin's head went back a bit. His eyes were not blinking. His cheeks did not flush as they usually did with alcohol. He simply closed his mouth and swallowed.

"He is intoxicated. He'll be fine," the king insisted.

"I've seen him drunk. This isn't it," Adam insisted. "Robin, are you all right? Can you hear me?"

"He'll be fine," James said. "Relax. Pour him another."

"No." Adam kept an arm around Robin, keeping him up in his seat. He shot a look at the British officer. "He's drinking as his king's guest. This isn't happening. *What the fuck* have you put in his drink?"

"Keep it down, Mr. Hudson," James said.

Finally, Robin wet his lips. He managed to look at Adam closely, at his shoulder. "Adam, calm down. It is only absinthe."

"Are you all right? What is happening?" Adam urged, turning Robin's chin to look him in the eyes. "What do you need?"

"I do wish you would stop…glowing," Robin told him. "If you would please, Mr. Hudson."

The others laughed.

"Why are you really here?" James questioned Robin then, leaning forward aggressively.

Robin slowly turned his head toward the Brit. "For the hot springs, of course."

"He's resisting it," James said.

Robin squinted and shook his head.

"Have a bit more." James sipped his own.

Adam grabbed Robin's glass and set it down on the table beside him. "No. You are not drugging him further. I thought absinthe was green."

"Quite protective, are you not?" James asked Adam. "Absinthe is not always green. Van der Kellen, what was your real mission on that French ship?"

"Keep it from abandoning us." Robin switched to French to say, "It's a passenger ship. Defenseless except for that 9 pounder. Can't leave us to the will of the Goddamn British."

"9 pounder? You did have munitions on board," James said angrily.

"Hell, they had two cannon balls. One moron barely knew how to set the charge. I don't think they knew how to keep powder dry," Robin blurted out in Dutch.

"What do you know about the London steam engines? Who was on that deal?" Collins asked.

"This is not fair!" Adam insisted. "You drug him and then question him? He's mixing up languages. You're not fit to wipe his boots."

"Very protective. Why is your assistant so loyal to you?" James asked.

The king and James' assistant just watched all of this.

Robin had to breathe for a minute, trying to focus. He tightened his grip about Adam's shoulders. "Adam is in love with me, and it is all right."

"You're not here to assassinate the king?" James asked.

Robin smiled slowly. "Sorry. No... I haven't done an assassination in years."

"A marksman like you? Why did you bring pistols into the palace then?" James asked.

"Well, I've been shot. Wouldn't I arm myself on the road?" Robin tried to loosen his ascot. He'd have hit the floor if Adam didn't hold onto him.

"I must get him to bed," Adam announced. "The show is over. You're not clever at all. You're only rude. And I feel sorry for you, Mr. Collins, when Robin recovers."

"That's Commander Collins, to you," Evans snapped.

"Help him," the king said to the butler.

Adam looked up at the butler. Together they lifted Robin's feet up onto the sofa and slid a pillow beneath his head. "Are you all right? Robin?"

"That suit looks good on you. Almost as good as it does on me," Robin said.

Adam sat down on the edge of Robin's sofa. He looked at the king, the two British men, the butler. "I literally can't believe you did this. Where is the honor? He came here as a barrister to plead his case to the highest legal authority in the land. You sent prostitutes to his room. You sent lavish food. You made him wait all day. And finally, when you give him the chance to do his sworn duty, you drugged him!"

"I cannot believe a servant, an American valet, has just scolded the king of the Netherlands and Belgium," James exclaimed.

The king stood up and strolled closer to Robin. "I do believe he is quite sensitive to absinthe. He has no tolerance. James, it was a foolish stunt. This man is what he seems. This isn't fun anymore. Return to London."

James stood up at the table. "You're not serious."

"Go on. Keep your damn island. I don't want it," the king said. "Now." He nodded to the butler.

The butler moved to escort Collins and his assistant out. After they had left, the king was alone with Robin and Adam. Robin's eyes had closed, and he held onto Adam's arm.

Adam looked up at the king defensively.

"My apologies, Mr. Hudson. Prostitutes, food, beverages, merely luxuries of the aristocracy. For my part, it was only meant to relax Mr. Van der Kellen, so that he would reveal his true purpose," the king said. "I believe he did. And you have proven yourself a most loyal companion, whatever you may be to him. No harm shall come to you or him. No one shall enter this room. As it would be ungentlemanly to carry him back to his room, we will let him rest it off here until all the guests have left. You have my word."

"Thank you, your highness. I'm sorry that I raised my voice."

"Well, I'm sorry Mr. Van der Kellen has gone to sleep. I would like to have heard more of his stories," the king said. "I will go talk to James and see him out. I will return to check on your companion. Do stay here with him. No one shall disturb. But come to the door if you need assistance. Does he need my physician?"

"I don't want Paula. I don't want Paula," Robin said. "I didn't sleep with her. I slept with Adam."

Adam felt Robin's forehead. "Ha. If only he had."

"Who is Paula?"

Adam looked at the king. "Our maid on the boat."

"Marie just won't let me yet," Robin blurted out. He rolled toward the back of the sofa.

"Paula...Marie...Adam...must be wonderful to be as beautiful as he is." The king reached in and loosened Robin's ascot, opened the top button of his shirt. Then he gave a thoughtful touch to his hair before stepping back. "Mind him. I'm sending for my physician."

Robin awoke the next morning, staring down into a tin pail. He raised up onto his elbow and focused on the room. "Adam? Adam, are you there?"

Adam scrambled into Robin's bedroom. "Are you all right?"

Robin was on the edge of the bed, lying on his stomach. The pail was on the floor beneath him. He rolled back and put both hands to his forehead. "Oh my God. My head hurts so."

"Shall I send for the physician again?"

"Again?" Robin asked, alarmed. "What the hell happened?"

"That British asshole drugged you with absinthe last night. The king threw him out. Sent him home to London."

"Absinthe? I have a terrible reaction to absinthe. Oh no. I didn't throw up on the king, did I?" Robin sat up, shirtless in the bed and looked around.

Adam smiled. "No, you threw up on the physician. Just on his trousers really, and your own, and mine a bit."

"What did I say when I was drugged?"

"Just the truth. Collins thought you were here to assassinate the king. That's why he did it. Thought you'd just blurt it out after a few drinks."

Robin rubbed his eyes. "The king sent him back to London?"

"Yes. He likes you. He apologized for this. You said something in French about how you got the French to protect our ship. Can I get you some coffee?"

"Yes, please," Robin said.

Adam went into their parlor to pour coffee and cream into a cup. When he returned, Robin had sat up against his pillows and headboard. He pulled his covers up to his waist. Adam handed the cup and saucer to him.

"What happened to my... clothing?" Robin asked.

"They had to be laundered," Adam said.

"I didn't take them off in front of the king, did I?"

Adam smiled, shaking his head. "No. You peeled them off here in front of the physician and me."

"I took them all off?"

"Yes, and I put you to bed." Adam smiled and folded his arms. "Enjoyed the dance though."

There was a knock on their front door. And someone called out to them.

"That's the doctor." Robin let out a deep breath. "Why not? Let him in. Just him."

"I will say though, I admire Marie's will power. How she can resist you, I do not understand." Adam smirked at him.

Robin pulled up his covers. "Waat?"

Adam went to the door. He found the butler and the same physician from last night. Adam held out his hand to stop the butler. "Just the physician."

"Who's there, Adam?" Robin called.

"The king's butler," Adam replied.

"Let them both enter," Robin called.

Adam stepped back from the door, allowing their entry. They spoke to each other in Dutch, and then the doctor said to Robin in the bedroom, "Are you well, sir?"

"Ha! It is a good thing I am. That could just as well have been arsenic not absinthe in my drink. I trusted that I would not be poisoned at the king's table," Robin blurted out.

"I beg your pardon, Mr. Van der Kellen." The butler stood at the foot of Robin's bed. "The king is far too lenient with his friends."

"Lenient? Or a fool?" Robin asked.

"Don't use that word when you speak of the king, sir," the butler said.

"How are you feeling today, sir?" the doctor asked.

"Like I had a hard night of drinking," Robin said. *"Only I didn't!"*

"Rest. Take some water. Eat if you are able." The doctor opened his medical bag on the foot of the bed. "Hangover remedy? Laudanum? Opium?"

"I would speak to the king. My whole reason to be here was to speak with him about my case. And I was starting to until I was drugged," Robin said. "I am due a serious audience with his majesty."

"He is not here."

"Waat?"

"He left this morning for his palace in Brussels."

"Get me my clothing, Adam. I need to get home then. And give me that hangover remedy."

Chapter 8: My Punishment

Robin and Adam exited the grand entrance of the palace, down the stairs between two fountains, toward an awaiting carriage and team of four horses. This was not the same carriage that had brought them from Robert's estate.

Out of the carriage stepped a tall blonde man in black suitcoat. He extended a hand to Robin.

Robin looked from hand up into the face of James Collins. "I thought you were off to London."

"As my punishment, I am to escort you home," James said.

"How is that not my punishment?" Robin asked.

Adam outright laughed.

Two footmen loaded Robins' and Adams' bags into the boot with one chest of James' as well. Adam held Robin's briefcase as he looked from Robin to the Commander and back.

"Where is your uniform?" Robin questioned.

"Obviously it offended you. It is packed away."

"Are you armed?" Robin asked.

James revealed the holster and pistol on his hip beneath his coat. "You can show me that revolver once we get moving."

"Don't you dare give him a hard time after poisoning him last night," Adam said firmly.

"I intend to make it up to him, Mr. Hudson." James indicated the carriage. "Shall we, before it rains."

Robin glanced up at the heavy clouds above. Then he reached for the handle and stepped up into the carriage. He sat back in a plush seat facing forward. He held a hand to his stomach.

"How long was your journey here in the dry?" James asked.

Adam climbed into the carriage and sat facing Robin, holding the briefcase in his arms.

"Two hours to arrive here," Robin said.

James entered and ordered the drivers to get them going. He closed the door and chose to sit beside Robin rather than Adam. "Should it rain, it will take longer than that. You came from Amstelveen, did you not?"

"That region, yes," Robin said.

"Other side of Amsterdam," James said. "It is a very flat country, is it not?"

"Yes, well, so it is," Robin said.

Adam crossed his legs, turning his feet away from Robin. "Are you going to throw up again?"

"No. How could I? I didn't eat anything," Robin shot back.

"I put biscuits in here," Adam said. "Just say when."

"Now."

The carriage took them down the driveway from the palace and began a journey over countless bridges to cross many canals and rivers. Windmills along the way powered flour mills everywhere.

"The whole country must be baking," Adam commented. "All these flour mills."

James pointed. "Pistols are in there, are they not?"

Adam looked down at the briefcase in his lap. He then laid it down beside him on the seat.

"Where did you get such a loyal assistant? He was like a bulldog last night, standing guard over you," James said. "Such that he is."

"Such that I...?" Adam shot back.

"People tend to speak the truth on absinthe. And he certainly did," James interrupted.

"He was speaking the truth without the absinthe," Adam said. "He's a gentleman. And you...."

"Are not fit to wipe his boots. That's what you said last night," James said.

Robin laughed. "He said that?"

"You accomplished what you set out for, Van der Kellen." James looked at Robin beside him. "The king has gone to Brussels to verify for himself where Wout Van de Berg was on that particular date of the bank robbery. And he's sent me along with you to see what other assistance I can provide."

"That's why the king has left?" Robin turned in the seat toward the Brit. He brought one boot up onto his other knee. "You're joking."

"Certainly not."

Thunder resounded above and around the carriage. The rain came down very hard then. The drivers pulled out their roof top overhead and the horses continued on, over another bridge.

The carriage jolted and suddenly pitched downward on James's corner. All three of them were thrown together onto the side wall and windows.

Adam landed on Robin who landed on James. He got up on his hands and minded the briefcase. "Are you injured? Robin?"

Robin grabbed Adam by the arm and scrambled to sit up. "I'm fine. James?"

"All right, I suppose." James sat up, finding Robin's hat and returning it to him as they all got off one another. "Bit of a thrill for you, was it not, Adam?"

"Was that my knee in your crotch? Sorry," Adam said.

"Gentlemen," Robin scolded.

A driver looked into their windows from outside in the pouring rain. "We've thrown a wheel. Everyone all right inside?"

"We're all right," James called back in Dutch. "What happened?"

"What is it?" Adam asked, handing the British East India Company pistol to Robin.

Robin took the pistol. "We lost a wheel. Just sit tight. If they can, they will get the spare on. Try to balance the weight to help them."

Adam climbed to the opposite side, the high side, and held on to stay there.

Robin moved back to where he'd been sitting.

James braced himself up beside Adam.

Another carriage came alongside, and two men assisted the drivers. They braced the broken side up, somewhat leveling out the carriage. In another moment there was a knock on the door. Their driver called in, "Axel is broken. We must transfer to another carriage for a ride to the nearest inn. It will take time to fix this. I'm terribly sorry. They recognized this royal carriage and offered to assist."

"Adam, mind that briefcase." Robin tucked his pistol into belt, hidden by his vest.

"Won't let it out of my hand," Adam said. "You suspect robbers?"

"You never know," James added. "My job is to look after you both, I confess. I'm an excellent shot. Not as good as the marksman here, of course."

In the pouring rain, they climbed down onto cobblestones and mud, and up into another carriage where they squeezed inside with an elderly couple. Their bags were transferred and soon they were moving on again. Over another bridge they went.

"Are you royals? You have the King's Mark," the elderly man asked in Dutch.

"We are not. We were traveling from Soestdjisk to Amsterdam proper," James replied in Dutch.

The elderly woman provided her handkerchief and began wiping the rain from Robin's cheek. "Goodness, you're soaked through. Here, make use of this."

Robin accepted the handkerchief to wipe his eyes. "Thank you, madam. Most kind of you."

"My delight. You must stay at our inn tonight while your carriage is repaired. We insist." She continued to pamper Robin by straightening his lapel and his dripping hair.

"We insist. It is not far," the elderly man said. "We are Mr. and Mrs. Rasmussen."

"Robin Van der Kellen. My assistant Adam Hudson from America. And…." Robin looked at James.

"James Collins. Pleased to meet you both," James said.

"Van der Kellen? Are you of the Amstelveen Van der Kellens with the big horse farm?" Mr. Rasmussen asked.

"Yes, indeed. That's my brother's farm," Robin said.

"Delightful."

It seemed to rain even harder as they emerged from the carriage and brought their own bags inside a small stone inn along a canal. "Take your rooms upstairs and get into dry clothing. We shall see you for lunch down here when you are ready."

Robin, Adam, and James climbed the stairs. The rooms all had cozy beds and fireplaces. There were six rooms. All of the doors were open and obviously they were the only guests.

"Is your powder wet?" James asked Robin in the hallway.

Robin laid his hand on his own vest, feeling the pistol inside it. "I do not believe so."

"I think mine is. I shall clean it out and be downstairs shortly," James said. "This room is as good as any."

"Marie will be looking for me today," Robin said. "I'll be lucky to make it home even tomorrow."

"Take this one." Adam pulled Robin to one on the end. "It's larger and the fireplace will be above the one in the kitchen. You like that."

Robin's boots sounded on the wooden floor as he followed Adam into the large room. Adam opened the suitcase and laid out a dry suit for Robin. "Do you wish me to sleep on the sofa in here?"

"No. Go ahead and take a room. I don't think we have to worry about James anymore," Robin said.

"You are not suspicious of him?" Adam asked.

"Not overly much," Robin said.

"You should be. Mark my words." Adam nodded definitively and took his own suitcase into the next room and closed Robin's door. Adam changed into the other of Robin's old suits. He then returned to Robin's room to offer assistance. Robin was already dressed in his newest suit. They set out Robin's wet trousers and jacket by the fireplace to dry. Together they walked past James's door down to the parlor.

A cook was at work in the kitchen and Mrs. Rasmussen was setting the table herself. Adam stepped in to help her with plates at the far end. She patted him on the shoulder. "What a fine young gentleman, helping with the women's work."

Robin smiled. "Adam has many talents."

Adam folded napkins and set out the silverware at one end while Rasmussen did the other end.

"Are your rooms to your liking?" She asked.

"They are most comfortable. You will allow me to pay for our stay, of course." Robin extracted gold coins from his pocketbook, inside his jacket.

"Oh, I couldn't." She stood and took Robin in, in all of his fine black suit and crisp white shirt. Of the three of them, clearly Robin was the wealthiest. Gold cufflinks. Silk ascot. Elegant manners.

"Yes, you could." Robin placed the coins in her hand. "Thank you for coming to our rescue."

"This is too much," she declared.

"Not nearly enough for all your trouble." Robin stepped away from her and chose to sit nearer to the fireplace at one of the place settings Adam had laid.

She pocketed the coins.

Adam brought over the tea pot and poured for Robin and himself. He also offered it for Mrs. Rasmussen.

"Thank you, Adam. I'm sorry he cannot understand me," she said.

"He doesn't speak Dutch, but he understands your intent very well," Robin said.

Adam sat beside Robin and put cream into both of their cups.

The cook handed to the lady a basket of rolls for the table.

It was then that James and Mr. Rasmussen entered together.

The inn keepers both compared handfuls of gold coins and realized at once, "Oh we've both been paid."

Robin and James met eyes across the table. At the same time, they both said, "Keep it."

James moved down the table to sit across from Robin. He was just wearing white shirt and black vest, black trousers. "I apologize. My jacket is quite wet and hanging in front of the hearth upstairs."

"We are not so formal here that one needs jacket and white gloves to take a meal," Mr. Rasmussen said. "Make yourselves at home and let us hear what your business was with the king at Soestdijk palace?"

James met eyes again with Robin.

Adam poured tea for James then, reluctantly.

"Thank you," James said in English. "They're wondering what our business was."

Adam passed the basket of rolls around the table. "Imagine if they knew the entertainment of evening last."

"Not going to forgive me, are you?" James said.

"Not so fucking likely," Adam replied softly.

"Ah, pleasant American jargon. Must have evolved after we left the Americas to the savages," James said. "Why is it you do not restrain your assistant, Robin?"

Robin exhaled. "Ha! I'm finding that very difficult to do, of late."

The cook brought over bowls of mashed potatoes and boiled vegetables.

The Rasmussens sat at either end of the table.

Robin said in Dutch, "I was summoned to speak to his majesty about a law case I am working on. His majesty is of course, head of the courts as well."

"You must be quite a famous barrister then, to be summoned to the king and to travel with two assistants. Or is one your bodyguard? This one, most likely." Mr. Rasmussen indicated James beside him.

James grinned. "Oh, do not let his youth fool you. Mr. Hudson can mount quite a defense."

The Dutch speakers laughed. Bowls of pea soup were passed around until everyone had one. When the lady began to eat, they all began to.

Robin moved his teacup to the left side of his plate. He spooned his soup with his left hand. "I've been in America for so long, that to enjoy real Dutch pea soup is a luxury on a cold wet day as this."

"How many years in American then, sir?"

"Six years. I married there. My wife and daughter will miss me today," Robin said. "They await me at my brothers, of course."

"I'm sure your carriage will bring you home to them tomorrow," Mrs. Rasmussen said. "Such handsome young men at my table. This is wonderful. Please say if there is anything you are lacking."

"This is wonderful. Thank you so very much," James said.

Other than the bit of salt pork in the pea soup, lunch consisted of no other meats. It was potatoes with butter, boiled carrots and peas, array of cheeses, fresh baked rolls, and dessert of white cake. The guests did not know that the cook would leave after lunch for the market with some gold coins to buy a haunch of pork for supper that night.

"Does it always rain like this in the spring?" James asked. "It is almost like summer at my home."

"Then you will be at home in the wet," Robin said with eye contact.

James nodded. He tried to hide his accent when he spoke Dutch. He took his tea with no milk or cream in it, like an Englishman to Robin's eyes.

"How old is your child, Mr. Van der Kellen?" Mrs. Rasmussen asked.

"Frida is almost three months old. She was born just before we made for the Netherlands. Born in America," Robin said.

"You'll be looking for some quiet sleep then," she said, making them laugh. "Does she look like your pretty wife or your handsomeness?"

"Ah…" Robin looked to Adam. "Does Frida take after Marie or me, do you think?"

"Oh Marie of course. Like a tiny version," Adam said.

"Adam says she's a tiny version of my wife," Robin said. "She has her greenish eyes."

After dinner, Adam brought forth a bottle of brandy and set it on the table.

"How thoughtful, Adam." Robin looked up at him.

"Can't expect us to drink anything Cmdr. Collins has brought," Adam remarked.

James nodded. "I deserved that. Can I expect greater tolerance for brandy then?"

"Considerably." Robin poured glasses for the four of them. He offered one to Mr. Rasmussen as well, who refused politely on the grounds that he was going to bed soon.

In the flicker of firelight and the two oil lamps on the table, Adam watched Robin and James match each other glass for glass. And they passed a tobacco smoke between them. Adam continued to nurse his first glass of brandy and a cup of tea.

James tried to refill Adam's glass but was waved off. "Not much of a drinker, Mr. Hudson?"

Adam shook his head. He picked up something from the floor between himself and James. He held it up to examine a very nice lead graphite for writing. "Did you drop this?"

"I must have. Keep it if you like. I have plenty," James said. "Where were you in India, Robin? Pulicat? Didn't go well for you there."

"No, it didn't. Pulicat, mostly. We were trying to hold the port and well... you know." Robin sipped and savored his drink.

"India? The most exotic location you ever saw, I'd imagine. Still more civilized than East Indies or Singapura or Brunei."

"Been all over the world, have you?" Robin asked.

"Yes. Literally," James said.

Adam was still studying the graphite writing device. Finally, he pocketed it.

"You have never been in rural Netherlands before?" Robin asked. "Mind that accent. It will not be received well here. Better let me do the talking."

"I will have to differ to your judgement," James said.

"Well, better than how you would be treated in Canterbury, Connecticut. When I first met the local constable, he almost throttled me just for having my East India Company pistol," Robin said.

"I don't doubt that," Adam chimed in.

"Took me by the collar. Thought I was a spy," Robin said. "What did you hear about my voyage from America?"

"About the Dutch hero from the Erasmus? Well, the British Navy assumes all vessels traveling from America to Europe are carrying munitions, weapons, or at the very least cotton to supply the French or the Dutch or even the Portuguese." James finished the smoke and put it out on a saucer. "Heard a passenger ship sent a Dutch war hero of some sort over in a rowboat, in rough seas, to the French war ship. This Dutchman successfully pleaded for French protection as the British ship had fired on them. Heavy fog laid in. The Dutch ship Erasmus was able to disappear into the fog. Did you pay them? You are quite wealthy, I hear."

"What? No, of course not."

"Bribe the French captain?"

"No." Robin shook his head. "I told him there were French women and children on board. It wasn't a lie. My wife is half French. I'm half French. What does that make my child?"

"American." Adam blurted out.

James glared at him.

"He gave me his sword, matter of fact, for my collection," Robin said.

"You have a collection of swords?" James said. "I have one from the Qing Dynasty, Hong Kong."

"Really?" Robin sat forward then. He reached to refill his glass. Then he grabbed a rye roll from the basket to munch on. "I have a Moghul sword from India with real ivory handle. Spectacular fellow."

"The Qing Dynasty sword has a handle made of some kind of muskox tusk," James said. "How did you come by this revolver?"

"A dear friend gave it to me in New York. They were still very rare then. Just invented, and very expensive," Robin said. "I still love the elegance of the Land Pattern. The Colt is efficient. It is not anything beautiful to behold."

"Have to wonder how it was invented in America of all places," James said.

"Well, necessity really. Cut off from Europe made them have to fire up their own ironworks. And parts of the country still have wild native societies unfriendly to the white man." Robin sipped his brandy.

"I've been to San Francisco," James said.

"Really? How so?" Robin asked.

"We pulled in for supplies. They're mining gold there, you know?"

"They let a British war ship dock?" Robin questioned.

"For a price. Right between a Chinese ship and a Portuguese," James said. "Anything goes there. And anything did in the tavern that night."

"And the women there?" Robin asked.

Adam's mouth fell open and his eyes turned to Robin.

"Anything goes there." James nodded. "Every race you can imagine."

"I can imagine a lot," Robin said.

James laughed.

"Did British troops in India have their own harem?" Robin asked.

"Didn't the Dutch?" James said. "We heard you guys did."

Robin grinned. He held up a finger at Adam. "Now you won't be telling my wife any of this? He's good friends with my wife."

"Don't let him be too good a friend," James said.

The warriors laughed, and Adam sat back, observing them as one would yet another species. How Robin could appear to befriend this man made his blood boil.

"How did you come by this boy?" James indicated Adam.

"Adam? Oh...He made his own destiny, indispensable to me."

James offered another smoke and Robin lit it up from the lamp beside him. Robin puffed on it, his full lips looking beautiful. Then he passed it to James who smoked it.

"Do you smoke, Adam?" Robin asked Adam.

"Barely," Adam said. "Surprised. I never see you smoking."

"It's not as if I don't have the skill," Robin replied. "Oh man, with a baby at home, it has been a long damn time for me. What a drink and a smoke makes me want next..."

"Try a year at sea," James said and refilled his glass. "Been married long?"

"About a year," Robin said. "I've just been so busy with this case, out late at night, gone all day. Have not had time for holiday here with her. That was what this was supposed to be. A trip to show her my homeland."

"Planning to catch the trade winds back in the Fall?" James asked.

"Yes. Exactly. Before winter comes," Robin said. "Depends on if she's... with child again by then. We have to make it across before...before that."

"Well then, you best keep working late," James remarked.

Robin laughed. "My wife is very beautiful. It's not an easy thing to resist."

"Never is."

"We have steamer travel from London to Halifax you could consider. It is much faster than sailing," James said.

Adam had his head on his hand.

"Adam, you can go up to sleep if you wish. We're all right," Robin said.

"I'm not sure about that," Adam said.

"You can be sure. I mean him no harm," James said. "You're welcome to stay, Mr. Hudson."

"Adam, we will just finish this bottle and be up to sleep soon," Robin said.

"You're certain? I did not get much sleep last night." Adam stood up.

"Of course. Get a good night's sleep then. And thank you." Robin patted him on the arm. "Well done."

"You're not drunk, are you?" Adam leaned to see into Robin's eyes in the lamplight.

"No. Not drunk," Robin insisted.

Adam walked around the table and up the stairs to his room then.

"How did you acquire him? He said he was working for a friend of yours."

In the morning, Adam felt a hand weighing down his shoulder and he awoke with a start.

"Hey, it's just me. It's morning." Robin stepped back from the bed.

Adam looked back at him and then rolled over to run a hand through his own hair. "What time is it? I overslept?"

"You're fine. The carriage is here. We'll be able to start for home again," Robin said.

"You've shaved already. You are dressed." Adam sat up. "I'll get right to..."

"I still remember how to use a blade." Robin put his hands in his jacket pockets and strolled around the bed toward the door. "Listen, I just wanted to tell you, before we start the day, you have really done a great job on this trip. You really can never go back to being just a valet, you know?"

"Your boots have mud on them," Adam said.

Robin looked down at his boots and shrugged. "My valet found another job."

Adam threw back his covers and reached for his trousers. "Well, you're not getting another one."

"I guess I'm not."

Adam dressed, shaved, packed his suitcase and Robin's. He carried their two bags and Robin's briefcase downstairs. He set those beside Commander Collins's in the parlor. There was male laughter in the kitchen. Adam lingered in the doorway with his hands on his hips.

Mrs. Rasmussen brought to Adam a cup of tea.

"Bedankt." Adam entered the room.

Robin and James were sitting at the table, having syrup waffles and tea. The two drivers were there as well, also having breakfast. Adam brought his teacup to the table and sat across from Robin, beside one of the drivers.

"So, the carriage has been repaired?" Adam said.

"Good as new," the driver beside him said in English. "And the rain stopped. It will be a pleasant journey today."

"Wonderful," Adam said. A plate of waffles was set before him.

James was just finishing his plate. He reached to refill his tea from the pot in the center of the table.

Robin poured more syrup on his waffles. "Adam, before we leave can you run to the mercantile next door and pick out something for Marie? I can't return a day late without a small gift for her."

"Of course. I can do that." Adam nodded.

"Do you have money?" Robin asked.

"Yes. I've got it." Adam shoveled more waffles into his mouth and rose from the table.

"You can finish first. There is time," Robin said.

"I'm finished. I'll take care of this," Adam said.

"Adam. Money." Robin reached forward and put coins with a note into his hand.

Adam nodded and exited for the parlor. He went straight outside and opened the note. He read it twice. Then he pocketed the note and went to the mercantile. Inside he bought a tin of black powder, a bottle of lavender water, and a tin of chocolates.

Adam,

You may have been right.

The axel was cut. Get me black powder.

R

The drivers were loading the bags into the boot and securing them with rope. Rope? Adam thought that was excessive until he saw Robin emerge from the house with his briefcase in his hand. The butt of his pistol was extending out from his belt.

James came out and got right into the carriage.

Robin indicated for Adam to get on board.

"Your gifts..." Adam blurted out.

"Give me the one. You know which." Robin followed Adam to the carriage.

Adam slipped the tin of black powder into Robin's pocket and secured the gifts for Marie into Robin's briefcase. They climbed inside.

The carriage began to move quickly away.

"Think Marie will like chocolates and lavender water?" Adam asked.

"Yes. Thank you. Mind them for me." Robin slid closer to the window to look about outside. The carriage rolled alongside a canal, and Robin brushed out and reprimed his pistol with the fresh black powder.

A gunshot rang out.

The carriage took off faster. Robin and James both looked out windows, pistols drawn.

"I refuse to drive this carriage while being shot at!"

"Get inside and get out of my way!" Robin yelled back, climbing out of the carriage and up to the driver's seat.

The two drivers scrambled into the back and James barely got up beside Robin before the horses took off.

"Cover me," Robin said.

James grabbed the reins from him. "Hell no. You're the marksman. You cover me."

"You don't know how to yell at them in Dutch."

"Well yell for them to go while you cover me."

Chapter 9: Mr. Hudson the Gentleman

Connecticut, April 20, 1841

"No! You must not be afraid of the weapon in your hand." Robin rushed in on Adam, wrapped his arms around him from behind, grasped the pistol in his and Adam's hands. And he fired it. He didn't let go but said then into Adam's ear, "It does that every time it is fired. Just that. You see? It kicks back in your hand. It shoots a flame out the side and a bullet out the front. It's hot now. All right? That's what it does. Now try to hit the target." Robin stepped back from Adam and to his side.

Adam nearly shook. But he turned his eyes to the gun and cocked it again. He held it out in both hands and aimed at the wooden target nailed to a tree.

"Breathe normally. Keep both eyes open. On the exhale, pull that trigger back so slowly, so slowly," Robin said.

Adam inhaled again, let out the breath and gently started to pull the trigger. The gun fired and he cringed. His shoulders went up.

Robin stepped in and took him by the shoulder. "Look. You nailed it."

Adam opened his eyes. "I did? Oh my God. I did!"

Robin laughed. "Again. Do it again. How many bullets do you have left?"

"Ah. I don't know. Four?" Adam looked at him.

"Four! Of course, four. In an emergency you must keep count," Robin said. "Take another shot at the target. Empty the gun at the target. Then we will reload and try again."

Adam looked down at the gun and for a moment he was shaking. As he held up the weapon, his hands shook.

Robin stepped in then and closed his hand hard around Adam's wrist. "Hold on. Stop. Give this to me."

Adam released the Colt into Robin's hand.

"Sit down. I didn't mean to frighten you," Robin said. "This has been enough practice for one day."

"No. You don't have to stop. You can train me just like anybody else," Adam insisted.

"No, I cannot." Robin removed the bullets from the revolver and pocketed them. "Anyone else I trained in the cavalry already had a lifetime with guns. You do not."

"I thought you meant... the other reason why." Adam looked down and sat down on a rock. He wiped his palms on his knees.

"What other reason?" Robin questioned.

"Maybe you thought if you put your arms around me, it would bother me," Adam said, looking at the ground between them.

"There's no other way to teach someone how to hold a gun than to get in there and show them." Robin finally sat down on a tree log facing him. "It bothered you? I do apologize."

"I didn't say it bothered me," Adam said.

"You are very clearly bothered."

Adam got up angrily and started to walk away. His hand wiped everything away in the air.

Robin picked up his rifle, holstered the Colt and chased after him. "What?"

"Just forget it!" Adam declared.

Robin grabbed him by the arm. "What is it? Stop."

Adam stopped but turned away from him. "Maybe you think I can't learn this. I'm too stupid. I'm too timid."

Robin put his hands on his hips. "No. I do not think any of that."

"Sometimes you forget that I've never been treated like that."

"Treated like what? Do I treat you any differently because I know? No, I do not," Robin said firmly.

"Sometimes maybe you should," Adam said through his teeth.

"You're angry with me." Robin stepped back. "I shouldn't lay a hand on you? I am sorry."

"And I can never lay a hand on you except to give you a shave or haircut. Right?" Adam said angrily. "It is just not fair that you think you can touch me however you like but I have to...."

"Have to what? You want to hit me, go ahead," Robin said. "I deserve it."

"I don't want to hit you!" Adam said.

"How have I been treating you?" Robin questioned. "I believe, I have only been treating you like a friend. If I am mistaken, if I have treated you like my servant, like a person of lesser rank...."

"No. Of course not!" Adam shouted. "You've treated me like one of the guys. And I never...." Adam turned away from him and put his hand to his face. And he sobbed. "Nobody ever did before. And I like it. And I liked your arms around me. There. I said it."

Robin let out a breath and looked around at the forest and the river alongside them. "So, I'm a little confused. Am I to continue treating you like one of the guys? Adam?"

Adam nodded.

"I asked you before if you can live with us being friends. If you can't do that, we have a problem," Robin said.

"It is just difficult, sometimes," Adam admitted. "But you don't have to be afraid to be alone with me."

"I wouldn't be afraid of you," Robin said. "We will continue target practice tomorrow. And I won't lay a hand on you. Won't ever again."

"Well just suck all the fun out of it!" Adam threw his hands open in exasperation.

Robin burst out laughing.

Adam wiped his eyes.

"Hop into that cold river over there. It would do you some good," Robin told him.

"It might."

"Yes, it might."

Adam wiped his eyes again, turning away. He laughed a little.

"You have every right to learn how to protect yourself," Robin said cautiously. "I don't see you as much of a fighter. I thought, you could learn how to use a pistol. That was all I meant by this."

"Legally, when can I shoot somebody?" Adam asked, turning to face him. Around his eyes was a bit pink.

Robin gave him a double take. "Ahm, wasn't expecting that. When someone attacks you, takes aim at you, or threatens someone else in the house. You don't ever pull a gun on a man unless you are willing to kill. And I would have you announce your intentions, if there is time."

"And if I had shot my father?"

"It would have been a self-defense case, somewhat complicated by the fact that you were to inherit his fortune. But I'm assuming you were under eighteen years of age," Robin said.

"Fourteen."

They began walking back toward the house then.

"I am sorry about that, you know. I think you must be lonely. You would not think of me that way if you had somebody. You know, Adam, you are my best friend in the world, my confidant, if not Marie of course."

"I thought it was Constable Poole."

"Oh no. He's a friend of course. But you and I were both raised to be gentlemen. We'll always have that in common."

"I think you lost them." James stood up to look over the roof of the carriage. "That turn was fantastic. We were on two wheels."

"Yeah. If anyone's alive inside," Robin remarked. "I know these roads. Grew up riding the hell out of them. You handled the team pretty good for a sailor."

"Anyone else grabbed the reins from me and I'd slap him." James reached over and tapped on the roof. "All right in there?"

"Are we even on a road? What the hell?" Adam declared out the window.

"Robin was the driver," James shot back. "We've escaped them."

"Best driving ever!" Adam called.

James crawled back down to sit beside Robin. "The case you're on...he was really framed and they stole 42,000 guilders. Do you know who did it?"

Robin shook his head. "Working on it."

"They don't sabotage a carriage and shoot at me for being English," James said. "Granted some Dutchmen in the country might think about shooting me."

Robin said, "In town too."

James looked at Robin and burst out laughing.

"Oh, I'll get you back for that absinthe, you limey."

The carriage turned into a cobblestone driveway lined by tulips on either side. There was a bridge over a little stream that came past a horse fountain.

James Collins took all this in, sitting back in the driver's seat, one leg crossed over the other and his elbow on the back of the seat. "You grew up here? And you left this for the cavalry? Loan me a jacket for dinner or I shall have to wear my colors."

"Don't you dare wear that in my mother's house," Robin said. "And don't drink anything clear."

James patted him on the arm. "I apologize again for the absinthe and your childlike intolerance of it."

"I threw up half the night."

"You're right. I must apologize to Adam. He had to hold your hair back all night," James said.

"Don't you say that to him," Robin said.

"I won't. I won't."

In the barrel-vaulted entry to the Van der Kellen estate, Robin turned the horses over to the stable master. He climbed down after James onto the steps and opened the carriage door. "Are you all right in there?"

Adam picked up the briefcase and climbed out. "Sort of my typical ride with you."

The two royal carriage drivers climbed out. "I could kiss the ground. I've never been shot at and escaped so close a disaster."

"Really? I do all the time," Robin told them. "Please come in. Take some rest and drive this team home tomorrow."

"Thank you, sir."

Inside the house they were met by Wout, Tess, Marie, and Mila.

"Darling." Robin took Marie into his arms to kiss her. "I'm sorry. We were delayed by the weather. The carriage threw a wheel."

"Really? Are you all right?" Marie asked him.

"Of course. My wife, Marie, this is James Collins. He is a...." Robin began.

James held out his hand to her. "Royal council. I was sent to help Robin with his case." He kissed Marie's hand. "Pleased to meet you, the beautiful Marie. He could think of nothing save getting home to you."

"This is my sister Mila. My sister Tess," Robin went on.

James bowed and kissed their hands as well.

"My brother-in-law, Wout Van de Berg," Robin said.

James shook hands with Wout. "Pleasure, sir."

Robin turned to the butler and said, "These are Royal Palace drivers. They've been through a terrible ordeal, with the broken carriage and the rain and all. Can we put them up for the night and send them back in the morning when the horses have rested?"

"Absolutely, Mr. Van der Kellen. Right this way, gentlemen."

"And one more thing." Robin drew the butler aside. "Adam will take a guest room as well. He has an elevated rank as gentleman."

"Explain that to Robert yourself. But I will have his things moved downstairs," the butler said. "Come along, gentlemen."

"Robin, your wife is even more beautiful than you said," James said.

That made the women smile.

"You speak English very well," Wout said.

"I handle many cases that involve English law." James followed Robin's example and took a seat on one of the parlor sofas.

"How did it go with the king? Will he help us?" Wout asked.

"I believe so," Robin said.

"He has sent me to help. And he went to Brussels himself to confirm your story and to attend some personal business at his palace," James said. "He is the Belgian King as well."

"I am Belgian. I'm delighted, sir," Wout said. "And where are you from?"

"A small island off the coast. You wouldn't know it," James said.

Robin let out a loud breath. "Can we have some brandy? I'm still cold from the soaking rain yesterday."

Marie slid her hands up Robin's arm. "And your shoulder? You ache so when it rains. Bring them some brandy."

"Bring it and can we have supper earlier? Why make them wait? Their travels have been hard," Mila spoke up.

"Where are Lynn and Robert?" Robin asked.

"Upstairs. Lynn is having a rough time of it. But she's all right so far," Mila said.

"Send her my wishes and tell Robert I need a word with him," Robin said.

Another of the butler's staff took off to do this.

"Mr. Collins," Mila said. "As eldest daughter of the family, welcome. Our brother Robert, a surgeon, is tending his expectant wife upstairs. She's very much in need these days. In their stead, I shall welcome you to their home. Your things are brought up to a very fine guest room. Tess is Mrs. Van de Berg. And my husband Jonas will be here shortly. What can I do to make you feel comfortable?"

Zoey served brandy to James, Robin, and even Adam. She could not take her eyes off the valet wearing Robin's expensive suit and sitting in the parlor. Adam's blue eyes met her dark ones. She blushed so pink and the smirk on her lips made him wet his.

Robin and Adam bounded up the stairs and round to Lynn's bedroom. Robin knocked on the door.

Robert stepped out and closed the door. "You needed to speak to me."

"How is Lynn?"

"Holding on. The baby is still kicking. She must hold on until this child is ready to come," Robert whispered.

"Send her all our love, will you?" Robin said.

"Of course. How was your visit with the king?"

"Robert, I am sent back with a British Commander James Collins. He claims to be here to help Wout's case on behalf of the king. But I believe he is here to spy on me. To report back to the king and I don't know why," Robin whispered. "I feel it in my gut."

Adam gasped. "But…" He grabbed onto Robin's arm.

"And I am to do what?" Robert said.

"Don't let on. Follow my lead. It's all for Wout at this point."

"Shall we remove him from the house? Are we in danger?"

"I don't think anyone is in danger from him, except me. I can handle him." Robin shook his head.

"Good Lord, Robin."

"Why did you not alert me any of this?" Adam whispered harshly.

"He's too much of a gentleman to do anything in this house or anything to women and children. He saved many on a train wreck just days ago, and they were all Dutch strangers to him. It is a strange code of honor we tread," Robin said. "Only him and I can comprehend it."

"Robin, what have you brought into my house?"

"Our carriage was sabotaged with a cut axel. Most likely James had to do with it. Oh, by the way, Adam is a gentleman now. He will take the room across the hall from mine."

Robert looked from Adam to Robin. "Why?"

"Because he was a gentleman in the king's palace. He can't go back now and certainly not in front of James. I'm borrowing a dinner jacket for James. Otherwise, he has to wear his British Navy colors."

"Not at my table," Robert said.

Adam held out his lapels. "Shall I change back into mine?"

"Keep them. They fit you well. These jackets interchanged with your other vests and trousers will make a good set for you," Robin said.

"He's wearing your clothing?" Robert asked, finally looking Adam over from head to toe. "The costume of a gentleman?"

"Couldn't have him dining with the king looking so plain," Robin said. "Tell the staff he is to be called Mr. Hudson now."

"I did let your trousers down one turn," Adam admitted.

"Saying you're taller than me?" Robin put his hands on his hips.

"Is there any other way to take that?" Adam said.

Robert snapped his fingers to get their attention. "I'll be down for dinner. You get down there and keep an eye on your guest."

"I will."

Down in the dining room, alone with Simon, Robin opened a cabinet in the sideboard and laid his Colt revolver inside on a shelf. "Tell the staff I need that there and they are not to touch it. Adam knows it is in here. Tell them also that Adam is to be called Mr. Hudson from now on."

"Mr. Hudson? The valet?" the butler said.

"Mr. Hudson, the gentleman," Robin said firmly.

"It shall take an adjustment, sir." Simon walked out.

Robin exited the parlor where James and the others were gathered. Jonas had arrived. Robin leaned in toward James to say softly, "In your room you will find a dinner jacket."

James stood up. "Thank you. Very much."

"Shall I show you the way so you can settle in?" Robin asked.

"Yes, please. That will be splendid." James followed him out and up the stairs, pausing to take in the painting of young Robin and the horse. Robin had to wait for him on the landing. James only smiled and kept climbing until he was beside Robin. They walked down the hall and Robin opened the door to James' guest room, not telling him where anyone else would be.

James walked in, seeing his bags and the jacket laid over the bed. "Thank you. This is lovely."

Robin waited in the doorway.

James opened the bag, revealing the glint of blue jacket among other articles of clothing. He laid his pistol there and emptied his pockets of ammunition.

Robin stepped inside and shut the door behind him.

James began unbuttoning his vest. "No need to worry, Van der Kellen. The pistol will stay where it lays. I have no intention of harming any of your family, or you for that matter. Think I had my own axel cut as a ruse?"

"It had occurred to me," Robin said.

James pulled off his vest and unbuttoned his shirt. When he turned to pull off the shirt and take another from his bag, Robin saw the scar of a bullet wound on his upper left back. James had some difficulty pulling on the fresh shirt and began to button it. "Yes. Something else you and I have in common."

Robin picked up James's vest to examine the buttons. They were brass buttons with anchors on them. British Navy buttons. "Can you find your way down to the dining room?"

"Of course," James said.

Robin backed out of the room and shut the door.

Marie met Robin and took him by both hands down the hall a bit. "Robin, everything is so strange."

"What is so strange, darling?"

"James and Adam." Marie looked up at him and adjusted his ascot for him.

"Adam masqueraded as a gentleman, my assistant on this trip and he was indispensable to me. Couldn't have done without him." Robin raised his chin for Marie to primp his collar.

"Jealous of Adam yet again," Marie remarked as they walked down the stairs. "And James? I know when you don't trust someone."

"I will tell you more tonight. Right now, continue to look after Lynn as you have. Does Robert tell you how wonderful you are?" Robin followed her down and around the landing beneath the painting.

"Yes, all the time. I've had a baby, remember? I know exactly what she's going through," Marie said.

"I've brought you a present. That is, if it survived the carriage ride here. Did Adam give it to you?" Robin asked.

"No," Marie said.

James entered the hall from the stairway, taking in the husband with wife doting on him. He approached them.

"The drivers set them on the table in the parlor." Robin looked from him into the parlor and saw the perfume and box of chocolates on the table. "Darling." He drew Marie with him in there and handed them to her with a kiss.

"Oh Robin. I love them." Marie kissed him on the mouth extra warmly.

James met Jonas and Wout in the parlor entry then. "Good evening, gentlemen."

"Evening, Mr. Collins," Wout said. "Are you a barrister then?"

"Merely a scholar of law. An advisor," James replied. "I can assure you, Mr. Van der Kellen is very highly regarded in his profession, in multiple countries. You are in very good hands. I'll help if I may, but more likely I am to inform his majesty on the outcomes of the case. Mr. Van der Kellen piqued his interest."

"Wout, it is all right to speak frankly about the case to his majesty's representative," Robin said. "As long as you stay in this household, or I go to jail in your stead."

Wout draped a drunken arm about Robin's shoulders. "Wouldn't do that to you, brother. Wouldn't think of it."

"Tell me you haven't finished off the brandy while I was away," Robin said.

"Oh God no. Jonas brought us more," Wout said.

"Robin, Robin look what I found." Mila hurried up to him and held out ribbons. "Father didn't burn them all. Mother saved some."

Robin's face lit up and he sorted through colorful ribbons in his hands and many with bronze medals hanging from them. "Mila, thank you. Ever so much. Look, first in the province steeple chase, 1820."

"1820? You were fifteen then." Marie clung to his arm.

"Yes, and so full of himself," Mila said. "With so many little girls cheering for him from the sidelines. Once he was thrown over a gate in a refusal and still landed on his boots. The stands emptied of little girls, running out to see if he was all right."

"Therefore, I can still say that I never fell off," Robin said, to much laughter. "Rather, bucked off like a cannonball right over the gate and the moat. Stuck the landing though."

James laughed, looking on. He moved deeper into the parlor to examine various artifacts decorating the room, or to appear to, at least. There were other awards on the walls for the prize horses that were bred. Oil paintings of fine horses lined the walls.

Tess moved in and hugged Robin again. "I'm just so glad you're home again. I know you can save Wout. I just know it."

Robin met eyes with Wout over her head. "I will be back at work first thing in the morning. I'm to see Judge Janssen again. I must tell him that I have an audience with the mayor and the appointed commissioner. The king is setting them up for me."

"I will get word when those are to take place," James spoke up. "You will know immediately. And I've met the commissioner. I can advise you on dealing with the tosser."

"He's not a nice man?" Tess questioned, worried.

"No, but he will have heard already how much favor Robin carries with his Majesty," James said.

"Carries favor with the king? You only just met him." Robert had just entered the room. "Does it take any more than that? My brother's popularity has no bounds. He should enter politics himself. It's a wonder the ambition hasn't occurred to him already."

Robin blurted out. "Think I'd make a nice Governor of Connecticut."

"If women had the vote, you'd already be." Marie broke up the room with laughter.

"Let us take our seats in the dining room, if you would please. Mr. Collins, I thank you for coming to the aid of my little brother." Robert held out a hand to the Brit.

James shook hands with him. "And thank you for your hospitality, Dr. Van der Kellen. You have a lovely estate."

Robin sat on the side of the table with his Colt in the cabinet behind him. James sat across from him. Wine was poured. Robin arranged his glass to the left side of his plate. Several courses of vegetables, cheeses, rye bread rolls, beef brisket and sausages were served by maids who listened in on conversations and giggled equally about the handsome visitor and the fact that Mr. Hudson was now a gentleman at the table.

"You were shot at? How do you know you did not lead them here?" Robert questioned.

Robin almost dropped his wine glass, the stemware catching the edge of his plate. "Well, Robert…."

"Robin took care of them," James spoke up. "Was he always such a marksman?"

"Ahm, yes. It started when we went hunting together and he was about as tall as his musket," Robert said. "I believe in the cavalry they had him training other boys when he was not yet through his own boot camp."

"Is that how you men define it? Robin took care of them. What does that mean?" Mila asked. "Something awful?"

"That is all that must be said at the dinner table," Robin said. "Mother had her rules. No yelling. No fighting. No pulling of girl's hair. And no talk of war."

Marie took another sip of wine. "He didn't pull you hair, did he?"

"Oh. He dunked my braid in an ink well," Mila replied to much laughter. "Still black spots on the walk there. Adam, have you siblings?"

"I have two sisters, one older than I," Adam said. "I would add to the rules: No mud. No animals. No spiders or bugs of any kind."

Robin leaned forward to see Adam on the other side of Marie. "What animals did you bring to the table? And spiders? You did not bring spiders to the table. You passed out when the cat ate one."

That broke the table up laughing.

"I did not bring animals to the table, but my sisters always had stray dogs underneath and sometimes a cat or two," Adam said. "I've never…I've never intentionally touched a spider. Just may have allowed one or two to encounter my sisters."

"Mr. Hudson, Adam, are you the transcriber for Robin's case? Do you keep the notes?" James asked.

Adam looked at James beside him at the table. "I think you would find my writing a mystery."

"Did you not learn to write elegantly?" James questioned.

"Of course. But Robin dictates very rapidly and I have my own short cuts only I can understand," Adam said.

"Then that means Robin needs you to...translate them?" James asked.

Adam nodded. "Job security." The gathering laughed.

Robin entered his room late that night to a lit fireplace and an oil lamp flickering. He began to unbutton his vest. It was then that he noticed his bed covers move. He met eyes with Marie in his bed. "It is late. I was going to let you sleep."

"Frida is being looked after. I came to wait up for you."

Robin peeled back his jacket and laid it over the chair. "Are you all right?"

"I'm fine. How do you like the lavender water you brought me?"

"I'm delighted." Robin removed his vest and then his shoes. He unbuttoned his cuffs.

"Let me help you." Marie sat up in black silk lingerie.

Robin sat on the edge of the bed to kiss her mouth. He felt her gentle hands opening buttons on his shirt, opening his cuffs. "You smell like Provence... the... south of France where all the... lavender grows." Her hand slid inside his shirt and around him, distracting him.

Marie kissed his mouth hungrily.

Robin moaned and leaned over her, leaning her back as he reached down to undo his belt. "Darling are you all right?"

"I missed you. That's all."

"Are you certain that is all?" Robin let her help remove his shirt. He tossed it onto the chair.

She pulled her night gown off, over her head.

"Marie?" Robin paused. "What is this?"

"Robin Van der Kellen, this is you being seduced," Marie said.

Robin stood up to unbutton his trousers and removed them. "Well I... shall endeavor to do my part."

"I understand, sir, you have a way with women," Marie said seriously.

"As a matter of fact, I am well certified in such matters. Banned even in some countries, my lady," Robin said.

"I can see why," Marie told him. "Remove that. You see the guilders on the dresser? I shall get what I've paid for."

Robin glanced and actually saw coins there in the lamplight. "My darling, in the morning I expect you to double that."

Marie pulled back the covers for him. "Triplicating that is in the realm of possibility. You do have a reputation."

Robin slid into the bed with her. "I must warn you. If we start this, I shall have to take you. It's been so long. I won't have any choice."

"I give myself to you, sir."

Robin kissed her before she could even giggle.

Adam awoke in his luxurious sleigh bed of French oak, finding it almost as amazing as the bed in the palace. He rolled over in fine linens to find his fireplace still crackling. Someone had restocked it during the night, just as he once did at the Millers. Dawn light was just coming through lace curtains and velvet drapes. He sat up against four pillows. Suddenly the situation dawned on him, and he threw back covers to hop out. He dressed in his own black trousers, blue shirt, and Robin's jacket. He washed his face and shaved a bit under his nose and chin. Then he popped across the hall to Robin's room, giving the door his characteristic knock followed by walking right in. He went straight to the wardrobe to take out a suit for Robin, a shirt, underclothing. "Robin, I'm getting your suit out. Wake up there." Then he started to carry these across the room toward the vanity closet to prepare the bath when he saw Robin naked in the bed and just awakening.

"Oh, forgive me. You're never in here." Adam backstepped. Only then did he see the long black hair of Marie across the pillow and her bare shoulder and lovely back. "Oh my God. Forgive me. I have your suit right here. I'll go out through the servant's door."

Adam disappeared into the vanity room. He shut the door so quickly he almost caught his own shoe. Buckets of hot water were beside the tub. He laid the suit over the rack and exited immediately through the other door to the hallway. There in the hall and only there, he bowed low and grinned ear to ear. He rose with a fist pump in the air and performed a double twirl down the hallway and skidded to a halt in front of Zoey.

Zoey giggled at this, especially the twirls. She went to him and wished him, "Goedemorgan, Meneer Hudson."

"Goedemorgan, mooi," he said to her. "I don't care if you saw that, by the way. That was not dancing. I'm actually quite a skilled dancer but that wasn't it."

Zoey called him handsome and said she missed dining with him. She knew where Eva was and indicated for Adam to follow her to the stairs.

"Oh, good morning, Eva," Adam said.

"Well. You left here a valet. You returned some sort of gentleman, or so I heard. Did the king elevate your rank himself?" she said. "Have a seat. I'm told I must explain this to the staff. This is Zoey."

"You have to help me talk to her." Adam sat down at the kitchen table where he had dined with the staff previously. "Actually, the king had something to do with it."

Zoey poured him some coffee and served a bowl of pastries to him.

"Mr. Hudson, you have a bit of a problem," Eva said.

"Only one?" Adam added cream to his coffee.

"This girl is in love with you."

"She is? We hardly know each other at all." Adam's eyebrows rose. "Really? Really." He smiled warmly as that sunk in.

"Why are we to treat you like a gentleman now?" Eva asked.

"I am a gentleman, or rather I was raised one anyway," Adam said.

"Well, I hate to tell you this, sir, but as valet you could have courted miss Zoey. As a gentleman you cannot."

"Sounds more like your problem, than mine," Adam said. "Tell her I like her very much. She has been very kind to me ever since I arrived, and I appreciate her."

Eva translated this.

Zoey brightened. She sat down across from Adam with her own cup of tea and listened to the explanation about Adam's rank.

Robin rounded a corner and surprised a couple in a passionate embrace. The young man was the taller and the girl had arms wrapped around his waist. The male supported her head and neck with both hands. The two suddenly looked at Robin in breathless surprise.

The girl, in a maid's apron, hopped back from Adam. Adam's cheeks had blushed. His mouth was red from kissing the girl. She started to hurry off.

"Wait. Hold on now," Robin said in Dutch.

Adam straightened his posture and wiped his mouth. He buttoned his jacket closed in front because the girl had been inside of it.

"Wait. I must talk to you both. Just hold on," Robin said in Dutch. "You, sit down over there. Don't go anywhere." The maid sat down on a sofa in the parlor. Robin gestured for Adam to come with him to the other side of the room. Robin looked away from him and said, "Adam, what are you doing?"

"Sir, I like her very much. It is not what you think. She has been so nice to me, so kind. Always helping me," Adam blurted out.

"It's her job to be kind to you. You can't even speak the same language. What are you doing, Adam? You can't take advantage of a woman this way," Robin scolded. "You do realize, you get her with child, and you will marry her and take a wife home with you. You realize that, right?"

"I was just kissing the girl."

"You stay right there. Don't move." Robin turned and approached the young woman.

She rose and looked up at Robin Van der Kellen in all his finery.

"Miss, I do not even know your name," Robin began.

"My name is Zoey Rameloo, Mr. Van der Kellen." She gave a bit of a curtsey.

"All right. Zoey. I will take care of this. He is my assistant. He is my concern. Has he done anything inappropriate?" Robin asked in Dutch.

"No. No, of course not. He is a perfect angel, really. Please do not punish him. It is my fault. I kissed him," Zoey insisted.

"Sit down. Calm down then." Robin turned back to Adam. He put a hand on Adam's shoulder and steered him around so that the girl could not see his face. "Adam, she kissed you?"

"Yes, but I kissed back," Adam said. "I like her very much."

"Adam. Jesus. You can't mean to court her? Really?" Robin asked. "I mean meet her father, and all that? You have never been with a woman before. Are you out of your mind? You can't even talk to her. You don't even know if she wants to leave this country to go home with you."

"I wasn't thinking of all that. I mean, is it all right if I'm a gentleman to court her? When I'm not doing my work, of course. I like Zoey very much," Adam said. "Robin, come on."

"You do not even know how impossible that is here. I do. You'll do what I say, everything I say, or your behavior reflects on me." Robin looked up at the ceiling. "As if my behavior can shock any further in this house." He returned to the girl and again she stood up.

"Sir, please do not punish him. I just love him."

Robin's eyebrows rose. "Miss, you do realize if your courtship progresses, you will have to return to America with him. There his employment lies."

"If our courtship works out, I will go anywhere he goes. Please, will you speak to your brother for us?"

"You realize he will appoint a chaperone? The butler seems reasonable. But you will not carry on again the way I just found you," Robin said. "You do not want a reputation in this house. Let me handle it. You go on back to your work."

She looked at Adam and he blew a kiss to her. She smiled and hurried away.

Robin put his hands on his hips, looking at the young valet.

Adam smiled. "I always wanted to do that."

"Boy, you're in up to your neck. Do you know how close you came to having to marry the first girl you ever kissed?"

"Marry? What makes you think this is the first girl I ever kissed?"

"Lower your voice. If the butler or my brother saw what I just did... I'm taking yours and her word that you did not have intimacy with her. They would not be so generous." Robin gestured a throat cutting with his right hand. "You're going to start learning some Dutch. You need to be able to speak a few words to meet her father. Let me go talk to the butler and then my brother. They've got a tutor teaching the children some English. We need her to teach you some Dutch."

"She already has been. Eva. Goedenmorgen," Adam said. "You had company last night. I would have thought you'd be in a better mood today. I do apologize for walking in like that, but you have to admit the chances of it have been very slim in past months." Then he smiled. "Remembered how?"

Robin met his eyes intensely. "Chances of you walking in on us will be greatly diminished as I confine you to your room from now on."

"Love is in the air apparently." Adam shrugged. "You will tell me how to be with a woman, won't you? What's the trick to it?"

"Adam, Adam, you...you behave like a gentleman. Keep your damn trousers on. Do you understand me? You're not experimenting with that girl. This is serious. You'll break her heart."

"Didn't it go well last night? Over too quickly?" Adam asked. "You sound a bit cranky."

"I'm cranky with you. Marie was wonderful. I was wonderful." Robin smoothed a hand down his own vest. "Wonderful. Are you ready to go to work? Little shit."

Adam reached forward and straightened Robin's ascot. "Of course."

Robin slapped his hand away. "Not that work. I can't read your damn writing."

"Translate before James comes to listen?"

"Yes, before that."

"You slapped me. I can't believe you did that. I must show you something." Adam followed Robin to the library, and they sat down on either side of the desk. "I was practicing writing something just like the note I found about the combination. And look at this." Adam opened

Robin's briefcase to produce the charcoal impression note and another from a drawer in the desk. "...ames combination 22-14-11-80"

Robin pointed to the one that came from his briefcase. "That is the original."

"Correct. But look how close I got with this fake one." Adam pointed to the other. "Robin, I was using that graphite that belonged to Collins. He said he had lots of them. It fell on the floor at the inn. Remember?"

"That's weak. Circumstantial at best." Robin slid the fake papers back to Adam and returned the original to safekeeping in his briefcase. "Good work, though. It is that way of thinking that will solve this case."

When Adam looked up from the paper, he found Robin staring at him.

Robin sat back in the chair. "Adam, what are you doing?"

"What?"

"The girl?"

"I can't be curious?"

"No."

"She smells so good, like flowers. She's so soft. I can't believe how much I'm flying right now. Kissing her is like..."

Robin rolled his eyes. "I should have gotten you a prostitute in Norwich."

"Don't make fun," Adam shot back. "No, I've never been with a woman. Do you think she's a virgin?"

"Yes, I do," Robin said. "Don't you ask her that."

"As if I could. Does it feel different with a girl?"

"Does it feel different with a boy?" Robin's brow furrowed. "Where do you put your...? Don't answer me. Don't you answer me."

"Curious, aren't you? You're awfully cranky for a man who finally had intimacy last night." Adam sat back in the chair, smirking. "Are we going to work, or you are just going to yell at me?"

"You were raised to be a gentleman, were you not?"

"Until I was homeless, sleeping in an alley, and swatting rats off my back," Adam said. "Anything else you want to know?"

Robin looked down at the ledger and flipped some pages. He slid the inkwell and pen closer. After a long exhale, he said, "Go back to your notes about the commissioner. What was it the king said?"

"You don't trust James, do you?"

"No. You remember how to use the Colt, do you not?"

Adam met his eyes and saw the seriousness in them, in the way he was not blinking. "Yes, I do. And I know where it is. I'll slip it into your briefcase when we go to town."

"I have considered telling you to keep it on you. But I think it's best you don't," Robin said. "I don't want you using a gun in this country, without me there. Do you understand?"

Adam nodded.

Chapter 10: Contempt of Court

Robin looked at his watch once again as he stood on the courtroom floor.

"Mr. De Vries, how were you hired by Mr. Van der Kellen?" Mr. Anholts, the prosecuting attorney, paced in front of the witness box.

"We knew each other in law school. He was my senior," Mr. De Vries said.

"And he hired you as a legal assistant?" Mr. Anholts asked.

"No, he did not."

"What did he hire you to do then?"

"I was hired to look into the backgrounds and financials of various personnel in Mr. Van de Berg's bank," De Vries said.

"Don't look to him for your answers." Anholts pointed toward Van der Kellen. "You look at me and remember that you are under oath."

"And keep it brief," Robin spoke up. "I need him to locate Mr. Hudson."

"Well, I apologize but this man is on the witness list for today, Mr. Van der Kellen," Anholts said. "Mr. De Vries, which personnel at the bank were you looking into?"

"Mr. Helmen and Mr. Mahoric," De Vries said. "As well as the secretaries."

"And how did you look into these people? Did you follow them?"

"Yes."

"Did you see where they live?"

"Yes."

"Did you see records at the bank? Such things as salaries and hours worked?"

"Yes."

"Did you ever look into these things regarding Mr. Van de Berg himself?" Anholts asked.

"Not intentionally." De Vries glanced at Robin again.

"How much money does he earn?"

"From the bank or his wealthy family?" De Vries asked.

"Objection." Robin stood up at his desk. "Irrelevant testimony meant to waste time and keep Mr. De Vries from doing his job."

"You are the only one this is irrelevant to, Mr. Van der Kellen. Sit down. Go on Mr. De Vries," the judge ruled.

"How much money does Van de Berg earn a year?" Anholts asked.

"From the bank in question, 45,000 guilders a year. His family is worth about 1.2 million guilders, mostly in Brussels. He stands to inherit," De Vries said.

"Were you told to investigate his financials?"

"No. But I was curious."

"About whether he stole from his own bank?" Anholts asked.

"Objection!" Robin stood up. "Unless you're trying to build my case for me by eliminating Wout's motive. Your honor, I need my hired detective to locate Mr. Hudson. I fear for his safety. You must release the witness and let him do his job."

"Well, I have never seen a lawyer object to helpful testimony for his client. Don't think you can lay seeds for malpractice, Mr. Van der Kellen. I'm not falling for it," the judge said. "Do you have further questions for Mr. De Vries?"

"I do not, your honor." Mr. Anholts returned to his own desk.

"Mr. Van der Kellen, this is your witness. Do your duty."

Robin wet his lips and strolled forward. "Mr. De Vries, you were investigating the bank records. What did you find out regarding the steam engine transaction?"

"The records regarding that were very strange. Names of individuals were inked out. I couldn't tell you who stood to gain from the transaction, besides Mr. Van de Berg. There were two other men who signed the documents," De Vries said.

"Did you hold it up the light?" Robin questioned.

"Of course. I made out a few initials. One had the first initial of J. Another an M. Last name of one began with a C," De Vries said.

"J.C. or M.C?" Robin asked. "Anything else?"

"Something struck me as rather...maritime about the document," De Vries said.

"Maritime? How so?" Robin asked.

"Speculation," Anholts said.

"Just describe the document," Robin said.

"It had an unusual stamp in the bottom corner. Not really a stamp but more of an impression, as if a button on a cuff or jacket got some ink on it and touched the corner. That's it. Looked to me like a ship's anchor."

"Did the anchor have a chain rather serpentine about it?" Robin asked.

"Yes. The sort worn by the British Navy," De Vries said. "It is a London steam engine company. I put two and two together that way."

"Yes, Mr. De Vries. But the British names were all blacked out, you said?" Robin thought about Collin's vest buttons. "On the copies the bank held, but what about official copies at the exchange office?"

"Mr. Hudson was going looking for those today, sir," De Vries said.

"And at what time today were you to meet with Mr. Hudson?"

"Ten o-clock this morning. He was to meet me at the tax office right after going to the exchange," De Vries said.

"That's very interesting. Do you suppose the copies held at the exchange or tax office would not be blacked out with ink?" Robin questioned.

"They couldn't be. They hold the originals there," De Vries said.

Robin Van der Kellen returned to his desk and slammed his note book down so hard that even Wout beside him jumped. "This is outrageous! Mr. Hudson has gone alone to find the very records proving who else knew the dates and times that the steam engine profits were to be deposited into the bank. And now he is six hours overdue. Six hours, your honor. You must let Mr. De Vries go find him!"

"Mr. De Vries may stand down, that is if Mr. Anholts has no further questions for him," the judge said.

"Oh, I've got a hundred or more." Anholts stood up, straightening his jacket.

"Jesus Christ. I just require a delay here," Robin insisted.

"Take your seat, Mr. Van der Kellen, and hold your tone, or I will hold you in contempt of court," the judge said.

"Then send police officers to look for Mr. Hudson," Robin insisted. "Or must I send my wife?"

"Hold your tone, Mr. Van der Kellen!" the judge yelled.

"The key to this whole case could be bleeding out in an alley right now, and you won't let De Vries or myself go find him!" Robin outraged with a finger held up in the air.

"Conjecture. You won't be so arrogant after spending a night in jail with your client, sir. Let us see you come to court tomorrow morning wrinkled and unslept."

"Don't hold it against me that it took you three times to pass the law exam," Robin pressed on.

"That's it!" The judge slammed his gavel down. "You're in contempt of this court!"

The audience swooned.

"Take the elegant Robin Van der Kellen into hand cuffs and intrigue him to one night in our jail. And if you open that mouth of yours, Van der Kellen, it will be a week in jail. I have plenty of time."

"Robin, no!" Marie cried out.

Robin turned to face the jury and held out his hands dramatically to await being handcuffed. His gold cufflinks shimmered. The scalloped embroidery on his cuffs even glimmered with gold thread in them.

Ladies in the audience cried out for him.

The judge stood up. "De Vries, your testimony will continue tomorrow. You may stand down."

Two bailiffs walked out to Robin. "Best give those to your wife, sir. They won't last long down below."

"I see you plan to ensure our safety." Robin removed his gold cuff links to allow the handcuffs to be locked about his wrists. Then Wout was also put in cuffs.

De Vries passed Robin and just nodded to him. He quickly left the courtroom.

Robin leaned over the rail to steal a kiss from Marie. "See you in the morning, darlin. Go home and stay safe." He slipped the cufflinks into her hands as she removed his pocketbook from inside his jacket.

"Do you want me to find Adam?" Marie asked.

"Don't you dare. Stay home. Oh bailiff…" Robin pulled a dagger out of his inside pocket and another from beneath his right pant leg. He handed those to Marie as well.

"Anymore?" a bailiff questioned.

The other bailiff patted Robin down in front of everyone. He patted down his sides, his pockets, his pant legs, and everywhere except his crotch.

"Enjoyed that?" Stripped of his gold and his money, Van der Kellen was still cocky in his finely textured black suit, high white collars, and silk ascot.

The ladies in the crowd called out his name and he winked at his wife.

The jailers opened the cell door and first unlocked Wout's hand cuffs, releasing him into the cell and then they turned to the lawyer.

"Hope you get on with your brother-in-law, as there is only one cot for the both of you. We have a full house tonight. Don't usually get fancy lawyers down here."

Robin rolled his eyes. "I trust your accommodations will be first class."

"Any complaints? Mind you, I have no specific orders to unlock your cuffs for the night."

Robin blanked his expression.

The guard grabbed his wrists and yanked him forward a step before he put the key into the cuff and turned it. The cuffs scraped his skin as they opened and clanged on the floor.

That made the other jailed inmates burst out laughing and yelling with various taunts about the handsome lawyer.

"Pick them up," the jailer said.

Robin simply walked into the cell with Wout and leaned there against the bars.

"Think you're funny, fancy ass barrister, do you?" The guard snatched up the hand cuffs and slammed the cell door shut. "Have a good night, gentlemen."

Robin folded his arms until the guards left them. Taunts from the inmates continued.

Wout stood closer to him. "I'm so sorry, Robin. I can't believe what I've gotten you into."

"Save your apologies. I got the delay I needed. And this making the headlines will certainly draw the attention of the king. I hope to see him in court tomorrow." Robin looked down at his wrists to rub at the bruises and red marks. "Besides, we are perfectly safe in here. And the family is safe because we are away. Are you all right?"

"Well as can be, I suppose," Wout said. "Do we have any chance?"

"We have every chance. I just hope Adam is all right. He's been away all day and I expect some trouble came to him."

"While I appreciate your economy of panic, I do wish you would share with me your plans before you half ass your way through them. He plans to humiliate you, the judge. Make you appear in court in the morning without a clean suit or shave or decent meal even," Wout said.

"Well..." Robin looked around at their small cell, one cot with a pillow, one bowl of water and a towel and the chamber pot in the corner. "When the king lays eyes on me unshaven in the courtroom, I'll have every sympathy in the audience, and perhaps the jury." He rolled his wrist over and showed the bruise to Wout. "These will still be here."

"Try not to make ladies faint, will you?"

"If I thought it would help the case…."

Jailers brought someone down the hall of cells and knocked on Robin and Wout's bars.

"Holy Jesus." Robin shot off the cot and went to the bars. "What are you doing here?"

"My only brother is incarcerated. You don't think I would be here? We may never see you again." Robert held onto the bars, looking inside at Robin and then Wout.

"Oh my God." Robin moved closer to the bars. "Go home, Robert."

"Robin, what is wrong with you? Getting thrown out of court?"

"With Adam in trouble, this is the only way to protect Wout and myself, and your household as a matter of fact. Don't you see, Robert?" Robin said. "It's a ruse to get the king's attention. It's the only safe place to keep Wout. I needed a delay. Has Adam been found?"

"What I see is that it's a ruse that can get Wout in prison for life."

"Go home Robert. Find Adam. See if Mr. De Vries has found him. Send him to me here."

As the drunk in the next cell sang tavern songs most of the night, Robin sat up on the cot, thinking through his closing argument, if he had to do it without the London men with initials M. C. or J. C. Would he have to use the charcoal note with the combination?

Wout slept beside him, leaning against his shoulder. Farther down the cells, someone was vomiting. And then the yelling started at the other end. Guards came down the line to quickly squash the disturbance of inmates. And then they paused beside Wout's cell.

Van der Kellen was sitting with his arms folded, just looking at them.

Van de Berg was still asleep with his head on Robin's shoulder.

"Give me one reason why I should let your assistant in to see you," one guard said.

Robin quickly stood up and approached the bars. "Mr. Hudson is here? Is he all right?"

"Not exactly."

Wout fell onto the cot and looked up in shock.

"What do you mean by that?" Robin asked.

"You'll see."

"You got women waiting outside," the other guard said.

"Women? Not my wife and his?" Wout asked.

"About twenty of them." The other guard laughed. "You married to all of them? How many of them are you sleeping with?"

Robin looked at Wout. "Well, none of them tonight."

After a moment both guards laughed. "I'll bring your assistant in. I'll be patting him down such that he has no blades or keys on him. Just play by the rules, barrister."

The following morning, Robin Van der Kellen rose at the desk beside his client as the judge entered the courtroom. Robin's unkempt hair curled into ringlets from the humidity in the jail house. And as always, he grew quite a bit of stubble overnight. His shirt cuffs were unfastened without cufflinks so that bruises would be visible when he pushed at his hair or straightened his ascot.

Reporters were quickly making note of all this, and the number of females gathered outside the courthouse.

The courtroom doors opened, and an entourage entered. Van der Kellen turned and looked on with growing confidence until he met eyes with James Collins beside the king.

"All rise for his Royal Highness."

"His Royal Highness, King William II, wishes to observe today's proceedings."

"Delighted to have you, your highness. You may be seated," the judge said.

Van der Kellen was the only one in the courthouse to remain standing.

"What is it today? Mr. Van der Kellen? Did you sleep well last night on a cot in my jail? I'll bet you missed your feather bed and eider down pillows."

"Well, you do keep quite a nice jail, your honor. Hardly any rats," Robin said to much laughter. "As the reason for my appearance is widely known, I shall not waste his majesty's time. I petition the court to enter new evidence into the record."

"I'm supposed to cross examine Mr. De Vries. New evidence cannot be entered now," the prosecutor cried out. "You're just grandstanding for the crowds again, as if you haven't made enough headlines in the papers."

"I urgently call a new witness, Mr. Adam Hudson to the stand," Robin said.

Adam rose and waited at the gate. His forehead had a bruise on it, above his left eyebrow. He too looked like he slept in his suit that night, as he had spent the night in a chair waiting to see Robin in the jail house. De Vries was actually holding Adam up by the arm.

"This had better be good. Admit the witness," the judge said.

The bailiff opened the gate and Adam walked unsteadily to stand in the witness box, nervously looking out on all the gathered people in the courtroom, including the Dutch King and Commander Collins.

"Do you swear to tell the truth under oath?"

"I do," Adam said, in response to question in Dutch. He sat down in the witness box.

"Enter into the record, the witness, Mr. Adam Hudson only speaks English. Therefore, this segment of the trial shall be conducted in English. You can speak English, can you not, your honor?" Robin strolled in front of the court, still looking handsome to spite his whiskers and no one could hear his growling stomach.

"Proceed in English then and bring us to the point."

"And enter into the record that this witness is also in the employment of Mr. Van der Kellen," the prosecutor announced. "I must be allowed to cross examine him and Mr. De Vries."

"Entered as such."

"Very well. Mr. Hudson, please state your full legal name for the court." Robin looked at Adam intensely. "And occupation."

Adam stared at him. His mouth pursed shut. His eyebrows fused.

"You are under oath, sir. *Full legal name*," Robin articulated.

"Adam Theodore Rothschild III, of New York, America. I serve as valet and legal assistant to Mr. Van der Kellen," Adam said.

"Thank you. You have worked for me for over a year now. Why is it I only know you by the name Adam Hudson?" Robin said.

Adam rolled his eyes. "I intend to legally change my name to Hudson, sir."

"Very well then, Mr. Rothschild the third, you paid a visit to me in the jail house last night, did you not?" Robin strolled in front of the judge's desk.

"Yes, sir."

"You were not there to give me a shave." Robin stroked his whiskers and played to the crowd for a moment. "You were there to tell me what?"

"To tell you that someone hit me over the head and tugged a grain sack over me. I was struck in the stomach such that I could not catch my breath. And then he carried me over his shoulder. I wasn't knocked unconscious. I knew it was not far away before I was dropped," Adam said. "Round some corners and into a building near the tax office."

"Objection. What makes this relevant? What makes you so sure it was a man?" the other lawyer said.

"Really? Does anyone think a woman carried him off over her shoulder? He is handsome." Robin looked around at the audience and jury as they laughed a bit. "This will become highly relevant. Who did you see when the sack was removed? Is he here in this room?"

"Mr. Helmen. Secretary to..." Adam pointed to the man.

"Objection. Conjecture on the witness's part," the other lawyer said.

"It's not conjecture," Robin reminded. "Clearly, Mr. Rothschild recognized him from his testimony. What happened next, Mr. Rothschild? Could you breathe?"

"I hurt pretty bad. But he handed me a sack of gold coins," Adam said.

"Do you have those gold coins in your possession now?" Robin asked.

"I do, sir."

"Offer them into evidence." Robin glanced down at his missing cuff links. "You might get them back."

Adam produced a handful of gold coins and placed them into a basket the bailiff offered. Then the coins were brought to the judge.

"This has all the appearance of a bribe," Robin said.

"Appearance of? *It was a bribe*!" Adam shot back. "And a kidnapping and an assault!"

"Easy now." Robin made serious his face and turned toward the judge. "I ask that your honor examine the coins on both sides please. What do you find there?"

The judge turned over a few coins. There was ink on some of them. "All right, Mr. Van der Kellen. Tell me why these coins have a RVB written on them?"

"Because Mr. Wouter Van de Berg marks some of the coins in his vault. And as you know, Mr. Van de Berg has not been back into his bank since his arrest. Therefore, these coins were marked a priori. In plain language, they came from his vault before that arrest. They came from the very public funds that he is accused of stealing. I also refer to the ledger held in evidence, the one with the handwriting that is not Van de Berg's but actually that of Mr. Mahoric." Robin walked the ledger from the evidence display to the judge. "If you will, please examine the entry in question, you will find that Van de Berg marks the ledger in the upper left corner with the mark that he puts on the coins that day. Flip through the pages and you will see, he changes the mark with the deposit, sometimes using the initials of his children and even those of his dog, Rufus Van de Berg."

That made the crowd and the king laugh. As long as the king was laughing, the judge had no choice but to pause.

It was the other lawyer who finally said, "Are we now to sit through the testimony of a dog?"

"Allow the prosecution to examine the coins and ledger please," the judge said. "Move it along, Van der Kellen. Point taken Mr. Anholts."

"When did you receive these coins, Mr. Rothschild?" Robin asked.

"Ten o-clock yesterday, sir."

"And from whom?"

"Mr. Helmen," Adam said. "I just told you that."

"Why would Mr. Helmen give you one hundred guilders in gold, exactly?" Robin questioned. "Did he say?"

"It was a misunderstanding!" Mr. Mahoric cried out. "That Adam Hudson was acting as a spy on our premises. And you don't even know his name! It's the testimony of a discredited liar!"

Robin raised his eyebrows. "A spy? A liar? Deceived me about his name? Well, that leads this witness open to my discovery. Mr. Rothschild, you work for me. What were you doing at Mr. Mahoric's house yesterday?"

"I was walking down the street in the general same direction Mr. Helmen was, leaving the tax office, when I was hit in the head. A bag was thrown over me. I was picked up and carried off. When I was able to break free and pull the bag off my head, Mr. Helmen was standing before me. He yelled at me for following him. He didn't want me to give you documents," Adam said. "He shoved this paper into my mouth, to be exact."

"I object. This is outrageous," Anholts said. "When do I get to cross examine?"

"What documents?" Robin asked. "What paper?"

"Quiet. I will have order in this courtroom. There shall be no further interruptions by the audience. Your Royal King is present."

Robin gestured toward Adam. "I enter into evidence a sample of Mr. Mahoric's handwriting."

"We already have samples of his handwriting. How is this new evidence?" Anholts asked.

"This wrinkled paper has writing in English, has it not? Please read it, Mr. Rothschild," Robin said. "The third."

Adam took a deep breath first. "If you will, Mr. Hudson, please withhold these documents in your possession and keep this money as only a down payment of the fortune that will follow. Fortune is spelled with three o's." Adam showed the paper to Robin.

"This is the paper that was shoved into your mouth by Mr. Helmen?" Robin delivered the paper to the judge. "The fact that the bribe is written in English points to the fact that it is meant for Mr. Rothchild's eyes, misspelling and all. What the bribe actually says is of very little importance given that the bribe itself consisted of some of the very gold coins from the public funds that Mr. Van de Berg is accused of stealing."

"What documents were meant to be concealed?" The judge asked.

"What documents, Mr. Rothschild?" Robin asked.

Adam held up more papers.

"When they hit you and bagged you, why did they not take these documents from you?" Mr. Anholts asked. "If that's what they wanted."

"They were hidden in my underclothing," Adam said.

Robin looked at him, looked at the audience, shrugged and finally picked up the papers. "Uncomfortable but effective. Where did you steal these papers from?"

Even the king laughed aloud again.

"These were filed copies at the registrar's office. Available to the public because they are tax records," Adam explained. "They can have them back. I only borrowed them."

"You are correct. Where taxes are due, records are public." Robin took them and flipped through them. "Deed to a home in Paris. Deed to a yacht in Stockholm. Horses. Coaches. Women. How I wonder does a bank manager afford all of this? He's spending the stolen gold! Who hit you and bagged you, Mr. Rothschild?"

"Ask Mr. Helmen! Someone tall and smelling of rosemary aftershave."

"I object! He's making that up!"

"Oh, and I made up this wound on my forehead!" Adam shouted back, his lack of sleep catching up with him. "Who hit me, Mr. Helmen?"

"Did you have a chance to visit the exchange, to see an original unredacted version of the steam engine deal before the assault?" Robin asked.

"The documents were missing. They said they had a break in. They couldn't find them, so I went to the tax office. You know what happened after that. I woke up in the alley several hours later," Adam explained.

"The exchange had a break in? Are you well?" Robin asked.

Adam met eyes with Robin. "Not exactly."

Robin looked up at the judge. "The defense has no further questions for this witness."

"Does the prosecution wish to cross examine the witness?" the judge asked.

"No, your honor. I do not wish for this witness to say another word."

"Mr. Hudson stand down. Do you wish to cross examine Mr. De Vries, now, Mr. Anholts?"

"I do not, your honor."

"This court is in recess while the jury and I examine these coins and ledger. We will reconvene for closing arguments in three hours. Please do get shaved up proper, gentlemen, before you return to my court room. And have his forehead attended by a physician."

Lawyer Robin Van der Kellen entered the courtroom for closing arguments in a crisp brand new stylish French suit of bluish black vertical striped wool, a brilliant white shirt, black silk vest, and a black ascot with white polka dots. His black leather ankle boots were also the latest fashion from Paris, with pointed toes and almost a two-inch heel. He was perfectly shaven, and his hair styled with part on the left and falling to a bell at his shoulders.

Robin gave a look to Marie in the seating area with the family. She was holding hands with Tess. Even Robert was with them today. Robin straightened his ascot and checked that his suit coat was buttoned properly. "Your highness, your honor the judge, gentleman of the jury, I have presented evidence demonstrating that Mr. Albert Mahoric, bank manager, altered the bank ledger, removed funds from the safe on April 22nd, and framed Mr. Wouter Van de Berg of the crime of retaining public funds. Mr. Mahoric bought a new carriage. He bought a new home on Canal Street and one in Paris. He bought a Swedish yacht. He bought diamonds for his mistress Madame la Prostituée. All of those purchases far exceeded his income. Mr. Helmen and an unknown assailant kidnapped my assistant Mr. Rothschild and bribed him with a letter in Mahoric's handwriting, with funds from the very bank theft. I have presented Mr. Mahoric's motive for framing Mr. Van de Berg. He had received a poor review, was reprimanded for arriving late to work on several occasions, was denied a promotion to senior manager. And I realize this case is strictly about Mr. Van de Berg. The facts are simple. On the date the money was taken from the safe, Van de Berg was in Brussels at his mother's funeral. The handwriting in the ledger is not the handwriting of Mr. Van de Berg. It more closely resembles the handwriting of Mr. Mahoric and you saw that with your own eyes. Mr. Mahoric writes with his left hand. The slant is to the left. His spelling is poor. The investment of these public funds in steam engine development was a guaranteed money maker for the government. Van de Berg knew that. That is why he invested in steam engines. That's why it made forty-two thousand guilders, and those funds belong to the government, not Mr. Mahoric with the Swedish yacht. And we yesterday, saw that Mr. Helmen attempted to bribe Mr. Rothschild with gold coins from that very bank robbery, to prevent him from demonstrating how much money Mahoric has been spending. A convenient theft prevented Mr. Rothschild from viewing the steam engine documents at the exchange. I'm afraid we are all left to wonder what other names would have been found on the original documents. Adam Rothschild still bears the wound on his forehead from that encounter. Yes, 42,000 guilders have been stolen. But it sure as hell wasn't by Mr. Van de Berg. The defense rests."

The prosecutor Mr. Anholts rose as Van der Kellen took his seat. He paced in front of the jury, the judge, the king and the audience. "I confess, the elegant Mr. Van der Kellen has taken all the wind from my sails. I am forced to withdraw my warrant for Mr. Van de Berg and instead issue ones for Mr. Mahoric and Mr. Helmen."

At that the audience roared approval.

The king rose from his seat in the audience.

Van der Kellen stopped hugging Van de Berg and Adam Hudson.

"His highness King Willem II shall approach the bench."

The king walked down the stairs and passed through the gate onto the court floor. He met eyes with the prosecuting attorney first, who bowed. To Van der Kellen, he did not look. He went past to the judge and spoke privately to him.

Robin laid a hand on Van de Berg's shoulder.

"What's happening?" Marie whispered to Tess and Jonas.

"I don't know. Brace yourselves," Jonas whispered back.

"Van der Kellen, approach the bench," the judge said.

Robin did so at once, finding himself standing beside King William II. "Your Highness," he said and bowed formally.

"I want all $42,000 returned to my government as soon as possible," the king said softly. "Announce this to the press the moment you exit this court room."

"Yes, your highness," the judge said. "We shall seize the funds of both men."

"You have the wrong man in custody. Release Van de Berg. Arrest Mahoric and Helmen immediately and find out who the rosemary aftershave man was. Arrest him as well," the king said. "And you, Mr. Van der Kellen...."

"Yes, your highness?" Robin said.

"Continue your investigation until you find out what Englishman was involved in the London steam engine deal. You and your wife shall guest in my palace in town," the king said. "And bring that Colt revolver with you and Mr. Rothschild the third."

"Yes, your highness," Robin said.

The king leaned close to whisper to Robin, "Mr. Van der Kellen, magnificent work." The king and his entourage left the courtroom entirely.

"Return to your station, Mr. Van der Kellen," the judge said.

Robin walked back to stand beside Van de Berg, behind the desk.

"All rise," the judge said.

Van de Berg stood up, glanced at Tess behind him and then looked at Robin in fear. Robin put a hand on his arm and gave him a good solid pat to the chest.

"All charges against Mr. Wouter Van de Berg are immediately dismissed. Mr. Albert Mahoric, Mr. Helmen are to be taken into custody immediately, as the charges are now against them. Their assets are frozen immediately in order that the 42,000 guilders be returned to the state. Mr. Van de Berg, is to be released. Jury, thank you. You are dismissed."

Wout's family cried out with glee. Wout and Robin shook hands and embraced as brothers. Wout then hugged Adam off the floor. And Robin turned to look at Marie in the stands, with a triumphant smile.

They entered Robert's house to hugs and cheers, into the parlor with all the family.

Adam dropped to the carpet. Robin spun and hurried to him.

Robert called out to Simon, "Bring my medical bag."

"Adam?" Robin knelt over him, putting fingers to the side of his throat.

Robert leaned over him. "He is breathing. What is this welt on his forehead? He took a blow to the head?"

"He managed to hold up in court today and lost it only now," Robin said.

"You didn't check this head wound? You just went to court with him this way? Ice pack. Bring an ice pack." Robert raised one of Adam's eyelids. "How is his pulse?"

"Rapid," Robin said. "He said he was all right."

One of the maids hurried off but Zoey stood over Adam and began to cry. Marie took her by the arm.

Robert leaned down to lay his head on Adam's chest.

The butler entered with the black leather bag. "Here, Doctor."

Robert opened the bag and rifled through. He opened a bottle of smelling salts and held it beneath Adam's nose. In a moment, Adam jolted awake.

Robert held him down. "Easy. Easy, young man. You had a fall."

Adam blinked blue eyes up at everyone.

"Can you hear me?" Robert asked.

"Yes."

"Follow my finger, if you will." Robert moved one finger from right to left over Adam's face. "Is your head in much pain?"

"Yes. All day," Adam said.

"I am told you also took a blow to the mid-section. Any pain here?" Robert pressed a hand just below Adam's ribs.

"No. Ooof...."

"A bit there. Have you eaten?" Robert asked.

"Can't manage to eat anything," Adam whispered. "May I please get up? This is terribly embarrassing."

"You will get up slowly. Robin, take that arm. I'll take this one. You will take some laudanum for the pain, have some broth or soup. And you are to be put to bed with ice on your forehead," Robert said.

"Is he all right? What happened?" Zoey asked in Dutch.

Mila explained to her.

A tiny golden cordial glass was brought to Robert as they sat Adam on a sofa. Robert measured out laudanum and offered the glass to Adam. "Drink this all. You were up all night with no sleep. That was fortunate for you with a head wound. Tonight, however, you must rest."

Robin sat beside him. "Are you certain he can sleep tonight? We never let head wounds sleep for very long."

"Are you also a surgeon, Robin? The boy is exhausted. He hasn't eaten. And he has a bruise on the head. I do not believe he has a concussion," Robert said. "His pupils are functioning normally."

"Then why all the laudanum?" Robin asked as Adam tipped the golden glass back, drinking the tincture of opium.

"To let him sleep." Robert closed his medical bag. He switched to Dutch. "Zoey, you will serve him tea and soup up in his room. Keep an ice pack on his forehead. He'll be fine."

"Yes, Doctor," Zoey said.

"Can we assist you up the stairs, Mr. Rothschild?" Robert asked.

"I'll help him," Wout said. "I thank you, Mr. Hudson. I owe you. I mean Mr. Rothschild."

"Now, please, Zoey," Robert said.

"Yes, Dr. Van der Kellen." Zoey left for the kitchen.

Wout and Robin helped Adam to his feet again. Though Adam's eyes followed Zoey leaving the room.

"I can make it up stairs, all right," Adam insisted.

"Of course, you can, with Wout and I to ensure it." Robin switched to Dutch to say, "Robert, are you sure Zoey should be the one to serve him in his room? You know she has affections for him, right?"

"With all that laudanum in the boy, tonight is not the problem. It's tomorrow night you should be worried about. I must check on Lynn."

Robin pulled the covers up over Adam in his bed, and he picked up a small book from the night table. Adam sunk back against pillows and clenched his hands over his eyes.

Robin stepped back, flipping through pages in the book, pages of handwritten poems and thoughts and drawings. He turned away from the bed and gently turned more pages. The drawings were nearly all of him, beautiful drawings of his face, his eyes, his hands, the way he stood with a hand on his hip. Robin looked at Adam in the bed.

"You didn't open that?" Adam sat up in horror. "Oh no. Oh my God."

Robin gently laid the book down on the nightstand where he'd found it. "They're very good, you know? Your drawings."

Adam closed his mouth, his eyes welling as they looked up at Robin.

Robin put a hand softly down on Adam's shoulder. "I did not mean to intrude. How...how did you do all that without me ever knowing?"

"Had nothing else to do on the boat," Adam barely managed to say. "I'm so sorry. I never meant for you to see that. I..."

There was a knock on the door.

Robin said gently, "We'll talk." He walked to the door and allowed Zoey and another maid into Adam's room.

They brought a tray of soup, tea pot, teacup, cookies, and bowl of ice into Adam's room.

Mr. Hudson sat back in bed, leaning back against four eider down pillows, wearing his silk sleep shirt with covers pulled up to his chest. He covered his eyes with both hands again.

"Adam, come and wake me at any time tonight? You hear me?" Robin said at the door. "Zoey, if he is in any distress, wake me."

"Yes, sir."

"Robin...wait."

"I know. Get some rest." Robin exited the room, closing the door behind him.

The girls set up on a table nearby. Then the other maid stoked up the fireplace and blew out two lamps on the other side of the room before leaving them. That left only the lamp beside the bed for light.

Zoey put a bed tray over Adam's lap, a lovely wooden tray with four legs. It had a place mat and napkin on it. She served him a bowl of soup with a spoon and fresh bread. "Can you eat this?"

"Bedankt," he said.

Then she poured a cup of tea for him, with cream, and brought that to his tray.

He was watching her placing ice chunks into a napkin and tying the corners up, making an ice pack. He tried the pea soup with ham. It was spectacular, for soup anyway. He drank some tea to get rid of that laudanum bitterness on his tongue.

She sat nearby in a chair properly, waiting for him to finish. "Are you in much pain? You poor thing. I heard you got kidnapped yesterday. Someone didn't want you helping with the law case."

Adam enjoyed the soup. He drank some of the tea. "Are you waiting to take this so that you and everyone else on earth leave me?"

She got up and leaned in to see that he was almost done with it. "Maureen makes really great soup, doesn't she? We need to get this ice on your head. I can't believe someone hit you. Such a wound on your pretty forehead. Your work must be very important."

When Adam put down the spoon and his teacup was empty, she picked up the tray. She set it over on the table and brought the ice pack to him.

"Lay back." She gestured for him to scoot down into the bed. When he did so, she moved one pillow out from beneath his head, so that he was comfortable on one of them. Then she sat beside him and gently placed the ice on his forehead. She smoothed his hair back. From his closed eyes and dark lashes, some tears welled and finally escaped. And the girl caught them on fingertips.

The ice pack stayed put and she could release it. She explored his curls and how they came down just past his ears. His sideburns were very light, and his cheek so smooth with youth. She wiped his tears away and leaned in to kiss his cheek.

That made Adam look up at her. His eyes were a dark blue, ringed in dark long lashes. There were freckles beneath his eyes, small light freckles on very fair skin.

She continued to pet him, in a way, with light fingertips on his throat down to his silk collar, down buttons, until her hand met his. Adam's hands lay on top of the blankets over his chest. His fingers sought to link with the girl's.

Adam held her hand as he fell away into sedation. He didn't know that she stayed for some time after, replacing his ice pack with a fresh one, adjusting his pillows, pulling up his sheet and quilt. She even went to sleep on the sofa in the room. When she awoke, she replaced his ice pack again, saw that he was breathing normally in his sleep, and slipped out quietly to her own room.

"How old is he?"

Robin looked from Zoey to Adam, as they sat together at a table on the terrace. His teacup rang as he returned it to the saucer.

Marie tugged on Robin's sleeve. "Just help them talk to each other, Robin."

"I will. I will." Robin switched languages to talk to Zoey. "I believe he has 21 years."

"Has he anyone at home in America? A girl waiting for his return?" Zoey asked.

"No. No, he does not." Robin switched to English. "What last name are you giving her when you marry her?"

"I just met the girl. I like her," Adam said. "Are you forced to tell her things about me?"

Robin shook his head. "I would tell her what you would have me to."

"Thank her for looking after me last night," Adam said.

Robin did so and added that he was feeling better.

"Is he your valet? I thought he was. And then all of a sudden..." Zoey said.

"Adam was my valet. Still is, I suppose. But he is learning to become a very good legal assistant as well," Robin said.

"I still can't believe that's not your last name," Marie said.

"I do apologize," Adam told her. "It was for my own safety. My father would have had me taken away to an asylum. Would you ask her about her family?"

Robin talked with Zoey fluently in Dutch for a moment and then told Adam, "Well you're in luck there. She has no family except for a married sister in town. Her parents have passed."

"Does that mean then that she has few ties, here? In the Netherlands?" Adam asked.

"You know you have few ties in America," Robin said to him.

"Would I have to do that to bring her home with me? Legally change my name to marry her with the name Hudson, if I was to do that anyway."

"Legally?" Marie asked.

"His father is not dead." Robin drank some more tea. "Adam ran away from home at 14 years. You must change your name here before you marry her. You cannot travel together unmarried. She can work in our home if need be."

"How wealthy is Adam then?" Marie asked.

"Not at all at the moment. As a legal assistant, could I afford a wife?" Adam asked.

"Of course, you could. Especially if you live with us," Robin said. "Adam, slow it down."

"I'm just considering my options," Adam said softly.

"You have an option here for another life. But is it true to yourself?" Robin asked. "You need to slow down, Adam."

"I know. I know. The fact is I have very much enjoyed doing the work for you on this case. I want to continue," Adam said.

"I would love it if you did," Robin said. "You've done a great job, and you will receive a significant bonus for this. You do not have to go back to being a valet when we go home."

"You're not hiring another. Nobody can cut your hair like I can," Adam said.

That made Marie laugh. "I agree with that. But a maid can iron his shirts. I did a fine job of it, I think."

"Is everything all right?" Zoey asked.

Robin explained they were talking about how well Adam did on this case.

Adam dabbed the cuff of his sleeve to the mouth of the ink well and watched the black wick its way up through the white cotton fibers. Then he closed the ink and wandered out into the hallway. Robin and Robert were talking in Dutch in the library. Adam continued along the hall until he found a parlor where Zoey and another girl were dusting glassware in a cabinet. They looked at him.

Adam strolled up closer to them and said gently, "I'm afraid I've had an accident." He turned his wrist over, demonstrating his ink stain.

"Oh, no." Zoey handed her duster to the other girl and went to him. "Come along immediately. Come on."

"Bedankt." Adam followed her.

Zoey gestured for him to hurry after her, down the stairs to the kitchen level. The kitchen was busy with bakers and cooks. Past this room was the laundry. Zoey hunted the shelves above the soaking tubs for a chemical bottle. It was a pale liquid. She waved Adam closer.

"Oh, you must remove the shirt. I'll give you another."

When Adam just stood there, Zoey moved past him to close the door. Then she selected a clean white man's shirt from the ironing and held it out to him.

"Oh." Adam nodded. He peeled back his jacket and Zoey collected that from him. Then he unbuttoned his vest and opened that as well. Zoey held it for him. He blushed a bit as he pulled his shirt up from his trousers.

Zoey smiled and laid his jacket and vest on a drying rack.

Adam's back was to her as he opened his shirt off his shoulders and down his bare arms. He turned to hand it to her, shirtless there in the laundry room. The sounds of cooks walking past in the hall came to them. He was slender and smooth of chest. His arms were lean. His stomach was flat.

Zoey giggled and shoved the clean shirt to him.

Adam laughed.

She busied herself laying his shirt down on the worktable. She laid the ink stain down on some white rags and poured the chemical onto the opposite side of the stain.

Adam pulled on the shirt and started to button it. It was large for him. Who knows who it belonged to in the house, one of the cooks perhaps. He tucked the shirt down into his pants and pulled on his vest and jacket. As he buttoned the vest, he strolled closer to her and picked up the chemical bottle to examine it. He held it closer to his nose.

"Oh, don't." Zoey waved her hand at him.

"It is the alcohol you put on my wounded finger, gin perhaps, or wood alcohol," Adam said. "You're taking the stain out with alcohol." He returned the bottle to the table his shirt was laid out on. "Do you think it will work?"

Zoey checked the progress by lifting up the sleeve. Indeed, the ink was seeping out into the rags beneath it.

"Wow. And to think, I was willing to destroy this shirt just to get you alone, miss Zoey," Adam said in his breathy intimate voice. "And you are saving my sacrificial garment."

"It will take a while. And then it must be soaked." Zoey moved about the table to help button up his collar as Adam leaned ever closer to her. When she looked up, his mouth found hers.

Adam kissed her lovingly, sliding his tongue over hers. The girl's arms slid about his waist, inside his jacket. Her hands pulled him to her. One hand slid down his backside and he let out a breath, lifting his mouth from hers in surprise.

She reached up his chest, up to his shoulders, and into his hair. Adam had wavy locks that tumbled from the top of his head beyond his ears and hair from underneath just reached his collar. She did not know that he cut it himself with his head upside down. She fully enjoyed sliding her fingers in that hair.

Adam giggled and squeezed her to him. The girl was soft in his arms. She smelled like vanilla cookies. Both of his hands felt down her skirt, over her little backside, pulling her up against him.

They met eyes as she surprised him further. She pressed her hand to his belt and down in the front, feeling how aroused he helplessly became. He stepped back from her hand. But he didn't leave. He looked at her through a loop of his bangs.

Zoey moved to open another door behind him. It was a storage closet, but large enough to store mattresses, pillows, blankets and such. She went inside and gestured for him to come.

Adam stepped inside the little room, seeing one window, shelving, linens. The door opened inward. He grabbed a chair and pulled it inside with them.

Zoey closed the door and Adam shoved the chair up beneath the doorknob. She giggled. She grabbed blankets off the shelf and tossed them down onto a pile of mattresses behind the shelving. Adam stepped around into the seclusion with her. He let the girl touch him, open his clothing, kiss him in places as he gave in to her. And as she undressed herself, he found wonders he'd never seen before. And he felt their bodies fit perfectly together. The thrilling feeling of warm smooth skin on skin was heightening. Twice he tried to stop from ending it too soon. And when the girl had an orgasm beneath him, Adam could not stop it again. But he pulled off of her and finished into his handkerchief.

Zoey rolled over and comforted him. She kissed his damp forehead. He quickly caught his breath and calmed down. He slid his hand onto Zoey's cheek. "Are you all right, Zoey?"

"Yes, Adam. Darling. We'd better get dressed," Zoey said.

They dressed each other and then laid down on the blankets again just to hold each other close for a few more moments. She combed Adam's hair with her fingers. She kissed his mouth. And Adam squeezed her tightly in his arms. He fixed her hair up into a perfectly neat bun with half a dozen little hair pins. And before they left their little room together, Adam kissed the back of her neck and released her to the hallway.

Chapter 11: Robin's Handkerchief

A day on the ship

Robin returned an astronomy book to the shelf and selected another to browse through. He flipped a few pages into it.

Paula entered behind him, observing him silently for some time.

"Where is Frida?" Robin asked, when he saw her.

"Mrs. Van der Kellen has her," Paula said. "Thought you might be here."

It was a small room with bookshelves that had edges on them, to keep books from falling off during most conditions at sea.

"I must be going. It's been a pleasure." Robin started for the door.

Paula blocked him. "You must be really needing it by now."

Robin stood up straighter. "Miss, may I remind you that you are an employee of this passenger line, and I am a passenger. This conversation cannot happen."

"Cabin 15. Level beneath yours. I have three roommates I can throw out anytime I need to. When your wife is sleeping with Frida, it won't take us long," Paula said.

"For what?" Robin exclaimed.

"Your wife is obsessed with her new baby. She won't even know you are missing. And I can make your toes curl," Paula whispered to him.

"Step aside that I might leave."

"It's been months and months, hasn't it?" Paula reached a hand forward and stroked Robin's trousers.

Robin pushed her hand away. "Girl, I won't have a prostitute caring for my child."

"I'm not charging you nothing," Paula said.

"Oh."

"Not as handsome as you are, Robin."

"Step aside please."

The girl was slim, young, and blonde like his first wife had been. He could look at her and see exactly what her body would look like and feel like.

The change in his expression made Paula step back, folding her arms to her. "I'm so sorry. You won't tell the captain, will you? I can be fired when we get to port."

"And my wife can be hurt by even rumors of this. You will make it up to her by being the best nanny you ever imagined," Robin said.

"Then pay me."

"Extortion?" Robin said.

"One hundred dollars."

Robin stepped toward her and said, "You're not worth one hundred dollars."

"Fifty."

"Oh, the minute you dropped your price you cheapened even further," Robin told her. "Mind that the next gentleman you do this to."

"You won't tell?"

"Don't tempt me. And don't come out of this room for ten minutes." Robin dropped his book on the table and left the library.

Robin drew Adam aside and into his brother's library. He closed the double doors. "Sit down."

Adam walked toward the desk and stood by the chair he usually sat in. "Is there more work to do? How do we find that Englishman?"

"Where were you?" Robin asked. "For the last two hours, where were you?"

Adam met his eyes.

Robin stared at him until Adam moved around the chair and sat. Then Robin stood beside the desk and folded his arms. Adam said nothing. Robin continued to study him.

Adam sat back, crossed his legs, and just stared out the window, desperately trying to mask hormones and endorphins rampant through his body. His cheeks were pink, and his breathing was elevated.

"You...deny it?" Robin finally questioned.

"Deny what?" Adam asked.

Robin stepped closer to him, bent and sniffed Adam from right at his throat. Then he stepped back around behind the desk.

"Did you just *smell* me?" Adam rose out of his chair.

"You smell like a woman, like, like you just *had a woman*," Robin said.

Adam shook his head, exhaling and wiping his palms down his jacket.

"You have almost always been honest with me," Robin reminded. "Mr. Rothschild?"

"I feel, there are some things a man should keep to himself."

"Yes. Well, when you actually grow into a man, certainly," Robin said.

"You are my employer, need I remind you? Not my father," Adam said then.

"You had Zoey. You will marry her," Robin told him.

"Do I have to marry her if I pulled out?"

Robin gasped.

"I want that bonus you talked about." Adam drummed a finger on the top of the desk between them.

"You're not getting it. Not yet." Robin paced behind the desk with folded arms. "You'll take it and run away. I'm not letting you do that. You will face your responsibilities and marry the girl."

"I'm not marrying any girl. That's going to mean children. Don't you see what's happening in this house? Marie used to run your household and travel with you. Now she's stuck here with a baby. And you're all about giving her another one. Look at Robert's wife, bed ridden with her third," Adam said.

"That's what normal people do. They marry and have children."

"Well, I'm not normal, am I?" Adam said.

Robin unlocked his arms and made fists. He finally sat down behind the desk. "Sit down, Adam."

"Isn't that what you wanted me to do? Try a girl and see if I can be normal. Well, I can't." Adam leaned on fists on the desk.

"Doesn't matter. If she'll have you, you are marrying her." Robin looked up at him.

"I don't think she was a virgin," Adam said.

Robin cursed in Dutch.

"I know what that means!" Adam pointed at him. "And I am not!"

"Adam, you are out of control."

"Don't worry. I'm sure I disappointed her enough that she doesn't want me anymore," Adam said. "I didn't let her trap me into marriage. She probably thought if she could, she would go to America."

"You don't know what she thought. You can't even talk with her," Robin said. "I want you to return to me every coin I gave you. Put it all on my dresser. And there it stays. Go iron everything in my wardrobe. Now. It should take you all day. Get moving."

"I'm demoted to a valet now?"

"No. You're incarcerated. Sentenced to ironing. And you're not to come out of my room all the rest of the day until I parole you."

Adam stood up, mumbling, "I didn't see any trial."

Robin stood up. "You're not running away?"

"No. Not without any money. I've done that before! Remember? I'm not doing that again!" Adam shouted at him and stood there shaking. His voice broke.

Stunned, Robin remained behind the desk.

Adam looked down at the fist he had almost brandished at Robin, and he opened the fingers as if they were not his own. He let out a breath as he walked toward the closed doors. And he did not turn around to look at Van der Kellen. But he stopped with his forehead almost against the door, catching his breath. When he spoke again, his voice was calm and quiet. "Adam Theodore Rothschild II is my father. He is a German immigrant. His brother, Girard Rothschild, is one of the richest men in the Americas. Coincidentally, they are bankers. When I turned eighteen, I was to inherit 20,000 dollars. Except that my father disowned me when he caught me with Lucas. Called me a freak. Inhuman. Sick. Said he would beat it out of me. Am I a little fucked up? Sure. Look how I was made."

Robin let out a breath and said very gently. "That argument is with him, not me."

"I will put your money on your dresser now."

"Adam." Robin stepped around the desk and walked closer to him. "Turn around."

Finally, Adam did so. He slowly raised his eyes to meet Robin's. There was still the dark bruise on his forehead. His eyes were dry, but his cheeks were flushed.

"Perhaps you should lay down for a while," Robin suggested. "You are injured."

"May I hide out in your room?" Adam asked. "Zoey won't find me there and I can't see her disappointment right now."

"I...think most women are pretty forgiving on ones' first."

"I don't think I can deal with anything right now," Adam admitted.

"Need I be concerned about my gun in there?"

"No. I'm not suicidal," Adam said.

"Adam, your bonus is going to be one thousand dollars."

His expression softened a bit. His eyebrows moved and then he reached into his pocket to find it empty. He wiped his nose with the back of his hand instead. "Does make my head throb somewhat less."

Robin pulled his handkerchief out of his jacket and offered it to Adam. "You'll get it when I can trust you not to harm yourself, by running away. All right? It's not that I mean to keep you. I only want to protect you, mentor you. You are not ready to be on your own yet."

Adam wiped his eyes and nose on the fine cloth and coveted the embroidered RVK in the corner. "I am not."

"I regret things I have said to you. I was angry. I have my flaws," Robin said softly.

"Awfully few." Adam looked down and hid away that handkerchief into his pocket. "I am still in love with you. What you said hurt me. But I

241 The Dutchman 2 Test of Character   By Susan Eddy

deserved it. I was jealous that you were with Marie. So, I was with Zoey. But I did not make her with child today."

They heard running footsteps in the hallway then.

Robin moved around Adam and pulled open the doors. He saw the butler. "What is it?"

"Gun shots on the property. Didn't you hear it?"

"Revolver is in the dining room. I'll get your rifle." Adam started running for the stairs.

Robin ran for the Colt in the dining room cabinet.

As Adam reached the second floor, he could hear Lynn crying out at the far end. He ran toward Robin's room but met Marie in the hall. They grabbed hands for a minute, blurting out at the same time, "There are shots fired outside!" "Lynn is having the baby now!"

Adam opened Robin's door and burst in, looking about quickly for the rifle and pistol.

"Where is Robert?" Marie said to him.

"I don't know. Robin needs these."

"Adam!" Marie urged.

Adam grabbed her by the arm and led her to the hallway. "Go to Lynn. When I see Tess or Mila or Robert, I'll send them up."

"Oh my God." Marie separated from him in the hall and went back to Lynn's room.

Adam dashed down the stairs, the British pistol in his belt, and the rifle held by the barrel and stock. He hit the main floor, gripping the rifle in both hands, holding the barrel up. He looked both ways and listened.

"I'm here to see Adam. Where is he?" James said.

"Adam? I don't know. Off with some girl someplace," Robin said. "Did you hear that gunshot?"

"No. Gunshot?" James puzzled.

"Must have been just something in the barn then." Robin walked out. "What business have you with Adam?"

James was beside a carriage in the barrel-vaulted entrance to Robert's home. "I think you know."

The door behind Robin opened and Robert called out, "Robin, did you hear that?"

Robin held up his left hand but kept his eyes on James. "It was nothing, Robert. I was just about to invite James to see the horse show. We call it that. It's the barns really."

"We call it what?" Robert started to step out the door.

"Rob, can you go tell Adam that James is here to see him. Tell him we're going out to the barn. He'll know where we are," Robin said.

Robert turned back into the entry parlor where he saw Adam standing behind him with a rifle. Adam held a finger up to his lips. Robert said out the door, "Robin, I will go find Adam then."

"Come along, James. You'll like the tour, I'm certain," Robin said.

"I don't think so right now, Robin. I'd much rather wait in the parlor for Adam. It's quite hot outside, you know," James remarked.

Adam whispered something to Robert who then suggested out the door, "Cold lemonade on the terrace, perhaps."

"Wonderful idea. What do you say, James?" Robin said.

"Very well then." James moved with Robin slowly through the vaulted way toward the back of the house. "Robert, you are joining us, are you not?"

Adam whispered to him again.

"You wanted me to find Adam," Robert then said through the doorway.

"Send a servant to find him. Come on along," James said.

"I shall meet you on the terrace after I alert the kitchen," Robert said.

Adam pulled Robert back and shut the door. "Doctor, Robin is sending all manner of signals. He has his revolver. Get to your wife."

"I must do this," Robert said.

Adam nodded and they separated.

Robin strolled around the house toward the stairs to the terrace. His back left side he kept toward James, trying to conceal his weapon on the right. "You said I know what you are here for."

"I'm sure you do," James said. "Adam tells you everything, does he not?"

Robin opened his jacket buttons, to close his right hand about the pistol tucked into his belt. "Lately, not so much. Very insolent lately."

"Sounds typical for him," James said.

"You have no idea..." As Robin rounded the corner, he was hit in the head and knocked to the ground.

James drew a weapon at the same time as Mitchel Evans backed off from having struck Robin with the butt of his gun.

Van der Kellen rolled and came up shooting. He shot the weapon out of James' hand, who fell, screaming out. That left Robin on the ground, looking up at the men with a suddenly jammed revolver. Click. Click. Click.

Robert came running from the terrace above, Robin's rifle in his hands, running right for the stairway above Robin and James.

Adam rounded the corner behind with Robin's British pistol extended out in both hands. "Don't anybody move or I'm shooting!"

The man over Robin began to turn his gun toward Adam. It was Collin's assistant, Mitchel Evans.

"Mitch, wait!" James called out.

Adam halted and inhaled. He kept both eyes open. On the exhale he pulled the trigger and was quite startled when the pistol fired. The flame shot out the left side. The pistol kicked back into his hands.

Evans jolted backwards, shot in the chest.

Robin scrambled for Evan's weapon and aimed it at James. He got to his feet just as Robert reached the bottom of the stairs and Adam still held the smoking pistol.

James looked over, holding his right hand in his left. He looked at the three of them.

Adam blurted out, "Robin the note. It was James and the combination. The ames was James! James stole the money! J. C. James Collins. He was there!"

"Put the gun down, Adam." Robin moved the man's head with his boot. "He's dead. Robert, get up to Lynn now. It's done here."

Robert handed the rifle to Robin and ran back up the stairs then, shouting orders to his staff.

James sat up. He removed an ascot and began wrapping it about his bloody hand.

"Adam, can you reload?" Robin switched to aiming his rifle at James on the ground.

"I don't have it..." Adam looked at the pistol in his hands and lowered it. It felt very hot, and he chose to set it down on the steps to the house. And then he sat down beside it. He looked at the man, bleeding out in the flower bed.

Robin looked about. "James, what were you talking about?" He saw workmen running from the barn with pitchforks and muskets.

"He knows what I was talking about. Don't you, Adam?" James looked up at the both of them.

Robin pointed that rifle at James. "Stay where you lay, James. You don't stand a chance against a marksman." The workmen were still running. They needed a moment. "You know, I've assassinated men from two hundred yards away. Doing it at pointe blank won't be any trouble."

James looked up at Robin. "Robin, it's me. What are you doing?"

"This is your assistant, Mitchel Evans," Robin said. "What's his part in this? Oh, I see. The M from the combination note."

"Why did you shoot me, Robin? I need your brother the surgeon out here," James said. "I need your help."

"He's the one who threw a sack over my head and hit me with his gun!" Adam pointed at James, his hand shaking. "It was James. I know that aftershave. Rosemary. Just took me a while to place where I smelled it before." Adam pulled out a second gun from his inside vest pocket.

"What is that, Adam?" Robin said. "Where did you get that pistol?"

James crawled a bit closer to the steps and toward Adam. He looked up at what he saw as the shaking boy on the steps.

"Drop that gun, Adam!" Robin warned more harshly. "One more move, James and I am shooting you dead. I have given you fair warning. I won't do it again."

James held up his hands, the right one bleeding down his arm. "Where's that money, Robin? You send Adam inside for it. You got a safe? Empty it. Put all you have in a satchel and bring it down here. Bring Robert down here to patch up my hand."

Robin saw the workmen had them surrounded. Several had muskets also pointed at the British Commander. "You had to leave England. Didn't you? Did you get shot while stealing from a Navy vessel? Did you lose your commission? You set up those steam engine deals only to steal the profits. I'll be telling the king you're a common thief."

Adam cocked the small, elegant pistol and aimed it at James.

"Toss that gun away, Adam. None of you men do anything but don't let James out of here alive." Robin moved around James so that he and Adam were not aligned. "Adam, go for the money as he said."

"I did see you, only for a second before you hit me!" Adam screamed. "I saw you there!"

"You're the only one who can place me with those idiots. I had such a great plan until you." James pounced on Adam and brought him down on the bottom steps.

Robin bolted to the side for a clear shot and found one. He fired and heard Adam's pistol also firing. Both Adam and James cried out. Both of them jolted.

"Adam? Oh my God." Robin yanked James back, dropping him onto the walkway. He found blood all over Adam's chest. "Adam?"

The men closed the circle around them against the house.

Adam Hudson scrambled back, slamming against a window to the kitchen where most of the staff watched in horror. He dropped his pistol into the flowers. His shirt and trousers were covered with blood too. He leaned his head back, gasping for breath. And his slender white fingers spread in the air as if to free themselves of the blood they dripped.

Robin stepped over James. "Are you hit? Adam, are you shot?"

"No! No, I'm not." Adam looked down at his own bloody chest and trousers. He inhaled the scent of iron and gun powder with every full breath. "This isn't mine."

"You had a gun? You fired it without any practice with me?" Robin went to him, leaning over him.

"I still shot him, didn't I?" Adam yelled at him, over their deafness from all the weapons firing.

"You're not hit? Are you sure?" Robin looked him over, pulled at his shirt and trousers, looking for holes in the fabric. "James was in it with Mahoric? He was there. He planned it."

"He's the one who threw me over his shoulder. It's the smell of him. It's his height and strength. It was him. He thought he hit me before I saw him. But for a split second, I saw the mother fucker! You heard him ask for the money. You heard him say it was all going well until me."

Robert appeared at the top of the stairs, another rifle in his hands. Jonas and Noud were beside him. They looked down on this scene below.

"I did. He was here to kill us both." Robin dropped his rifle and spun the carrousel on his revolver until bullets moved into place. He aimed it at James but his hand shook. He put both hands on the revolver and stepped closer to James, aiming straight down at his head.

"Robin!" Adam called. "He's dead enough!"

Van der Kellen cried out in an anguish none of them had ever heard out of him. Robin emptied his revolver into the air, out over the red tulip fields. For a moment he saw the battle fields of India, horses down, artillery explosions sending dirt high into the air, and his boyhood friends lying dead all about him. Instead of tulips, the fields were bathed in blood.

Adam glanced over his own shoulder into the kitchen and saw Zoey with the others. He knocked on the glass and leaned to the opening to say, "It's over. It's all done here. Het is gedaan." Then he went to Robin and took the gun out of his hands. "It is over, Robin."

Van der Kellen swallowed hard. "Account for everyone," Robin said to the men. "That first gun shot? Was someone hit out there?"

"I fired the shot. Saw these two on the property with weapons. I fired a warning shot for the house," one of the workmen said.

"Very good but still account for everyone," Robin ordered as he padded a hand to the side of his mouth. He found blood from his lip.

"Yes, sir, Mr. Van der Kellen."

Robin walked around James and ducked to call into the kitchen, "Send someone to check on Marie and Lynn. Now. Robert, get up to your wife." Then he turned back to the men. "Leave the bodies where they lay. Saddle a horse and get the police out here."

"When I got there, Marie had the baby girl in her arms. I have a daughter!" Robert declared, to a room of applause.

"Marie brought the baby?" Robin brightened.

"All by herself. Marie saved them both." Robert embraced Robin. "Thank you, Robin. Thank you for your fine incredible wife."

"I'm so proud of Marie and happy for you," Robin said.

Zoey shook her head and stepped back from Adam, who stood there wiping blood off his hands with a towel. "What did she say?"

"She says she saw you kill that man. She can't look at you," Robin translated. "I'm sorry, Adam."

"I didn't have any choice," Adam replied in a hard voice. And then he softened it almost to a whisper. "I didn't have any choice."

Robin grabbed Adam by the back of his jacket. "Where did you get that gun?"

Zoey gathered with some of the maids and started out of the parlor.

"Zoey? Please don't..." Adam looked at her.

Robin said in Dutch, "Zoey, if ever he needed you, it is now."

"I'm so sorry, sir," Zoey said and hurried away with the maids.

That left Robin to meet eyes with Adam. He pulled Adam's arm around his shoulders to prop him up. "You used a pistol you did not show to me. Where did you get it? Do you have any idea how dangerous that was?"

"I bought it in town, one of those days I was tailing Mr. De Vries. You said you considered keeping a gun on me. Remember? How is your head?"

"You bought a gun? You can't even speak Dutch." Robin secured his hold on Adam tighter, holding him up. "My head is fine. I was faking it when I hit the ground, mostly. I wasn't as sure about James as you were. My judgment was incorrect."

"Adam shot the British Commander?" Robert said. "And the other man? Good lord."

"So did Robin," Adam said.

"None of this blood is yours?" Robert asked Adam, searching him.

"James was the one who knocked Adam out and carried Adam back to Mahoric's house. There was a note in the bank that said, James and the combination. James planned the fraud and the theft," Robin said. "They fought over a gun and Adam pulled the trigger."

Adam looked at Robin and faltered a bit. Robin held him. "Let's get you out of these things. You'll feel better."

"I must go back up. Let me know the police arrived," Robert said. "They may have to come up for my statement."

"Follow Robert up. Simon, Noud, pour a bath for Mr. Hudson. Get him some clean clothing," Robin ordered. "I'll wait for the police." He passed Adam into Simon and Noud's hands.

Adam scrubbed himself in the bath, dressed in his old plain suit, and went straight up into the attic to knock on Zoey's door. It opened with one of the other maids blocking the entrance. She looked him up and down. "May I see Zoey?" Adam asked softly.

The door was closed on him. "Ga weg. Ga weg."

He finally turned and walked to the stairway, with a look back at her door. He returned downstairs, seeking to be with Robin and hearing his voice ahead.

The Van der Kellen brothers were with the police in the main parlor.

"Adam, come in," Robin invited. "The detective speaks English."

Adam entered and stood very formally beside Robin, facing the officers. Two were taking notes. Adam's hair was still wet and slicked back from his forehead.

"Mr. Rothschild? Tell me your account of it?" the detective asked.

"The first one, Mitchel Evans, had hit Mr. Van der Kellen and knocked him to the ground. I didn't know if he was hurt badly or not. He took aim at me and so I shot him with Robin's pistol," Adam said. "The other jumped on me, James Collins. I shot him too. My own gun."

"You shot the two men out there in your own defense then?" the detective asked.

"Yes, I did. And to save Dr. and Mr. Van der Kellen, if I might," Adam said.

The detective leaned in to examine the bruise on Adam's forehead. "He did this to you, sir?"

"As a matter of fact, he did," Adam said. "You should see the one on my wrist."

The detective did examine Adam's wrist. "Powder burns there. Get some ice on it, young sir. Captain Van der Kellen shot which one of the men? None of you say anything. Let the boy answer."

Adam glanced at Robin. "Captain Van der Kellen shot Commander Collins while I was wrestling with him for my pistol."

The detective held out the small, elegant silver pistol. "Is this your weapon?"

"Yes," Adam said cautiously, looking at Robin.

"Came in handy, didn't it, boy?" The detective returned it to him with a pat on the shoulder. "Sign this, if you will."

Robert saw the police out and then followed Robin out of the parlor.

Adam Hudson saw the two brothers embrace and pat each other on the back as they moved into the hallway.

Hudson, in exquisite aloneness, made his way into the dining room after them and pulled out a chair at the far end of the table.

"No. Down here. Come on." Robin gestured. "Try to eat something."

Adam lowered his eyes and his chin. "Am I paroled?" He moved down to the chair beside Robin. He sat down and could not look at either of them. He saw a plate of tenderloin, peas, potatoes, and gravy set down before him. The beef was pink.

Robin rested his left hand down on Adam's forearm. "Most gratefully."

"Mr. Rothschild, I am in your debt," Robert said. "You enabled me to get up to my wife and newborn. I shall give some thought to ways in which I may reward you. You remembered well your weapons training with Robin. Kept your head together most extraordinarily."

Adam ran a hand up through his wet hair. "I'm afraid I'm not doing so well as all that, at present."

"I suggest a sedative for the night," Robert said. "I will pour you one before you leave the table. Try to take a little food."

Adam looked at Robin's plate. Robin was able to eat. Robin could always eat. Adam's hand shook on the table and rattled his fork against his plate such that Robin tapped on that wrist.

Robin poured a snifter of brandy for himself and one for Adam. He slid it over beside Adam's plate. "Try a little of this. Settle your nerves. Police are guarding outside, just in case. We are safe tonight." He kept his left hand on the back of Adam's chair.

Adam picked up the crystal gold rimmed brandy snifter and had a sip. Then he tipped it back and guzzled it all down in several swallows.

The brothers met eyes.

"Let me show you this pistol of yours," Robin said.

"I don't know...." Adam shook his head.

"I saw it when the detective pulled it out of the flowerbed. Do you know what you have?" Robin produced it from his pocket and laid it on the table between their two plates.

"It's Belgian," Adam said.

"It is Belgian. Single shot. Walnut handle. Only a couple years old. .44 caliber," Robin told him. "Six inches long. Fits in your pocket. You see this right here? Made in Leige, Belgium. This is a good pistol, Adam."

"It is?" Adam asked. "I thought you were going to yell at me again for buying it without you."

"I would have preferred that we went together. But you did all right. The range is short. Within this room, perhaps. I'll get you plenty of shot for this. You may have trouble finding it in America," Robin said. "I want to test this out back and verify the range, so that you will know."

"Can we talk about something else, please?" Adam said.

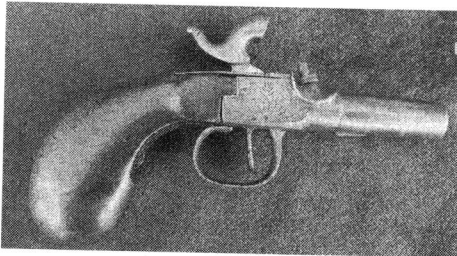

"When will you bring the boys back from Uncle Pieter's?" Robin asked.

"Leave them a week. They can attend school there. It will allow Lynn and the baby time alone to bond and nurture," Robert said. "Latest research shows quite a lot of importance in the first few days of mother and infant bonding. It is essential to the health of both."

Adam tried a bit of the beef and nearly threw up. He changed to the peas.

"Who delivered your Frida?" Robert asked, watching Adam. He pushed the basket of rolls across to him. "Try one of these."

Robin laid a napkin over the pistol on the table. "Alice Poole, the midwife, and seamstress. She's the wife of Constable Poole. Good friends with Marie."

"I must say, she taught Marie well," Robert said. "Until now, I did not have much confidence in the work of midwives. They are not physicians but do very well when all goes as it should. Did you have a physician at all there in Canterbury?"

"Yes. He came to visit Marie and the baby two days later," Robin said. "We had to get word to him that we had the baby."

"What do you do in an emergency, living that far from town?" Robert asked.

Robin looked around. "Well, what do you call this? You're the only physician around here for miles. What if you need a doctor?"

That made Adam look at Robin.

Robert shrugged. "But there is a hospital just ten miles away, in town. Where is the nearest hospital for you? You need to move back to Boston."

"I have friends in Canterbury. When I'm old and feeble I'll move into town," Robin said. "Norwich has a hospital."

"You're thirty-six, Robin. You are not getting any younger," Robert said.

The look on Robin's face made Adam spit brandy into his napkin. He burst out with a laugh.

"Do you believe that? He thinks me an old man. And I'm five years younger than he is," Robin said.

"I wish you would reconsider and buy an estate here," Robert corrected. "That is really my point."

Adam tore a roll in half and took a bite of it.

"When steamer travel across the Atlantic is common, I might buy a second home here. The journey across is just so long," Robin said.

"Well, your wife will look after you," Robert conceded. "Do you ever think that you would have a six-year-old son now?"

Robin lowered his chin.

Adam was about to butter his roll, but stopped.

"He should be playing with your sons," Robin admitted. "I must visit Adrianna's parents. I must before I leave."

"I'll go with you," Adam said. "You know, I didn't tell you I saw Paula."

"What? Where?" Robin turned toward him.

"I apologize. On my investigations I went to the address of an inn that had posted a letter to you," Adam said.

"Did she see you?" Robin asked.

"Who is this?" Robert asked.

"The nanny on our boat overseas," Robin said.

"She had a vile affection for Robin. Tried to trap him into money," Adam interrupted.

"Extortion is the word for it," Robin said. "Where did you see her?"

"She is still working at the inn where you set her up with employment," Adam said. "Still the most rude woman I ever knew."

Robin turned to Robert to explain, "She was fired from the ship line, and I did her an anonymous kindness. I set her up with employment at a friend's inn. I feared she was on the verge of prostitution to survive."

"Did you sleep with this woman?" Robert whispered.

Robin threw down his napkin. "No, I did not."

"I just asked," Robert explained.

"Why does everybody ask me that?" Robin asked.

"Because the twenty-year-old Robin slept with every woman who moved," Robert shot back.

Adam laughed aloud. "I'd like to have known him then."

"I can't be alone tonight. I can't." Adam stopped on the stairway beneath the painting of young Cavalry Robin.

"Did you take your sedative?" Robin whispered.

Adam nodded. "I can hardly hear out of this ear."

"I know. It will pass." Robin extended his arm to him. "Adam, we did not finish our conversation from the library."

"No. I was entirely in the wrong. Forgive me." Adam clung to his arm and started up the stairs again. "I don't know what is wrong with me."

"Adam, I'm so glad we did not lose you today. We will deal with your situation in the morning. Come here. We're all right. Marie is exhausted and sleeping. The nanny has Frida. Take the sofa in here." Robin drew Adam into his room. Marie was already asleep in Robin's bed. Robin held a finger up to his lips.

Adam nodded.

Robin indicated the sofa by the fireplace.

By Susan Eddy

Adam sat down on it and pulled off his boots.

Robin brought him a pillow and blanket from the chest at the foot of his bed. Then he poured two brandies and brought one to Adam. He sat down on his own bed, beside Marie, and held up his glass to Adam.

Adam pretended to clink his to Robin's. They both drank.

Robin pulled off his boots, laid his Colt on the nightstand. And he and Adam just looked at each other by the firelight. The day's battle replayed before them both. What Robin did not know was that Adam looked on him in his grand bed, and the curve of Marie's hip beside him, with such envy.

Chapter 12: World Upside Down

Marie awoke and reached for Robin. His head was beside hers on the pillows. She found him on top of the blankets and still dressed in untucked shirt and trousers. She freed her hand from beneath the sheet and laid it on Robin's chest. His hand came up onto hers. Sunlight filtered by white lace sprinkled across the bed.

"You all right?" she whispered.

"Just couldn't sleep," he whispered and kissed her forehead. "Adam is over there."

"He is?" Marie lifted her head a bit.

"Forgive me. He was frightened," Robin whispered. "And sedated."

"Get him out of here and I'll make love to you." Marie opened a button on his shirt. She raised up, on her elbow, and smoothed his hair back from his eyes.

"I have to see the king. Adam and I have to get to him," Robin said in more of his normal voice. "You want to come with us? He did invite you to the palace."

"It's dangerous," Marie said.

"Two are in jail. Two were taken away dead from here. I think you're safe to come along." Robin sat up, running a hand through his hair to straighten it out.

Adam sat up on the sofa.

The two men met eyes.

Adam unwrapped himself from the blanket. "I'll get started." He left for Robin's vanity room, poured Robin's hot water into his bath, and then exited for his room across the hall.

Hearing the water pouring into the copper tub, Robin finished unbuttoning his shirt. "Bring Frida and Zoey will be her nanny."

"Zoey? Adam's girl? But she is mad at him." Marie sat up.

"Yeah well, fitting punishment for him then. And we can't take the nanny from Lynn, now can we?" Robin stood up and stepped out of his trousers.

"Isn't he going to marry her?" Marie asked.

"I'm working on it."

Their door was knocked on.

Robin grabbed his robe, pulling it on as he crossed the room. He opened the door to find Simon the butler. In Dutch Robin said, "Adam, myself, and Marie must go see the king. We shall require Zoey to mind Frida. Get her packed and ready to work. Get a carriage ready. And I need so much coffee right now. If you would, please?"

Simon reached in and patted Robin on the chest. "As you wish, Sir Robin."

Marie returned to her room to dress and pack, with the nanny, all that she and Frida would need.

Robin, however, was sitting in his hot bath when the butler came in with coffee for him. He then went about preparing a suit for Robin and packing his things. When Robin rose from the tub, the butler draped his robe about him. "Shall I give you a shave or go see that Mr. Hudson is packed? Noud is getting him dressed."

"Help Mr. Hudson. Thank you."

"You look so tired, sir. Did you not sleep last night? What can I get you?"

"I'll sleep in the carriage. I guess that means I need a driver." Robin let out a sigh. "I have to tell the king his friend robbed him of 42,000 guilders and I had to kill him."

"Perhaps he does not find him such a friend, after all," the butler said.

Robin's eyebrows rose as he considered that.

"You must sit for breakfast before you leave. I insist. If nothing else, you must agree that Marie needs a moment to eat."

Robin looked at the suit on the rack. "Is that new?"

"Yes. The tailor delivered more for you. Good timing. It will take a week to get all the blood out of your clothing from yesterday. I won't mention Adam's." The butler poured another cup of coffee for Robin. "Start dressing. I will be back to check on you."

The dining table was set for five for breakfast. Wout was at last home with his family. Jonas and Tess were at their home. The lady of the house, Lynn, had just had a healthy new baby.

After a quick glance at the table, Robin took his usual seat. Marie sat beside him.

Adam Hudson, dressed in one of Robin's suits, took the seat across from Robin.

And Zoey entered. She was dressed in a grey broadcloth for travel and her dark hair up in simple bun. The butler ushered her to the chair beside Adam and pulled it out for her. She sat down nervously.

Marie met her eyes kindly from across the table, with a warm smile.

Adam sat back in his chair, looking at her. Dressed very plainly only made the perfectness of her face and skin more noticeable. The simple bun of hair was shiny in morning sunlight. Her lips and cheeks were blushing.

Zoey looked down at china, silverware, and glassware that she had only set before, never ate from. She saw Adam hold his hand out for her between them, but she folded her hands tightly into her lap. She just looked down at her plate.

Robin rearranged his place setting, moving water and coffee cup to the left side.

Adam sat back dejectedly and unfolded his napkin on his lap. He was biting his lower lip.

"Sorry, sir. They keep forgetting," Simon told Robin.

Robin indicated the head of the table. "Is this for..."

"Me." Robert said as he entered.

"How are Lynn and the baby?" Marie asked.

Robert moved around behind Robin and sat down at the end. "Lynn is quite tired as this new girl has quite a set of lungs on her. She's quite demanding. I think she will take after her auntie Tess in that regard. Though you certainly screamed a lot as a baby." Robert looked at Robin. "Already demanding attention."

Marie laughed.

Robin only smiled and drank his coffee.

Plates of waffles, sausages, cheeses, and rye bread were set before each at the table. Tins of warm syrup were set at each place. Bowls of mixed fruit were also provided, and the fruit included orange slices from Spain, dates from the Middle East, and strawberries from the garden.

Zoey picked up an orange slice to taste in such a way that Adam knew she'd never had one before. Adam looked away from her eyes.

"Robin, you must convince the king that James Collins was an evil man. I will go with you if necessary. He tried to shoot you," Robert said. "He demanded all the money in my house."

"You must stay and look after Lynn and the baby. I will pass on your comments to him. By the way, haven't you got a name yet?" Robin said. "Can't keep calling her the baby until she marries."

"After discussion with Lynn, and with your approval, we have decided to name her Julia Marie Van der Kellen," Robert said.

Robin turned to Marie and laid a hand on her shoulder. "I love it."

"I am so honored," Marie sighed.

"And I wish you to explain to the king that if not for Marie, this man holding me at gun point downstairs nearly killed my wife and infant, preventing me from being there at the critical moment of birth," Robert said.

Robin nodded. "At least you were there for the critical moment of conception."

Adam burst out laughing.

Robin met eyes with Adam. "You, sir, may not laugh at that. Saving my life and yours last night did not get you out of the boiling pot, as it were."

"What is he in trouble for?" Robert asked. "Need I ask?"

"He had Zoey," Robin blurted out.

"What?" Marie said. "I thought they just kissed."

Adam sat back and lowered his chin. "This is the only time I'm grateful that she can't understand English."

"You did?" Marie asked Adam.

Adam put his forehead in his hand. "Oh my God."

"Well, you're not taking her with you? They can't even speak the same language," Robert said. "You must separate them."

"I think forcing them together will do far worse," Robin said.

"What I told you was in confidence," Adam complained.

"I say a lot when I haven't had any sleep." Robin poured syrup on his waffles and then used the fork to move strawberries on top. "I'll sleep in the carriage."

"You are going to insist they marry?" Robert asked.

"She hates him. He's attracted to men. Forcing them together will surely drive them apart. And then their lives go back to the way they were," Robin said. "And so... will mine."

Robert's brow fused. "My brother is an idiot."

The brothers looked at each other.

Marie burst out laughing.

A burgundy painted brougham pulled by two Friesians was loaded with luggage and trunks. One driver waited beside it.

Robin assisted Marie up into the carriage first and then handed up the basket containing baby Frida. Marie took her seat facing forward on the far side and set Frida on the floor right beside her.

Zoey was assisted in next, and she sat across from Marie with another basket containing baby clothing, blankets, diapers, and jars of applesauce and jars of sweet pea soup.

The butler handed a pillow to Robin, and then Robin climbed aboard. He sat beside Marie and positioned his pillow against the wall and window.

Adam climbed in with Robin's briefcase containing the two pistols. Robin's rifle was laid across the floor at Adam's feet, as he sat across from Robin and beside Zoey.

The butler handed up a second pillow to Robin.

"So kind. Thank you." Robin packed that pillow on top of the other.

"Here, sir." The butler leaned in to grab at a handle beneath Robin's seat. "This pulls out to make you a bed. I thought you'd like this carriage."

"O mijn God." Robin immediately pulled it out.

The butler closed the door and told the driver to get them underway.

Robin stretched out on his bed and his boots were up beside Adam, making Adam and Zoey sit closer together. Robin made use of his pillows and reclined on his side, facing Marie. He let out a sigh and closed his eyes.

"Robin, is that really so necessary?" Marie asked gently.

"Absolutely." Robin did not open his eyes.

"I think Frida is like Robin in this way. Sleeps well in a moving carriage," Marie said. "Adam, did you get any sleep last night?"

"Some. Sorry again for the intrusion," Adam said quietly.

Marie smoothed out her skirt on her lap. "I understand. Adam, aren't you going to ask her to marry you?"

"She does not want me," Adam replied, in his quiet breathy voice.

"She's afraid of your guns." Marie indicated the briefcase.

Adam set it down beneath Robin's pull-out bed. "She does not know Robin's guns are in there. She's just afraid of me, really."

"She probably knew you to be so gentle," Marie said.

Robin's eyes opened.

"Then she saw you fighting Mr. Collins," Marie added. "The first time I saw Robin shoot somebody I was terrified. And I'm not like other women. So I'm told, anyway. She must be even more frightened than I was."

"Intimacy tonight would help me sleep," Robin remarked.

Marie and Adam met eyes.

"Good luck with that," Adam told him. "I don't think either one of us will be that fortunate on this trip."

"Speak for yourself," Robin said. "I would have had it this morning if not for you."

"Marie, they gave us prostitutes that night in the palace," Adam said.

"What?" Marie outraged.

Robin got up on his elbow and pointed at Adam. "You tell her I didn't touch them."

Adam made a show of folding his arms and sitting back.

"You should have wet your carrot on them. You wouldn't have to get married now." Robin laid back down.

"I pulled out."

"Oh my God!" Marie slapped her hands down on the seat. "I am not hearing this. You men talk to each other this way? This isn't a tavern. You can't just say such things in front of me. Now shut up both of you!"

Robin looked at her. He laid his head down and closed his eyes. But his cheeks were flushed, and his mouth pursed tightly closed.

Adam sat tight with arms folded.

Zoey quietly took all this in, and finally settled eyes on the beautiful Van der Kellen reclining across the carriage, wondering why Adam and he were arguing. Marie certainly had the better of them both. She leaned her elbow on the arm rest and watched the scenery in the yellow sunlight of morning.

Robin's dreams

Royal Palace of Amsterdam

Robin emerged first from the carriage to speak with the delegation that met him at the bottom of the steps, and the six well-armed guards.

"Mr. Van der Kellen, your arrival is unannounced and ill advised. Your presence here is alarming," the butler said. "You shall get back on board and leave at once."

"I see by the flag that his Majesty is here. I must bring him bad news of a friend of his," Robin said.

"You will bring it no further than to me," the butler said.

"It is private. I must speak to his Majesty himself." Robin opened his jacket to demonstrate that he was bearing no pistol on his hip. "My wife and child are in the carriage. See for yourself. His majesty invited me to bring my wife to the palace. I am following his very instructions."

The butler pointed to the carriage.

The infantryman approached the carriage and got onto the step to look inside. He stepped back down and approached the king's butler. "Mrs. Van der Kellen, I believe, and infant. Also Mr. Hudson and a maid or nanny, I presume."

"He carries two pistols and a rifle. Collect them from him," the butler said.

Robin called to the carriage. "Adam, give him my weapons, if you would. It's customary."

"Customary, it may be." Adam handed the rifle to the guard. He opened the briefcase to allow the guard to extract the two pistols. Then he stepped down from the carriage. "Ill advised, however."

The guard also opened Adam's jacket and patted him down for weapons. He patted him so hard on the sides that Adam was pushed this way and that. Remembering his training, Adam tried to look bored and let out a tired breath.

"Do you plan to shake down my wife that way too?" Robin questioned.

"Your bluntness may amuse his majesty, but it pisses me off," the butler said. "Come with me. Your wife and assistant will be shown to their rooms to get settled in."

Robin glanced back at them and then walked with the butler and three of the infantrymen up the steps.

"We can't speak Dutch," Marie said.

Zoey took the baby in her basket as Marie stepped down. Then she handed the basket to Marie and the other basket to Adam. She pulled up her skirt and looked down at the step.

Adam took her hand with his free one. He assisted her from the carriage.

They were spoken to in Dutch by the butler's assistant.

Zoey let go of Adam's hand and responded to the man. "Thank you. It has been a long journey. The baby needs rest."

"Right this way, if you please."

Adam reached out again to Zoey's hand, but she took the basket of baby supplies from him instead. He followed the two women into the palace.

Marie, Adam, and Zoey were led to a grand gilded stairway that wound upward. The baby basket was carried by a maid. Their luggage followed them up with a team of porters.

They were shown to rooms that adjoined in a central parlor. Adam dug his sliver pistol out of his luggage and immediately glanced out the window. He slipped that pistol down into a jacket inner pocket. "They took Robin in the other direction, up the other stairs, to that wing over there. He'll be trying to indicate to me where, by a window if he can."

Marie looked about at the gilded chair and table, candelabra, chandelier above, and the gold frame of a huge painting above the fireplace. "Good lord. Have they run out of gold? Does Zoey know how to change the baby?"

Adam shrugged. "I never asked her that."

"No. I don't suppose you did. Keep it in your trousers, would you? Now that you know what to do with it."

"Marie, I have to talk to you," Adam insisted.

"Not now, Adam." Marie followed Zoey into another room where Frida had been carried. Frida was crying and Marie set about to change her diaper. Zoey unpacked the necessary towels and powders. And then Zoey demonstrated that she knew babies very well. Marie ended up standing back and watching. Then she patted Zoey on the back. "Bedankt, darling."

Zoey laid Frida down for a nap inside the canopy bed. She set out the bottles of applesauce and pea soup. She had small baby spoons laid out beside them.

Adam was still staring out the window, holding back the curtain and drapes. "Wherever he is, he's unarmed. I'm so thrilled about that."

Marie moved to the doorway between the two rooms. "He'll be all right. The king liked him, you said."

"The king liked him in a way I don't think he's willing to succumb to," Adam said.

"You're joking," Marie said. "There are other men like you? Like that, I mean."

Adam let down the drapes and dropped hands into his pockets. He straightened upright. "Not nearly enough men, in my opinion."

"She doesn't know?" Marie asked. "But you like her?"

"Liked her, very much," Adam said. "She hates me now. Didn't I say I had to talk to you?"

"Adam, did you force her to do anything?" Marie asked very seriously.

"Marie!" Adam shot back.

"Someone has to ask her this," Marie said.

"No, I didn't force her. We just started to kiss, and it very quickly became very...we just...well she..." Adam flustered and ducked his chin down. He almost wept. He stood near the table and turned his back to her.

"Adam, you know what you did, right? You were never with a girl before? Are you sure that you..." Marie said more gently to him. She entered the room to stand beside the table. "Robin knows what you did with her?"

"Yes," Adam insisted.

Marie held onto the back of a gilded chair. "Adam, look at me. You didn't become so aroused with her that you forced her to let you have her?"

"Marie, no! She started everything. She took everything to the next level. I was helpless to stop. And then I told you I got off of her and finished it," Adam admitted, breathing hard, his cheeks flushed. He brushed his bangs back from his face.

"Did she force you, Adam? Is that what you're telling me?" Marie questioned.

"No. No, I completely wanted to," Adam told her. "Why does she hate me now?"

"No, she doesn't. You just continue to be nice to her. She'll come around. I'd better be alone with Frida while we have time. Zoey," Marie went toward the bedroom where the baby lay. "Go sit with Adam for a while. I have to nurse her."

With a hand gesture, Zoey understood and passed Marie in the doorway.

Adam turned quickly around, his back to her. He wiped his eyes with Robin's handkerchief and then quickly hid it away in his pocket again.

Marie crawled onto the bed with the baby.

Zoey closed the door and looked about the parlor. She could see the side of Adam's face and how flushed he was beneath his eyes. He avoided looking at her. Zoey glanced back at the bedroom where Marie was. She'd heard their raised voices and the emotion in Adam's voice.

In Dutch, Zoey said, "Well. I think she just let you have it. Doesn't seem like she's a woman you want mad at you. They're both mad at you because of me, aren't they? I've put you in a terrible position. And you don't want to marry me, do you?"

Adam took a deep slow breath and finally looked at her with his chin tucked down.

Zoey made a look into the other two bedrooms. While Robin and Marie's room might be the grandest of the group of rooms, in royal blue and gold, there were rooms finely appointed in moss green or lavender. "Where will I be staying? Do you know where the servants' quarters are?"

Adam picked up her bag and carried it into the lavender room. "Why don't you take this one? I've seen you wear this color. I've seen me wear this color."

She looked into it again. "Really?"

It was definitely a question. Adam nodded. He watched her look about inside the room, at lavender sofa, chairs, and canopy bed. He watched her slide a hand over fabrics and upholstery, and he shivered at the thought of her touch. He folded his arms to his chest. He lowered his chin.

When Zoey came back to him and stood before him, Adam said softly, "Pardon?"

"Het spijt me ook." She laid her hand on Adam's forearm, on the sleeve of his suitcoat. I'm sorry.

"I don't understand," Adam said in his breathy soft voice.

Zoey looked up at him. "You were so brave, like an American cowboy. I was frightened at first. But now I see what an effort it was for you to fight that man, how treacherous it was for you, that it was not your nature. I wish I had been a comfort to you. I'm so sorry."

"Easy, darling," Adam said gently. "Ah, ga langzaam. Slow down. Take your time. Neem de tijd."

"Ja schat, Adam." Zoey stretched up and kissed his mouth briefly. Yes, my love.

That surprised him completely and he brightened.

She wrapped her arms about his stomach and felt him breathing hard. He folded around her and rocked her in his arms. Every breath that escaped him ebbed out the relief and agony he felt.

There was a knock on the outer door. Adam and Zoey released each other, and both went to the door. He urged her to say something.

"Who is it, please?" she asked.

"Tea for you, ma'am."

She looked at Adam and nodded.

He opened the door.

A cart of refreshments was wheeled into the room. And then they were alone again.

Zoey set out three teacups on the table and poured two of them. She set out the cream, sugar, and pastries. Then she sat down.

Adam sat across from her and they both reached for the cream.

Zoey gestured for him to take it.

Adam poured cream into each of their teacups, hers first.

"I asked around. I know why you did it that way, when we were together. You were acting for my benefit. We were not married, and you didn't wish to...you know," Zoey said to him in Dutch. "I suppose you must have been so disappointed to find that it wasn't my first. You must understand, he promised to marry me. He swore that we would. And then he took a job in Zeeburg. And I didn't mean to with you. It's just that other men are so forceful. And you were... almost reluctant.

Somehow, I found that impossible to resist. It was as if you'd never been with a woman before. I was your first, wasn't I?"

Adam wet his lips and looked about. "Sure wish Robin would come back." His left hand was on his vest, on his heart, near his hidden pistol.

"You're frightened," Zoey said. "We're in some danger, aren't we?"

Adam smoothed that hand down and then picked up his teacup with it.

"Very well. I shall do what you say. Just...point it out to me," Zoey said.

Marie emerged to find Adam and Zoey sitting silently at the table together. Adam was biting his lower lip. "Frida is sleeping. No Robin yet?"

"No."

Zoey poured some tea for Marie and refilled her own.

Marie sat with them. "Well. You wanted to talk, Adam."

Adam looked from her to Zoey and back. "Are you crazy? After that?"

"I'm sorry. Someone had to ask you that. Did Robin?" Marie asked.

"No. He knew I didn't," Adam said. "He saw us together. He didn't have to."

"And you're not happy now?" Marie said.

"Well, she's upset with me about the shooting, and you just gutted me." Adam looked down at buttons on his vest, Robin's vest. "I don't think I can feel much lower."

"Adam, I'm sorry. I believe you," Marie said. "You were intimate with her. Go on..."

"Now? I couldn't possibly," he replied.

"How did that happen?"

"How did it happen for you?"

"Ah." Marie sat back. "That was different. He immediately said he'd make me his wife. What did you say to her?"

"I'm… tossing this handkerchief into the nearest fireplace."

"What?"

"Nothing. Marie, you knew you were in love with him, right? How did you know it?" Adam asked.

"I think I knew it the minute I saw him," Marie said. "Didn't you?"

"Ah…" Adam looked down and smiled nervously. "Ouch. That hurt."

"Adam, this girl is in love with you. You can't just not marry her now."

"I…"

"I've known you to be so sweet. How could you do this to a nice girl like her?"

"I have nothing to offer her. I am a valet masquerading as a gentleman," Adam said.

"You can have your father's $20,000," Marie said.

Adam sat back in his chair. "How do you know that?"

"You were raised a gentleman. You were educated. You have a gentleman's manners," Marie told him. "You know you have to marry her."

When Adam's blue eyes teared and he sniffed, Zoey laid her hand on his forearm.

He lowered his chin.

"You see? She won't refuse you," Marie said gently.

"How do I ask her? I can't even talk to her," Adam whispered.

"You will learn. You love her?"

Adam nodded.

"You have to be encouraging to her, supportive. Remember that she has far more at stake than you. You know you can earn a living even without your father's money. She doesn't know anything about you, except what you shared with her. Trust your heart and hers," Marie said.

Adam and Zoey met eyes.

He pulled a handkerchief from his pocket to wipe his eyes and didn't let anyone see the RVK embroidered into the corner.

By Susan Eddy

Robin Van der Kellen waited in a huge parlor, looking up at the ceiling far above him, and wondering how they painted the scene of the accension way up there. The room was so vast that it was quite cold. He plunged his hands into his jacket pockets. The throne was at one end of the room.

And then doors behind him opened. He turned to see fourteen armed infantrymen enter on either side of him and march all the way across the room to the throne, spanning out across the room, with Robin left standing in the center.

Robin let out a breath and took his hands from his pockets. *Probably too nice a tapestry for them to shoot me on it. Right? Heirloom, perhaps. Gift from another dynasty.*

Then there were trumpets. Four trumpeters entered and marched up the middle, past Robin, and up to stand beside the throne.

This was followed by no less that fourteen well-dressed men who entered outside of the armed servicemen and went to stand up near the throne.

The trumpeting stopped.

King Willem II entered from a door behind the throne and quickly took his seat.

The room went silent.

Robin suddenly remembered to bow, from the waist, as low as he could. He breathed. He breathed again. Belt was tight on the waist. *All right they can shoot me now. I do have to stop eating like this.*

The king said in a loud authoritative voice, "You may rise, Captain Van der Kellen and approach the throne."

Robin stood up with a bit of a flourish of his right hand. He sauntered forward, deliberatively slowly, as if he were balancing his cavalry hat and wearing a sword. Unsure of how far forward he should stop, he watched the king for any signs. There were none. He left a little more room than he thought necessary and stopped.

"I am told that you are bearing bad tidings for me. How is that possible when you won your case so magnificently?"

"Your majesty, I must inform you of the death of Commander Collins."

"James Collins has died? How? I just saw him days ago. How did this happen?" the king said.

Robin hesitated.

"Sir?" the king insisted.

"I had to shoot him, your majesty," Robin said.

At that, every single infantryman raised and aimed his rifle at Robin.

Robin raised an eyebrow. "Waiting for that." He swallowed. "Your majesty, James Collins was behind the whole plot to steal the 42,000 guilders from Van de Berg's bank. He knew when the money was being deposited. His name and that of his associate Mitchel Evans were on the steam engine papers. Collins was the one who kidnapped Mr. Hudson. Then Mr. Collins and Mr. Evans showed up at my brother's estate. They held my brother and I at gunpoint and asked for all our money. First, I shot the gun out of his hand. He would not surrender. Mr. Hudson had to shoot Mr. Evans. Then Collins wrestled with Mr. Hudson for a pistol. I was forced to shoot to kill. I do apologize, your majesty. I know you were friends."

"I wasn't friends with the asshole. He stole from me before!" the king blurted out. "Lower the weapons. This man is your war hero, Captain of the Royal Netherland Guard. You owe him your allegiance."

Robin let out a hard breath. With his eyes closed, he could hear the weapons being lowered and stowed.

"I really enjoy testing your character, Van der Kellen," the king said.

"Wonderful. I hope you would be so good as to offer me another pair of trousers then," Van der Kellen said, making everyone in the room burst out laughing, especially the soldiers.

The king stood up, laughing. He walked forward and extended his hand. "Please accept my apologies and partake in every amenity my palace affords."

Robin dropped to one knee and kissed the back of the king's hand. And for a moment he leaned his forehead to it.

"Their guns were not ready to fire. You knew that, did you not? They were not cocked. You and I were the only ones cocked in here."

"May I... rise, your majesty?" Robin immediately regretted his choice of words.

"Please do." The king met eyes with Van der Kellen when he stood up. The king said to him alone, "I'll bet you are beautiful when you do."

Robin paused, thinking carefully. "I did not forget your invitation and brought my wife and child."

"And Mr. Hudson?"

"And Mr. Hudson. And the child's nanny," Robin said. "The girl and Mr. Hudson are..."

"What are they?" the king asked.

"I caught them together. They have been intimate."

"He is to marry her. How does he feel about that? Does that make you the slightest bit jealous, I wonder? Why didn't you bring them here to meet me immediately upon arrival?" the king asked.

"Did not want my wife to see my head blown off from several directions. It's a helluva sight."

The king laughed and flopped an arm loosely around Robin's shoulders. "Come, come. Let us get you some champagne. A lot of it. And no absinthe, I promise you."

Robin let out a breath.

"I frightened you? I would not think I warrior like you could be frightened."

"Well... amazing what a firing squad can do."

The king laughed heartily. "Ceremonial. Ceremonial, I assure you, Van der Kellen. You amuse me so!"

Robin burst into their parlor and all three of them stood up at the table.

"Are you all right?" Marie hurried round the table and into Robin's arms.

"I am. I told him Collins was dead and that he was responsible for everything. I thought he was going to have me shot right there. And do you know what he said?" Robin's voice rose. "Said that asshole stole from him before!"

"What?" Adam said.

"He knew the guy was a thief and a phony. Test of my character, my ass!" Robin blurted out. "If I could belt the king I surely would. Twenty-eight infantrymen took aim at me! I almost had more holes in me than cheap stockings. Jesus. Did they bring my guns back to me?"

"No," Adam said.

Marie bent to pull up her skirts, revealing ankle boots, lovely calves, knees, a bit of thigh and the bottom of her pantalettes. She pulled a pistol out of the right side and stood up, dropping her hem down to the floor again. She handed the pistol to Robin.

"Still warm." He held it to his cheek. "From your inner thigh."

"Outer thigh. You didn't watch very closely," Marie remarked.

Adam's eyebrows rose. "Surely you want to know where I have mine."

"Your luggage, I hope. That's where I told you to keep it." Robin tucked the small pistol into his inside pocket. "And then the king put his arm around me and made a lewd remark to me."

Marie looked at him.

Adam put hands on his hips. "You didn't believe me. I spoke plain English. I don't have any accent, that I'm aware of..."

"I'm sure you misunderstood," Marie told him. "What did he say?"

"He said I'm sure you're beautiful when you rise," Robin said.

Adam turned away from Robin, laughing.

"What does that mean?" Marie asked.

Robin looked at Adam. "Shut up, Adam. And, well Marie, just see for yourself when we go there. We're all invited to dinner. Zoey too. Tell her to put on whatever she has that's best."

"You have to tell her that, silly," Marie said. "I'll loan her a gown."

Robin went to the table, poured himself a brandy and drank it in three gulps. He looked around at them. "Twenty-eight infantrymen. Did nobody hear me?"

"Oh, poor Robin. Sit down. I thought you were joking." Marie hurried to him.

Robin sat down and finished his glass. Then he poured another.

Zoey sat down across from him. "What has happened, sir?"

Robin looked at her, dazed, and said in Dutch, "The world is upside down. Twenty-eight infantrymen just took aim at me. I can't trust my king. My king is insane. Test of my character? I don't know what my that means anymore."

"Sir?" Zoey said.

Robin reached across and patted lightly on her forearm. "Forgive me. I ran on. We are invited to dinner at the king's table. My wife will lend you a dress. Brush your hair. Do whatever it is that pretty girls do for dinner. And...and don't ask me because I'm a stupid, stupid man."

Zoey looked at him for a moment and laughed. "What...what about the baby?"

"They are sending some women to look after her so that you may join us," Robin explained.

"That is so kind of you."

"It was the king's idea. Do you know how to curtsey? You will need to," Robin said.

"Yes sir. Of course, sir. Every little girl practices to curtsey. You know, in case she ever meets a prince. Is Adam angry with me?" Zoey asked. "For walking out on him that way? I never should have done that."

"Oh. You and Adam. Not at all." Robin downed a second glass of brandy. "Not nearly as angry as I am with him. What did you do to him? Adam?"

"What?" Adam said.

Robin had a good look at him. "You look upset."

Adam met eyes with Marie.

Robin turned to look at her. "What happened?"

"Robin, I want you to ask Zoey one question. Adam, go into your room and close the door. Go on." Marie stood up.

"Oh God." Adam sulked out of the room and closed his door.

"Now." Marie moved close behind Zoey and set her hands on her shoulders. "Robin, you didn't ask her if Adam forced himself on her. I want you to ask her that. Let's get it over with."

"No way he forced himself on her, Marie," Robin complained. "The guy is...."

"It's a formality. You must ask her," Marie said.

Robin pulled out a chair across the table from Zoey and said in Dutch very gently, "Zoey, Marie insists that I ask you if Adam forced himself on you. Were you forced at all? I did ask if he did anything inappropriate but obviously, he did, after that occasion, because he told me he was intimate with you. Forgive me."

"Oh no. No of course not." Zoey looked from Robin to Marie over her shoulder. "Please tell her Adam was so shy and sweet and timid. We kissed and just could not stop. He's so wonderful. Please do not punish him."

Robin translated for Marie.

"I made him cry. I'm sorry," Marie admitted. "Somebody had to ask her that. I also asked if she forced him. For the record."

"Really? A man can't have unwilling relations, Marie." Robin walked to knock on and open Adam's door. "Adam, get out here."

That made Adam emerge sheepishly.

Robin pulled him into his arms for a brotherly hug. "My wife gelded you, as only she can. You'll be needing a good shot of brandy."

Two maids took over the watching of baby Frida. Marie dressed in her silk evening gown. Robin put on his tuxedo with the shirt of a million pearl buttons. Adam put on his best suit of Robin's. And Marie loaned Zoey one of her travel dresses which was far superior to anything she owned.

The butler knocked on the door. "Good evening Mr. Van der Kellen. We are to escort you to dinner now. Please allow me to remind you of etiquette. Gentlemen bow low at the waist. Ladies curtsey as low as possible. Everyone holds this until the king says they may rise. Ready?"

"What drug should I be expecting tonight?" Robin asked him.

"Oh. Sir. I had nothing to do with that. You do know that. Right?" the butler said in Dutch.

"I threw up on you, I heard." Robin said.

"I believe so, yes sir."

"Well, I'm still not sorry about that," Robin said.

"I...can only hope to make it up to you, sir."

"Then be extra nice to my wife and our nanny. Do you understand?" Robin told him.

"Absolutely, sir. My pleasure, sir."

Chapter 13: Jumping off a Cliff

One table in the grand dining room was set for the king and queen, just a couple of the king's friends, and Robin's party. All of the men who were in the throne room earlier, were seated at other tables nearby. Enormous flower arrangements dominated each table. Golden candle sticks held lit candles. Violinists played on the balcony above.

Robin's party was shown to their seats. When the king arrived, they all had to bow or curtsey until the king took his seat at the head of the table. Robin was at his left. Adam was at his right. The queen was at the far end with a number of her friends.

Marie looked on her place setting of gold rimmed china and crystal. She looked down to the far end of the table at the queen in her jewels. "This is magnificent."

"I am pleased you are happy at my table, Mrs. Van der Kellen," the king said in English. "You are a most lovely couple. I knew that Robin Van der Kellen would be with a young and beautiful woman."

"Thank you, your majesty," Marie said meekly.

Robin laid his hand on her thigh and smiled warmly at her. He gave her a wink.

"And Mr. Hudson, I am pleased you were not injured in the encounter with my former friend," the king said. "Are you well?"

"Yes, your majesty," Adam said.

"Some of the infantry men were hoping to see a demonstration of your famous marksmanship, Robin," the king said. "Would you be willing to give us a show after dinner?"

"Anytime, your majesty. I would prefer to use my own weapon, of course," Robin said.

"Oh, you will have that back. And I have arranged a gift for you. Bring it forward." The king waved an infantryman over.

He brought forward a rifle box and two other infantrymen were prepared to hold either end while Robin opened the case.

"All the way from America, just like you. This weapon has just been invented. I give it to you, a man worthy of its tremendous advantage," the king said.

"Before dinner, your majesty?" Robin asked.

"Yes. Open your present. You can play with it later. Just have a look. I cannot wait," the king said.

Robin opened the brass latch and raised the lid. After a moment he said, "Is this a Mississippi Rifle?"

"The captain knows weapons," the infantryman said. "A muzzle loading percussion rifle. Percussion lock is said to be more weatherproof than flintlocks. It is .54 caliber and 1:66 rifling inside the barrel. V-notch site. It is said to have a 500-yard range."

"How did you come by this?" Robin gasped. "I only heard about these. Is this the ammunition?"

"Yes. Have a look," the infantryman said.

Robin opened the small wooden box inside the gun case to examine the acorn shaped ball. "Colonel Abrams said he had seen one. A friend of mine, an American Colonel."

"This is my gift to you, for what happened this afternoon," the king said. "Let us put this away and Robin can try it out after dinner, in the gardens. Go set up some targets. Two or three hundred yards?"

"Five hundred," Robin said.

"Magnificent."

The gun case was closed and taken away.

"I have my connections in America," the king said. "A number of these were given to the Infantry and they can spare one. And not to be rude to my other guests..."

Another servant came forward with a tray of three wrapped presents. The king selected the gold foil wrapped one and said, "This is for Mrs. Van der Kellen. I thank you for tolerating the time I had taken your husband from your home."

The present was set before Marie.

"What do I do?" Marie whispered.

"Open it. It's all right," Robin whispered.

Marie unwrapped the ribbon and opened the gold paper. Inside, she opened a box to find a diamond and pearl necklace. It was a long necklace and would fall further down her cleavage than the sapphire necklace she was wearing.

"Allow me to put it on you," Robin said. "Thank you, your majesty. It is beautiful."

Robin clasped it behind Marie's neck, and she looked down at it. Her fingers touched the diamonds.

"This one is for Miss Zoey, for looking after the Van der Kellen baby," the king said.

A smaller box was given to Zoey.

"And this one for Mr. Hudson, for looking after Mr. Van der Kellen." The king placed the last gift on Adam's plate. "What an amusing position you now find yourself in, young man."

Adam averted his eyes from the royal down to the gift before him. "Robin is just telling everyone now, it seems."

"Does the young lady speak any English?" the king asked.

"She does not, your highness," Adam responded as he watched Zoey open a box with a modest pearl choker necklace.

"One does wonder, how did you get the young lady into bed with you when the two of you cannot speak the same language. Do tell," the king said.

"Yes. Wouldn't we like to know," Robin added.

"Haven't yet gotten her into bed." Adam glanced at Robin and avoided eye contact with Marie. "Laundry room, however..."

The king burst out laughing, urging Adam to open the wrappings and find inside a gold pocket watch with pearl inlay and diamonds in the four corners.

"Tell me, Mr. Hudson, was it your first?"

Marie couldn't believe she was hearing that or seeing Adam answering so coyly.

"She was, yes." Adam smirked. "She's a little angry with me at the moment."

"What is the predicament then? And remember, I adore your bluntness, Mr. Hudson," the king said. "Please don't disappoint."

Adam shot him a look. Then he laid eyes on Robin who offered him no assistance whatsoever. "She saw me fighting with Commander Collins and is afraid of me now. I apologize. I didn't have any choice."

"Well. That is something," the king said. "I am pleased that we did not lose you. That was a very accomplished foe that you battled, and Robin had to shoot."

That made Adam and Robin make eye contact.

"You know what can remedy everything for you, young man?" the king said. "There will be dancing tonight. Do you dance, Mr. Hudson? Dance with the girl."

Adam nodded. "I am an excellent dancer. If she'll have me. I don't know how much success I will have. May I ask you a favor?"

"What favor?" Robin sat forward, alarmed.

"Please ask it, Mr. Hudson," the king said. "Anything."

"May I please drink this champagne now?" Adam asked sheepishly. "I'm scared to death."

"Of a great many things, I would imagine." The king picked up his own glass of champagne. "We shall all drink to the young lovers."

"To the young lovers," Robin said, in two languages.

That allowed them all to drink and Adam downed his entire glass, only to find a server quick to refill it.

"I cannot wait. The gun is nice, but I can't adorn Robin Van der Kellen with it. This is for you." The king had a fourth gift brought out and he gave it to Robin.

"This is most generous, your majesty. All of this. I do not know what to say," Robin said.

"My wife picked these out. Except for the gun," the king said.

Robin's gift was an elaborate gold cross pendant with a big red gemstone in the middle.

"The queen said it will keep you safe. It belonged to her late brother," the king said.

"This is too precious. How do I accept such a gift? How do I thank her Majesty the Queen?" Robin said.

"You dance, do you not, Mr. Van der Kellen?" the king asked.

Robin swallowed. "Of course, yes."

"Then you must reserve one dance for the Queen. Put it on. Put it on. Bring the first course. Drink up everyone."

Marie put her hand on his thigh.

Adam still smirked, feeling the king's eyes on him and on Robin. He lowered his chin and saw Zoey extend her hand to him beneath the table. At last, he took her hand in his and his heart was in his throat. He ducked his chin down and looked at her with the warmest smile.

"Is...is this a ruby, your majesty?" Robin asked, as he danced with the queen.

"It is a red diamond. Very rare. Almost as rare as you," she said. "You're not sleeping with the king, are you?"

Robin was speechless.

"Of course not," The queen went on. "You are a real man. A magnificent man. A war hero. A leading barrister in Amsterdam, I hear."

"Oh, I only tried one case, your majesty," Robin said.

"Look your wife is dancing with the king. Let us dance another. I'll bet every inch of you is splendid. Are you faithful to your wife, sir?"

Adam stood and offered his hand formally to Zoey. She looked up at him. "C'mon. Dance with me. Why not?"

"You mean? Really?" Zoey stood up. Her left hand went to the pearls about her neck and her right fingertips touched Adam's palm.

He took her hand into his. "I know this one. Come with me."

"I hope you know what you're doing." Zoey held his hand and followed him through the dancing couples until they were near Robin and the Queen. Room was made for them on the dance floor.

Adam set her left hand up on his shoulder and he held her right hand out at a respectable distance, letting her arm relax. "Ready? One, two, three." Adam drew her into the dance with him and in just a few moments, they were synchronized with the other couples around them, even the twirls. At the first twirl, Zoey giggled. At the second, she outright laughed. Adam laughed too.

Zoey forgot entirely that her dress was the most plain, that everyone probably knew she was the nanny. She looked up at her American lover, and she laughed with him. He led her so well. He danced so finely. He smiled broadly. His laughter made her laugh. How did he know this? She looked over at Robin and how elegant he was, as he danced with the most glittering woman in the room, the queen.

Then Robin and Marie danced together such that it would melt the hearts of all. Their stolen kisses, their embraces, their affection for each other...

Adam would glance over his shoulder, judging distance to others so quickly, and then he guided Zoey into the space, making her giggle. For song after song, they saw only each other. He guided her as much as he let her decide when to twirl or turn or step into him. A long lock of her hair had come loose from her bun and coiled down to her shoulder and bosom. There was no pause in between the songs, merely a softening and then a new tempo began. The young couple were reading each other so well, their bodies moving closer together, their endorphins visible to all around them. They were an intimate couple.

Robin put a hand on Adam's shoulder, stopping them. He leaned into Adam's ear. "Stay if you want. Marie is tired." Then he repeated it in Dutch.

"Oh. Zoey? Do you want to stay or…" Adam said.

"My feet hurt," Zoey blurted out. "But I loved it so!"

"I think she wants to get out of those shoes," Robin told Adam.

Zoey nodded. "Oh, but tell him I loved dancing with him."

Robin patted Adam on the shoulder. "Where did you learn to dance like that? She loved it, Mr. Hudson. You thrilled her."

"Thrilled?" Adam let out a long breath. "Hated it when I was a boy. It's a lot more fun now that I like girls."

"You what?" Robin said.

Marie grabbed hands with Zoey. "Are you having fun? She's having fun."

Zoey giggled.

They left the ballroom, the two women holding hands. Robin had to carry his new gun case. Adam skipped along beside him, giving a twirl as he passed into the hallway. He held out his hand to Robin. A sidelong glare from Robin made him laugh.

Back in their suite that night, the two couples enjoyed more wine, still enthusiastic about the party and electric about it. The room had a warm glow from the oil lamps and the fireplaces.

"Should have seen the look on the king's face when you hit the target," Adam said.

"Hey, nobody was more surprised than I was. I've never had a weapon that accurate for that distance. What a spectacular invention," Robin said.

"Did you hold your breath for a shot like that?" Adam asked.

"Fired at the bottom of a breath, before I inhaled," Robin explained. "You have to take into account the wind on a long shot, but we didn't have any wind tonight. Sure didn't want to miss with all those infantrymen looking on. It's a Cavalry thing."

As Zoey transferred Frida from her arms to Marie's she said, "Thank you for the gown. I should give it back to you now."

Robin translated.

"Are we going home tomorrow?" Adam asked.

"Not until I get my weapons back. Let's get some sleep, huh?" Robin said.

Robin refilled two wine glasses and carried them to their room. They saw Adam go to the green room and Zoey to the lavender one. Marie set the wine down on the table in their room. She met Robin's hungry kiss, and he took her down on the bed.

Zoey twirled about in her room for a time and then changed from gown into sleeping dress. She pulled the palace robe on and tied it. Then she laid the gown over one of the dining chairs.

Adam sat down on the edge of his bed for a time, ran a hand up through his hair. He buzzed with wine in his head, but he reached down to pull off his shoes.

After Adam had removed his suit, Robin's suit, he pulled on a sleep shirt over his head and opened his bedroom door partway. Then he retreated to his bed to fold down fine linens and slide into them.

Zoey opened his door, her long dark hair down and flowing, her white robe wrapped around her. She closed the door.

Adam sat up. "Zoey? I'm so glad you're here." He hurried to fluff his hair up and open the collar of his sleep shirt a bit. "Come. Komen."

Zoey walked in and sat down on the edge of his bed. "There is no way a valet could know how to dance like a gentleman that way. I just don't know what to make of you. First you arrived and lived in the attic with us, a valet. You ate with us in the kitchen. You worked hard. The next thing we knew you're to be addressed as a gentleman. You are moved into a guest room. You dine with the family. You turn out to be a gun fighter, of all things. What do I make of you?"

Adam smoothed his hand on her arm. He stroked it through her hair. He found she was still wearing the pearls. "I want your kiss. Come closer to me."

"Oh, how I want more of that sweetness you gave to me. I don't even know you. But I had such a wonderful time with you tonight. How do our bodies move so well together?" Zoey said sadly. "What do you want? Should I return to my room?"

Adam leaned forward and kissed her mouth very lightly, looking into her eyes the whole time. He sat back to look at her in the light from the fireplace. He smoothed strands of her hair back from her face.

"And Robin is so mad at you. You don't want to get married, do you?" she whispered. "I'm sure Marie was asking you about us earlier. She upset you very much. She had to ask us these questions."

"I have to hear if there is any trouble. The only weapons he has are Marie's tiny pistol and that huge rifle the king gave him. He needs his pistols back." Adam reached over and pulled back the covers on the other side of his bed. He then crawled out, walked around the bed, and opened the door just a bit. But he heard Robin and Marie and the squeak of their bed in the very next room, and he quickly closed the door again. "Oh my God."

"You don't want us to do anything," Zoey thought aloud. "Do you want me to leave?"

Adam crawled back on the other side of the bed and folded down the blankets on her side. He invited her to get in with a pat to the pillow. His heart raced. His breathing increased. He fluffed up his curls again.

Zoey removed her robe, laid it on the chair, and slid in with him in her night gown. She'd never laid down in a bed with a man before. How electric would their first touch be? What would their first touch be?

"I can't think of anything more erotic than this moment in my life." He slid his feet down and stretched out. "What are you going to do when Robin enters in the morning? And you know he will."

"I watch your eyes go to him," she whispered. She touched Adam's cheek, his ear, his fluffy hair and watched his eyes close. His dark lashes were long like a girl's. "He is beautiful. Do you want me, Adam? Me and only me?" She kissed his neck, in little kisses, up to his ear.

Adam opened his arms to her. His mouth found hers and he kissed her deeply. Her hand pulled up his shirt. His went up her gown. He soon found himself on top of her and before he knew it, he was making love to her again. And this time, Adam set his passions free. *Was Robin doing this very same thing? Was he feeling this?*

Zoey thought of their evening of dancing together in the royal ballroom, the sight of all the gowns and glittering jewels. The evening was so perfect. If only she could tell him, so she made love to him passionately.

Adam's back went wet. He was losing control. He moaned into the pillow. He held Zoey down and climaxed helplessly. He shuddered. And he struggled to keep quiet.

Zoey kissed him. "You needed that."

"Oh my God," he sighed. "Never felt that in my life."

She giggled quietly. "Are you all right?"

Adam giggled too. "No that did not happen. I think I love you. Ik hou van jou, Zoey."

Robin Van der Kellen emerged from his bedroom, dressed in his fancy pin striped suit and tying on a cobalt blue silk ascot. He stopped in his tracks when he found Adam and Zoey having breakfast together at the table in their palace bathrobes.

Adam looked at him. "Well good morning. Sleep well?"

Robin strolled closer to them and slipped his hands down into his pockets. "I seem to be intruding."

Zoey started to get up. "Sorry, sir. I'll get dressed immediately."

Robin switched to Dutch. "Stay. Stay seated. This is quite all right." He changed back to English to add, "On some planets."

"Everything changed last night," Adam told him enthusiastically. "Everything."

Robin moved closer and pulled out a chair beside Adam and across from Zoey. "I see that. Proper attire is optional. Rank is reversed. I had to change a diaper. Marie gets to sleep in. Deserves it after last night. I think, strangely enough, I've become the nanny."

"House entertainment, more likely." Adam laughed. "Zoey and I would have talked all night if we could. We've been dying for you to get up. It was all I could do not to burst into your room and shake you awake."

"Really?" Robin glanced at them both as Zoey poured him some coffee. "Surprised you didn't."

Adam laid a gold watch on the table and slid it in front of Robin's cup and saucer.

"I actually gave that to you." Robin gestured to take it back.

"It's your father's. I can't keep it," Adam insisted. "Robin, I want you to tell her about me."

"Tell her what?"

"I can't go forward with her if she doesn't know," Adam said. "And I can't tell her. I don't know the words. There's no children's primer that has these words."

"You should let me have some coffee before all we grab hands and jump off that cliff." Robin poured cream into his coffee cup and then stirred with a beautiful silver and pearl inlayed spoon. He looked at his father's plain gold watch on the table. "Are my weapons here yet?"

"Your crazy ass king is not going to harm you now. Not after last night. You danced with the queen. He danced with Marie," Adam said.

"I danced with the queen while she massaged my shoulder and rubbed her hip against mine, telling me what rare a jewel I am, what a real man I am," Robin said. "I wonder how many men they can get into a firing squad. Hmmm."

"Knock it off," Adam said.

"I still don't know what that means," Robin declared.

Adam burst out laughing.

"You want me to tell her what? You were...are attracted to men?" Robin asked.

Adam pointed at him. "You do that without making me sound like a freak."

"Don't blame the messenger. Let me find a way to start in that general direction." Robin changed to Dutch. He picked up that watch and opened it to check the time. "Zoey, there is something Adam wants me to tell you. Ahm, he likes you very much. You are the first girl he was ever with. You probably knew that. He said everything changed last night."

Zoey smiled brilliantly. "He is so wonderful. Will you tell him? I absolutely adore him. He's so shy and sweet and passionate."

Robin raised eyebrows. "Is he? Well. Well. First, first can you both go get dressed? And then I can do that. Adam..." He changed languages again. "*God, I hope this is English!* Go get some clothes on so you two don't look like you *just* got off each other."

"We did." Adam grinned. "So did you two, for that matter."

"Go!" Robin urged through his teeth.

"Tell her you're joking." Adam pushed his chair out.

"What makes you think I'm joking?" Robin snapped. Then he changed to a friendlier tone of Dutch. "I'm playing with his head. It's an amusement I highly recommend. Please get dressed. I'm terribly uncomfortable with the robes."

"Yes, sir."

Adam and Zoey left the room.

Robin sipped his coffee alone, drank the whole cup and poured another. He reclined back and crossed his legs comfortably. He looked at that watch. He let out a long slow breath and savored the absolute silence, the aroma of coffee, satisfaction...and then the bedroom doors opened again.

The couple returned much sooner than expected, as if they threw on clothing in their rooms and hurried back to each other. They met behind Robin with a noisy kiss and giggles.

"Knock it off. Is that proper use of it?" Robin remarked.

They sat back down, moving their chairs closer together.

"Well, you are finally learning American," Adam said.

Robin indicated the watch on the table. "If my father caught me kissing a girl like that..."

"That's the least of what we've been doing." Adam moved a napkin over the watch. "First tell her that this is not just physical. I know we can't talk to each other but there is so much more communication going on. It's spiritual. It's...*I am flying.*"

"Are you touching her beneath the table?" Robin's brow furrowed.

"*No! I'm holding her hand!*" Adam shot back. "You are *really* enjoying this, aren't you?"

Robin laughed out loud. "My skin is crawling. When Frida is of age, I'm buying a cannon."

Adam laughed. "You are not pointing a cannon at her beau. Didn't you ever have to coach your young regiment on the art of romance?"

"Romance, no. Syphilis, yes." Robin let out another uncomfortable breath. "What am I supposed to tell Zoey for you? And let's keep me out of this. I'm merely the translator." Robin looked down into his coffee as he stirred cream into it. And then he poured brandy into it.

"You're in the middle of this. Not unlike the way you were in that bed last night. How many times? Tell her about Lucas. Tell her about you and I, but we have this agreement. I think...I think she might know anyway," Adam said. "What are you doing with that brandy?"

"Nothing. Tell her what about you and I?"

"You know. Zoey is different," Adam said. "You're different. Maybe every time we love it is different. You did it at least twice last night. Not bad for your age."

"I...." Robin let out a long breath. He gulped down a good shot of brandy from the bottle and set it down. "Miss Zoey, Adam wants to be completely honest with you and tell you something most would consider shocking. Prepare yourself. He has never been with a girl before because...he was with, Adam had a boyfriend before."

Adam lowered his eyes.

"He was very young. 14. And he cared for him very much. But his father caught them together, and Adam had to leave home. Nevertheless, he says that there is a spiritual connection to you. He loves you. He...is not sure he can change. He has had...attractions to men," Robin said gently.

"To you," Zoey said quietly.

Robin raised eyebrows. "Though he knows we can only be friends."

"Is he saying he only wants to be friends with me?" Zoey asked.

"No. He loves you. That much is certain. And he clearly found enjoyment in being with you. Says you two communicate somehow.

Spiritually, I'd imagine." Robin met eyes with the girl. "I do apologize. These are things I should never know about your relationship. There's plenty he shouldn't know about mine."

"Do you think he can change?" Zoey whispered, her voice shaking and nervous.

"I..." Robin thought a bit and looked down at his coffee. Then he studied the young man whose long brown curls hid his eyes at the moment. "He doesn't need to change. I think he can love a man or a woman. He just...has a different heart than the rest of us."

"He never intended to marry?" Zoey asked.

"Before he met you, he never wanted to marry. I don't know how he feels about that now. But he just told me this morning that everything has changed." Robin saw Adam raise his chin to make eye contact with them both. "And he is flying."

That made her smile. The young couple held hands beneath the table, fingers linked tightly.

"Ahm, I am compelled to tell you that his childhood was difficult. There was a falling out with his father over that boy. His father beat him, and he ran away from home. He survived on the street. That's when he reinvented himself as a valet. It is quite possible that your comfort is the only he has known in a long time, or the only he has ever known."

"Oh my. That is exactly how he behaves. No one has ever cared for him. Every touch. Every caress. He melts. Can you tell him, it is all right if we take this slowly, and we continue?" Zoey said. "If he wants to."

"That is exactly what I've been telling him to do," Robin said. "I mean to go slowly."

"And I want to go to America," Zoey said. "It has been my dream my whole life."

"Really?" Robin said.

Adam finally said under his breath, *"You're killing me over here."*

"Adam, she's all right with it. Okay to take it slow. She wants to go to America," Robin summarized.

"Really? She knows what I am?" Adam wiped his eyes and looked to face Robin. "But you brought her along so that we would fight and split apart."

Robin sat back in his chair. "No, I didn't."

Adam wiped his eyes again, with that precious handkerchief of Robin's.

Robin did a bit of translation again for Zoey. Then he asked Adam, "What happened last night? The dancing?"

Adam shook his head. "I mean that was wonderful, magical even."

"Everything changed?" Robin asked him, searching his expression. "Adam?"

Adam sat back and nodded. "Well, ladies and gentlemen, I must marry her now."

"Oh? Oh. Did you like it?" Robin searched the blush on Adam's face and laughed. *"How many times did you like it?* More than twice? Little shit. Guess I'd better give you that bonus so you can buy her a ring and a dress, and..."

"I think I may faint." Adam started fanning his face with his napkin and pulled at his collar.

"A house...."

"I can't live with you anymore?" Adam asked.

"Of course, you can."

"Don't terrify me that way. Is it hot in here?"

"No. I'm going to terrify you further. You must meet her sister. You're about to marry her and take her away to America, one month from now. What name are you planning to give her? Legally, you're a Rothschild."

"Can I change my name in court here? Will that be legal in America?" Adam suddenly sat forward at the table, enthusiastically.

"Ah...Yes. I have to check some law books, but if memory serves, yes," Robin said. "Then would you marry her here and use the name Hudson?"

"If she'll have me," Adam said.

"One step at a time. All right?" Robin said.

"What is the next step?"

"I take you outside and teach you to propose to her in Dutch. Then I petition the court for your name change. Then you meet her sister. Get all new clothes made for her, and luggage to travel to America. Assuming she wants all of this, and I think she does. You marry her here where her family and friends can witness. They may never see her again."

"And so, I take a wife home with me? I can't say that wouldn't please my mother," Adam said.

"I'm sure it will. Be certain you are doing it to please yourself."

"Mr. Van der Kellen? May I ask something?" Zoey asked.

"Yes, of course. I apologize," Robin said.

"He said everything changed. Can he be happy with me, if I'm merely...a girl? And it...might mean children," Zoey asked timidly.

"Zoey, he is clearly very very happy right now, and it is all because of you," Robin said.

She smiled and then she started to tear up.

"Adam, comfort her. In there. Go on. She wanted to know if you're happy with her. I said very much so," Robin said.

"Then why is she crying? You said it wrong," Adam said.

Robin smiled. "Adam, you've got a lot to learn."

Adam stood up and took her hand. "Dutch is what I need to learn." He drew her away into the lavender bedroom and closed the door.

May 10, 1806 The Confrontation with Paula

"You left as soon as Paula came in," Marie said.

"He always does." Adam was folding Robin's shirts that Paula had just delivered from the laundry.

"Why? Do they say anything about it?" Marie pointed toward the dining room. She looked from Robin to Adam and back.

The look on Robin's face made Marie put down her blankets. "They did? What did they say to you?"

"Ahm, just that it is inappropriate for a gentleman to…be alone with…the maid," Robin said.

"Robin, have you been alone with Paula?" Marie asked.

"No. Only fleeting moments."

"There's nothing wrong with that," Marie said. "Why do you look so nervous? You know that's how you and I got together. Oh Robin."

Robin slid his hands onto her upper arms. "I never laid a hand on her. But…."

"But what? Oh Robin."

"Nothing happened."

"What happened?" Adam urged.

"You were tempted to? Because I'm not letting you?" Marie started to cry.

"No. I wasn't tempted. She put her hand on me," Robin said.

"Robin, where?"

Robin just shut his mouth.

"She grabbed your…" Adam blurted out.

"She touched you there?" Marie asked him. "Robin, I will knock her overboard."

"I believe you could." Robin exhaled hard. "I think you should just continue to be her boss in here and keep me out of it. I shouldn't have told you."

"I should leave you alone for this." Adam stood up.

"Don't you dare go anywhere. I won't have any woman touching my husband."

Adam tried to leave but Robin grabbed him by the arm. Adam blurted out, "What did I do?"

"We can have her duties exchanged with another maid," Robin offered. "I almost went to the captain. It's rather embarrassing."

"We can tell her when the voyage is over that her tip would have been bigger if she hadn't grabbed your trousers, with you in them," Marie shot back.

Robin drew her into his arms. "I love you darling. I won't try to keep any secrets from you again. I'm terrible at it. Whatever you think is best in this situation and we will do it. Just, I don't want you to confront her alone."

"We'll do it together."

Robin let out a hard breath. "Greatly feared you'd say that."

"I'd really like to be here for that," Adam urged.

"Get out," Robin and Marie both said in unison.

Paula was invited into the cabin and handed Frida to Marie, but it was then that she noticed Robin sitting cross legged in the far corner of the bed, cleaning his pistol.

Paula backed up against the wall. "What is this?"

"Sit down, Paula," Marie said. "We just want to talk to you."

"About what, mum?"

"About what happened in the library," Marie said.

"He pressed me up against the wall. I pushed him. I'm sorry. He said he wouldn't again...."

At that Robin made the pistol sound as if he cocked it. He didn't. He then completed loading it.

Paula sat down on their trunk and burst into tears.

"I think we all know that's not what happened," Marie said.

"You won't tell the captain, will you?" Paula asked.

"I wouldn't like to. I'd like the three of us to come to an understanding that you are the maid and a nanny, and you will keep your hands off my husband," Marie said.

"So, you're going to pay me to be quiet?" Paula asked.

Marie looked at Robin in shock.

"I'm not going to pay you shit," Robin said. "Don't get up off that trunk."

"All I have to do is tell the captain he got on me," Paula said. "I told Robin, I want one hundred dollars."

Marie faltered then, her second shock.

Robin slid off the bed quickly and got between the two women. He left the pistol on the bed and urged Marie to sit down next to it. The seriousness of him, registered once again with Marie and she sat with her hand near that gun.

"That's an interesting sum of money. That's more than you make in a year," Robin said. "How did you arrive at that figure?"

"You're rich. You won't miss it," Paula said. "I saw her diamond ring."

"Extortion at sea is a maritime crime. The captain alone can send you to jail at the first port without a trial. I don't wish to do this to you. I think you're a young girl, in trouble, looking for a man to save you or a man you can extort money out of. Why do you need money? You have a place to live, work to do, you get a payment at the end of the voyage," Robin said.

"Forcing yourself on me would also be a maritime crime," Paula said.

"Except that I didn't," Robin said. "You won't win this case. I'm a lawyer in two countries. I can tell you, you will not win this."

The girl did cry again then. Her cheeks flushed. "Not against the man who saved this boat."

Robin softened his voice as he often did while questioning female witnesses in court. "Why don't you tell us why you need a hundred dollars?"

"I'm not being asked back on the next voyage. I'm being left in Amsterdam with my twenty dollars and not even a place to stay," Paula admitted. "I thought you were so beautiful. Your wife just had a baby. You're not doing it. I could romance you and you'd take pity on me, leave me with some money perhaps."

"The first truthful thing you said since you entered this cabin," Robin said. "Why are you not being asked back? You were a fine maid and nanny. You didn't need to grab my trousers."

"Oh... Marie, I'm so sorry," Paula said.

"Answer him," Marie urged. "And excuse me. What the hell makes you think we're not doing it?"

"The rich men usually just sleep with me. Sometimes they give me money, a bigger tip at the end. But enough of them have complained," Paula said. "I wash your sheets, remember? They hardly need washing except that he sweats, probably from not getting it."

Robin let out a loud breath.

"Robin, this is all mine. This is very simple, Paula. Your choices are few," Marie said forcefully. "You can be good and receive our help or you can go to jail."

The girl looked from Marie to Robin and back to Marie.

Marie said, "I do know what desperate situation you are in. I don't know how you were selected for us on this ship. Especially given your reputation. But you're damn lucky you got me."

Robin folded his arms and looked at Marie. "You need a job you can live on. Not in my house. But I do have friends in Amsterdam. Or do you need passage back to family in Poland?"

"I have no one." Paula looked up at him and her eyes teared.

Robin looked at Marie.

"Can you help her?" Marie asked.

Robin put his hands on his hips and stood upright in the only part of their cabin where he could. "I can get you a job as a maid. You'll make more money as a nanny, but you'll never meet anyone but married men. And you can't be doing this again. I think you'll be happier as a maid."

"Can you really do this?" Paula asked.

"If I give my good word on you, you will not let me down," Robin said to her.

"I swear, sir, I will do my best."

"Our settlement is this. You continue to work for Marie on this voyage, and for God's sake care for the baby. You do that and I will put you up somewhere in Amsterdam until I can get you work at one of my friend's homes. Not mine or my family's. Not a place I will see you again. But you can start a new life," Robin said. "You fail here, you do any lack of care for my child, and you'll get escorted off this ship in hand cuffs."

The girl nodded and just put her head in her hands and cried.

"Calm down girl. And you can't be seen walking out of here crying." Robin stepped back to lean against the cabin wall. "Did you steal from us?"

She shook her head.

"Why should I believe you?" Robin asked.

"Because your trunk is locked," Paula said.

Robin shook his head in exasperation. "At least she's being honest." Then he said to the girl, "What I don't understand is why you didn't think you could ask us for help."

"You? Only the most perfect couple ever."

That night, Robin dropped back hard into the bed and sunk his head into the pillow. "I'll be awake all night...not sweating."

Marie burst out laughing, handing him his nightcap of brandy.

Chapter 14: The Dowry

Robin brought Marie to see the art gallery, and as they strolled into a room of Rembrandt and similar artists, Robin told her, "Adam plans to propose to her out there."

"He does? What changed his mind?" Marie asked.

"She did, apparently. You saw how happy he was," Robin said.

"Yes. He was. He's making love to her?" Marie asked.

"All last night, yes," Robin said.

Marie wrapped her arm around Robin's waist and slipped beneath his arm. "I'm amazed. Do you think he can be attracted to both men and women?"

"I think so." Robin hugged her. "You know, love is in the air. And Frida is being tended to."

"Find the nearest place we can be alone."

"Adam and Zoey did it in the laundry room."

"Laundry room? Oh, we can do better than that."

Adam and Zoey held hands, strolling through the tulip gardens of the palace. Pink tulips on the left, yellow on the right, red ones straight ahead. A spicy aromatic flavor of tulips filled the air. Zoey's dress was plain, dark brown with a white lace collar. The white pearls fell around her neck just inside the collar. And one strand of dark brown hair had fallen free of the bun in the back. The breeze made it tickle against her cheek. Adam slid it behind her ear for her.

"You know, I am going to tell you something in Dutch, but I have to start with something easier," Adam said in his soft breathy voice. "I thought you were pretty, the first time I saw you in the kitchen. And you were so kind, bringing me food at the table down there. I know you work very hard, and I know how hard life is being a maid. I know I am 21 years old, and you are eighteen. I have been very very wealthy. And I have had nothing. I have gone without…most everything. I have gone without anyone caring if I was even alive for six years, until I met Robin and Marie. Robin has been withholding my salary lately because I've been rather crazy. But all that has changed. Technically I make enough money that you do not have to work anymore, just take care of wherever we live. I don't know how you will feel about it, but I don't want to leave Robin's house yet. We can work those things out later. I have feelings for him but it's different than with you. I don't know how I sense it, but I sense that we can be friends. And I know that we can be lovers because of last night. Wil je met me trouwen?"

"Ja ik wil, Adam."

He smiled.

Zoey wrapped her arms up around his neck. "Ik hou van jou. Take it slow, Adam."

He let out a breath. And he kissed her.

She said to him in Dutch, "Since my parents died, I've been very alone too. I think you were very brave to run away from home when you were so young. I have great friends there in the house. And I have my sister, but I hardly ever see her. I hope we can marry here so they can share it with us. I think Robin and Marie are so very kind. I think you met them so that you could meet me. I love your voice. I love your eyes."

"Well, so we're both trying to learn each other's language. That's really good, right? I need Robin to tell you I will buy you a ring. I will meet your family. I don't know what the customs are, but I will do whatever I have to, to marry you," Adam said.

"I loved dancing with you." She wrapped her arms around his neck again, lifting her feet off the ground.

Adam laughed and swung her about in his arms. "That's definitely happy right?" He twirled her down the aisle in the tulip garden, all the way to the end, until they were both dizzy and laughing.

Adam and Zoey,

Meet us for lunch, at the terrace dining room.

Ontmoet ons voor de lunch, terras eetkamer.

R

Robin and Marie were seated beneath an umbrella at an elaborate table. Robin immediately stood up. "Here they come."

Adam led Zoey by the hand, to the table. He lowered his chin, and he smiled the biggest smile they'd ever seen. "Ladies and gentlemen, we have consented to be married. To each other."

Marie shot out of her chair to hug Zoey, who giggled.

Robin said in Dutch, "Did you consent to get married?"

Zoey laughed. "Ja, ik ben dol op hem!"

"Just checking." Robin reached out to shake hands with Adam. "It's official. You are getting married."

"Tell her I will get her a ring, and dresses, and all that?" Adam said enthusiastically.

"Yes, give me a chance. Have a seat," Robin offered. "Hij zal je een ring geven, bruidsschat, jurken…"

"He doesn't have to do all that. I have a little saved," Zoey said.

"It's all right. I owe him quite a lot of money. He and I will take care of everything. I'll work things out with Robert. You won't need to work for him anymore," Robin said. "You're the bride to be of a gentleman now."

"Oh Mr. Van der Kellen, I don't know what to say. You and your wife are so kind to me, and to Adam. I will continue as your nanny, won't I?"

Robin looked to Marie. "You want her to continue being Frida's nanny? She'd like to."

"Oh yes. If she wants to. She's wonderful, at least…when she's not busy ravaging Adam." Marie made the men burst out laughing.

Robin selectively translated. "Yes, you are wonderful with Frida. Continue if you want to. You will receive a salary for it, of course."

"Do you mean no more laundry or floor scrubbing or…." Zoey asked.

"None of that anymore in Robert's home. He has plenty of maids," Robin said.

They were served tea and lemonade, rye biscuits and berry muffins to begin their lunch.

"Please tell Zoey about my name change. I want her to be assured it will be Hudson, but to know what we must do first," Adam said.

"You're changing your name?" Marie talked to Adam in English while Robin talked to Zoey in Dutch.

Plates of beets, roasted carrots, and herbed peas were served.

"Adam, do you think you will visit your mother?" Marie asked.

"I'll write her first. I'll post her a letter from here. At least, father will never expect it to be from me when it comes from Amsterdam," Adam said.

"And tell her you are a legal assistant on an important case in the Netherlands, where you met your fiancée," Marie coaxed.

"Ah, yeah and I'm dining with the king tonight," Adam mocked.

"Well, aren't you?" Robin said. "It's not an exaggeration. I'm really proud of you."

Adam nodded. "Thank you, father."

Robin bristled.

"Did you tell her you're planning to meet all Frida's beaus from the sights of a cannon?"

"All her beaus? She's not having more than one."

"Well, coming from the both of you, don't bet on it," Adam said.

Adam held packages as he walked with Zoey through the market district in Amsterdam. Zoey had a wrapped new dress over her arm. They walked past a candy shop and looked in through the windows. Adam drew her inside immediately. He went straight for the chocolate display.

Zoey giggled and wrapped her arms around him, when she found that pistol inside Adam's vest. She drew back to look up at him.

He patted that vest pocket. "If you take a peek inside my pocketbook while I buy a ton of Swiss chocolate, you'll see why I have a gun. Here, look." He opened the leather purse to take out some guilders.

"Oh my," Zoey commented.

"Uh huh. Yeah, we're not done shopping." Adam pointed to something behind the glass.

Zoey said in Dutch, "He wants that dark chocolate. A lot of it."

The woman behind the counter picked up her scoop and a box. "How much?"

"Just start scooping and I hope he says when," Zoey said. "He doesn't speak Dutch."

"No? Cute as a button, isn't he? Let's get him all cranked up on chocolate then," the woman said.

Zoey laughed.

"Here try this," the woman offered.

They stopped at Robin's tailor. Adam ordered a suit and asked to have more dresses made for Zoey. He paid for these and would have them delivered to Robert's house. He explained that he was wearing Robin's suits. Just make the trousers an inch and a half longer, and he could use Robin's measurements. Since the tailor spoke both languages, he asked, "Can you do me a favor? Ask her in Dutch if she needs anything else? Boots? Hats? And ask her if she is hungry."

"Ask her if she is hungry? You are getting married, and you cannot speak to her?"

Adam nodded. "That's right."

"Arranged marriages can work. Don't you worry, young man." The tailor patted him on the back.

Adam just raised eyebrows and turned to watch Zoey with the seamstress. "I'm not worried about that."

"What are you worried about, young man? The wedding night?"

Adam laughed. "I'll, I'll do my best, I suppose."

"That's the spirit, young man."

Adam popped another chocolate into his mouth. He offered one to the tailor.

Meanwhile, the seamstress was talking to Zoey in the corner. "He's a handsome young thing. Does he have the money for all of this?"

"Oh, yes to both. He is a young gentleman and works for Mr. Van der Kellen as a legal assistant," Zoey explained. "He does law things. I do not know what."

"He's asking over there if you need boots or hats or anything. I think you absolutely do. And corsets. And pantalettes. Lots of things if he's buying." The seamstress giggled.

"Where can I get lingerie for my wedding night?"

"It is the pleasure of this palace, to reserve this dance for the young couple who became engaged today. Please welcome, Mr. Adam Hudson and Miss Zoey Rammeloo to the floor."

"Oh no." Adam looked at Zoey. Even in Dutch he understood it.

The room applauded.

"Tell him I don't know how. He has to lead," Zoey insisted.

"Go ahead, Adam. You danced just fine with her last night. Lead on," Robin encouraged. "Besides, you're American. If you make something up, they won't know the difference."

"Ha! You'll know. Amazing what one remembers from when they were twelve." Adam took Zoey by the hand and walked her onto the ballroom floor. She was wearing her new pink ball gown. As long as Adam did not look at Robin, he could do it with a straight face, though he still felt as if playing a part in the theater.

"Mr. Van der Kellen, Robin, are you certain about returning to America? I could really use a man of your many talents right here," the king said to him as he smoked from a hookah.

"I am honored. However, I do have a farm and a practice to return to."

"How about this? Should I have need occasionally for a Dutch ambassador in America, could I count on you to travel to Washington or New York, to represent me in affairs?" the king asked.

"Of that you may depend on. I would be delighted," Robin said.

"Oh wonderful. Then you are not lost to me forever. Leave with my butler where I may write you." The king offered the hookah pipe to Robin.

"Of course, your majesty." Robin accepted the pipe. "Don't tell my wife."

The bedroom door was banged on. "Mr. Van der Kellen, please come. I'm so sorry, sir. Mr. Van der Kellen?"

Robin threw back the covers, grabbed his pistol, and hurried to the door. He opened it. "What is it?"

"It's Adam. Something is wrong with him. I can't ask him what. I'm so sorry, sir," Zoey declared.

Robin turned and grabbed his robe. He set down his pistol, and followed Zoey out, pulling his robe over his sleep shirt and bare legs.

Marie sat up, worried and listening.

Zoey led him into the green bedroom where Adam was sitting up against the headboard, both knees up under the blankets and his arms wrapped around them. He was struggling to breathe and shaking.

"Adam? Are you all right?" Robin asked.

"Oh my God. Such a horrific dream." Adam wiped his eyes. "I'm so sorry."

Robin sat down on the side of the bed. "He's having night terrors," he said in Dutch. "Zoey, get him a glass of brandy."

Zoey left the room.

Robin put his hand on Adam's knee. "The shooting?"

"How did you know?" Adam shook. "It was so awful."

Robin nodded. "You don't think I got those? Used to all the time."

Adam grabbed onto his arm, ducked his head and just shook.

Robin allowed this and patted him on the shoulder. "This can happen a few days after, when you are safe." He watched Zoey enter and set two glasses down on the night table. Then she lit a lamp there.

"He's not upset with me?" She asked meekly.

"No dear. That shooting was his first. It terrified him. He will need some time to get over it. He wrestled with a British Commander for a weapon," Robin explained. "And he won. Here, darling. You drink this one. He drinks this one. And you comfort him. He'll be all right." Robin stood up.

Zoey stood there with her arms folded in her palace robe.

"Zoey, the man that you love needs you."

Zoey hurried onto the bed with Adam and took him into her arms.

Robin backed off. He closed their door.

Dear June and Marta,

You will not believe where I am writing from - the Royal Palace in Amsterdam. One of the king's valets is translating and writing English for me. Hope he does well at it.

We will be leaving for home in one month's time. Robin has won his case magnificently, saving his brother-in-law from charges of banking fraud. He has the favor of the king himself, and you may take that in every way you can imagine. Frida has grown and enjoys eating applesauce and mashed potatoes. I am learning to cook Dutch foods in the kitchen each day. And Robin's older brother Robert and his wife welcomed finally a baby daughter after two boys. Lynn was so hoping for a girl. She gave her my name as her middle name, and I am so honored. Please tell Alice, if you see her, that I delivered the baby all on my own. Luckily, she came easily, though I was terrified. I did not let on of course.

Here is the biggest surprise of news for you. Adam will be returning with a wife. Yes, read that twice. Adam has fallen in love with a maid in Robert's house. Her name is Zoey, and she is adorable. She is most infatuated with Adam. They are both trying to learn each other's languages as they cannot even speak to each other yet. Explain to me how two people fall in love without ever talking to each other. But I see it in their eyes. Until two weeks ago, I never saw Adam look at anyone that way until Zoey. Well, perhaps at Robin a little bit.

Robin has promoted him to legal assistant. He has a change of status now in that he is welcome at Robert and Lynn's dining table with all of us. I'm certain Zoey is confused as to what his status is. So am I really. I'm not supposed to tell anyone, but he is legally changing his last name to Hudson. I do not know what it was before.

Hope all is well at home. Please prepare Adam's room for the arrival of Zoey as well. She is my nanny right now and hopefully will continue as such. I suppose that all depends on what exactly Adam's status becomes.

With love, Marie

In the morning, Marie was the first to emerge to the salon between their rooms. She carried Frida with her and set the baby into her basket beside the table. She had heard a cart being wheeled in, and now found the cart set with coffee, tea, biscuits, muffins, waffles and sausages. She made herself a cup of coffee.

In a few moments Robin joined her, sat down at the table still buttoning his vest.

"You could have slept more, darling. It's early yet," Marie said.

"I'm hoping to talk to Adam, and Zoey for that matter," Robin admitted.

"Did you tell him that might happen?" Marie set up coffee and cream before Robin.

"No. Because sometimes it doesn't," Robin said. "We use a wait and see approach in the cavalry."

"But he was so scared that first night. He had to sleep in our room," Marie said. "He had to be sedated."

"Yes. And that might have been the worst for him. But now it seems last night was," Robin said.

"Sounds like a wait and see is not the best approach."

"Well, we're talking about men, here, Marie. You tell a man he may have this problem and he will. On the other hand, if he doesn't know about the problem, doesn't have it, why should he worry about it? He can fight on another day," Robin said. "Very often men in combat don't get enough time sleeping to dream. This kind of thing happens much later, even years later."

"And the remedy then?" Marie questioned.

"I'll let you know when I find one," Robin said.

"It's a good thing men go to war because this all sounds stupid to me," Marie remarked. "You should have warned him there may be night terrors following that gun battle. You knew he almost passed out at the sight of blood on your shirt when you got shot. He has a delicate heart."

Robin lowered his chin. "Well, he didn't faint this time, did he?"

"Did you have bad dreams about shooting James too?"

"No. Not once he wrestled with Adam for a gun. Oh, hell no," Robin said. "Commander against valet? Oh hell no. I wanted to blow him away. And I make no apologies for it."

"Not when you put it that way," Marie said. "I don't like the way Adam's been raising his voice to you. Why do you allow it?"

"He's stretching his legs as a man. That's all," Robin said. "Did you put your little pistol back into your under garment?"

"Wouldn't you like to know?"

In a few moments Frida started crying and Marie took her into their room to change her. But that shrill sound had Adam and Zoey start moving. Zoey wrapped in her robe and scurried across the parlor to her room, saying she was so sorry to Mr. Van der Kellen.

"It's all right. Are you well?" Robin asked her.

"I'm fine, sir. I'll dress and be right back to care for Frida." She ducked into the lavender room.

Robin got up from the table then and went to Adam's door. He knocked. "Adam, may I have a word with you?"

The door opened.

Robin went inside.

Adam had trousers on and was buttoning up a pale blue shirt.

"What did you dream?" Robin picked up Adam's paisley vest and held it out for him to slip arms into.

"Oh God. Myself shot, insides falling out. You shot. James standing there laughing," Adam said.

"Nice touch, the laughing," Robin said.

Adam buttoned his vest, looking down. "Not in my opinion."

"The mind likes to fuck with you, when it has the time. Especially with one part of your life being wonderful, I believe it gets jealous," Robin said.

"I didn't think of it that way," Adam admitted. "Shooting a man does not offend you?"

Robin picked up his jacket and held it for Adam to slide arms into. "Not when I need to. Adam, he planned to use you as a shield and shoot me with your gun."

Adam started breathing harder. "They both could have killed us."

Robin took him by the upper arms. "We're too good for that. All right? You see where my arrogance comes from? Experience. Training. Instinct. Teamwork. You and I have those things nailed."

Adam slowly raised his eyes up to meet Robin's and see his mouth so close to his own.

"It wasn't luck that saved us. It was us that saved us, including Robert, including those farm hands who surrounded us. And I thank you for your first shot finding its mark. The second one, wrestling for your pistol. You already had it pointed at him. It was more effort for him to turn it on you than for you to hold it on him. We teach soldiers that every day. The advantage was yours in both cases and you took it. I commend you for it. Pin a medal on you right now if we were cavalry."

"Really? Sorry about last night." Adam looked at him sheepishly. "Zoey must think I'm crazy."

"Right after the shooting when she ran off, she was afraid you were a gunfighter. It is the mild mannered *you* she prefers." Robin tapped him on the chest with one finger. "Finish getting ready. We leave for home soon."

"Not a bad valet, Robin."

Robin shook his head as he left the room.

Robin was the last to climb into the carriage and lay his rifle down on the floor behind Adam's feet, the barrel facing away from the baby basket. Adam's blue eyes looked at him across the carriage, as the wheels began to roll across the cobbles of the palace drive.

"Do you expect trouble on road?" Adam questioned.

"Expect it? No." Robin shook his head.

Zoey bent forward to pull the baby blanket up over Frida, between her and Marie. And Adam's hand touched her back as she sat up. Zoey put her hand on the cushion between her and Adam so that they could hold hands.

"Adam, I don't think I have ever seen you so happy," Marie said.

"I am happy," he said in his breathy soft voice.

"You seem to have really changed in the last few weeks. Are you taking this all too quickly? Are you all right?" Marie asked. "You are challenged with many things right now."

"Right now, I believe, the only way I am getting through all of this is with the guidance of Robin and the caring and affections of Zoey. I have some life experience to draw on. I've been in some fights before, living on the streets. I'm not so frail. But there was no way I was going to let James shoot Robin or myself without a fight."

"Adam." Robin cautioned with a handheld out in a gesture to be calm. "If it eases your mind any, I shot him in the back, right through the heart. Mine finished him immediately. Yours would have in time."

"Doesn't matter. I definitely killed the other." Adam shrugged a bit. "Don't think it hurts my heart any that I did."

Robin thought a moment before saying gently, "You do not need to regret any of your actions that day. I regret that I did not finish them both off a few moments sooner. You and Robert were at risk. Lynn too, I suppose. Risk alone is not proper justification for veteran soldier to fire first, however. The law holds me to a higher standard."

"I fired first. Am I to expect charges from the police?" Adam asked.

"No. Self-defense is different. You as a private citizen were fully justified to shoot first with two weapons aimed at you," Robin said. "James attacking you made me incredibly furious. It was hard to only kill him once."

"Well, all of that is awful. And you two are lucky it turned out as it did. You want to see terror? You should have been delivering a baby alone like I was," Marie said.

Adam smiled.

"Incredible accomplishment." Robin leaned over and kissed his wife. +*

Robin did a bit of translation for Zoey, to catch her up in the conversation. "Zoey wants to know if you were frightened, Marie."

"Terrified. I just did what Alice Poole would have done. I hope," Marie said.

Robin said to Zoey, "She said she was terrified. But to be honest, I've never seen a stronger woman when it comes to it. That's why I married her. Well not the only reason." Robin smiled handsomely.

Zoey leaned closer to Adam, smiling. "I can't wait until I can talk to Adam. At least, I need a woman to translate for us. Nothing against your translation of course. Some things are so hard to say to a gentleman."

"I'm happy to help but I completely agree with you. I'm sure the tutor in Robert's house will assist you, even teach both of you some basic conversation in the next month. I will pay her for her time," Robin said. "I'm trying to think of what I can do as a wedding gift for you both."

"Taking us to America with you should be quite enough," Zoey said.

"Not nearly." Robin shook his head.

"That sounds wonderful. Could you explain to me Adam's name change? I don't understand," Zoey said.

Robin said in English, "She wants me to explain your name change."

"Simple, I don't want my father's name," Adam said.

Robin said to Zoey, "He chose the name Hudson for himself. He doesn't want his father's name. So, I must help him get this done legally here so that Hudson is the name he will marry you with."

"My mother used to call me Teddy," Adam said.

"You are keeping the middle name, aren't you? How else can we call you Teddy?" Marie asked.

Adam raised his eyebrows. "I should have expected that. I like the name Zoey. Never heard that name before."

"It's from Zoe, in Greek meaning 'life'," Robin said. "She may have Greek or Jewish relatives."

"We were German and Italian," Adam said. "Again, I only know the curse words."

They stopped partway along the journey, to have lunch and let the baby take some rest, at the Rasmussen's Inn. Mrs. Rasmussen was delighted to meet Marie and Zoey and doted on baby Frida. No mention of James Collins was made. And then they continued on to arrive at Robert's estate mid-afternoon.

"Robin, may I ask a favor? And you know I never ask for anything, right?" Adam asked, as they drove up the entryway.

"Anything," Robin said.

"Can you ask your brother to move Zoey to the room beside mine? If you saw the room she shared with three other girls in the attic, you'd understand. It's so hot up there in the summer," Adam said. "I don't know how anyone can sleep up there."

"I'll do more than that. She also will not need to work in the house anymore. She is your bride to be now and you're a gentleman. She can still tend to Frida if she would like to. Good practice for her," Robin said. "You and I still have some work to do. We have some business in court, as you know."

"Thank you."

"Well, it's time I swallowed my tail and let Robert know he was right." Robin stepped down from the carriage. "Boy, I don't do humility well at all."

Marie took his hand and climbed down. "Not at all, really."

Robin smiled.

Zoey handed the baby basket down to Robin and Marie.

The drivers were met by the butler and staff to carry in the luggage and all of Zoey's packages.

"Happy to receive you back home, Sir Robin," Simon, the butler said. "Mrs. Van der Kellen, Mr. Hudson, if that is still to be your name. Zoey, welcome."

"About that, is Robert home?" Robin asked.

"Yes, they are all home. The whole family," the butler said.

"Put Zoey's things in the room beside Adam's. It will all be explained shortly," Robin said.

Simon looked from Robin to Adam with displeasure.

Adam rapped the butler lightly on the chest. "Cheer up. You can call me Teddy, if you'd rather."

Simon wrinkled his mouth up and exited. Didn't even need to understand English.

The family cheered and welcomed them into the parlor with hugs and kisses. And then Robin drew his brother aside to talk with him. "In the library, if you will."

Robert held him by the arm. "No. You're not getting away with a private admission. I see what's going on here. The girl is on his arm. She is wearing a new gown. Did you buy it?"

Robin let out a breath. "Adam did."

"Right here. You tell everyone," Robert insisted. "That I was right."

"It is my great pleasure," Robin began to announce, waiting for everyone's attention. "To announce the engagement of Adam Hudson to miss Zoey Rameloo. They got engaged in the King's palace and even had a bit of a ball in their honor."

Zoey was then welcomed by the family and the men shook hands with Adam, patting him on the back.

"You forgot to say that I predicted this whole thing before you left," Robert said.

Robin nodded. "Yes. And how is you had better insight into my assistant and good friend than I did?"

"Because you are more beautiful than intelligent, my brother," Robert declared. "Just as always."

The family broke up laughing.

Robin blushed and laughed. "I could use some of my brandy now, if Wout left any."

"I've done better than that. I have champagne awaiting your return. And now we use it to toast an engagement," Wout declared. "As well as your victory."

Zoey spent some time drawn to the edge of the room where the staff were in the hallway to talk to her. The girls hugged her, and they talked excitedly about what was happening. They kept glancing over at Adam as he stood beside Robin. Adam kept looking over and finally couldn't stand being with the gentlemen and ladies while she had to stand in the doorway to talk to her coworkers. He joined her there in the threshold, reaching for her hand. Some of the cooks were men, and they shook his hand. None of them spoke English, but Adam picked up a word or two.

It was then that Robin's sister Mila joined them. She put a hand on Zoey's shoulder. "We all just want you to know how happy we are for you, Zoey. We will miss you so much when you leave with Adam for America. How are you getting on, when the two of you really can't speak the same language? I'm afraid we are all curious."

"Mr. Van der Kellen translates for us. But we are both trying to learn each other's language," Zoey told her.

"I would love to help, if I may," Mila told her.

"Oh please, if you would. Some things I just cannot say to Mr. Van der Kellen," Zoey said.

"I'm delighted to help two young lovers." Mila gleamed and then laid a hand on Adam's arm so that she was between them. "Will you get married here? We would love to have it in our church in town or in the tulip gardens, wherever you wish it to be."

"That would be Adam's decision. Where does he wish to be married?" Zoey asked.

Mila then asked Adam, "Have you thought about where you want the ceremony to be? We can reserve the church if it agrees with your religion."

"I just want Zoey's sister and her friends to be able to attend. I'll marry her anywhere she wants me to. I just know I must marry her to take her overseas with us. And I can't bear leaving without her," Adam said softly.

Mila swooned and changed to Dutch. "Oh Zoey, this man is so romantic. He says he will marry you wherever your sister and friends can attend, and he can't bear leaving without you."

"Oh, I love him so," Zoey said.

Adam smiled, ducking his chin down at that. "Ik hou van jou, Zoey."

"What is your religion, Adam?" Mila asked. "Our church is Protestant. Is that all right?"

"I was raised Catholic, but I'm not very religious. I'm happy to marry her in any church," Adam said.

"Do you have family besides the sister?" Mila asked.

"Distant cousins, yes. I'll write my sister first thing tomorrow and post it, if that is all right?" Zoey asked.

"Yes, you must. Invite her and her family here to visit. I know I can speak for Lynn and Robert, and they have a whole other guest wing they can open up." Mila changed to ask Adam, "Are you feeling well? You still have a bit of a bruise on your forehead."

"I'm fine, thank you, Mrs. Bakker," Adam said.

"You're very brave. Robert told us what you did in the incident. Robin was right to retain you as valet or assistant or whatever you are exactly. From what I heard, you played a part in saving Wout as well. How ever did you get along in town on your own, not speaking Dutch?" Mila asked.

"Ah, I grew up in New York. Every neighborhood speaks another language that I do not. I'm not afraid to try some kind of communication," Adam said.

"That is fascinating. You are very brave again." Then Mila translated all that to Zoey. Then she told Adam, "I think you are telepathic, Mr. Hudson."

Adam smiled. "Perhaps."

The height difference between Adam and Zoey was greater than that of Robin and Marie. The top of Zoey's head only came up to Adam's shoulders when she wore her boots with heels. It was acceptable now for Zoey to lay her hand on Adam's arm or hold hands with him as they talked, as long as there was some daylight between their bodies. Adam was observed placing his hand on the back of her neck, beneath her hair bun, and Robin had to warn him not to do that in front of others.

They were sipping champagne, awaiting the dinner service, mingling in the salon with the family.

Adam said softly to Robin, "Forgive me. Um. Everyone knows I'm American and do not know the customs of engagement in the Netherlands."

"Or in America," Robin whispered back.

"Or in America," Adam conceded with a nod and a wink.

"Adam, it would all be much better if you have your honeymoon closer to when we take the ship home, if you know what I mean. You should try to wait until then," Robin said.

"I will if you will," Adam said.

Robin shot him a look.

"I know what you're worried about. I do. I will try," Adam said. "You'd be advised to do it as well."

"You know, Marie said she was concerned at the way you have been raising your voice to me lately," Robin pulled him aside. "She thought I should be correcting your behavior."

"I think you know that I mean you no disrespect and I have been in a serious crisis lately," Adam replied. "It won't happen again."

"Well, I basically said our boy was growing up." Robin smiled. "No raising of voices in front of females."

"Marie yelled at us pretty good that time she told us both to shut up," Adam said.

"I wouldn't remind her of that," Robin said.

My Dearest Mother,

I apologize for how many years have passed since I last wrote you. I hope this letter finds you and my sisters are well. I long to find out if they have married and gone on with their lives.

I am writing you from Amsterdam, where I have traveled on business. I'm in the employment of a famous lawyer from Boston. I am working as legal assistant now. I'll admit I am still also his valet but that is because he will not let anyone else cut his hair. Perhaps you read about him in the New York papers, Robin Van der Kellen, the famous bank robber catcher. I'm certain uncle heard of him.

Here in Amsterdam, he is visiting his family with his new wife and child. Which brings me to the news I wish to inform you of. While here, I have met and fallen in love with a maid in his brother's house. Her name is Zoey Rameloo, and we are to be married.

Zoey is a beautiful brunette, two years younger than I am. She is anxious to see America with me and I shall bring her as my wife.

I hope you can be happy for me. Now that I see Robin and his family, I long to introduce Zoey to mine, at least to you and my sisters. I do not know if any extended family would even speak to me, nor do I care, really. I will be returning to America, or at least starting the voyage home in one month. We will be living in Canterbury, Connecticut with the Van der Kellens. I shall write to you again once I am home. You can send me letters there in Canterbury, care of Robin Van der Kellen. I am changing my last name. Please do not think that reflects on you in any way.

Your loving son,

Teddy

Adam Theodore Hudson

Adam sat down in Zoey's room, with the door to the hall open, and watched her sorting her old clothing from her new things that Adam had bought for her in the city. She was unpackaging her new ball gown and the new black boots. Adam finally got up from the chair and crossed to the bed where she had some of her old clothing.

"I have a suggestion for these." He picked up old stockings and a worn, slightly singed black skirt to drop them into the waste basket. "I'm buying you all new things. You don't need any of these."

Zoey moved closer to him.

"I understand. You should have seen what I discarded when I went to work for Robin. We may not be wealthy at first, but you will not need to wear anything burnt or worn or anything mended to the point that it won't hold together anymore." He dropped an old sweater of hers into the basket.

Then Zoey grabbed up a few more things and dropped them in herself. She grinned at him.

Adam laughed a bit. "There you go. Now you're catching on. Look um, just so you know…" Adam reached inside his jacket and opened his leather purse to show the guilders inside. "At the soonest possible occasion we will go to town to buy you more new clothing. Robin gave me part of my bonus."

Zoey looked into his purse and pushed it back into his pocket. She went to her carpet bag and dug inside for a moment before showing him what appeared to add up to about fifteen guilders. She tried to give them to him.

Adam shook his head. "Keep it. We're not married yet and even if we were, I would not take your money." He let out a breath. "I think he would have given me all the bonus if he wasn't afraid I'd run away with you here, in Europe. I think he does mean to look after me, or us. It is not about control. He has no interest in controlling me. And I…I really have no interest in suing my father for my inheritance. I hope you are okay with being the wife of just a legal assistant. On the other hand, if he has died, I'm taking it all. Every cent. But I will look after my mother and sisters of course."

Zoey laid her hand on his vest, on his shell buttons. Her fingertips came up higher than the vest, onto his shirt where she could feel his warmth and his heart beating. Adam set his hands on her waist.

"Ah ah ah." Robert paused in the doorway. "You are not married yet, Mr. Rothschild."

Adam stepped one pace back from her. "I was just helping her unpack, Dr. Van der Kellen. You will not call me Mr. Hudson?"

Robert entered the room. "Not until after that court date."

Adam lowered his chin.

Zoey clenched her hands in front of her, tightly to her stomach. The contrast of the pink silk ball gown and the brown or gray work skirts on the bed was like night and day.

Robert strolled across the oriental carpet toward the sofa at the foot of the four-poster bed.

"Is there something I can do for you, Doctor?" Adam asked.

"I believe there is something I can do for you," Robert said.

Adam straightened his posture. "I beg your pardon?"

"My brother left here almost seven years ago, a war hero for certain, a barrister, a husband. Yes. All of that was true. But that vain, arrogant, snob, yes, I say that of my brother, that snob would never have befriended and elevated in rank a young man such as yourself," Robert began. "He immediately called you a friend when you both arrived. Simon and Noud have worked for me for a decade and yet I know nothing about either one of them. If they have ever been married, I do not know. If they have friends, I do not know. But Robin does not see people in classes anymore. He does not classify people except perhaps as good or bad. But that he has always done. His relationship with you has enlightened me."

"Doctor, I…" Adam began.

"I know what you would say. I understand your relationship with him is different than his with you. But you and Zoey are to be married. Can you assure me you will give the girl a good and happy life?"

"Absolutely, Doctor, I want nothing more than to give her a good life as she has given me the only happiness I have ever known," Adam said.

Robert extracted an envelope from his pocket. He held it out to Adam then.

"Doctor?"

"Please open it."

Adam took it and opened to find a thick stack of paper guilders. "I...I do not understand."

"You can exchange them, of course, for any currency you choose. You will find 500 guilders there. I wish to supply Zoey's dowry," Robert said. "I give this to you, in the hopes that you will have a happy marriage and one day be able to get over the anguish of shooting those men outside. You made it possible for me to rush upstairs to my wife and baby girl. Do look after Zoey. Be a good husband to her. Be a good friend to Robin."

"I...I do not know what to say. I am so humbled," Adam sighed. "I dedicate my life to Zoey and to Robin."

"I know you never killed a man before. I know from Robin that it will always be a dent in your armor. You will never forget it, the way I shall never forget the first patient who died on my table. I wish to instill in you the link, that killing that man also saved my wife and infant. I know Marie delivered the baby excellently. But had a surgeon been needed, I had to get up there. You know what happened to Robin's first wife and son."

Adam looked at him.

"Well then, live well with Zoey and look after my little brother." With that, Robert walked out of the room. "Mr. Rothschild."

Chapter 15: Missed Road

Prior to the French Ship Mission:

Marie was shown to the stern of the ship, past other second-class cabins, past ladders up and down through the ship, and to the master cabin which spanned the entire beam of the ship at the stern. Doors were opened for her to reveal a dining table of twelve crewmen, and her husband seated beside the captain's chair at the head. A chair was left empty beside Robin, presumably for her. All of the men rose when Marie entered the room in her green velvet gown.

Robin went to her and took her by hand to the chair. "Everyone, my lovely wife, Marie."

"Mum," many of them said at once.

Marie smoothed her skirt beneath her and sat. Robin pushed her chair in for her and sat beside her.

"Pleasure to finally meet you, Mrs. Van der Kellen. I am Captain Ericcson."

"Thank you," Marie said. She reached for Robin's hand beneath the table. "Are you all right? You look drenched."

"I am drenched. I'm just fine, though," Robin said, so some laughter around him.

The first mate said, "Your husband has eyes of an eagle."

"And when we hand the spy glass to him, oh Lord," another seaman said, to much laughter.

They had their dinner, drank some wine and then the captain began with, "Mrs. Van der Kellen, we must borrow your husband for a mission at first light. I hope you don't mind. The sea will be calmer then."

"What has happened? We heard there was a British ship firing out there," Marie said. "Robin?"

"Marie, it's not British Navy. It's a privateer, flying a British flag. And it's targeting ships like ours up and down the corridor," Robin explained. "There is a French Naval vessel not far off our starboard. If she's still there at daybreak, we plan to signal her."

"And then what? What's the mission?" Marie sat more upright.

"Madam, Captain Van der Kellen and my first mate will be taken over to the Frenchy to convince him to escort us out of here and into port in Amsterdam," the ship's Captain said.

"Why you, Robin?" Marie asked.

Robin said to her in French, "Because you know I can negotiate with the French. None of these crewmen speak it well enough. They speak English and Dutch only."

"Robin, in a small boat? One of those row boats?" Marie questioned. "On the ocean?"

"It's the only way to talk with them," Robin said. "They're not going to come over here. This is a commercial vessel, a passenger ship with a Dutch flag. I need to tell them half our passengers are French."

"I'm the only one speaking French on board," Marie said.

"Madam, your husband will be perfectly safe. We'll row him over there and back. We'll be armed," the first mate said.

"What if the French ship is gone?" Marie urged.

"Fog is settling in. She'll be there," the captain said.

"In the fog you're going to put my husband in a rowboat? Are you men crazy?" Marie said.

Robin sat back with a smile. "I told you. My wife doesn't miss a thing. Darling, I must do this."

"Why? You can't lie worth a damn," Marie said.

The crew laughed. "Lucky wife."

"I can't lie about myself. About this ship being full of French citizens, I sure can," Robin said gently. "You cannot tell anyone on board. We don't want to cause a panic,"

"That privateer will come after us? And do what?" Marie said.

"Rob everyone on board. Kill some. Throw the men overboard. Take the ship," Robin told her. "There would be a gun battle. We don't have but one small cannon in the stern. We can't beat her without that French ship."

"Then what are you waiting for? There's still some daylight now, isn't there?" Marie said.

"The kitchen said they are making something special tonight for dinner as the whole family will be over again, even the children. We need a second table set up for the little ones. And it might be nice to have that violinist over that you mentioned. Lynn could use some music for a little peace," Marie was saying to Simon when Robin entered the dining room that morning.

Robin met eyes with her and pulled out his seat beside her.

"Excellent idea, Mrs. Van der Kellen. I will summon the musician immediately and get the other table set up in the second parlor for the children. The adults would appreciate having them in another room, would they not?" Simon asked.

"If you do not mind? We've had them running all over the house lately. I suspect that's how the vase in the stairway went tumbling." Marie sipped her tea.

"Yes, ma'am." Simon exited toward the kitchen. "Bring out Mr. Robin's breakfast if you would please."

"What?" Marie looked at Robin beside her.

"Are you running this household now?" Robin remarked. "I believe you could keep a battalion organized."

"I already do," Marie said. "Lynn is not up to running the house yet but I'm sure she wants appearances kept up."

"Thank you, darlin," Robin said. "I like the violinist idea."

"Well, that was for me." Marie grinned. "I do not get to hear music often enough."

Robin sat back with a smile as Adam and Zoey entered holding hands.

They took seats across from Robin and Marie.

"Goedemorgan." Adam unfolded a napkin onto his lap. He glanced up as maids brought Robin and Marie's plates first. "What are the plans for the day?"

Robin looked down at his waffles and sausages. He did not pick up a fork yet. "You and I go to petition the court for your name change. That should be fun, given my behavior with the judge."

"Perhaps you should explain why you required that night in jail," Adam said.

"Ah, he'll probably still throw the book at me," Robin said.

"You may begin, you know," Adam told him.

"They will bring yours shortly," Robin replied.

Marie just drank her coffee and noticed the kitchen door swing open.

The maids brought out breakfast for Zoey and Adam, whispering to her to come into the kitchen later. They also set down bowls of fruit for all four.

"Once we get a court date then I'm sure we can arrange a date at the church, if that is where you want to do it." Robin then started to eat his meal, pouring warm syrup on his waffles.

"Yes. That would be wonderful. We posted letters to her sister and my family today," Adam said. "Where are…where are your brother and his wife?"

"Robert, as usual, went to the hospital early this morning. Lynn is upstairs with the baby. I think the boys come back tonight from their uncle's," Robin said. "Listen, Zoey must need a lot of things, including a wedding dress. Marie can take her to town for that. The tutor can go with them. Marie has the money. Do you have time for that today?"

"Yes, we should get her measured for the dress. That's going to take a while to prepare," Marie said.

"You know, you two didn't really have the sort of wedding you deserved, with your family," Adam said. "Zoey and I agree, you should take your vows again, with us."

Marie and Robin looked at each other.

"Oh no. That is your day. We're already married," Marie said.

"We'll be standing up there with you anyway, if you are worried about needing a translator," Robin said.

"No. No way. You two need to be married here for your family to join you and celebrate your love," Adam said.

"Please," Zoey said in English. "Marie?"

Robin sat back and looked at his wife. She looked at him. "It's not proper here, you know? For a married couple to take vows again."

"Hmm. I know how you like to be disruptive," Marie said.

"Get the gown you always wanted," Robin told her with a kiss.

"Really?" Marie smiled.

"We'll surprise everyone. They won't know until they see it. Zoey and Adam will go first."

Adam looked over at Robin as he drove the team of Friesians along the canals, over the bridges, through the tulip fields toward Amsterdam center. The sunlight was shining and making him squint his dark eyes beneath his hat. As they slowed at an intersection and met another carriage, Robin would tip his hat to the others. As they passed ladies walking with their parasols, Robin called out, "Goededag," to them.

"What?" Robin finally looked over at Adam. "You usually talk my head off all the way along. You're not changing your mind?"

"No. About what?" Adam said.

"Name change. Marriage. All good?"

"Yes. In fact, I don't think I've ever been more at ease in my life," Adam said. "And you, I've never seen you so calm."

"Well. I'm not looking forward to this judge. Can you imagine if I'd let you testify as Adam Hudson and now, I want to change your name to Adam Hudson?" Robin laughed aloud.

"Are you going to bring a case against my father?"

"Because he owes you $20,000?"

"That's why you did it, isn't it? To get me to tell you my name?"

Robin shook his head. "That's for you to decide."

"This would be a good day for you to visit Adrianna's parents," Adam said.

By Susan Eddy

"No." Robin looked out ahead of the horses. "This is the last day on earth I would do it. This was the day they died."

"Robin, I'm sorry to remind you." Adam grabbed onto his arm. "Now you look so sad."

Robin patted Adam on the hand. "I need your distraction today. If you would."

"Oh, I have the perfect thing." Adam returned his hands to his pockets and looked out ahead of the horses. "Could be the first day you ever kissed a man."

Robin looked at him and Adam burst out laughing.

"Nice try."

Adam stood by as Robin spoke to the administrators at the courthouse, as he filled out paperwork, and then they waited inside a courtroom as that same judge was hearing cases, all in the Dutch language.

There was a prostitution case, some sort of theft case, and a number of boring property transactions. Adam was so bored he was reading one of the children's English-Dutch primers, occasionally asking Robin for pronunciations. Finally, their case was called.

The judge spoke up, "What did you just say?"

"Petition for name change of Adam Rothschild III, your honor," the bailiff repeated it.

"Rothschild and Van der Kellen, approach this bench," the judge said, searching the audience. "Now."

Robin and Adam rose. Robin led Adam down the stairs to the gate at the bottom. The bailiff opened the gate for them. Both gentlemen removed their hats and went to stand in front of the judge.

The judge gestured for Robin to step closer where he said very quietly to him, "I know you are far from stupid, so you must have balls of solid iron."

"May I explain, your honor?" Robin asked.

"No. You may put your fancy hat back on and make tracks back to your horse farm, sir."

"Your honor, I had to get Mr. Van de Berg into jail that night. It was the only place on earth where he was safe. Mr. Rothschild was missing, beaten and kidnapped at the time. It was the only way I could think of to ensure Van de Berg's safety," Robin whispered urgently.

"You wanted to delay the proceedings…. Let me understand this. You got yourself thrown into jail on contempt of court, to keep your client safe in jail?"

"Yes, your honor," Robin said.

The judge searched Robin's face and then Adam's. "You want his name changed?"

"He wants to be married, your honor."

The judge sat back and banged his gavel down. "In my office, Mr. Van der Kellen, and Mr. Rothschild. Bailiff, show them to my chambers. The court is in recess for one hour."

Robin and Adam were shown the way behind the judge's platform, down a hallway, and into a grand office overlooking Amsterdam and the canals. Midday sunlight was not shining directly through the windows, though windows were open and breezes gently swayed through sheer white curtains.

"What is he going to do?" Adam whispered.

"Shhhh…" Robin warned. "Just wait as you are."

"Sweating in terror." Adam pulled at his vest and moved closer into the breeze.

Assistants were setting up a table in the next room, jingling silverware as they laid it out. There was the aroma of delicious food that made Robin's stomach growl. Robin rubbed at his vest. "I was really planning we would take lunch and then visit the tailor today."

"Are you getting a new tuxedo?"

"Of course. So are you. I thought of buying all of the first-class tickets on our voyage home so that it would just be us in there. Marie would love that, I think," Robin said. "Haven't really spoiled her yet."

"Getting shot rather ruined your honeymoon to New York," Adam remarked under his breath. "Besides, you became filthy rich afterwards. She deserves to be spoiled."

A few moments after the table was set, the maids and butler left the chambers. Only the aroma of food lingered.

Robin glanced around at the volumes of law books lining the walls of the office. Dutch ones. Belgian ones. French law books. One was out of order and Robin quickly moved it.

And then the judge entered with a resounding clomp of the door closing. "Van der Kellen, and Rothschild, you are joining me for lunch."

When Robin just stood there, Adam remained at his side.

The judge gestured them to come with him into the next room. "Are you that suspicious?" He laughed aloud. "I had a long talk with Judge Janssen."

Robin let out a breath and patted Adam on the back. They entered the judge's dining room and set hats and briefcase down on a sofa. They took seats with the judge. Lemonade and tea were the beverages of the meal. Plates of dumplings, roast lamb, and peas were waiting.

"I apologize for the deception in court," Robin said, in English.

The judge left the table for a moment to retrieve a bottle of brandy from the cabinet. He returned and poured three glasses in the middle of the table. "You will go to no ends to win your case or save your clients, it seems. Janssen explained the whole thing to me. He said you are the most interesting character he has ever met and I am to keep my wife from ever, ever meeting you."

Adam smirked as he looked at Robin.

"What did you do to his wife?" the judge asked.

Robin lowered his chin until it touched his silk ascot. "She was a secretary at the law school. I had an affair with her before they married. Night before. Spoiled her first, you might say."

Adam burst out laughing.

"You know, I really wanted to laugh at that 'not to give me a shave' bit," the judge laughed. "But enough of all that. Why does this young man want to change his name? You know it will be binding in America as well? If you do plan to return there with this new name, there could be difficulties down the line."

"What sort of difficulties, your honor?" Adam asked.

"First things first. Why the name change?"

"My father beat me so badly when I was 14 that I ran away from home. I lived on the streets. I slept in the rain. I went hungry. I shined shoes for money. I gambled in the streets for money. Finally, I took work in a wealthy home as a valet," Adam said. "I cannot bear my father's name any longer. I won't wish it on my wife either."

"Very well then. Your name is now changed. I'll sign your papers," the judge said. "Contingent on one thing. Why did he beat you? Did you steal from him?"

Adam shook his head. He looked to Robin for guidance.

"It is a delicate matter," Robin explained.

"Have a drink and tell me," The judge ordered. They all three had a drink of fine brandy. "I don't imagine anything would surprise me from either of you."

Robin then swirled and sniffed his glass, savoring the essence of charred French oak. "It is all right, here, Adam. America is far more puritanical than Holland ever was."

Adam said, "My father caught me with another boy. He beat me so terribly that I had to crawl out. I was 14. I chose my own name. I feared encountering my father again, until I met Robin, I mean, Mr. Van der Kellen. He taught me that you can lose everything else, but if you still have your dignity, you can hold your head up against any tide."

Robin had to bring the napkin to his nose. "You are a poet, Mr. Hudson."

Adam smiled a little. He nodded. "You have no idea. Well, some idea."

"Who is this girl?" the judge asked. "After all this you wish to marry a girl?"

"Her name is Zoey. She is the most wonderful thing. You have to let me marry her with the name Hudson," Adam said, enthusiastically. "You have to."

Robin smiled.

"And so, you shall," the judge said. "You hang onto these papers. You will need them for your overseas voyage. You will need them should you ever inherit under the name Rothschild, if that is a possibility. And hold onto your marriage certificate. These are the documents of your life, young man."

Robin stopped the carriage in front of some shops. He set the brake and handed the reins to Adam. "Wait here a moment." He stepped over Adam, across the carriage.

"What do I do?" Adam said in a bit of a panic, looking up at him as their knees passed.

"Nothing. The brake is on. Just sit there." Robin climbed down and entered a store. The sign over the door said, "Kunst Winkel."

Adam looked about, watching people strolling past. He checked the king's pocket watch and then slid it back into his silk-lined vest. He looked at the two horses in front of him, their tails swishing at flies.

349 The Dutchman 2 Test of Character   By Susan Eddy

In a few moments Robin returned with a package wrapped in brown paper and a ribbon about it. He climbed up and over Adam to the left seat again.

"What did you buy for Marie this time?" Adam asked.

"This is for you." Robin offered the package to him. "Open it."

"Now?"

"If you would like, yes."

Adam looked down at the ribbon and pulled. On the seat between them, the bow came apart and the paper could be opened now. He flipped it over and opened the paper. Inside he found a package of graphite, pencils, pens, an ink bottle, and a sketch book of fine art paper. Adam shot a look at Robin.

"I thought you could start a new one," Robin said.

Adam nervously lowered his chin and his eyes.

"This one is... more worthy of your drawing skills. Perhaps you will draw some of Zoey and really impress her. I'm certain she would love that. I can't speak for your poetry. I didn't get a chance to read very much of it," Robin said.

"I'm so sorry you saw that. I'm so horrified." Adam's hand shook on the drawing book.

"I'm not. Ahm, what...what do you write about?" Robin adjusted his own ascot into his vest, looking straight ahead.

Adam wrapped up the drawing supplies back into the paper with the sketch book and tied it back up with the ribbon. "Sometimes I wrote things that I could not say. Wrote about things I could not feel. Can we get going now?"

Robin wet his lips and took off the brake. "Lopen op." The horses started forward again. Robin glanced over to make certain no one was in the road. He pulled the team away from the storefronts. "You are still very young to get married. She's quite infatuated with you."

"Thank you for the book and the pencils. Can we leave it at that?"

"Of course," Robin said.

They continued over a canal, round a corner. Robin stared out at the passing scenery.

Adam sniffled and drew out his handkerchief.

"We must set her expectations about the farm in Canterbury," Robin said casually. "Don't want her to expect a palace and find it a..."

"Ah, you sound as if you're embarrassed about the place." Adam said into the cloth as he disguised wiping his eyes with blowing his nose instead.

"It's a hay farm," Robin said.

"Well, it is a hay farm," Adam said.

"I know. But it's not even a nice hay farm." Robin gave him a quick wry look. "Not even one moat. No tulips."

Adam's cheeks had flushed, and his eyes were wet. His lips were red. Some of his color was even flushing on his throat. With a chest so thin it was easy to see it heave within his suit.

"Well, ahm, we will have a lovely stone mansion in about another year. It takes a while, this construction," Robin rambled on. "What do you think if I had bridges and fountains? A windmill perhaps?"

"Don't forget tulips. You could bring some bulbs home with you," Adam said. "You don't think Zoey would like my room on the end?"

"I think we could build your own cottage on the estate," Robin said. "I also think we could sue your father for your 20,000 and you could buy the estate next door."

Adam shot him a look.

"All right. One day when you are ready to," Robin said. "Your call. It's just that someday you may have children. Marie wants another child. You will want your own home."

"My children can play with yours," Adam said.

Robin smiled. "I would love that. I would. Adam, I just want to understand something. How can you just turn from, forgive me, from being attracted to men to marrying a woman?"

"Or do you mean from loving you to loving her?"

"Stoppen!" Robin set the brake when the horses abruptly stopped, and he turned to grip the back of the seat between them.

Adam slid away from him, and then he scrambled to get up without spilling his package.

Robin grabbed him by the arm. "Stop. Stop it. Sit down!"

Adam sat back down.

"Look at me, Goddammit," Robin said harshly. "You think me so vain that everything is all about me all the time? That's fucking bullshit. And you don't say that about me again. How can you not know me at all after all this time?" Robin let him go. He cursed in Dutch.

In the anger, Adam blurted out, "You told me maybe I would not think of you that way if I had someone."

"Oh my God!" Robin looked at him.

Adam wept and shouted at him, "I am never going to have you, am I? So, am I never to have anybody for myself? And that's how this started. But that's not where this resides now. I want...I want someone for me. And she surprised me. She came to me. She awakened something in me I didn't know was there. And she liked me when I was an insignificant valet. She doesn't even know my father is worth at least $200,000, and I'm nephew of one of the richest men in the world, and best friends with one of the richest men in New England. Except that he hates me right now."

Robin let out a long breath. He dropped his forehead into his hand.

Another carriage was approaching from behind them. It drew up alongside and the driver called over, "Trouble there, sirs?"

"Thank you, no. Just, just discussing something," Robin said to him.

"In the road?"

Robin looked at the other carriage, closed up with people inside and a driver in the front. "Yes, in the road. Thank you, very much. Have a good evening now. If you would, please."

"Well good evening to you!" The other carriage driver snapped back at him and pulled ahead.

Robin took off the brake. Looking straight ahead, he said angrily, "Lopen op. I know my brother gave you 500 guilders. And I gave you 250. I owe you more. You see, you can't run off with the girl while I owe you money."

"No, I suppose not. That wouldn't be right, to take away your chance to settle," Adam said. "Would not be honorable."

"I shall only pay you 999 of the thousand I owe you," Robin said. "And always owe you a dollar."

"Then you can be sure I will never run away from you."

"Very well then," Robin said.

"Settled then."

Robin reached over and wrapped his arm around Adam's shoulders. He pulled him closer.

This allowed Adam to fold toward him and finish his cry out.

Robin held the reins in his left hand and held onto Adam with his right. "I never know when something I say to you will be so hurtful. I am so sorry, Adam. I want you only to be happy. I love that giant laugh you have. All right? So, I will suffer until that laugh happens again."

Adam laid his hand on Robin's chest, on his vest and the shirt Adam ironed for him so many times.

"Can you love her?" Robin whispered.

"Yes," Adam said into Robin's right shoulder. "I do."

Robin thought it over for several moments before finally giving Adam a warm and lengthy kiss on the forehead, with a caress of his chin on those dark curls. "I'm sorry. I find this friendship the most challenging...but most worthy."

After he stopped, Adam sat upright, sat back on his side of the bench. He looked at the Dutchman.

Robin looked at him sideways.

Adam burst out with a laugh. "And there it is, ladies and gentlemen. This is the day Robin Van der Kellen finally kissed a man."

Robin pointed behind them. "We just missed our road!"

Chapter 16: Marrying Robin

The following day.

Adam followed Robin out to the stables where they found twenty or so men gathered in the show barn, the place where they held auctions and demonstrations. Two young horses were in the ties and the men stopped brushing them when Van der Kellen entered the barn. The men were all dressed for horse work. Some quickly set aside the tools of their trades, the pitchforks, the hoof trimmers, and leather straps.

The foreman spoke first. "All assembled, Mr. Van der Kellen."

"Where are these two horses going?" Robin asked.

"Sold to Von Maur, sir," the foreman said. "At a fine price as well."

"Very good then." Robin turned about to take in all of the men.

Adam stood beside him, confused as to why he was brought along to the barn. He looked at Robin in his fancy new riding trousers and boots, standing among these workmen.

"As you know, I am returning to America in a few weeks. When I do, I have decided to begin my own horse breeding concern in America. I am looking for two men with expertise in selecting horses, breeding horses, and selling them. They must, of course, be willing to relocate permanently to America or give me at least a two-year commitment," Robin began.

At least eight of the twenty immediately raised their hands and called out in Dutch such things as, "Take me, sir! To work for you, sir? I'm the one you want."

Robin smiled. He turned to glance at Adam who threw up his hands and paced around in a circle.

The second in command of the barn said in English, "You'll be wanting me then, Mr. Van der Kellen. I'm the one who bred these two horses. I'm the one who got the price for them. Does your brother know you are doing this?"

"Yes. This is with my brother's permission. Just a moment, I have not decided who I will take yet," Robin said in English and then changed back to Dutch. "The two men that I choose, will have to hire and manage stockmen, purchase livestock, and of course travel a bit to secure the best breeding stock we can find. And I must make you aware that living conditions will be quite rustic for at least the first year. I need to build a barn such as this. I need to build a new home for myself and in time the farm home that is there will be where these staff will live. My property in America is a very successful hay farm, but not much to look at."

That made the men laugh.

"Are there women? Are they much to look at? Pretty as yours?" one man asked, to much more laughter.

Robin burst out laughing. He remarked to Adam, "He's asking if there are women in America."

Adam smiled and set a hand on his hip.

"No. No there are no women in America. I married the only one," Robin said. "You men are fine horse breeders and you know some of the best around. You know them from auction and shows, I am certain. This competition to work for me will not be restricted to his barn. I'm taking the two best men. Since I know, you do not wish to share this information with the surrounding farms, I'll see to that. Saddle up two fine horses for me, if you would, please."

"What have you in mind for this competition, sir? You don't expect any of us to outride you," one of the men said.

Again, they roared with laughter.

Robin smiled. "As if any of you could. Of course not. It is a test of character. I shall conduct interviews. Oh, and one of you must give Mr. Hudson here, a flash course in how to ride."

"What?" Adam bounded closer to Robin. "I'm to what? Ride a horse?"

"You're going to learn to ride a horse. Why do you think I put you in those boots?" Robin said to him.

"Because they make your ass look great," Adam said just to Robin.

Robin burst out laughing. "No, certainly not. Because they are functional. Keeps your foot from sliding through the stirrup should you fall off." Robin turned to the men. "Bring me a good ride and bring a learner's horse for Mr. Hudson. Who's the best teacher among you?"

"Me, sir." A man stepped forward. "I speak a bit of English as well."

"Perfect. You get Mr. Hudson into a saddle and take him round the pen a few times while I have a talk here," Robin instructed.

"Never rode before, Mr. Hudson? You'll need a horse that takes to new folks."

Robin patted Adam on the shoulder. "Go with him. You want to ride like a cowboy, don't you? I can't train you as these experts can. Get some basics under your belt and you'll ride with me to neighboring farms today."

"Ride like a cowboy? You must be joking." Adam followed the man down the row of stalls.

Robin and the foreman stepped outside the barn to speak privately. "Robert tells me I will not be able to convince you to go."

"I am sorry, Mr. Van der Kellen. I have a wife and family here. This is where I must stay," the man said.

"I can respect that. I don't wish to deprive you of your best help either," Robin said.

"I can tell you who not to choose. You don't want trouble. You don't want ignorance or laziness," the man said. "If you are going to neighboring farms, the man you need to persuade to run your operation is Miles Champagne. He's the best around. Bit of an asshole though. It would please us all to see him leave the country."

Robin laughed. "And what farm does he run?" He could observe Adam mounting a horse in the distance.

"Vervaeke Farms. He's the head breeder. He's ambitious and smart. Don't know if he has a desire to go to America though. Another you might consider Jasper Scheffer. That's the son of Scheffer farms over in there. He's not the eldest son so is not to inherit. But he's got a good eye for horse flesh."

"You don't promote any of your own men? You do not wish me to take any?" Robin asked.

"You want men to work well together. You cannot choose two who are the best. You choose one good businessman and one with horse instincts. But choose two you can live with, if I may be so bold. And you know better than anyone what it takes to succeed in the new world. Look for those qualities. I will be sorry to see you go, sir," the foreman said. "With your love of horses, it broke my heart that your father did not leave this to you. Your brother never even looks this way."

"I should have mentioned I will need to hire native Americans to build the barn and new home. These two men must be open-minded."

"Well, that rules half of this lot out."

Robin stood at the fence and watched the trainer leading Adam about the ring, the two of them on mild mannered horses. The trainer was instructing him on what to do, how to communicate with the animal.

"Here you are, sir. Not Gris, but a spirited ride you can enjoy a day on."

Robin turned to look at the animal for him. "She's beautiful."

"This is a Hanoverian, sir, recently acquired from Germany. A dapple-grey four-year-old mare. We'll breed her with Gris, the stallion you liked," he said.

Robin moved around the mare, sliding his hand over her spotted gray neck and shoulder.

"Zware Mist, is her name."

"Yes, I shall enjoy riding this beauty." Robin moved around to the left side of the horse and stepped up into the stirrup. He pulled himself up and gathered the reins.

"I have taken the liberty of adding a canteen for you, a flask of brandy, and a pistol."

Most of the men looked on, gathered around Robin.

Robin looked about his saddle to take in these items. "What more could a man need? Thank you. I shall bring Zware Mist back to you, all in one piece."

"She's not in season. You do not have to worry about polluting her at the other farms, sir."

Robin laughed. "Good to know. I won't be needing that pistol then." He rode into the ring and brought his horse alongside Adam's. "You look good, sitting there."

"You're joking," Adam said. "I'm a cat on a roof here."

"Ready to go?"

"Now? Go how?" Adam said in a quiet panic.

The man training him handed over the guide lead he'd been holding on Adam's horse, to Robin. "Take it easy on the boy. He's never ridden before. His horse will trot if you lead her. But that boy can't stay on her if you ride like you usually ride, sir."

Robin took that lead and gathered it into his left hand. "Don't worry. I'll bear that in mind. Relax Adam. Just sit the horse." He rode out of the pen and onto the driveway.

Adam's horse had no choice but to keep pace beside Robin's, at a slow trot. "What does that mean? Sit the horse?"

"Just let the horse do its pace. It's going with mine. I'm controlling mine. Relax," Robin said.

They rode toward the house and beneath the balcony where Marie and Zoey were sitting out with Lynn.

Robin waved his hat. "Hello, ladies."

"Robin, where are you off to?" Marie called.

Zoey looked down at her Adam in the saddle, admiring him from above, unable to see any of the stress on his face.

"Off to the farm next door. We'll be back for dinner," Robin called up.

"But it is not yet even lunch. You'll be gone all day again?"

"I'm sorry, darling. I have business to attend to. Back for dinner."

They rode, side by side down the lane between farms. There was a narrow canal on one side of the lane. "Why did you not say anything about your plans, Robin?" Adam asked.

"They've only been coming to me through the course of this case for Wout," Robin admitted. "Though I will continue with law cases, I realize, it is horses that I really love. Look at this magnificent animal. I don't want to just grow hay. I don't want to live in Boston all the time and try cases."

"And get shot at," Adam added.

"Yeah, well, that is a good point too. What do I do with all of my money? Buy a ship? A fleet of ships? That is not for me," Robin said. "I want my brother's horse farm, but done my way, and in America. I think that is why my father made me move out from Boston. He knew I wanted this. He gave me the land to make it possible."

"I like it. New house. New barn. You have an endless number of acres there for a new enterprise," Adam said.

"We'll build a lovely home for you and Zoey. One day, you'll want your own home. You'll see."

"Wonder what June and Marta will think of all this," Adam said.

"Horse farm will bring plenty of available men around for them to choose from. I think they'll approve."

Adam smiled and nodded. "I agree."

Robin looked over at him and reached to pat him on the knee. "Loosen up. You don't have to hold on with white knuckles. With boots in the stirrups and knees bent, your legs are holding you on."

"They are?"

"Relax, Adam. The horse knows what to do."

At the next farm, Robin's dappled Hanoverian was the first thing that drew the men around. Robin stepped gracefully down from his horse and then held tightly to Adam's. "Stand on your left foot, swing the right over the back of the horse and step down on the horse's left side always. Always that side. One smooth motion. Come on down, Adam."

Adam Hudson did so, but his left boot stuck in the stirrup enough that Robin had to free him.

Some of the men laughed so Robin remarked to Adam, "There went their chances."

Adam smiled shyly and followed Robin from between the horses.

"Fine animal here, sir. To whom do we owe this pleasure?" A blonde man removed his hat and offered his hand to Robin.

"I am Robin Van der Kellen. Robert's brother," Robin said.

"Ah, the cavalryman?" He shook hands with Robin. "Miles Champagne. Pleased to meet you."

Robin shook his hand firmly. "Pleasure is mine. Is Mr. Vervaeke at home? I have some business."

"He's away to Norway, buying horses," Miles said. "I'm in charge in his absence. What can I do for you?"

"Norway?"

"We're looking to breed bigger stronger draughts. They have a breed up there we're looking to acquire." Miles was sizing up Adam Hudson and not quite favorably. But Robin Van der Kellen drew his full professional admiration.

"Oh. Forgive me. This is my assistant, Adam Hudson. An American. He speaks only English," Robin explained.

Adam shook hands with Miles.

Miles said in Dutch, "Terrified of horses. What made you bring him along, Mr. Van der Kellen?"

"That would be my concern. May I speak to your men for a moment. I have a business offer to make." Robin looked at the men gathering with them on the cobblestone drive between several barns.

Adam studied Miles Champagne, an attractive blonde Dutchman, about Robin's age as Robin gave the same speech as he'd given at his barn. Miles was smoking tobacco.

After the speech, Champagne said, "Vervaeke won't like you looking to take any of his men away. I don't care for it myself."

"You would be the main one in consideration for such a venture," Robin said.

"While I am interested in running my own outfit, such as you described, I'm not interested in America. Not a bit," Champagne said. "You want to start an outfit here that would be a different story. I know your cavalry reputation. I also rode with you in a few competitions about twenty years ago. Don't know if you remember."

"Is that right?"

"I was junior to you, of course. I remember you jumping hedges and turning your horse on a coin. Still ride like that, do you?" Miles said.

"When I have the chance," Robin said. "Got a jumper at home I'm particularly fond of riding."

"Looking to breed him, are you?"

"No. Looking to purchase all new horses," Robin said. "How would you like to choose them?"

"Well talk to me while I give you a tour of the barns," Miles said. "Is this a small breeding concern you are starting or a more substantial venture?"

"I'll tend your horses for you, Mr. Van der Kellen."

"Adam." Robin indicated for Adam to walk with him. They strolled through barns with Miles pointing out various horses. Adam ducked to look through the stall at a small colt and its mother. A Collie dog began to follow along with them. At first it barked and ran toward them, making Adam turn and back into Robin.

Miles told the dog to sit. And it sat right down and shut up.

Robin went on talking about the horses with Miles, who watched Adam stoop to pet the collie. Then the dog suddenly went for Adam's face, to lick him.

Miles continued to watch all of this. "Haghen, zitten."

The dog sat down again.

Adam wiped his face on his sleeve. "It's all right. He's beautiful. That means sit? Zitten?"

"Yes," Robin said.

As they continued to walk, Adam patted his thigh and Haghen trotted alongside him, letting him continue to pet him.

"Mr. Champagne, I like my brother's stables well enough. I want my own in America and I want it substantial enough to enter the competitions again," Robin was saying.

"Is that right?"

As they left the last barn and walked toward their two horses in the middle, Miles said to them, "Join us for lunch, Van der Kellen?"

"Ahm, no thank you. We have to cover more ground today. But thank you," Robin said.

Adam had not said a word the whole time, but he finally remarked quietly, "Never known you to turn down lunch."

"Can you get on your horse?" Robin said to him.

"Hold him for me." Adam held onto the left side of his saddle. "Don't hire that man."

"Don't worry," Robin remarked. "He's not interested."

Adam mounted his horse and looked about, managing to balance on top of so tall an animal.

Two other men came to talk with Van der Kellen. They were interested.

Miles Champagne held onto the Hanoverian and looked up at Adam beside him.

Adam looked bored, as practiced, though his heart raced.

"Well, good day to you Mr. Champagne. Thank you for the tour." Robin shook hands with the other two men and then with Miles.

"Again, why did you bring the boy, Van der Kellen? All he does is look at you," Miles said.

"To assess your character, sir. And it was very telling." Robin swung gracefully up onto the dappled horse.

"Van der Kellen, two years, you say? I'd like to think on it. May I call on you tomorrow?" Miles said.

"Yes, you may. Bring your questions. Come round at noon." Robin reached over for the lead from Adam's horse. Adam held it and denied giving it to Robin. So, Robin let Adam go, judging the animal he rode to be trustworthy.

"Lopen op," Adam said, and his horse walked ahead toward the road. He looked back over his shoulder at the collie standing beside Miles.

Robin followed on his pretty horse, and out at the road, reached for and snagged the lead. "Very good, Adam. Good riding so far."

"Don't hire that man," Adam said.

"I know. I picked up on it. Picked up on a lot of things. He doesn't like America. He does know how to breed excellent horses. And I do remember him from my youth. He was a bully then and he's a bully now."

Adam looked over at Robin. "Still, surprised you turned down lunch. I can hear your stomach from here."

"Yeah, well, I know the next farm better. Better lunch."

Adam and Robin rode beneath an archway that read, Scheffer Paarden Boerderij.

The elder Scheffer came out when he heard that Robin Van der Kellen was visiting. He was a white-haired man in his sixties, but he hurried out to the barn. "Well, Robin Van der Kellen. What a famous man you have become in these parts."

"Mr. Scheffer, it is my pleasure to see you once again." Robin kissed him on both cheeks and he did the same to Robin.

"The younger Van der Kellen returns home at last. I was so sorry to hear about your father passing. Is that what has brung you back from the Americas? You're here to stay now?"

"I regret that I am only visiting. In fact, in less than a month I will be returning home to America. I would have paid a proper visit sooner except that I was deeply involved with a legal case for my brother-in-law," Robin said.

"Yes, I heard all about this case. Read it in the papers. You won magnificently. Heard about the shooting over at your place too. I'd have come calling but I heard none of you were injured and your brother has another child born. You'll stay for lunch, of course," Mr. Scheffer said.

"I would be delighted. I was just telling your men my business here. I hope that you do not mind. I am looking for a good horse breeder and a good businessman to start my own breeding farm in America. I have a very successful hay farm there as it is, but you know me. Watching hay grow will not amuse me for long."

The men all laughed.

Mr. Scheffer put his arm around Robin's shoulders. "Well, Robin Van der Kellen here in the flesh. You wouldn't take one of my boys away, would you?"

Jasper Scheffer was standing right there, a man a bit younger than Robin, blonde and quiet. Jasper met eyes with Adam.

"I don't wish to part you of one of your sons, however the younger Scheffer has come highly recommended to me," Robin said.

"Jasper, this is Robin Van der Kellen. Robin, Jasper."

The men shook hands.

"Why have I not met you before, Jasper?" Robin asked.

"I attended school in Paris. Perhaps that is how I missed you. Heard all about you though," Jasper said. "So, America? That sounds exciting. You'll have to tell me about it over lunch then, sir."

"This is my assistant, Adam Hudson. Adam, meet Jasper and Mr. Scheffer. I'm afraid he speaks English. Learning a bit of Dutch as he's about take a Dutch bride home with him," Robin said.

Adam shook hands with the men.

"Marrying a Dutch girl and he doesn't speak the language yet?" Jasper said. "He's handsome but I hate to ask how he wooed the young lady."

"More than meets the eyes, it would seem." Robin patted Adam on the back.

The men laughed.

"Who's he marrying? Someone from your brother's household?" Jasper asked.

"Yes, one of the maids. Zoey," Robin said.

"He's marrying Zoey Rameloo?" Jasper said.

Adam grabbed Robin by the arm. "He knows Zoey? How does he know Zoey?"

"Easy, Mr. Hudson. As I recall, Jasper speaks a bit of English."

Jasper said to Adam, "She is very pretty and that is all I know about Miss Rameloo. You are a lucky young man."

"Oh. Thank you. Bedankt," Adam said.

"Have a look at some of the horses and then we will retreat inside for lunch. That's a fine horse you are riding today, Robin. What breed is this one?"

Jasper held Adam's horse as Adam Hudson mounted for only the third time in his life. Jasper even had to push Adam's boot forward deeply into the stirrup once he got up there. He checked the strapping of the saddle and stirrup for him, from both sides of the animal. He patted Adam on the knee. Then he walked over to Robin's horse to say quietly in Dutch, "He's never ridden before today, has he? How will he be involved in this new business of yours?"

"He won't be. He's a legal assistant and valet of mine," Robin replied.

"Why did you bring him along today then?" Jasper questioned.

"To see if you would look after him, and you just did," Robin said. "Come over to the house tomorrow and we'll talk more. Come at noon for lunch. You must seriously consider this venture."

"I am, Robin. I'm thinking on it," Jasper said. "But if you hire Miles Champagne, I'm out."

Robin tipped his hat to Jasper and to his waiting parents behind him. "Good to know, Mr. Scheffer. Good day and come over for lunch tomorrow." Robin led his horse over to collect Adam's and they rode down the drive toward the lane back to Robert's estate.

Adam and Robin looked at each other.

"What?" Adam finally asked.

Robin shrugged. "Just wondering how exactly *did you* woo a Dutch girl without speaking with her."

"Someday when I'm either very drunk or very dumb I might tell you."

Robin laughed. "I look forward to the day."

They left their horses with stable hands in the barrel-vaulted entry to Robert's home. The first salon was full of packages and fine new dresses laid out over the sofas. But there was no one around.

"I see the damage has been done," Robin remarked.

"Damage?" Adam questioned.

"To our purses, Mr. Hudson," Robin said.

Adam set his hands on his hips, his jacket open. "Well, that was enough smelly horse riding for me."

"They do not smell," Robin said.

"What comes out of them all the time smells," Adam said.

"It's a horse." Robin shrugged. "Can you live and work with Jasper?"

"That's your decision," Adam said.

"I'm not hiring anyone you hate." Robin said as the girls entered the salon.

"They brought in all our things," Marie delighted. "How do you like them?"

Robin kissed Marie on the mouth. "Very lovely, my dear."

"How was your business?" Marie asked.

Adam had moved very close to Zoey, very close, and soon their mouths met. She snuggled into his arms and their kiss lingered on into a hug and embrace.

"I think I've found a horse breeder to bring home with us," Robin said. "I think I would be good with Jasper Scheffer and someone to run the business. I'm starting my own horse farm when we get back to Canterbury."

"Well, why didn't you say so? That sounds wonderful," Marie said.

"Wasn't sure I'd find the right man. There is another who is very good with horses but not much with people. They won't work together, it would seem," Robin said. "Are you still kissing her? Adam, are we to leave the room?"

Adam and Zoey stepped apart, laughing.

Adam sat before her on the bed, his shirt removed. His arms were lean with only light hair on the forearms and his chest was smooth. He had only a little hair beneath his arms. And Zoey could make out each rib and where they ended.

Zoey was topless as well, a soft young girl with small breasts. Adam smoothed her long black hair behind her shoulders. She squirmed out of her pantalets and into Adam's bed.

He remained sitting up, leaning on one hand and arm. His other hand pulled her covers down to reveal the curve of her hip.

Then he reached over to pick up the sketch book from the table and his graphite. To her amazement, Adam sat there in his underclothing and drew her portrait as she reclined there against his pillows. She watched him drawing her, his eyes almost entirely on her, only occasionally on his paper. Zoey could hardly stand it by the time he was done. She looked at his beautiful drawing, the way he blended with his fingertips, the way he portrayed her perfectly.

He started to wipe the graphite off his fingertips with a handkerchief, when Zoey started to kiss his hands, and his knee. She unbuttoned his underclothes, freeing his erection. Adam set aside his book and crawled onto her.

The following day both Miles Champagne and Jasper Scheffer showed up at the same time, noon. The two shook hands in the salon, and Robin joined them. "Gentlemen, good to see you. Welcome. I see you know each other."

"Indeed, we do. We do," Miles said. "You're thinking of hiring the two of us? Who's in charge?"

"I'm in charge. And I'm only thinking of hiring one or both of you. One as the horse breeder and one as the business manager," Robin said.

Miles could see beyond Robin into the hallway and the dining room where Adam was standing with his back to the door. Adam was talking with someone. "I heard about the shooting over here. I didn't realize he was the one who shot the two intruders."

"He?" Robin followed his eyes to Adam. Then he lowered his voice. "Still suffering for that. Never shot a man before. Can't be alone right now."

"So that is why you brought him yesterday. Shot a British Commander. Wrestled with him for a pistol, I heard," Miles said. "He's just a boy."

"Well, part of this job, if offered to you, is looking after Adam and the women on the voyage back to America. If you can't do that, you know where the door is." Robin set his hands on his hips.

"He is not your son?" Miles asked. "He's too old for that, isn't he?"

"No. He's my assistant," Robin said.

"What's...what's to be looked after on a ship? You are expecting trouble, Robin?" Jasper asked.

"It just seems to find me. I'm just saying. So, we are going to talk about horses. Join us for lunch?" Robin said.

"Very good then." Miles followed Robin first into the dining room.

"They want to move lunch onto the terrace," Adam said. "It's too hot in the kitchen and the heat is filling the dining room above it."

"All right then. Where are the ladies?" Robin asked.

"They went shopping again with Eva." Adam unbuttoned his jacket. "Good to see you again, gentlemen." He brushed his hair back from his face, also brushing the heat off his forehead.

"Goedendag, Adam." Jasper shook his other hand.

"Hey Jasper."

"Oh. Now I know how American's greet one another. Hey, Adam," Jasper said.

Miles shook his hand too, feeling obligated. "Mr. Hudson."

"Mr. Champagne," Adam responded.

"Are you joining us for lunch, Mr. Hudson?" Jasper asked. "As legal assistant, I want to know what you do for Mr. Van der Kellen."

"Can we save the trouble and use our given names from here on?" Robin suggested.

"Absolutely."

"Happy to."

Simon escorted the men out to the terrace.

The hot summer day was shaded by a festive awning over the terrace, and half the terrace was shaded by the house. The four men were seated in the shaded area at a table set lavishly with white cloth and crystal glasses. Lemonade with ice was served along with several courses of Dutch summer delicacies.

As the first course was being served, Robin said, "Jasper, you wanted to know what Adam did as my assistant. For my legal case, he interviewed people, took notes, located individuals, and at some point…"

"Was struck over the head, a bag thrown over me, and was carried off to be bribed by the bank robbers with gold from the actual robbery," Adam summarized.

"Thus, providing the evidence that won the case," Robin added.

"Spectacular," Jasper cheered.

"So it was related to this case, the men Adam shot?" Miles asked.

Adam sat back in his chair, looking down at vest buttons he longed to open.

"The one who hit him over the head and carried him off was the British Commander. Adam and I both had to shoot him," Robin said.

"How are you doing then, boy?" Miles questioned Adam.

"Distracted sufficiently by wedding plans," Adam replied. "We have to be married quickly before the voyage home."

"Have to be married? Did you have intimate knowledge of miss Zoey?" Jasper teased him quietly.

That made Miles laugh. Robin was awaiting Adam's reaction before a laugh escaped him.

"He's turning red. I think that's a yes," Miles said.

"Well, you weren't a very good chaperone, Robin." Jasper sipped lemonade.

"Confession, the heat is killing me." Robin suddenly stripped off his jacket, freeing white linen sleeves. "If anyone else wants to get comfortable, be my guest."

"Thought you'd never say so." Miles peeled back his jacket then.

Jasper and Adam did as well. Adam could finally unbutton his vest as well.

"Guess you're enjoying your first summer in Amsterdam." Jasper patted Adam on the shoulder. "Got laid anyway. That's more than I can say for my summer."

Everyone laughed.

"First woman, was it?" Miles questioned. When Adam only looked at him, Miles said, "Glad I didn't have to marry my first woman. She wasn't even dancing on the main canal down there but one of the side alleys."

That made Robin and Jasper burst out laughing.

"Not even a word? First woman? Come on, one word," Miles persisted. "Any detail?"

Adam looked down at his cold lemonade. "Only the best thing ever."

"There you go," Miles cheered. "Now I can relate to the boy."

The Amstelkerk Protestant church built in 1600s

Before the ceremony, Robin smiled. He opened his jacket and pulled out the pocket watch. He looked at it a moment and then told Robert. "Hold out your hand."

"What is that?" Robert did so.

Robin placed the watch into his hand. "Father's pocket watch. You should have it."

"Robin, he left it to you." Robert looked at it, admiringly.

"I think you will enjoy it more than I."

"Adam Theodore Hudson, do you take this woman to be your lawfully wedded wife, to honor her, cherish her, and keep her until death do you part?" Robin translated for Adam.

Adam looked at him and his eyes teared. Having those words coming from Robin's mouth was so much like marrying Robin. This double ceremony suddenly struck him as if he was marrying Robin.

Robin waited and finally whispered, "Just look at her and say I will."

Adam turned to Zoey and said, emotionally, "I will."

The pastor spoke in Dutch to Zoey then. She responded, and then Robin was permitted to translate.

"Zoey Rameloo, do you take this man to be your lawfully wedded husband, to honor him, obey him, and keep him until death do you part?"

"I will," Zoey said.

"You are now Mr. and Mrs. Adam Hudson. You may kiss your bride."

Adam raised the lace veil over Zoey's head and leaned in to kiss her mouth lightly. And then his round eyes went to Robin before he was asked to take his bride to sign the register.

Zoey in her gown of white lace and silk, glanced at the diamond ring on her hand, and went with her young husband to the back of the alter to sign.

Robin looked at Marie a few feet across from him on the altar and surprisingly, his heart raced. He even smoothed a hand down his vest and tuxedo coat. Marie blushed as she looked at him, in her pale blue dress, a new second wedding dress for her.

When Adam and Zoey returned to their side, the pastor announced them to the audience, and then he asked everyone to stay for the second wedding of Robin Lodewijk Van der Kellen to Marie Frances Longuiel.

The couples changed roles. Adam now provided a wedding ring for Robin to place on Marie's hand. This one was a blue sapphire.

Robin and Marie also signed the registry and were presented as man and wife.

In the surprise of it all, their family and friends cheered.

The wedding reception was in a hall near the Amstelkerk, in a ball room, with an orchestra playing during the dinner and the ball. All of Robin's family and friends were in attendance, as well as all of Zoey's. And in the early morning hours, Adam and Zoey were whisked away in a white carriage pulled by four white Lipizzans that Robin borrowed from the Scheffer barns.

Adam and Zoey would spend their wedding night in the luxury suite of a nearby hotel.

Meanwhile Robin and Marie would dance the night away with easily a hundred friends and family, including lawyers Robin knew, the judges he knew, women he did not marry, and the men he was considering hiring for his horse business. The ball went on until dawn when Robin and Marie left in another fine carriage, theirs pulled by four of the dappled grey Friesians. They were taken, as they slept in the back, to Robert's estate.

Zoey awoke to roses on the tables beside their bed, to sit up looking at the small diamond ring on her left hand, and the bare pink shoulder of her husband as he slept beside her. She touched the gold chain around his neck of the locket she gave him.

He moaned and awoke to wrap his arms about her. His wedding vows had been a poem he wrote to her in Dutch. She could think of nothing else and his gentle soul.

Chapter 17 Voyage Home

Times had changed in the months since the voyage to Amsterdam. Robin Van der Kellen and his group left Amsterdam on one of the King's sailing ferries to London. They stayed on two nights in London, and then boarded a Cunard line steamer bound for Canada, the RMS Britannia. A side paddlewheel on either side of the ship and three masts would propel the wooden vessel across the Atlantic in an expected fourteen days.

Robin held Marie's hand as they climbed the boarding bridge. "Is it safe, Robin? All that coal they are loading? Look at it all."

"Quite safe, my love. Long as no one lights a cigar down there. Look it has sails too, three masts of them. If the steam engines fail, we can always raise sails, and if the winds are favorable, I'm sure they use both," Robin said.

As the wealthy couple stepped onto the bridge, the steerage and second-class passengers waiting on the dock, remarked at her lovely gown and how handsome the gentleman was, how his silk top hat shined in the sunlight. They remarked that it was he securely carrying their baby across the narrow bridge.

Behind them, Adam held Zoey by the hand, and they were both looking this way and that. Adam seemed very young and slender. Zoey had a pretty floral shawl about her lavender gown. Fearful of the walk bridge, she tucked in close behind Adam, holding onto him.

Jasper Scheffer and Miles Champagne brought up the rear, both of them also well dressed.

"How long is this supposed to take? Six weeks?" Miles asked.

Robin stopped on deck and turned to see his group all make it safely aboard. "Two weeks or so to Nova Scotia. Then we'll find transportation to Boston either by steamer or train. We're saving a month at least."

"I don't know if it's safe to travel at such speeds. We'll blow right off the boat," Miles grumbled.

"Experimental? How many of these have made it?" Jasper asked.

A crew member stepped up to them. "We have made fifteen crossings ourselves on this very vessel. You are quite in good hands, sir. Built in Scotland just last year. 115 passengers maximum and a crew of 82. May I escort your party to your luxurious first-class cabins?"

They followed the man down a curved flight of stairs beneath a stained-glass ceiling, down and around into the wooden Salon deck. "This is the fore passage. First class only of course." Crewmen opened the doors to a salon surrounded by cabin doors. "Mr. and Mrs. Van der Kellen on this side in cabin number one. Mr. and Mrs. Hudson on the other side in cabin number two. These are the largest and finest of our guest cabins.

Mr. Scheffer you will be in cabin three and Mr. Champagne in cabin four. Of course, as you purchased all ten of the first-class cabins, you may move about as you please. As you can see, dining for all meals occurs here on the central tables as well as a rousing game of cards with the captain every evening. I will let you get settled in. I trust your belongings are stowed in your cabins as prescribed?"

"Yes, thank you," Marie told him.

"I'll take number eight over here." Champagne chose to be in the opposite corner with empty cabins between himself and anyone else.

Jasper quickly looked about and said, "I'll do the same. That one over there."

"Of course. We'll move your things straight away."

Zoey followed Adam into their cabin, seeing their little cast iron stove, the two bunk beds, each just wide enough for the both of them, the chair, the two trunks beneath the beds, the desk, the wardrobe. She examined the fine white linens and warm wool blankets. She sat down on the bottom bunk, spreading out her lavender silk skirt.

Adam opened the cabinet to find his suits and some of her gowns already hanging inside. On the desk was a pitcher of water and porcelain bowl. The edges of the desk had a rail to keep items from sliding off. They had a small window and two oil lamps mounted on the wall. "This will do, I suppose. Seems like we had more room on the sailing ship. But small price to pay to save an entire month on the open sea."

"Adam." Zoey sprang to the window and climbed up on the chair to see out. "Can we? Please."

"What do you want, darling?"

Zoey pointed up.

"Oh yes. Yes. Let's go up top to see the ship depart. Come on. Bring your shawl." He tossed the shawl to her and grabbed her hand. When they burst out of the cabin, they collided with Robin. "Oh. Sorry. We're going on deck to see the ship off. Coming?"

"Ah, she's doing something with Frida," Robin said. "Hold onto her. Don't let her slip."

"I've got her. Don't worry." Adam let Zoey wrap her hands around his forearm and he took her up the stairs.

Robin paced in the salon, looking at the sofas that lined the exterior, the two tables in the middle and plush cushioned chairs around the tables. Twenty people could dine here where only six would be.

Miles Champagne emerged from his cabin and set a bottle of brandy down on the table. He selected a glass from the cabinet behind him. "Have a brandy, Robin?"

"You're not going up top?" Robin asked.

"I've seen enough of London, that's for sure." Miles poured his glass and then another to offer to Robin. "Did the little fluff take his bride up on deck?"

"There is still time to eject you if you do not want to be civil, Miles," Robin snapped. "What happened to you in London?"

"I'll be civil to the boy." Miles handed the brandy to Robin. "Just hard to imagine him swatting a fly much less killing a man."

"Two men." Robin took a sip. "You will be respectful to Mr. Hudson and his wife, or you will find yourself swimming home."

"How do you reckon this British Commander lost out to Adam?"

"Underestimated him," Robin said. "You would do well to remember that."

"Indeed. I think he'll do just about anything for you, Robin. Took a wife, didn't he?" Miles said.

Jasper emerged, saw the brandy and picked out a glass for himself.

Miles poured for him. "Not that he isn't enjoying the experiment."

"What experiment?" Jasper asked.

Miles smiled. "Nothing."

Jasper tossed back his brandy. "I'm going up top. Never seen a steamer leave port before. And now I'm on one, thanks to you." Jasper patted Robin on the arm and bolted out of the room.

That left Robin to scowl at Miles.

Servants began setting the table for dinner, laying out cloth and plates and silverware. Bowls of oranges and the glow of oil lamps soon filled the middle of one table.

Marie emerged from the cabin with Frida on her hip. "Have we moved out yet?"

"Not yet, Mrs. Van der Kellen," Miles said.

"Let's go up and watch, Robin."

"Come along Miles. You're on a team now. Get with it."

"Going up top, then."

Chilled from being on deck for the launch, they gathered down around the table to enjoy hot tea, boiled potatoes, pork roast, steamed greens and carrots. Brandy and French wine flowed liberally. Servants who would have waited on twenty, were super attentive to six adults and one baby. Two of the maids tended Frida in her baby carriage, feeding her mashed potatoes with a bit of gravy. They quickly realized Robin Van der Kellen was the rich man who bought all the tickets, and he became the subject of special attention. His wine glass was kept topped off. He was served white cake first. And then it became known that there were newlyweds among them. The white cake became known as wedding cake then.

Robin sat at the end of the table with Marie on his left and Adam on his right. Zoey was beside Adam. Jasper beside her. And Miles sat beside Marie, looking at Adam across the table, watching the delicate way in which he held his wine glass.

After the dessert, the captain and some of the crew came in to start up a card game. Robin, Miles, and Jasper were pleased to join in. Marie relaxed on a cushy sofa on the side with Frida's baby carriage right up beside her.

"Adam, join the card game with the men?" Miles questioned.

"Ah, no thank you. I do not think I should." Adam rose from his chair.

"Good chance to learn the game," Miles persisted.

"I am quite familiar with the game, thank you," Adam said.

"Then join us. Bring some of the gold coins I know you have," Miles invited. "I think you should, boy."

"I really don't think you want me to," Adam declined.

"I think you don't know how," Miles said.

"Respectfully, I must decline," Adam said.

Miles stood up. "Respectfully, you must get your ass to this table."

"Miles," Robin cautioned.

"Very well then. Don't say I did not warn you." Adam sat back down with them.

Zoey moved to the comfy sofas with Marie. She folded her arms, worried.

Marie reached over and patted Zoey on the arm. "Robin will look after him."

"Will you Robin? There's no looking after any man at a poker table," Miles said. "If you're a man, you shall have to man up at a poker table."

The ships crewmen laughed.

Adam Hudson looked like a very young gentleman, likely too fancy to know how to gamble. His soft, slim hands picked up the cards he was given. Shrewd blue eyes saw what he was dealt, and hands closed up the cards tightly.

"Five card draw. Ante up with ten pence," one of the ship men said. "You men have British pounds, do you not?"

"Some. Some French Francs. Some Dutch gold guilders," Robin said.

"They are gold? Oh, we'll take those," the ship man said. "We'll take your gold, gentlemen."

The poker game carried on as the men chatted about Robin's war history and what he did for the ship on the voyage from America. Some of the younger officers played out and just looked on as the captain, Robin, Adam, Jasper and Miles played. A particular hand came down to Miles vs Adam. And stakes were raised when Adam laid down another gold coin.

"Awfully lucky at cards, Adam. Where did you learn to play? I don't imagine the wealthy of New York teach their children how to play poker," Miles questioned.

"No, but the alleys of New York provide such education. It made a better income than shining shoes," Adam said.

"You grew up wealthy. I can tell by your airs," Miles said. "What do you know about shining shoes?"

"I call. What have you?" Adam said. "By the way, mind that rat there."

"What?" Miles said.

Adam pointed.

Miles turned and the rat jumped on him. He shrieked and stood up, jumping around.

One of the ships company swatted it off him. And the men all laughed. Zoey pulled her feet up onto the sofa, beneath her skirt.

"Oh, don't worry about those. Just play the hand," the captain said.

Adam burst out laughing.

"You shut up." Miles looked down at the cards in his hand. "Rats. Three queens." He laid them down. "You can't beat that, kid."

"I wouldn't be so sure." Adam laid down two kings and three jacks.

"Fine hand. Find hand, Mr. Hudson." The captain applauded.

The pile of coins were pushed in front of Adam.

"Where did you get that third jack? Robin laid down most of the spades." Miles turned over the cards that Robin had discarded. There wasn't a jack. "Well, how many of them are in this deck?"

Adam displayed his three jacks. "Four, like there are in every deck of cards."

"These are my cards, gentleman. I assure you they are quite honest," the captain said.

Miles turned up Jasper's discarded ones and others.

"You can knock it off, Miles. It was Adam's hand." Robin began collecting cards to shuffle them and redistribute.

Miles reached toward the small pile of gold coins when Jasper blocked his hand. "What are you doing?"

"He doesn't get my coins. I'm out," Miles declared.

"I don't know how you play in Europe, but where I come from you have to pull out before it's over." Adam collected his winnings and pocketed them.

That made most of the men laugh, impressed with his inuendo.

"Well. We've got weeks to win them back from you," Miles conceded. "I don't imagine it will take that long."

"I don't know about that. He played like he's counting cards," Jasper said.

"Counting cards? How do you do that? What cards do I have here?" Miles hadn't given them all to Robin yet.

"You have your three queens, a two and a four. And the captain laid down his two eights, the queen you were hoping for, and a six and a nine," Adam rattled off.

Miles turned the cards over to reveal that Adam was exactly correct. The other men cheered. Miles picked up the card and held it up to the candlelight. "How did you do that? You can't see through these."

"I saw what everyone discarded. There's only four of each card. It's not that hard to figure it out if you remember them all," Adam said. "It's called a brain, Miles."

"It's a trick. Give me them cards." Miles held out his hand to Robin, who placed the deck in his hand. Miles looked through them.

Adam began to rise.

"You get back to holding that chair down," Miles told him. "Here." He shuffled the cards. He then laid down ten cards and turned them over one at a time, turning each up for a moment and then face down. With all ten face down he said, "Now what were they?"

Adam pointed from right to left. "Two of hearts. King of spades. Eight of clubs...."

Even as he was still listing them, Jasper was turning them over to find them all correct. Jasper sat back laughing. "He's a genius of some kind."

"Indeed. The boy's a genius," the captain chimed in. There was much laughter. "I can remember a couple of them."

"Not all ten," Robin said. "I had three."

Adam stood up. "I apologize. I tried to avoid the game, knowing I had you all at a disadvantage."

Robin laughed and patted Adam on the back. "You certainly did."

"Never playing cards with him again," One of the deck officers said.

Adam strolled over to pick up the wine bottle and he brought it to refill Zoey and Marie's glasses, then one for himself.

Miles shuffled and dealt cards again. "Very well. Let's just have mere mortals play for a while."

"Adam, have you done that before?" Marie whispered.

Adam nodded. "All the time." He stood near the women, sipping his glass of wine, wearing a fine new suit purchased in London. When he turned, he made eye contact with Miles across the table. Miles was still angry, but quiet for once. Miles even gave him a shrug. Adam took a seat beside Zoey and crossed his legs. He sat back with his fluted glass of French wine.

"You knew he could do that?" Jasper asked Robin.

Van der Kellen shook his head. "Never played cards with him before. Never will again."

That made the men laugh, Adam included.

Jasper picked up his cards and frowned at them. "We need to take that boy to a serious gambling establishment. We'll make a killing."

Miles rolled his eyes.

"They'll probably throw him out, he'll win so much," Jasper said.

Robin looked over at Marie and she at him. Robin looked at his cards and set down a coin.

Adam and Zoey retreated to their own cabin and shut the door. Zoey put some coal chunks into their iron pot belly stove. When she rose, she stood up into Adam's arms.

Zoey wrapped herself tightly about him and looked up at her husband. "Ik how van jou, Adam."

His breathy voice said, "I love you so, Zoey. I will look after you and you after me." He kissed her forehead. "Are you okay, darling? Not sick?" He pulled back and rubbed at her belly. "You okay?"

"I'm fine. Good. Okay." Zoey looked up at him. "I don't like that man, Miles. He's mean to you."

"Miles? I'm not worried about him. If he does anything Robin doesn't like, Robin will get rid of him." Adam began unbuttoning his vest and shirt.

Zoey hung her shawl up on a hook on the wall. She turned and looked at the small bed in the small cabin she shared with her husband.

Adam continued undressing. He set those coins he won into a drawer in the desk.

Zoey turned to allow Adam to undo her corset. He helped her slip out of it. And she climbed into the lower bunk, to the far side.

Adam sat down beside her and leaned in to kiss her. He slid into the bunk with her, and let Zoey come to him, to rest her head on his chest. He wrapped his arms about her.

The following night, Zoey brought Frida in her baby carriage into their room. "We're looking after her tonight and maybe for a few nights. Let them have time alone."

"Ah, what about the wheels?" Adam looked at this carriage. He got out one of his handkerchiefs and made a way to tie the carriage to the side of the bunk.

"Oh. Good thinking. The waves and all," Zoey said. "Adam, you will make a fine father."

Adam put chunks of coal into their stove. "She's probably cold. It's cold in here, on the North Sea. You know, we can hold her."

Once Zoey crawled into bed and indicated that she would be on the side by Frida, Adam just lifted the baby into the bed with her. He sat on the foot while he removed his boots. He unbuttoned his shirt and vest and pulled them off. He found a sleeping gown to pull on over his head and then stepped out of his trousers. Then he climbed into the bunk with Zoey, back against the wall with the baby between them.

"She's cold," Zoey said to him. "How did you know?"

Adam laid his head down and wrapped his arms around Zoey and the baby. "It's all right darling."

Zoey held the baby in her arms between them. "Adam, ik hou van jou."

"I love you, Zoey."

The servers poured hot coffee into the china cups for Robin and Adam who sat down together at the table in the morning.

"How did she sleep last night?" Robin asked.

"She was cold. You know that, right? That's why she was crying," Adam said. "She didn't stop until I crawled in and held her on my chest."

"You put out more heat than a Friesian."

"You compare me to a thousand-pound horse?" Adam asked.

"You do smell better." Robin stirred cream into his coffee. "Sorry you did not get much sleep."

"No, I slept all right. I'm just not used to sleeping with anybody yet. I trust that you made good use of your night?"

Robin smirked into his coffee.

"Well then it was all worth it, I suppose," Adam remarked.

Jasper joined them and pulled out a chair beside Adam. "You've got to do that card trick again."

"I don't think so," Adam said.

Jasper set the deck of cards down on the white cloth. "Come on. Just a few cards."

"Later."

"Can you teach me how?" Jasper asked.

Adam shook his head. "If you're not a freak already you'll never be one."

"Do you remember everything?" Robin asked.

"If I can see it," Adam said.

"Do you remember everything that you read?" Robin asked.

Adam nodded.

"God. That would make law school a breeze for you," Robin told him. "I'm just saying."

"I have not decided yet. Besides, I'd have to live in Boston."

"There's a fine law school in New Haven," Robin said. "Come home on the holidays."

"You're trying to send me away." Adam spread preserves onto a biscuit and filled his mouth with it.

"Tell me again what the status is of your new home in Canterbury," Jasper asked.

Miles emerged from his cabin and joined them, sitting down across from Adam, in Marie's usual seat. "Where are the ladies? Sleeping in?

Coffee is so much better with pretty faces to look at, rather than your mugs."

"I agree," Adam remarked.

"Tending to the baby, I believe," Robin said.

"The new house? What have you heard about it?" Jasper asked.

"Last I knew the foundation has been started. That was about a month ago. The granite blocks for the walls had been partially delivered. I would imagine the walls are going up," Robin said.

"And we get to shop for horses in Boston when we arrive?" Jasper asked.

"I would start with Boston. From there we can determine where the best breeders in America reside and purchase horses," Miles said. "How many are you looking for?"

"I want twenty horses in the barn," Robin said. "Of course, we'll need a new barn and a show ring."

They all stopped what they were doing and looked at him.

"I do want the business to be profitable, but I want breed standards. I want us to enter the competitions," Robin said.

"That's going to take time, Mr. Van der Kellen. It will take at least two or three years to get a horse we can enter," Miles said. "Two or three generations to win."

"I'm very aware of how long it takes to grow a two-year-old," Robin said. "It begins with good foundations, beautiful horses. I want to enjoy my farm, not agonize over when I can leave it next."

Adam shot him a look. "Really?"

Robin nodded. "Except for Marie, of course."

"I didn't think it was that rustic," Adam said.

"Oh, didn't you?"

"How rustic?" Jasper questioned.

"It's all made of wood. Rooms are small. The windows freeze up with ice in the winter. That would be my biggest complaint," Adam said. "How hot and how cold it is."

"We can install new windows in the old house," Robin said. "I thought the spiders were your biggest complaint."

"Well, yes, now that you mention it. At least rats are intelligent," Adam said.

"They carry disease," Robin said.

"Not by choice," Adam said.

That made Robin laugh and the others were just confused.

"Gentlemen, you show a profit, and I will give you each ten percent of the business," Robin said to Miles and Jasper.

"Give me 10% of the business? Why would you be so generous?" Jasper asked.

"Because I wasn't the eldest son either. We have to make our own fortunes." Robin met eyes with Jasper.

The ladies emerged from Marie's cabin and carried the baby to the other end of the table. They were laughing about something themselves. The servers poured coffee for them and doted on the little girl.

Adam blew a kiss to his wife, and she giggled. She whispered something to Marie and even the maid giggled.

"What? Seriously?" Miles questioned. "His wife doesn't speak English."

"She said his mouth is beautiful," Marie said. "I think."

"I think so," the maid echoed.

Jasper laughed and thumped Adam on the shoulder. "He didn't woo her with his mouth."

"Or maybe he did," Miles remarked.

"Gentlemen," Robin cautioned. "It is not even nine in the morning yet."

The captain said, "I know Mr. Van der Kellen is the Dutchman of the Erasmus. Some passengers may know this as well. Some may be angry that France and England almost came to war again over that incident."

"Some might say my actions diffused the threat of war between France and England," Robin countered.

"I personally happen to believe that. But there are others who do not. Why do you think I allowed you to buy up all the first-class tickets? You might not have been so well received by the other Englishmen," the captain said. "May I take coffee with you?"

"Of course," Van der Kellen said. "Please do be seated."

The captain of the private British vessel sat down in the middle of the table.

The server poured him a cup of coffee and one for Robin. She pushed the cream and sugar to them.

"Please sit, Mrs. Van der Kellen. A pretty face would be pleasing about now," the captain said. "Van der Kellen, do you mind my asking, why did you buy all of the tickets?"

"I wanted to spoil my wife," Robin said.

The captain smiled and drank his coffee. "I do find I enjoy your party very much. Perhaps we can persuade the boy to play cards with us again? And teach us his tricks?"

"With cards or with women?" Robin asked.

Chapter 18 Halifax

The arrival in Halifax, Nova Scotia happened at midday, and the captain ordered the first class departed before the doors to second class or steerage were even opened. Robin's party exited in their finery, down the bridge to the dock together and chose to board carriages to a hotel.

It was Sunday, September 19, 1841. They were three days late with seventeen days at sea. Surrounded by carriages with the names of inns and hotels on their sides, Robin chose one with "Luxe Herberg" painted in white lettering on black carriages. Black hackneys pulled the carriages. He spoke to one of the drivers in Dutch, "Is there a Dutch side of town?"

"Oh yes, sir. And we have a lovely Inn, speaking Dutch and French for you. Dutch Village, with a lovely view of the sea. How many rooms would you require, sir?"

"Four."

"Wonderful. We have a five room Inn with luxury accommodations. How long will your party be with us, Mister…."

"Van der Kellen. We shall reserve all five rooms for one week, if that is agreeable," Robin said.

"Most agreeable, Mr. Van der Kellen. Don't you want to know the room rate?"

"No. If the Inn is as lovely as your horses, we shall be most pleased," Robin said. "Load our things, if you would. The women are cold and wet. My child is about to get quite unreasonable if we do not get her someplace warm."

"Right this way, Mr. Van der Kellen."

They were taken by two carriages, Robin and Marie with Miles in one, Adam and Zoey with Jasper in another. The day was raining heavily. They passed storefronts offering brewing, coblering, haberdashery, glassware and all manner of trade goods.

The inn welcomed them, on the edge of town with a hillside view of the ocean and had a large fire in the parlor hearth with many staff to greet them. Robin tipped them so very well that each of them had an employee to gather their belongings and bring them to a warm dry room with a hot tea, glass of brandy, and help with dry clothing from their luggage. No doubt, hot baths would be a welcome thing for that evening.

Robin and Marie's room was on the end, with wide planked flooring, post and beam ceiling, a four-poster large bed, fireplace, and six windows with views of the ocean. A wooden rocking cradle was brought in for Frida.

Adam and Zoey's room was beside theirs, a bit smaller but also with a four-poster bed, fireplace, and views of the ocean and the side garden. It had a window seat.

After a half hour or so, they all gathered downstairs around the hearth and were invited to sit at a dark oak table, with pewter bowls of seafood chowder, crystal glasses of fruit juice, an array of cheeses, hot biscuits, fresh butter, red grapes, and fresh vegetables.

"What are we waiting for? Let's eat," Marie said.

"We will be here for a few days. I paid for the week. It will take me a while to find us passage to New London or Norwich." Robin rearranged his glass of juice and teacup to the left side of his plate. "Relax, ladies and gentlemen. Enjoy the pleasures of solid land for a bit." Then he said in English for Marie and Adam, "I paid for the week. Let us relax here a bit before continuing the journey."

"Solid land with pleasure," Jasper said. "How did you ever endure 6 weeks of that? And on a larger ship with all sorts of people in first class with you?"

"They have grapes in the Americas?" Zoey picked up a handful to taste. "They are wonderful."

Adam smiled at her. "Looks like she approves of the grapes."

"Well, we aren't exactly home yet. But at least if we take a steamer south, we will nearly be in sight of land the whole time," Robin explained.

"If we travel to Boston, would we then take another steamer to New London?" Miles asked.

"That is what I must find out. Perhaps we could take a train from Boston, if you are looking for a different adventure." Robin paused after a dip of biscuit into the chowder and sighed. "Oh, my this is wonderful."

"Bet you're glad to be off that ship." Jasper patted Adam on the arm.

"Glad to be off any ship. I can't exactly swim," Adam admitted.

"Now you tell us this?" Robin blurted out. "I thought you swam in the Quinebaug river."

"Waded in it. Washed my hair in it. Well, how do you think I got my name? Fell in the Hudson." Adam had a taste of the chowder. "Three homeless guys pulled me out. They were calling me that ever since. I've had enough fish for my entire life. It is good, but I'm telling you... I think I grew fins."

Jasper elbowed him. "Maybe you can swim now."

Jasper, Miles, and Robin laughed. Then Robin translated for Zoey.

"Tell us about June and Marta? Are they attractive, these women?" Miles asked in Dutch.

"Ah, both, yes," Robin nodded.

"Adam?" Miles encouraged.

"Ah. Marta is pretty. June scares the snot out of me," Adam said. "Handsome woman, I suppose. But tougher than I am."

"Tell us about them," Zoey urged.

"Well, Marta is about your age. Strawberry blonde hair. Timid girl. Housekeeper and very good nanny," Robin explained in Dutch. "June is more Miles' age. My age. She's running the place right now. Very intelligent. A handsome woman, yes. Says what she thinks. She's...good with a musket. So, mind yourselves."

They laughed.

"Musket or muskrat?" Adam asked in English.

"Both."

Adam smiled. "Pray I don't tell June you said that."

"You don't know what I said," Robin said.

"You said June is good with a musket," Adam replied. "Goed met een musket."

Marie laid her hand on Robin's. "Good thing he doesn't know any French. He'd hear all of our little whispers."

"I hear your little whispers all the time," Jasper said. "Robin's cute little ass and Marie smells so lovely he can't wait to get on her."

The group laughed. Then Jasper translated for Zoey.

"Will Zoey and I be able to go into town alone?" Adam asked.

"No. You will have to take Miles or Jasper with you," Robin said. "You are American."

"What has that to do with anything?" Adam asked.

"This is the British colony of Nova Scotia. Halifax used to be the headquarters of the British Navy until they moved to Bermuda," Robin explained. "Many Dutch settled on this side of town, our inn keepers, for example. You will find Dutch spoken here and French. You'll need a translator anyway."

"When did the British Navy move out of here?" Miles asked.

"1818, I believe," Robin said.

"You are not to go about anywhere without one of us yourself," Miles told Robin.

"Me? Why?"

"You're the meal ticket. Anything happens to you..." Miles made them laugh.

Adam smiled and blushed, thinking back to a conversation long ago:

Canterbury, CT March 20, 1841

"I would touch him all over, everywhere. I just want to feel every bit," Marta said.

"You don't know what you're talking about," June told her. "You've never been with a man."

"I'm so curious, you know." Marta giggled.

"Well Adam will show you. Open your trousers." June reached over.

Adam jumped back, blushing and doubled over laughing. "You touched me. You touched my boy parts."

"He has boy parts," June remarked. "I can confirm that."

"Of course, I do!" He laughed until he cried and had to sit down.

"You ever been with a girl, Adam?" June asked.

"Not unless that counts."

"No, it does not. What would you do if you had five minutes alone with him?" June questioned. "And he let you."

Adam smiled broadly. His cheeks flushed pink. "I would kiss him. I often look at him and wonder, no, I imagine what it would be like to kiss him. He has the most perfect mouth. I would kiss him all day. I do not think I could stop."

In the morning, Adam went downstairs to find Robin sitting at the inn keeper's desk in the corner of the parlor. He was writing elegantly and paused to acknowledge Adam with a nod. Then he continued to write his correspondence.

Adam strolled closer, sliding his hands deep into jacket pockets. "You wish me to post a letter for you?"

"Would you? I'd like to take Miles and try to secure our next passage South," Robin said.

"Of course. Who are you writing?"

"I need these to beat us home. Pay extra if you must but get these on the first ship to Boston or Norwich. I'm writing June and another to Michael Poole," Robin said.

"When you write June, do you tell her I've married?" Adam asked.

"I wrote that to her last month. But I am telling her to get your room ready for the both of you. Also, she needs to set up Miles in the corner room and Jasper across the hall from him. That should do until we can move into the new house," Robin said.

"Yes. I wonder what Zoey will think of our first room together," Adam mused.

"Is she feeling better now that she's on dry land?" Robin asked.

Adam nodded. "I think she's fine now."

"Take Jasper with you. Seriously," Robin said.

"And will Marie be going with you?" Adam asked. "Or with us?"

Robin shook his head. "Says she will tomorrow. Today she just wants to sit in the garden with Frida and enjoy the sunlight. You can take Zoey with you, if you want. She may need to purchase some things in town."

"We'll ask Marie if she needs anything then." Adam's brow furrowed. "You shaved already?"

"I'm perfectly capable. Why? Did I miss a spot?" Robin looked up at him.

"Not that I can see. I should trim your sideburns before we go to sea again. I wouldn't want to slit your throat or anything," Adam remarked.

Robin looked at him. "No. You wouldn't. What's the matter?"

"Nothing."

"You're upset that I shaved?" Robin asked.

"Well, you have been doing that a lot lately." Adam paced toward a cabinet and looked at the fine china on display inside. He also looked at his reflection in the mirror in the back. He saw himself in Robin's old suit, black vest, white shirt, and plain black necktie. He ran a hand up through his dark brown curls.

Robin folded his letter and sealed it with a drop of wax and his stamp. He gathered the two letters and stood up. "Adam, don't get me wrong. You're a fine valet. But you are a really great legal assistant. You've got an analytical mind. You can be anything. And when I get home, you will get the 750 that I owe you."

"The $749, you will give me." Adam smiled.

Robin put the letters into his hand along with some gold coins. "Yes. That would pay very well toward New Haven Law School and a room in town. Of course, you can apprentice in my office."

"You know, I have not decided yet. But I do appreciate that you have confidence in me to do this," Adam said.

"Oh, I have absolute confidence that you can post these letters." Robin patted him on the arm and moved past him toward the dining room. "No fancy vest or ascot today? You look quite plain."

Adam let out a breath. He pocketed the letters and the coins. "Thought I would blend in."

Miles came from the stairway and met Robin at the dining room door.

"You're with me today," Robin said.

"Yes, sir, Captain Van der Kellen," Miles mocked. "And what is our mission today?"

"Securing passage home, and a case of brandy, case of wine…." Robin walked in and took a seat. "I'll have a lot of money on me to purchase the tickets, so I need your accompaniment."

Miles demonstrated the pistol under his jacket. "Read your mind."

Adam lowered his chin, following them to the table. He waited to see where they took their seats.

Robin pointed at the chair across from him. "Adam. Sit. There's something else I need you to do. In the Dutch village you need to find some good Dutch-English books. This is likely the last chance to find any for yourself, Zoey, and well one day for Frida."

"Oh. Good point. Yes, I was going to find some books written in Dutch, maybe poetry or something. I can learn from those as well." Adam sat across from Robin.

"Borsten, benen, lippen…." Miles began listing female body parts.

Robin burst out laughing.

"Well, the boy won't get those from a children's primer," Miles said. "Just furthering his education."

"Je bent een eikel," Adam said to Miles.

"Yes, don't be a jerk," Robin echoed.

"I don't mean anything by it," Miles said. "He wants to read poetry to his girl. I get it."

"He writes his own. Did you know that?" Robin said. "And he draws very well."

"Very impressive. If his daddy wasn't rich, he'd never make a living," Miles said.

With that Adam stood up.

"Adam…"

Hudson almost walked out.

"As a matter of fact, he could make a very good living as a lawyer," Robin said.

"My daddy is rich, but he never gave me a dime," Adam shot back. "Klootzak."

Miles looked up at him. "Very well, kid."

The women came down then, Marie with Frida in her arms and Zoey carrying the basket.

Adam looked flushed. He was still standing with his chair pushed back.

"Robin, you were up early," Marie said. "Where are you off to?"

"Miles and I are going to the docks to make our next travel arrangements. Adam wants to take Zoey for some shopping nearby." Robin and Miles stood up for the women.

Then everyone sat down, including Adam, though he would not look at Robin.

Jasper arrived and breakfast was set out on the table for them, pancakes, muffins, sausages.

"I swear Miss Marie, you are prettier every day," Miles said.

"Well thank you." Marie smiled.

"Jasper, you are to look after Adam and Zoey today in town. Translate for them," Robin said.

"Good. I was going to post a letter home to my family that I'm still alive," Jasper said.

"Excellent. Adam is posting some letters for me," Robin said.

"You know, you forgot to write to your brother," Adam said.

"You're right. Ahm. Before we leave Halifax, I will write him," Robin agreed. "I need you to remind me of such things."

"Don't patronize me," Adam snapped.

The tilt of Robin's head changed, and he looked across the table at Adam. "Before we go, I will have a word with you."

"Just have a word with me here." Adam shrugged.

"Why did you just rip into me?" Robin questioned. "You are quite insolent today."

"You let Miles rip into me," Adam said.

"What is this?" Marie asked. "Who's mad at who?"

Adam sat back and folded his arms.

Miles just sipped his coffee and returned to eating.

Robin returned to eating.

"Miles, would you like to catch me up here?" Marie asked.

"I was teasing the boy. Didn't mean no harm. All right, Adam?" Miles said. "I don't know anything about your father and you. Figured you for a gentleman. Gentlemen like Robin, Jasper, and yourself, come from money. I figured. I work for a living."

"And you answer to Robin," Adam said. "And Robin said he would not hire you unless I agreed. So, I agreed."

"Against your better judgment?" Miles asked. "You whine like a rich boy."

"Miles," Robin finally cut him off. "That is enough."

Adam's chin was down such that his bangs hid his eyes. Zoey slid her hand into his beneath the table. She leaned closer and kissed his cheek, making him almost smile a bit. She kissed his ear, and he did smile.

"Technically," Jasper spoke up. "I said I wouldn't work with you. Then Robin opened his purse and changed my mind."

"Is that right?" Miles nodded. Then he laughed. "All right. Look. I apologize, Adam. When you all make money off this horse business, you'll have me to thank for it. Just remember how long it takes to grow two- or three-year-olds. Until then, we are spending money."

"My money," Robin added. "And for that, no fighting."

Adam held hands with Zoey and walked down the street toward Dutch Village. Zoey wore a coat over her black velvet gown with floral skirt.

Jasper followed them. "What's with the plain suit today? Where are your silks?"

"Didn't feel like getting beat up today," Adam replied lightly. "This town is quite plain."

"Well, I liked your matching vest and ascot. Didn't think you smell like a whore at all."

Adam turned on him.

Jasper play punched him in the stomach. "Just like a regular girl."

Adam laughed and wrenched Jasper's arm behind his back.

Zoey stepped away from the boys, laughing.

They returned to walking, three-wide now with Adam in the middle.

"What do you know about this Constable Poole?"

"Oh he's Robin's friend. Older than Robin. Helped him catch the bank robbers so Robin gave him a share of the fortune. If you thought Miles was rough, just wait," Adam said. "Poole will size Miles up in one glance and call him a dandy or something."

"Miles a dandy? What will he think of me?" Jasper said.

"Well, you are a dandy so what of it?" Adam said.

Jasper laughed. "Indeed. True enough. Not as much as you are."

Adam smiled and nodded easily. "Not even close."

They posted letters. They purchased books and soaps and lavender water. Adam purchased aftershave lotion after Jasper approved of it. Jasper purchased tobacco after Adam approved of it. They sat down at a café in town for lunch.

"Did you bring me along just to carry your purchases?" Jasper rolled up a tobacco cigarette.

"Of course not," Zoey told him. "You will look after him, won't you?"

"I will. But for the record, he looks after himself pretty well," Jasper said to Zoey.

"Oh look, they have those pastries Robin loves. Let's bring him a dozen," Adam said.

"Sorry you pissed him off this morning?" Jasper lit the cigarette.

"I pissed him off?" Adam said. "You think Robin is angry with me?"

"Oh yeah."

"Oh my God." Adam looked out the window. "We must get back and wait for him."

"Have your lunch first." Jasper gave the cigarette to Adam.

"But he's...angry with me." Adam most surprisingly, puffed on the tobacco.

"And starving your wife won't help that any," Jasper said. "Does she know about you...and him?"

Adam met his eyes across the table. "I don't know about me and him." He dragged on the cigarette.

Their lunch arrived, seafood chowder, biscuits, fried fish, and tea.

"What did you say? He was happy until you said something," Zoey told Jasper.

Adam looked down at his plate and bowl. He let out a long sigh. "Why is it always fish?"

"Why can't all of you just let him alone? He has such a great smile when he's happy. He laughs so. Why is it so easy to be cruel to him?" Zoey said.

"All I did was tell him he angered Robin this morning," Jasper said. "Don't worry. Robin won't hold it against him for more than a moment. So go ahead and cheer him up."

Zoey kissed her husband.

Jasper stole back his cigarette.

But Adam was sad. He ate his chowder because he was hungry, after not eating much breakfast.

And then they walked back to the inn, carrying their purchases and a dozen pastries from the Dutch bakery. Zoey took care of Frida for a while, letting Marie take a nap in a lounge chair on the terrace. Adam stretched out on another lounge chair.

By dinner time, Robin and Miles were not back yet. They ate without them. The kitchen would save some food for them.

Adam looked at his pocket watch again. Then he looked at Jasper. "Stay with them." He went upstairs and retrieved his silver pistol. He verified it was loaded, picked up his reloading supplies, and went downstairs with that pistol tucked into his belt.

"Jesus, Adam." Jasper saw the gun. "How American."

"They're late." Adam smoothed his jacket over the pistol. "Do you think you should go look for them?"

"I think he told me to look after you and the girls," Jasper said. "Maybe they found a poker game."

"With regular men?" Adam said.

"Well, there aren't any here," Jasper remarked. "That's the gun you killed that British officer with?"

"What of it?" Adam said.

Adam paced after supper. At the sound of every carriage on the road, he looked through the corner of the window.

"Adam, have a seat before you make the women nervous," Jasper suggested. "You don't drink much, do you?"

"No, I don't," Adam said.

"Have one drink and relax," Jasper suggested. "Just one. Come here."

Adam followed Jasper back into the kitchen.

Jasper poured himself a small glass of brandy. He poured another for Adam. "May I ask you one really offensive question?"

"Is there some reason you feel compelled to?" Adam asked.

"You talk just like Robin. But don't think I mind it. I just wonder something about you. Wonder if you might consider...an option. Wonder if you know you even have options." Jasper laid a hand on Adam's chest, but not in a manly pat, more of a feel of his heartbeat.

They looked at each other.

"You know, occasionally." Jasper smoothed his hand up Adam's throat and into his hair. "Relax. Your heart beats as if you are running."

Stunned, Adam turned away from him and sipped the brandy.

"Are you offended?"

"No. I don't know what you mean."

"All right. That's all right." Jasper glanced to see that they were alone in the dining room. He stepped in close behind Adam and slid his hand onto his shoulder. "If you change your mind, you won't be sorry."

Adam moved around the table from him.

"Robin is incredible..." Jasper said. "Is he ever...."

Adam laughed out loud. "No. Not in the least. Try that with him and he'll punch you."

"Punched you, did he? I don't think so," Jasper said.

"I was never stupid enough to come on to him," Adam said.

Jasper put his hands up. "I think they're here. I hear horses."

"I guess you would know." Adam returned to the parlor to look out the window. "They are here." He pulled open the front door and went out to the carriage.

Robin and Miles were laughing. Miles handed a case of wine down to Adam. "Can you handle this, boy?"

"I have a name, or are you too drunk to remember?" Adam held the case in his arms.

Jasper came out to take another case from Miles.

Robin climbed down from the carriage and went up front to tip his driver.

Miles came down with a case of brandy. "We're not drunk. We just...found a nice Dutch tavern to make use of."

"Carry them inside. They're heavy now," Robin urged.

The carriage moved away toward the barn around back.

Marie held the door open for the men to carry their cases inside. "How did it go, Robin? When do we go home?"

"We leave on another steamer for Boston on Saturday," Robin said. "From there, we will have to find a train South. Apparently, the trains are faster than a steamboat going around the horn of Cape Cod." He kissed Marie on the mouth. "You remember the map."

"Hmmm. You have had a few," Marie told him, sliding into his arms. "Can we get a train from Boston to Norwich?"

"I don't know if the Worchester to Norwich rail line is complete yet, or a line from Stonington to Norwich. Remember the Millers had to take a stagecoach from Worchester to New Haven," Robin said. "Of course, that was a year ago. They tell me there is one from Boston to Stonington."

"Stagecoach? I've heard about the American stagecoach, and the wagon trains," Miles teased.

"Excuse me, sirs, will you be wanting any supper tonight?" One of the maids asked.

"Oh. No. I'm sorry that we dined in town," Robin said.

"We have the pastries from town then. Perhaps you will all want a dessert."

"Pastries?" Robin said.

Zoey explained that Adam found them in town.

"I will serve them in the parlor for you," the maid said.

Robin sat down beside Marie and picked up his daughter from her basket. He cuddled her up to his chin and kissed her curls. The little girl held onto daddy by his long hair.

"Had any trouble in town?" Jasper asked Robin.

"No. None at all. Did you?" Robin asked.

"We were just fine. Zoey found books for them and for Frida," Jasper told him.

Miles had opened another bottle of brandy and poured a glass for Robin first. "Here, I'll set this on the table for you."

"Thank you," Robin said.

Miles poured one for himself, one for Jasper, and then looked at Adam. Seeing the bulge of a gun in Adam's belt, he poured one for Adam too but met eyes with him as he gave it to him.

They all sat down together, enjoyed plates of Dutch pastries. Robin shared his dessert with the baby.

"Adam walk with me, while they hitch up the horse."

"Yes, of course." Adam walked with him out through the picket fence the next morning, toward the hilltop overlooking the sea below. Adam walked beside him, silently, his hands in the pockets of his wool overcoat.

"It's definitely fall again. You can feel it in the air, here in the North. We'll have another month of almost summer down in Connecticut," Robin said.

"Weather? You're that angry with me that you begin with the weather?" Adam questioned.

"I'm not angry with you at all. I just don't understand what's happening with you. Thought you were just coming of age a bit and standing your ground more. That would be one thing." Robin's hair was tossed in the breeze. He had to turn facing the breeze and let Adam put his back to it to see each other. And then Adam's bangs were in his face.

Adam held out a black ribbon.

"Oh. Thank you." Robin took the ribbon to tie his hair at the base of his neck. "Zoey's?"

"No. It's one of yours. You never seem to remember one yourself," Adam said.

"All right, here's the deal. I won't have you yelling at me anymore in front of Miles or Jasper. As a Captain, nobody yelled at me in front of another person unless he outranked me. And I won't have it in business either," Robin said firmly. "In private, out here, yell all you want. I likely deserved it."

"I am sorry. I will hold my tongue from now on. I really never meant disrespect to you. You know that, don't you?" Adam said.

"You said I patronized you," Robin said. "I just don't know if you're my valet or what now? You don't want to remind me of things a valet would do and yet you hand me a hair ribbon."

"Is that why I don't do your shave for you?" Adam asked. "You don't want me to be your valet anymore?"

"I think you are quite more than that and I didn't want to demean you by asking you to groom me," Robin said. "I'm perfectly capable."

"Am I not better at it?" Adam lowered his eyes to the ground. "Your boots need blacking. You see? I'm neglecting you."

Robin looked down at his boots. "They're fine, Adam. When I went to town with Miles, you know that I carried good deal of money on me. I needed him as a guardian. He's bigger than me and rather imposing. I needed you to look after Zoey and Marie. You know that, right?"

"I don't care if you went to town with Miles, went to a tavern with him afterwards. I don't care. I have done that with you many times in Amsterdam," Adam said.

"I didn't say you were jealous," Robin said.

"I didn't say I was jealous," Adam said.

Robin looked at him with a bit of a smirk. "Come on. You're my best friend in the world, no matter how many companions I acquire."

That made Adam shrug. "I guess that will have to do."

"Have to do? Don't you think I'm a bit jealous that you took a wife? You didn't even tell me you liked women," Robin said. "Could have at least told me you are attracted to both."

"How was I supposed to know?" Adam said. "Then she kissed me."

"Kissed you? All right."

"And then opened my trousers," Adam said.

"Where did that happen?"

"In this little storage room off the laundry." Adam smiled.

"In my brother's house? By the laundry?" Robin nodded. "And you went all the way?"

"I can't imagine it could get any further."

Robin burst out laughing.

"But I pulled out that time, remember? It was that night in the palace that I couldn't manage that anymore," Adam said. "Seems to me that women come to a climax as well."

"Adam, you are a natural Casanova, and you didn't even know it," Robin said. "Most grown men go their whole lives without figuring that out."

"Not you, of course," Adam remarked. "I feel sorry for most women then."

"I happen to have a very good way with women." Robin nodded. "Do you want me to say anything to Miles? I thought you took care of him much the way you did Michael Poole, especially with that poker trick. He likes you. As a matter of fact, his opinion of you changed back in Amsterdam when he found out you shot two men."

"I don't take that as a compliment." Adam asked.

"Have you started that new drawing book?" Robin started to walk them back toward the inn.

"Yes. You were right. Zoey is a beautiful thing to draw. She takes off her clothing and lets me draw her."

Robin stumbled a bit in the grass and Adam caught him by the arm.

"Easily shocked, are you not?" Adam teased him. "I would have thought a Cavalry man would have seen a few naked women around the world."

"Oh, I've done more than see them. Just keep that book hidden away, all right? I have to look her in the eyes."

"Zoey likes my drawings of you," Adam said.

"She's seen those?" Robin said. "Are you...are you all right with Zoey? In general, and here alone for a bit?" Robin asked.

"Yes, of course. She can speak to the Dutch staff at the Inn. None of us can speak to the French without Marie here."

"And you're happy? With her?" Robin stopped him and turned him to look into his blue eyes.

Adam nodded. Then he smiled so bashfully.

"All right." Robin messed up his hair as he pushed him away. Adam stumbled ahead, laughing.

Chapter 19 The Storm

That evening a Nor-Easter rolled in, bringing heavy rain and winds to Halifax. Marie, Zoey and Frida had gone up to bed but there was something about the wind that made Robin concerned. He asked the men to stay up with him, and they were not drinking wine or much brandy that night.

The howling of the winds after dark became unnerving. Something hit the side of the house.

"You know, we are right on the coast. There is nothing to block the winds from the ocean here," Miles remarked.

Their inn keeper entered the dining room where the men were gathered. "No need for concern, gentlemen. We get these all the time.

We are closing the shutters. Have some brandy and relax if you will."
He went out the back door with the stock men.

Robin stood up from the table. "The upstairs shutters need to be closed from the inside." He gestured to Adam to follow him. But Miles and Jasper came along to close the ones in their rooms and the empty room as well.

"What is it, Robin?" Marie sat up in bed.

"The wind is quite bad out. We are closing the shutters. Perhaps you should put a dress on and have supplies for Frida ready in her basket just in case," Robin said.

"In case of what?" Marie slid bare feet to the floor and stood up.

"In case we must spend the night downstairs where there is more shelter." Robin moved from window to window to open each and pull the outside shutters over and latch them.

"Tell Zoey," Marie said.

"This room in particular is exposed. In case we lose the roof or a window, get everything into the chests or wardrobes to protect them," Robin said.

With just one quick knock on the door, Adam entered their room.

Marie had to grab her robe and pull it on.

"Zoey is getting dressed. She's worried." Adam went right to a window Robin hadn't done yet and worked on it.

And then the winds got even worse.

It took both Adam and Robin to get the last window shuttered and closed.

Something terribly loud crashed outside behind the house. And then there seemed to be a lot of commotion downstairs. The travelers met in the upstairs hallway.

"Women stay in the house and get downstairs with Frida. I think they lost part of their barn. Grab your coats gentlemen." Robin grabbed onto Adam. "I need you to stay in the house and look after the women."

"I can help you," Adam protested.

"Panicked horses and livestock are not for you. Stay here and protect the women," Robin insisted.

Marie retrieved Robin's coat for him and held it up for his arms.

"I'm counting on you, Adam." Robin donned the coat and ran down the stairs with Miles and Jasper.

Outside, in a flash of lightning, Robin saw that half the barn had come down. Stockmen were yelling in French and Dutch. Maids were running from their lodgings toward the main house.

The woman of the house was calling to the girls to hurry. To Robin, Miles, and Jasper, she said, "Get in the house. It's not safe out here."

"Get in the house, madam." Robin physically moved her into the doorway before he and his men ran toward the barn.

"We may lose the whole thing! Get these horses to the neighbors!" the man of the inn was shouting in Dutch.

Robin entered part of the barn and grabbed rope off the wall. He tossed a rope to Miles but ran toward a rearing horse with his, making a lasso out of it.

"Good God, Robin. Watch that animal!" Miles hurried around debris. They could hardly see inside the barn, but they could hear the horses in distress, their cries and poundings they made were louder than the wind.

In the fallen debris of the southeast part of the barn, stockmen were trying to free an injured horse.

Robin and Miles lassoed the panicked horse. Jasper brought an apron over to wrap over the animal's eyes and pull his head down. It took the three of them to lead the horse out of the barn.

The man of the Inn yelled to them. "Cross the field there. Neighbor's barn."

"I've got this one!" Jasper replied, taking the horse by Robin's rope and the apron. He was able to lead the horse into the field.

Robin and Miles went for the next horse, trapped in its stall.

The maids started making hot coffee and heating soup in the kitchen fireplace. Marie said to them in French, "Is there a root cellar?"

"Yes, it's over there."

"We need to prepare it in case we all must spend the night there," Marie said. "Show me."

Zoey had Frida in her arms.

"Adam come with me. Zoey stay right there," Marie ordered.

Adam followed her to the back of the house and carried a lamp for her down the stairs into the root cellar. It was large enough, with crates around the outside and stacks of potato and vegetable sacks, bushels of apples, barrels of beer and wine.

They both began clearing the center of the cellar, making room for mattresses.

"Don't move those. I've got them." Adam stopped her from moving crates. "Tell the maids to bring down mattresses. I'll get dry clothing for our men when they return."

"Good thinking, Adam."

A gunshot rang out. Or was it thunder?

"Oh my God. What was that?" one of the maids said.

"Stay in the house. Stay calm." Adam moved toward the door and opened it a crack to peek out. In the lightning, he could make out Robin's coat dashing toward him. Three men were behind him.

Adam opened the door when they arrived.

Robin, Miles, Jasper, and the inn keeper entered, wet completely and out of breath.

"What was that shot?" Adam asked, taking Robin's heavy wool coat from him.

"Horse didn't make it," Robin said. "The storm's getting worse out there. You should see how dark the clouds are, and they're coming this way."

Marie started to unbutton Robin's jacket. "Adam has dry clothing for all of you in the next room. We have the cellar ready to take shelter in. Hot coffee and soup ready for you downstairs."

The inn keepers talked to each other in Dutch, the man telling the woman what happened outside, that their guests saved the rest of their horses, two cows, the goats, and most of the chickens. Even their dogs were in the house now. The stockmen were finishing up outside.

Robin, Jasper, and Miles all went into the salon to find their clothing laid out on the sofas. Shivering and dripping wet, they each stripped down by the light of one oil lamp. They toweled mostly dry and hurried to put on dry clothes.

Adam started collecting wet clothing and hanging it on the dining room chairs.

Robin followed Marie down the narrow stairway into the transformed storm shelter. There were two oil lamps and three mattresses laid together in the center with quilts and blankets. The surrounding walls provided numerous crates and barrels for seating. And each person who came down was handed a cup of hot coffee.

Zoey was already cozy in a corner with Frida on her lap.

Marie sat beside her and took the baby into her arms. "I have her for a while. Have some coffee dear."

Robin suddenly felt tall in this room, ducking, and took his seat beside Marie, warming both his hands on his hot coffee cup.

Miles and Jasper took seats. Maids handed them bowls of soup and spoons.

Robin had to set his coffee cup down on a barrel between himself and Miles, to accept his bowl of soup. His long hair dripped wet down onto a towel about his neck.

Now the maids were distributing bread and pastries.

"I don't know how to thank you gentlemen." The man of the inn came down. He accepted his coffee and sat across from Robin. "I would have lost all my stock for certain, and my boys could have been killed in that barn, if not for you. I am overwhelmed." The man wept.

"I did not realize these are your sons," Robin admitted.

"Yes, sir. They're my boys."

"You're in luck. You had three of the finest horsemen in Amsterdam at your service," Miles said.

"And we are happy to do what we can, sir," Jasper added.

"We are still here until Saturday. We'll see what we can do to help with the clean up," Robin added.

"Your kindness overwhelms me. I so regret you do not have fine beds to sleep in tonight," the man said.

"Hopefully we will all return to our beds tomorrow night," Robin said.

They heard the house creaking above them.

Adam looked upwards, shoulders up.

Once the stockmen changed into dry clothes and came downstairs, with the two dogs, everyone was safely below ground. There were even axes and shovels leaning by the stairway, just in case.

Adam stood up and moved toward Robin to hand his briefcase to him. "Look inside. I think you'll feel better about this."

Robin unlatched the case and looked in to find his British pistol, his purse of a large amount of money, and two bottles of brandy. Adam's pocketbook was in there as well. Robin smiled. "You are a genius, Mr. Hudson." He pulled out the brandy.

Adam took the case to store it safely beside Frida's basket.

Robin opened the brandy and first offered it to Adam, who politely refused.

Marie held out her empty coffee cup. "Am I invisible, Robin?"

That made everyone laugh.

Robin laughed as he poured a splash into her cup. "Sorry darling." He then poured for Miles, Jasper, and himself before passing it to the inn keeper and the stock men.

They enjoyed their hot soup, sipped brandy and coffee as the storm raged overhead. There were some loud crashes, but as the night hours went on, the winds began to lessen just a bit.

In the center of the row of three mattresses, Marie and Zoey laid down on either side of Frida. Robin lay down behind Marie. Adam took his place behind Zoey. "Crowd in now. Don't be shy. We all need some sleep before a lot of work in the morning," Robin said. "In times of emergency one must forgo silly conventions."

Miles let out a sigh and laid down behind Robin, at one end of the mattresses.

Jasper crawled in close behind Adam. And behind him the inn keepers took places, the maids. The stockmen curled up in the corner. The dogs slept at the stockmen's feet.

One oil lamp remained burning.

Robin's arm around Marie had his hand on baby Frida, where it met Zoey's. He withdrew his. She withdrew hers.

Adam wrapped his arm around Zoey and folded behind her. He felt Jasper's knee against him, and Jasper's hand on his back, but he did not mind.

In the middle of the night, Marie had to nurse Frida, but no one knew except for Robin. They moved the baby between them.

Adam awoke to a hand up the back of his shirt. He sighed a little. Zoey kissed him. He squeezed her hands in his and kissed them. Then he lifted his head.

Jasper's hand massaged his back, and it did feel good, though it was a heavier hand than that of a woman's.

Adam laid his head back down.

Jasper's hand slid slowly around Adam's stomach and stayed there for a while.

Adam had both of Zoey's hands in his. He started to doze off again, feeling warm and sleepy.

Jasper felt Adam breathing and he did smell a bit like lavender but also a bit like Robin's bergamot aftershave. His stomach was flat. Jasper could feel his ribs and his hip. He was still like an adolescent, just a little hair beneath his arms and a little in his trousers.

Adam lifted his head again. He inhaled sharply.

Jasper withdrew his hand. He gave him a little feel of his backside and then laid his head down to sleep. He folded his hands between them.

Adam let out that breath. He rolled onto his stomach and desperately sought thoughts that did not make him aroused. In the lamplight he could see Robin's head beside Marie's. That did not help to lay so close to the man he desired so.

Zoey whispered to him, "Dream?"

Adam nodded.

She hugged him close.

When others began to get up in the morning, Adam scooted away from Jasper and helped Zoey to her feet. They both sat on the crates and let Robin through to go upstairs with the inn keeper and Miles to survey the damage. The stockmen followed them up.

That's when Adam shoved Jasper and took his foot out from beneath him, hard enough that he fell down on the mattress.

"Jasper? Are you all right?" Marie turned to see him down.

Jasper laughed it off. "Tripped. How stupid of me." He looked up at Adam.

Zoey looked at Adam, though to her credit, she said nothing.

Adam stepped around the mattress and climbed the stairs.

The men were dragging and lifting lumber from the wreckage of the barn, stacking, and sorting it to the side. Adam and Jasper were carrying either end of a heavy plank. Once they dropped it into the pile, Adam shoved him again.

"Hey! I get it, all right?" Jasper pushed him back.

Adam tackled him to the ground, and they rolled over, slugging each other, wrestling, struggling.

Robin and Miles ran to them in shock. They each grabbed one of them, unsure who they had even, as their fight was so entangled. But Miles fell back with Adam in a chokehold. Robin dragged Jasper to the side.

Both combatants sat on the ground, catching their breath, wiping noses.

"Stay there. You stay there." Robin moved between them.

The stockmen were looking on.

"What the hell is going on here?" Robin bent over to yell at them from their height. "These people have lost their whole barn. They have windows broken in the house. I had to shoot their horse last night. Just what in the fuck are you doing?"

Adam scrambled to his feet first.

Jasper stood up.

Miles handed a handkerchief to Adam for his bloody nose.

Robin looked from one to the other. "What is this? Who started this?"

Neither said anything.

"Are you finished then?" Robin asked them. "Adam?"

Adam nodded, pinching his nose closed in the handkerchief.

"Jasper?"

"Done," Jasper said. "Sorry about your nose."

Adam nodded.

"Get yourself cleaned up in the house. Tell Marie you...fell on your face," Robin said. "Go on. The rest of us get back to work."

At dinner that evening, after everyone had worked a long hard day, even the women with cleaning up inside the house, Robin's guys all looked at one another. Adam had just a bit of a black eye. Marie put her hand on Adam's arm. "How are you, Adam?"

He lowered his chin. "I'm fine."

"You couldn't get your hand up in time when you fell?" Marie asked. "Try not to hurt your pretty face, Adam."

He just nodded.

Robin looked over at Miles. "They have about twenty men coming over here tomorrow to build the barn again. How would you like to practice as foreman before you build mine?"

"I don't know. I think Marie is the one to keep men working," Miles teased.

As everyone got up to leave the table, Robin made sure to take a hold of Adam's arm, very gently. Marie moved around Adam and went to the stairway. Adam turned to face Robin in the corner of the room. Robin moved side to side a bit to see the black eye better.

Adam said nothing.

Robin finally said quietly, "You know, Adam, I don't want to fire him. I really don't."

"Don't. It's over. There's nothing to be done."

"What happened?"

"I really prefer to not say. There is an...unwritten rule I would be breaking," Adam said.

"Funny, that's the same thing he said outside when I asked him," Robin said. "I thought you would tell me."

Adam lowered his chin. "Forgive me. I cannot."

Finally, Robin shrugged. "You are all right?"

"I'm all right. I was in the wrong."

"That's what he said as well. Get some rest then."

Adam and Jasper sat across from each other on the train. Jasper held up a card.

"Two of hearts," Adam said.

"Damn!" Jasper put the cards down.

Adam burst out laughing.

"Did it again," Jasper declared.

Robin sat down beside Adam.

Miles sat beside Jasper. "We figured out how to play cards with you, boy."

"No, you didn't," Adam replied.

"We figured out two ways." Robin set a bottle of brandy on the table.

Miles set a bottle of wine on the table. "Either we get you shit faced...."

Robin set two more decks of cards on the table. "Or we play with all of these."

Adam and Jasper laughed.

Robin began to shuffle together all three decks.

"I don't have any money on me," Adam said.

Robin reached into his pocket and set a pile of silver and gold coins on the table. "I happen to owe you 720 dollars after this."

"719 dollars," Adam corrected.

Robin patted another pocket of his jacket, making in jingle. "Those are yours. I have my own."

"You know, I played a game once where everyone had to take a drink if they did not win," Jasper offered.

"I'll even open it for you, boy." Miles started working on the wine cork with his pocketknife.

"This is mean. This is just, very mean," Adam declared, but then he smiled and began scooting the coins across the table toward himself.

"Everyone starts with a glass of wine and then we move on to the brandy," Miles said.

After a couple of hands, when Robin won, Miles won, and Adam won a hand, Robin said, "You know, back there in Halifax when we were all working together after the storm, I was going to say that we were really starting to work well as a team."

"Until these two did a throw down," Miles said.

"You didn't tell Marie, did you?" Adam looked at Robin beside him.

"No, she still thinks you fell on your face," Robin replied.

That made the guys laugh. Three of them drank brandy while one drank a glass of red wine.

Many more drinks later, and more hands rather evenly split between them all had passed.

Robin looked over at Adam beside him as he shuffled cards. "Had enough to drink to tell us what Zoey did to you in that laundry room?"

Adam turned blue eyes at Robin, leaning back in his chair.

"Laundry room?" Miles said. "Do tell, boy. She found out what you had in the trousers, huh?"

Jasper waited until Adam had a mouthful of wine and said, "Average."

Adam spit wine onto his cards, on the table, and dropped his feet to the floor.

Jasper pretended to wipe off his face, sitting across from Adam.

Robin cried laughing and that made them all laugh. Others in the train car looked over at the laughter.

"But as slim as he is, average appears very significant." Jasper pointed at Adam across the table.

Adam burst out laughing.

"You beat him up for that, Adam?" Robin asked.

"I never meant to hit you in the face. Just so you know. You fell into my fist," Jasper said.

"I what?" Adam said, wiping his mouth with a napkin. "You hit me."

Miles tossed him another napkin for the table and the cards. "That's not what I saw."

Robin helped him wipe up the mess. "Let's not get this in my lap. You two must swear to me, you're done fighting."

"Hardly call that fighting, what they were doing. Ha, and you thought I would be the problem," Miles said. "I've seen whores put on a better fight than you two."

"Okay. You've had enough. You're cut off." Robin took the brandy out of Adam's hand and downed it himself.

Adam giggled and laid his head on Robin's shoulder.

"Yes, that much is certain," Miles agreed.

"Let's pick up these cards and get him back to our car," Robin said.

Adam sat back with a smile. "Did I win?"

Jasper grinned. "He's a pretty thing when he's drunk. But then, you're a pretty thing when I'm drunk."

"Now we've got two drunks to get across to the next car." Miles stacked and filled his pockets with their decks of cards.

"Never have been fond of being called pretty," Robin said.

"Thought you'd be used to it by now," Miles said.

"No, I am not!" Robin declared. "Which drunk do you want?"

"I want Adam. The little one," Miles said.

"Well, you can't have him. He's mine," Robin said.

"Don't offer a choice when none exists." Miles stood up and moved over to pull Jasper's chair back.

"Adam, c'mon, buddy. We're going." Robin tried to figure out how to collect Adam, picking up a limp arm and then leaning to look him in the face. "Are you all right?"

Adam wrapped his arms around his neck then. "Robin. Robin. Robin."

"Yes, do what Robin says and get your ass up now." Robin pulled Adam from the chair.

Jasper stood up on his own and walked into the aisle. "Oh oh. He's really drunk. We might have a problem here."

"Which problem is that?" Robin moved Adam into the aisle and they all four began moving toward the door in the back of the rail car.

"How do we get him across?" Jasper asked.

"After we throw you across, we carry him," Miles said.

"I'm not so very drunk," Jasper said.

"You're right, Miles. Get Jasper across and then help me with Mr. Hudson," Robin said.

At the door, Adam's knees gave out and he dropped almost to the floor.

"All he had was wine really." Miles opened the door. "Stay here. Drinks like a girl." He grabbed Jasper and moved him across to the next car and inside that door. "Don't move."

Robin pulled Adam up and waited for Miles to grab Adam by the other arm. Together they walked him across and through the door to their car. Jasper helped pull him inside, declaring, "Teamwork, buddy."

They managed to get Adam to his cabin door. Zoey opened it.

They carried Adam inside and deposited him on his bed, still warm from Zoey rising out of it. She stood in her robe and bare feet.

Robin, Miles, and Jasper stood in the tiny room with her. Robin said in Dutch, "Ahm...You see well..."

"What happened to him?" Zoey said.

"He had a bottle of wine," Jasper blurted out. "Mostly."

"He's drunk?" Zoey said. "What do I do?"

Robin held out a hand to her. "Let him sleep it off. And here." He looked quickly about and found the brass spittoon. He set that beside the bed. "He might throw up. Come and get one of us in the morning."

"Is he all right?" Zoey asked.

Adam was laying back with eyes closed and mouth open.

Robin laid a hand on his chest. "You all right? Spinning?"

"I'm good," Adam sighed.

"In the morning, have him drink some water. Oh, his winnings," Robin gave him a pat on the chest and moved away from the bunk. He reached into his pocket and pulled out Adam's coins, to put those into a drawer in their tiny salon. "Get me in the morning if he needs help. He'll sleep it off."

Miles, Jasper, and Robin went into the hall where Marie was peeking out of her cabin door. They closed Zoey and Adam safely into theirs.

Robin grabbed Jasper by the arm. "What did you do to Adam? The night of the storm."

"What? What do you mean?" Jasper said.

"He tried to beat you up after that. What did you do to him?" Robin asked.

"I just slept is all," Jasper said.

"Did you hurt him?"

"No, of course not."

"Then why did he tackle you out in the yard and start pounding on you?" Robin asked.

"I don't know."

"You said he was average. Was it just a joke?"

Miles took Jasper by the other arm. "Did you do something to that boy?"

"No. Of course not. It was a joke."

Miles and Robin looked at each other.

Adam and Zoey arrived late for breakfast, but well dressed and giggling together as they entered the dining car.

As the tables on the train sat four on one side and two on the other, Adam and Zoey sat across the aisle from their party. "Well folks, we arrive in Stonington tomorrow. How do we plan to get from there to Canterbury?"

"You are feeling all right today?" Robin asked him.

"Why wouldn't I be?" Adam sat back and crossed his legs beneath his small table.

"Ah, well, I thought we might hire a coach to Norwich. We may separate a bit in Norwich as these two need to purchase some horses for themselves." Robin indicated Miles and Jasper.

"I was studying your map. To travel from Norwich to Canterbury, how long is that ride?" Miles said.

"Half a day," Robin replied. "We need to get Michael Poole to pick us up with my wagon. We can bring all of our trunks and such home with the wagon. Getting word to him though...."

"Miles and I purchase horses. We ride out there. We get Michael Pool to bring us to your home and your wagon. We come back for you. The four of you get an inn to relax for a day or so," Jasper suggested.

"We need to pick up supplies in Norwich anyway," Marie added.

"You don't know the way to Canterbury," Robin said.

"Well, you take my ride and go with Miles. I'll look after the ladies and Adam," Jasper suggested.

"You mean I look after Jasper and the ladies. I know Norwich," Adam said.

"Yes. That may be the best plan." Robin nodded. "Any better ideas anybody?" He met eyes with each of them. "That is the plan then. Adam, you and I will go to a bank in Norwich to transfer money to you."

"You still keep your money in a Norwich bank? After what happened there?" Adam questioned.

"John Bradford at the Norwich Central wouldn't dare lose my money after the way he treated my father. Wouldn't dare," Robin said. "But don't think I put all my money there. No way. It's in multiple places. I thought Adam may want to start an account."

"I likely should, yes," Adam agreed. "We need to buy a few things for Zoey. Marie, do you know a place to get dresses that are more typical for Connecticut? I know some of her travel dresses will do very well. But she could use more."

"Oh yes. Let's get some skirts and blouses too," Marie said to Zoey. "Then you can mix them and make new out fits."

"Yes, I would love this," Zoey said.

"And think about winter coming. She needs warmer things. It gets much colder here than it ever does in Amsterdam," Adam said.

"It does?" Jasper asked. "Get myself a seriously warm coat while I'm here. How cold?"

Adam smiled as he stuffed a pastry into his mouth.

"Well, January, February, and March can be well below freezing with bouts of heavy snow," Robin said.

"Given your sketch of the barn, Robin, we need to get started on the new barn immediately if we are to get it up before January. We just can't get more than a couple horses for breeding into your father's barn," Miles said. "We need to secure timber, planking, and men."

"Agreed." Robin nodded, sipping his coffee.

"Adam and I can inquire in Norwich while you two are away. The ladies can shop for clothing. And then we will all four of us buy the dry goods and food supplies that we need," Jasper said. "You know Norwich, Adam?"

"I've been there a few times with Robin. There was a lumber business beside that place we got the bathing tub from," Adam said.

"Yes. Try there," Robin agreed. "Don't agree to anything without negotiation. They over price at first. You must reason them down. That's how they work here."

Jasper nodded. "Just as when purchasing a horse."

"Miles, what do you need in Norwich?" Robin asked.

"Sounds like I need warm clothes and… some dancing girls," Miles said. "Don't suppose you have those in Canterbury."

The guys laughed.

Robin said in Dutch that you can't expect from them what you can in Amsterdam.

Chapter 20 The Letters

They arrived back in Canterbury, settled into the old house, and dinner at the dining room table. Unpacking of crates of glassware and tulip bulbs from Amsterdam.

June handed out letters. Robin and Marie had one from Mila. Adam had one from his mother.

Wine and brandy were sipped while the letters were opened. "Oh, it's just Mila checking to see if we made it home before winter," Robin said.

Adam made an involuntary moan. And his breathing increased the more he read.

Jasper grabbed Miles by the arm and pointed across the table at Adam.

Robin reached over and laid a hand on Adam's forearm.

"What is it?" Zoey asked.

Adam gasped as he read his letter. "Oh my God. My father has died. My mother requests I come at once. My uncle is contesting my inheritance. Robin, he's throwing her out of her home." Adam stood up, shaking.

Robin rose too and held onto his arm. "What is the date of that letter?"

Everyone looked on.

Adam teared up. "Three weeks ago. This has already happened! There's nothing I can do!"

Robin took him by both arms and actually shook him a bit. "It takes one to two months to get anything in court in New York. And we can always appeal if we get there after the hearing."

"We?" Adam looked up at him, his head rocking as he held back sobs.

Robin looked at Marie.

Marie slid her hand up Robin's back. "Leave tomorrow and do this for him. You have to."

"You have to help the boy. Jasper and I will take care of things here," Miles insisted.

"Don't even unpack. You and Zoey will leave with me at first light," Robin said. "You will bring your legal name change, your marriage certificate. The three of us will travel as quickly as possible and get on a train in New Haven tomorrow."

Before dawn, Miles and Jasper had Genie hitched to Robin's father's carriage. They actually woke Adam and Zoey up when they entered their room to collect their trunk. The trunk went inside the carriage. Robin came down the stairs with two cases in his hands and briefcase under his arm. Jasper put these out in the carriage. June and Marta had food packed for them in a pail. That was set on the seat inside the carriage.

Then everyone met in the kitchen for coffee.

"I'll come behind you later today with Jasper and we'll collect Genie and the carriage from the livery," Miles said. "We'll tell Constable Poole what has happened when we pass through town."

"He'll help you with securing men to build the barn. You may have a good six-weeks before heavy snowfall," Robin told him. "I should be back in a few weeks."

"Send a letter as soon as you know anything," Marie said.

"Got your pistol?" Miles asked him.

"And my revolver." Robin nodded.

"Don't you worry about a thing here. I'll look after Marie and the baby. I'll keep your house building going while we start this barn project," Miles said.

As Adam and Zoey went out to the carriage, Robin and Marie exchanged a lengthy goodbye kiss.

After an hour on the road, Robin handed the reins to Adam. The red sun was only barely coming up.

"What?"

"Just hold these. Don't do anything. Zoey?" Robin turned in the seat. "What did they send for breakfast?"

Zoey reached for the pail and removed the towel from the top. "Rolls. Bacon. Cheese. What may I give to you?"

"Damn, your English is getting really good," Robin said. "Something of each, please."

Zoey made him a napkin with a selection of everything and passed it into Robin's hands. "I make for you Adam."

"Adam, turn right there." Robin pointed.

"Huh?"

"Pull on the right reins. Het recht. Het recht," Robin said.

The carriage turned onto another road.

Robin made a sandwich out of his biscuit with cheese and bacon in the center. "Give me those back. You go ahead and eat something."

"I can't eat. I feel sick," Adam grumbled.

"No, you don't. Eat something so that you can help your mother," Robin insisted.

Zoey handed a napkin of food to Adam. "Robin, we must stop for a moment."

"What's wrong?" Robin asked.

"Nothing. Just stop," she said.

"What?" Adam asked.

Robin brought the carriage to a stop.

Zoey began to climb out. Adam hopped down to help her. They were surrounded by thick woods.

"Go up front," Zoey told Adam. She pointed. "Go."

"Oh. Robin, she's using the water closet," Adam said.

"Oh." Robin turned his back to her. "Adam, make sure there's no poison ivy back there before she does." He ate more of his sandwich.

"Wait, Zoey. Okay fine. Go right there." Then Adam returned to the front to stand beside the horse and look up at Robin.

"What are you doing?" Robin asked.

"I'm going after she does," Adam said. "As it were."

"Just do it right there. I'm not going to look at you," Robin said.

Adam let out a frustrated sigh and opened the front of his trousers. He relieved himself there beside the carriage. "What about you?"

"I don't have to go." Robin shrugged.

And then the horse released a urine stream like a river.

Adam jumped back, doing up his pants again. He hopped to keep his boots out of the stream.

Robin burst out laughing.

"That's disgusting!" Adam shot back further.

"He's easily influenced," Robin said.

"Did you know he was going to let loose like that?" Adam asked.

"Of course. The carriage stopped. What do you think a horse is going to do?" Robin said. "Oh hell. Get up here and take the reins."

Zoey climbed back into the carriage. "What is happening?"

Adam climbed up and Robin down. "Robin's turn. Easily influenced as well."

"You just made it to the noon train," said the ticket office.

"It's one-thirty," Adam exclaimed.

"She's late. Those your bags?"

"Yes. Two first class cabins."

"Only got one left."

"We'll take it." Adam looked at Zoey beside him and saw Robin's carriage reaching the livery down the block. "We'll deal with it."

Adam had their bags installed into cabin five. He and Zoey nervously waited and waited and waited. As the train was just starting slowly to move out, Robin ran for it and jumped on into Adam's waiting grasp.

Their porter helped pull them both up the steps.

Robin and Adam were laughing.

"Never saw a gentleman do that, sir," the porter said. "Has he got a ticket?"

"Of course, he does." Adam shoved it into the porter's hand. He then drew Robin into their cabin and shut the door. "We have to share this one. It's the only one left."

"Oh? Very well." Robin sat on the sofa.

"I thought you'd be upset," Adam admitted.

"Last one. I'd have done the same," Robin said. "I'll sleep here. You two take the bunks."

"You take the bunk. We'll..." Adam said.

"No. You two take the bunks. We'll hang a blanket across. I'm fine here, besides..." Robin indicated the small bar beside the built-in sofa. "Oh, one thing. Zoey, listen please. My pistol will be on this bar at night. Neither of you are to touch it, ever. Do not touch my gun."

"Yes. Agree," Zoey said. "I'm sorry, Robin."

"Sorry? About the one cabin? I'm fine. I don't care. Nobody in the dining car will even know we are sharing a room. Let's just keep it secret," Robin said. "If anybody does ask, you're my son and daughter in law."

"What are you reading?" Adam asked.

Robin had a book open at the dining table. "Reasonable doubt in American law. Your uncle brought the case. He has to prove you are not you. I only have to create reasonable doubt that he is wrong. We need one person to verify your identity, a sister, your mother, a neighbor. Anybody. And we hunt down the doctor who signed your birth certificate. And you are in possession of the birth certificate. That alone can raise reasonable doubt."

"Oh my God." Adam sighed.

Zoey sipped tea, looking from Adam beside her to Robin across from him.

"Reasonable doubt is a doubt based upon reason and common sense and is not based purely on speculation. It may arise from a careful and impartial consideration of all the evidence, or from *lack of evidence*. Adam, we both know he has no evidence at all that you are not Adam Rothschild. He's going to recognize you. Your cousins are going to recognize you. I'm certain you are seven years older. Your voice has changed. Your eyes are the same. You bring into testimony some shared experience you had in his home. Start thinking of some occasions and details you can speak of."

"Will my cousins be in the courtroom?" Adam asked.

"Most likely, but he will not want them to testify. He will have them sign an affidavit before the case saying that you are not Adam Rothschild." Robin sat back with an exhalation. "Families become estranged when there is a lot of money at stake."

"May I study that section? I remember everything, you know?" Adam said.

"Of course. Remind me of these clauses if they come up. What do you remember about your uncle, aunt, cousins?" Robin turned the book around for Adam to read.

"Everything. He never liked my mother. This is revenge against her for being Italian. I remember parties at his home, birthdays, my cousin Erika's coming out party," Adam said. "Awkward giraffe in a party gown."

"Perfect. Don't mention the giraffe part. And I urge you to let me call your sisters and mother to the stand, if necessary," Robin said.

"I won't traumatize them. I will do this myself."

"Don't let your pride trip you up," Robin said.

"What if he falsifies evidence against me?"

"We counter it point by point. And be prepared, he may know why you left home and as a last straw try to have you claimed insane and unfit to manage the estate."

At that, Adam lowered his chin and shut his eyes.

Robin reached further across the table and laid a hand on his arm. "You are disproving all that simply by testifying for yourself in court. And it is here-say, what happened between you and another boy seven years ago. Is there any chance he finds Lucas to testify against your mental capacity, keeping in mind finding Lucas proves right there that you are Adam Rothschild?"

"Lucas is dead. He was murdered in the street about a year after," Adam said.

"That's horrible." Robin looked down. "Forgive me."

442   The Dutchman 2 Test of Character   By Susan Eddy

That night the three of them slipped into their cabin. Robin and Adam strung a blanket across the end of the bunk beds to the hat hook beside the cabin door, dividing their small compartment in two. Zoey retreated behind the blanket to get ready for bed and crawl into the bottom bunk bed.

Adam and Robin sat on the sofa. Adam handed him a pillow and blanket. It was dark except for the small oil lamp on the bar. Robin had his arm on the back of the sofa and was slouched back in a state of exhaustion. Adam was turned toward him with one knee up on the sofa.

The train rattled along on the tracks, backwards for them, with the occasional lights from buildings in the town on either side of the tracks. Mostly moonlight was the only illumination of the towns and forests.

"You've told me everything even remotely related to this case?" Robin asked softly.

"Far as I know," Adam said. "Like what?"

"What are your cousins like?"

"Bernard is an asshole," Adam said. "We fought all the time. He didn't like me."

"He has motive to do harm here," Robin said. "Other cousins?"

"Just Erika. She was so tall when we were young," Adam said. "She was never mean to me or anything. My father only had the one other brother. I only have the 2 cousins on that side of the family."

"Any on your mother's side?"

"About twelve. But they're in Philadelphia," Adam said.

"Your relationship with Bernard?" Robin asked.

Adam's face scrunched up. "He always called me names. Called me a girl. I suppose I had long hair when I was a boy. Always said the Italian in me was the problem."

"The problem with you? And how do you get on with your own sisters?"

"Always fine until I ran away from home and never wrote to them again. I guess that won't be good," Adam said.

"Perhaps they will just be glad to see you again," Robin said. "Do we go straight to your mother's house?"

"Start there. Do you think he threw them out already?"

"Probably tried to. Couldn't. Had to bring it to court," Robin said.

Adam got up and stood beside the blanket to say, "Honey, Zoey, are we keeping you awake with the talking?"

"No. I like the talk," Zoey said softly.

Adam looked at the bar and opened it. He pulled from it the whiskey and poured two small glasses of it.

Robin held out a hand.

Adam gave him a glass and then downed his quickly. He shook a moment and then poured himself another one before sitting beside Robin again.

Van der Kellen was looking at him. "Take it easy, Adam."

"How would you prove who you are? Have you thought about that?" Adam looked straight out into the darkness beyond their window. "It is something that has lived over my head for many years. It's something no man should have to do. I have to do it."

"Ah...I would ride a horse in some spectacular fashion or shoot a target some range beyond my weapon's average capability." Robin shrugged.

"Are you trying to make me laugh?" Adam looked at him seriously.

"No. I get it. I do. I have citizenship papers. I have a retirement certificate from the Royal Guard. I have the law exam in two countries. Signatures will match on all. But you see, the older you become the more accomplishments you have for your credibility. At your age, there is not so much of a paper trail." Robin patted him on the knee. "But you are you, are you not?"

Adam nodded. "Far as I know."

Robin set his whiskey on the bar with his pistol. He reached down to pull off his boots. Then he sat cross legged on the sofa and retrieved his drink again. "Get some sleep if you can. I'm sure you did not get much last night."

In the morning, Zoey pulled on her corset and tied it as best she could. She slid a dress on over her head and buttoned up the side of it. Then she stepped into her ankle boots. She brushed her hair and gathered it up into a bun on the back of her head, held in place with combs and hair pins. She peeked out around the blanket.

Robin was still snoozing, lying on his side beneath his blanket, his head on the pillow and his knees bent.

She stepped around the hanging blanket and pulled on the door handle.

Robin got onto his elbow immediately. And he started to reach for his gun, when he met eyes with Zoey.

"Sorry," she whispered.

"Where are you going?" he asked in Dutch.

"Just to the lady's room. I will be right back," she said in the same language.

While she was out, Robin stepped into his trousers and pulled on his shirt. He buttoned it. The sun was up, behind the train somewhere. He pulled on his ankle boots.

Zoey returned quietly with a pot of coffee in her hand.

Robin grabbed his weapon off the bar and set it beside him on the sofa.

"Koffie?" Zoey asked, taking cups from beneath the bar and setting them with saucers on top.

"Yes please. Is he sleeping?" Robin asked in Dutch.

"He finally got to sleep. It took him hours." She handed a cup and saucer to him. "Can you win this case?"

Robin looked up at her and nodded. "Yes. Nothing we can do today except rest up. Sit."

The blanket was folded on the back of the sofa. She sat back against it, only a few inches from Robin. She drank her coffee quietly, watching the scenery pass by the window.

"You have not said too much about all this. It is a terrible way to meet his family," Robin said. "His mother and sisters will welcome you. I'm certain of it. They already know he married you."

"Yes. I just wish there was something I can do."

"There is. Just be there for him. A man is twice as strong, with a good woman." Robin smiled a bit. "In court, just try not to be emotional. And stay near him. It will work to your benefit that you are not fluent in English yet. You stand up behind him when I give you the signal."

"What signal?"

"I'll give you a nod. You will likely know when, but just to reassure you." Robin finished his coffee and got up to pour another. "If I raise my voice in court, do not be alarmed. I do many things for the effect of it. There is a method to persuasion. And I'm schooled at it."

"I just feel so helpless."

"No. You just look after him. That's all you must do. That is why you are here."

"He's frightened. Can you reassure him that he is going to win?" Zoey asked.

Robin looked at her for a while. "I usually don't. But in this case..." He nodded.

Adam helped them select the carriage of a hotel near their courthouse.

"You take our bags and get us two rooms in that hotel. I'm going to the hospital where my surgery was, to inquire about this doctor," Robin said. "I'll meet you back at the hotel."

Adam grabbed a newspaper from a passing salesman and dropped a coin into his hand. "Robin, look at this first."

Robin leaned over his shoulder.

Zoey took it upon herself to summon the carriage driver of the chosen hotel to them.

"It's tomorrow," Adam declared. "We're the headlines."

Robin grabbed the paper from him and rolled it up. "You get to the hotel and stay out of sight. The two of you can dine in the hotel restaurant and wait for me. Do not go anywhere." Robin dashed off toward some awaiting taxi carriages, briefcase and paper under his arm.

"Yes, sir, two rooms at the hotel. Do you prefer suites or rooms, sir?"

"The name is Van der Kellen. Two suites side by side if you have them," Adam said. "These are our bags."

"We'll take those."

Adam Hudson claiming to be heir to Rothschild Fortune

If heir does not show up in court tomorrow, Gerard Rothschild will claim late brother's fortune for himself. Gerard Rothschild owns

several banks on Manhattan and Long Island. His brother Adam Theodore Rothschild passed away suddenly, leaving a widow and only daughters. Teenage son is said to have run away from home several years ago and has not been seen since. Two imposters have been disputed. One was way too young to be Adam Rothschild. The other was considerably from the wrong country, speaking with an uneducated tongue. Is this Adam Hudson the real thing? Mother claims he had name change overseas. Estate is said to be worth over $200,000, including a mansion, two factories, and bank accounts. Our reporters will be waiting at the courthouse to attend the hearing. Are you the long-lost heir? Seems every young man wants to be Adam Rothschild III.

"Hello, I am looking for a particular physician," Robin said at the front desk of the hospital.

"What is his name, sir?" the secretary asked.

"He would be rather an elderly man, perhaps even in retirement by now," Robin said.

"Come in and have a seat. This may take me a while." The secretary stepped to the end of the counter to open a door beside it. "Come this way."

Robin entered the office, holding hat and briefcase in his hands in front of him.

"Have a seat right here, hon. I'll be happy to look up his address for you."

Robin smiled warmly at the woman. "Thank you, Mrs…"

"Miss Johnson."

"Miss Johnson, I thank you very much, love."

"I'm not normally supposed to give this out. What are you looking for this doctor for, sir?" The woman sat down at her file cabinet, opened a drawer and began to sift through files. "You're not a policeman, are you? Policemen don't dress so finely."

"Ahm." Robin crossed his legs and fluffed up his ascot a bit. "You look like a woman of great strength. I believe you can handle hearing this as you do work in a dangerous position such as a hospital receiving ward. You see…"

She looked at him, hanging on his every word, watching his mouth as he spoke and his lashes as he blinked at her.

Robin rubbed at his right shoulder. "You see I was shot a few years ago. If not for Dr. Jones, who usually delivers babies, if not for him patching me up in the street I would not have survived."

"Oh my. Are you in much pain? Is there anything I can get you? Cup of tea perhaps?"

"Tea would be lovely."

"I'll get that right now for you and then I'll find his address. I'll just be a moment."

The woman left the room and Robin dove toward that open file drawer. Files were alphabetical. Allen Jones. Allen Jones.

Robin grabbed the file, removed its contents, put the file back and hurried out the door. "Sorry miss. No time for tea."

Across from the hotel was the courthouse, already with reporters gathered around the front steps.

Adam and Zoey were shown the way to the hotel desk. The ledger was turned toward Adam, and he signed in as Adam Van der Kellen. He took the keys to the two suites, paid for the first night, and was shown to the stairs with porters bringing up their trunk and Robin's two bags.

Their suites were facing the front street, and Adam moved a curtain aside to look out the window at the courthouse across the street. Robin's bags were put in the room beside them. "I think we would like to take supper up here. Can you send the maid up with a menu, please?"

"Oh, I can tell you everything on the menu, sir. I'll have the maids bring it up. We have turtle soup. We have beet salad. Our special tonight is the most amazing north Atlantic cod."

"You have got to be kidding me!" Adam declared.

"You don't like cod?"

"Anything else, please," Adam said.

"We always have beef soup and beef brisket. We have…"

"Bring that. Beet salad, beef soup, and brisket for three. Bottle of Cotes du Rhone red French wine. My father is joining us. Bring warmers to keep his serving warm. He'll be late. And leave word for him at the desk that we are here," Adam said. "Bring a dessert."

"Yes, Mr. Van der Kellen. My pleasure."

Adam put two dollars into his hand. "Put the meals on the room. Thank you."

Adam looked at Zoey across the table from him.

"You worry for him?" Zoey asked.

"He's been gone a long time. He's doing this for me." Adam sat back in his chair. "Yes, I'm worried about him."

"You do not think he will miss the court tomorrow?" Zoey asked.

Adam put a hand to his forehead and shut his eyes. "Oh, I needed another reason for bad dreams tonight. Can you imagine me representing myself? Holy fuck."

"You study the book, yes? You know the law here?"

"I read the book yes. But he has so much experience. He's tried so many cases. I could never..."

There was a knock on the door.

"Oh Jesus." Adam stood up and slipped his pistol into his pocket. He went to the door and stood beside it. "Who is it?"

"Porter with Mr. Van der Kellen, sir."

"I beg your pardon?" Adam questioned.

Another knock knock on the door. "It's me. Open up and put your damn gun down."

The porter hopped back in terror.

Adam unlocked and opened the door.

Robin walked inside, saw the gun in his hand and said, "I'm late. No reason to shoot."

"You are late," Adam said.

The porter hurried away and down the stairs.

Adam burst out laughing. "You terrorized him."

"Ah, he knows I'm joking. Right? I found your doctor. We're all set for tomorrow. Is that beef?" Robin said.

Adam shut and locked the door. He returned his small pistol to the corner of the table. "Yes, we kept yours as warm as possible here."

Zoey prepared Robin's plate, raising the lid and moving the plate off the warming irons.

Robin set his briefcase down against the wall and his top hat on the hook behind the door. "Took me awhile. Old fellow moved twice since he retired. But he seems agreeable to show up tomorrow."

"Agreeable? Is he going to show up or not?" Adam took his seat again. "Robin?"

"Of course, he is. Am I sleeping on the sofa again or did you get me my own room?" Robin shoveled brisket into his mouth.

Zoey laughed out loud.

"Of course, I got you your own room. It's right next door." Adam pointed at the key on the table. "Did you stop at a tavern on your way here?"

"Would if I could," Robin said. "I'm starving. Wasting away. Hardly keep my trousers up."

"You...what?" Adam exasperated. He looked at Zoey. "Unbelievable. Do you realize my name is on the headlines of every newspaper out there? I'm terrified without you here. And you're out there having a party of it all."

"Party? I was working. I went to one house. Was told where he moved to. Went there. Was told where he moved to. Finally, I met up with the old fellow," Robin said. "Oooh. Is that chocolate cake?"

"Cake?"

"Adam, listen to me. In court tomorrow, I want you to do this for me. Focus on this. Any time you feel the slightest bit of anxiety, you are to take hold of that pocket watch my king gave you, let out a long slow very slow breath, and remember what a fantastic team we were in

Wout's trial. I'm going to work the room. Win the room. Win the jury. You remember that. Hopefully this won't even become a jury trial."

Chapter 21 Trial of Adam Hudson

Zoey watched a woman in black enter the courtroom. She was a young blonde woman, dressed in the black plain dress of a woman in mourning, yet she had no hat or veil. She was looking for someone, searching, standing up on her toe tips just to see over the crowd.

"Adam." Zoey pointed at the woman.

Adam turned around inside the defendant's box. Zoey and his sisters were seated right behind him.

As Adam's eyes took in the people gathering in the courtroom, and as he saw the woman, the recognition crossed his face. "Mrs. Miller?"

Elizabeth Miller squeezed past people down the aisle to stand beside Zoey. "Adam Hudson." The wealthy blonde woman reached out to him, black gloves on her hands. "I saw this in the papers. I thought perhaps Robin and Marie would be with you. Isn't Robin representing you?"

"Robin is here. Marie stayed home with the baby. Mrs. Miller, it would please me to introduce you to my wife Zoey, and my sisters."

"You've married? Adam, that's wonderful. Marie wrote that you went with them to Amsterdam." Elizabeth was taken aback. She looked Adam and Zoey up and down. Her tone changed from surprise to something deeper. "Edward knew your father and uncle very well. We dined with your uncle many times. I had no idea, we had no idea, you were a Rothschild."

"I am pleased that it didn't show." Adam slipped his arm around Zoey's shoulders. "Zoey, this is Mrs. Elizabeth Miller."

"Oh. Oh yes." Zoey nodded, remembering the story of the Millers. "Pleased to make your acquaintance."

"Delighted to meet you, Zoey. Adam, do you have any idea how well I know your uncle? Your cousins? Your Aunt Sonya?" Elizabeth grabbed hands with the women beside Zoey. "And your sisters..."

"You know Adam?" His eldest sister asked.

"I've known him for years. You never said you had a brother."

"Why didn't you tell us where he was?" his sister said. "We didn't know where he was."

Elizabeth took in the clothing Adam and Zoey wore. "This is a beautiful gown your wife wears. Lovely pearls. How did you afford a diamond ring for her? I mean, before you inherit. She came with quite a dowry, I'd imagine. You make a delightful couple. I'm just so surprised. And I regret so, that I did not treat you better."

"I have no doubt, you would have treated me better had you known I was wealthy," Adam remarked.

"You have every right to be rude to me. Please remember that I am in mourning," Elizabeth scolded. "And Edward thought very well of you."

"I know what you asked of Robin," Adam said softly. "Though I have no doubt that you loved your husband. I cared for him as well. I was sorry to hear of his passing. I hope that my leaving gave him no animosity toward me."

"He was not surprised. None of us were very surprised that you followed Mr. Van der Kellen away. Where is Mr. Van der Kellen, Mr. Hudson?" Elizabeth said. "I mean, Mr. Rothschild. Oh I don't know how to address you."

"Van der Kellen?" Said a man across the aisle.

Robin had entered from the judge's chambers, onto the floor, past the judges' desk and witness box.

Gentlemen behind the plaintiff's booth stood up to beckon Robin toward them.

Elizabeth remained standing with Adam's little group of women.

To news reporters in the room, here was the famous bank robber catcher, perhaps the most famous lawyer on Manhattan. They rose also, calling out to him such things as, "Mr. Van der Kellen, you were shot. How are you now? How are you feeling? Are you representing Mr. Gerard Rothschild?"

Van der Kellen gave the audience a little bow, glanced to see that Adam was all right, and continued across to meet with Edward Miller's former banking friends. They chatted quietly and exuberantly, but Robin only talked about how he had just returned from Amsterdam to set up a horse breeding business.

On the other side of the courtroom, Gerard Rothschild entered with an entourage of attorneys, his wife, son, and daughter. The son looked at Adam with disgust. They locked in eye contact.

"Who is he?" Zoey whispered.

"My cousin Bernard. He's to inherit all of his father's fortune. Obviously has designs on mine as well," Adam whispered beneath his breath.

Gerard Rothschild was one of the wealthiest bankers in New York. Nearly everything he did made the papers. And a lawsuit to collect his late brother's fortune certainly made headlines and filled the seats with reporters.

"Excuse me. I must go to work." Robin Van der Kellen walked across the center to stand beside Adam Hudson, to the shock and amazement of Miller's friends and reporters alike. "Adam, remember."

Adam straightened his posture and blanked his expression. He smoothed a hand down his striped vest, found his pocket watch from the Dutch king, and let out a long slow breath.

Everyone rose as the judge entered. "A large audience for a simple inheritance case. I remind all of you to remain silent and allow the proceedings to roll on. On that note, I call the case of Gerard Rothschild vs Adam Hudson. Will both parties step forward and be sworn in? Mr. Rothschild."

"Gerard Rothschild, brother of the late Adam Theodore Rothschild II, your honor."

"And may we have Mr. Adam Hudson?"

Adam stepped around the desk, in his finest suit and one of Robin's pin striped vests. He held up his right hand. And he began his best Robin Van der Kellen impression, having practiced it many times. "Adam Theodore Hudson, your honor. Formerly Adam Theodore Rothschild III."

"Do each of you swear to tell the truth and the whole truth?"

"I do, sir," Adam said.

"Yes, I do." Gerard stood with his four lawyers.

"And who do we have representing the plaintiff?"

The law firm introduced themselves.

"And the defendant?"

"Robin Van der Kellen, licensed in the state of Massachusetts and the Netherlands," Robin said. "I can legally practice law in New York."

Applause went up in the courtroom.

The judge banged his gavel on the desk. "Silence the applause please. We've all heard of the Netherlands," The judge quipped, to some laughter. "Mr. Hudson, you have name change documents?"

"I do your honor," Adam said.

"May I present these to your desk, your honor?" Robin asked.

"If you would please."

Robin walked the papers forward and placed them on the desk with a well-practiced flourish. He stepped back a step, looking up at the judge.

The judge looked over the papers while the courtroom looked over the famous lawyer. "The name change took place in the Netherlands just over two months ago. How did Mr. Hudson return to New York so quickly?"

Robin turned and indicated to Adam to speak.

"On the Britannia, your honor, a steamer from London to Halifax. Two weeks at sea and then another steamer to Boston and trains to New York," Adam explained, holding onto that pocket watch. "Just arrived last night."

"And the reason for the name change in the Netherlands?"

Robin took this. "If you would be so good as to read the paper beneath it, you will find a marriage certificate. He had to change his name before he married."

The judge read over the second paper. Then he offered them back to Robin. "Very well. And what is the profession of Mr. Hudson?"

"I have been a legal assistant to Mr. Van der Kellen in Amsterdam," Adam said.

"Before going to the Netherlands, you lived where?" the judge asked.

"In Canterbury, Connecticut from May 11, 1840, to present. I grew up in New York and lived on William Street all my life until leaving for Connecticut to work for Mr. Van der Kellen," Adam said.

"Very well. Both of you may return to your desk." The judge then had a look at the wealthy banker and his four lawyers facing down the young defendant with such angry faces. "Mr. Rothschild, you have the burden to prove that Mr. Hudson is not your nephew. Do you not recognize him?"

The room laughed a bit.

Adam stood beside the desk, with regal posture, and looked from his sisters and Zoey toward the Rothschilds on the other side of the room. Robin Van der Kellen tried not to draw attention from Adam, but just by sliding his hair from his eyes, he actually drew a few sighs from women in the audience.

Mrs. Miller saw and heard this. She smiled. She sat forward more eagerly.

One of the lawyers spoke up. "This is absolutely not the son of my client's brother. That boy ran away from home at the age of 14 and has not been seen since. We have no idea who this man is."

Elizabeth stood up behind Adam. "I would not say never seen since. He worked in my household on William Street, since he was 14 years old."

"Is this your witness, Van der Kellen? You did not register her," the judge said.

"She is not my witness, but I'll take her testimony, thank you very much," Robin said.

The room burst out laughing, drawing a bang of the gavel again.

"I will not call a widow to the witness stand. Remain comfortable where you are and please state your name for the record," the judge said.

"Mrs. Elizabeth Miller, the widow of Edward Miller." She freely laid eyes on Robin before her.

"And by what name did you know the defendant when he was in your household?"

"Adam Hudson," she said.

"He worked in your household all those years? Doing what?" Gerard yelled at her. "You never said you had my nephew! You did not have my nephew!"

"Are you sure?" Robin said. "You just referred to him as your nephew."

"Mr. Rothschild, you will hold your tone in my courtroom and when addressing a lady, particularly a widow," the judge cautioned. "What work did he perform in your household, Mrs. Miller? Did you know he was a runaway?"

"Yes, we knew he was a runaway. He began work in the house two years before I married Edward. He was a wonderful valet. Hard worker. Did any chores we asked of him. We made him finish school. He was a very good student," Elizabeth said. "I did not know he was related to a friend of my late husbands. I know Edward would have been shocked to learn that Adam was Theodore's son."

"Theodore?" the judge asked.

"We knew Adam Theodore Rothschild, the second, as Theodore," Elizabeth said.

"And just where is your home, Mrs. Miller?" the judge said.

"Corner of Wall Street and William," she said.

"Across from the bank. Thank you, Mrs. Miller. You may take your seat," the judge said. "Mr. Gerard Rothschild, do you swear to the court that you do not recognize Mr. Hudson as your nephew?"

"Yes, your honor. I have never seen this boy before in my life," Gerard said. "He is not even old enough to be my nephew. Adam should be 21 years old now. This boy may have a wife with him, but he cannot even shave whiskers yet."

That made people laugh.

"Mr. Hudson, what is your age and birthdate?"

"21 years old. I was born June 3rd, 1820. And I have my certificate of birth," Adam said.

"Bring me this paper."

Robin selected the paper from the desk and sauntered across the floor to lay this down for the judge, with the same flourish.

"I protest. We will see this document," the lawyers said.

"For the record, the document says Adam Rothschild the third, was born right here in New York, in the household that is part of the William Street estate in question. It has the signature of a doctor," Robin told the courtroom.

"Yes, it does," the judge said.

"If I may, your honor, I call my first witness, Dr. Allen Jones," Robin said.

"Do you expect the good doctor to recognize the boy?" the judge questioned. "Twenty-one years later?"

"No, your honor. I expect him to recognize his own signature," Robin corrected.

Dr. Jones was shown to the witness booth and stood with his right hand raised.

"Very well. Dr. Jones, state your name for the record."

"Dr. Allen Jones," said the elderly man.

"Bailiff, bring the birth certificate to Dr. Jones."

The elderly man put on his glasses and examined the paper. "This is my signature. Yes. I brought three children into that house on William Street, two girls and a boy, as I recall."

Then the bailiff brought the certificate for the lawyers to examine before returning it to Adam's desk.

"This is not my nephew! I do not know where he got that paper!"

Elizabeth saw Robin made a hand gesture to Adam, very secretly down at his side.

"You know very well who I am, Uncle. The last time that I was at your house for dinner, it was my cousin Erika's coming out party. She wore a pink gown. I danced with her though she was a foot taller than I was," Adam said. "I am pleased to see that I am the taller now."

There was some nervous laughter in the courtroom.

Robin gave Adam a small smirk. He gestured to continue.

His cousin Erika stood up and was pulled back down by her mother.

"Hello Erika. Pleasant to see you again," Adam said, breathing hard though keeping his voice measured and his hand on his watch.

"Well, this is highly unusual." The judge sat forward at his desk, looking from Adam to Gerard. "Dr. Jones, you may leave the witness box now. Thank you. Mr. Gerard Rothschild, your wife and daughter Erika do not recognize this young man?"

"They do not, your honor," the lawyer said.

"These women, they do speak?" the judge asked.

"There is no need. I have their signed deposition," the lawyer said. "Unlike some lawyers, I will not take advantage of women."

Robin raised eyebrows, to the giggles of women in the courtroom. "No complaints so far."

"Mr. Van der Kellen," the judge scolded.

They roared with laughter.

"I will speak. I am Bernard Rothschild, and I can tell you that is not my cousin Adam!"

"Objection. They didn't register Bernard as a witness," Robin said.

"I'm allowing it because I allowed Mrs. Miller's testimony," the judge said. "Bernard Rothschild, please step forward. We have no signed deposition from you. Please take a closer look at Mr. Hudson. What do you see?"

Bernard and Adam were soon face to face.

"I don't know him at all," Bernard snapped.

"Still angry about that scar I put on your chin," Adam said.

"Objection. Anyone could have told him that detail, a maid, a butler in the house," the lawyer said. "Bernard Rothschild is not a witness here."

"Well, I'll take his testimony too!" Robin declared. "You can't hate someone that badly when you never met him before. Your honor, really!"

Gerard walked past Robin, giving him a mean glare.

"Ooo. That is a nasty scar. How did that happen?" Robin looked around Gerard to Adam.

"Oriental vase," Adam said.

"Oriental vase to the face? Remember that, Mr. Rothschild?" Robin set both hands on his hips. "Sounds memorable to me."

"Objection! We did not get to question Mrs. Miller," the lawyer said.

"Mr. Van der Kellen, you will not harass this witness," the judge cautioned.

"Oh, but he is not a witness, now is he? If he was, his backside would be in that box, and I could cross examine him!" Robin returned to his desk and stood beside Adam. "My client may be seven years older but every one of his family members recognizes him. Gerard Rothschild referred to him as his nephew. Bernard Rothschild hates his guts. What more do you need for reasonable doubt?"

The reporters were struggling to write all this down, hanging on every word.

"Mr. Van der Kellen, I would like to make this easy. Have you anyone in this courtroom who will swear to your client's identity, under oath?" the judge asked. "You had Mrs. Miller testify that he is Adam Hudson. Give me one person to swear that he is also Adam Rothschild."

Robin looked at Adam intensely.

Adam pursed his mouth and said nothing, even though his two sisters jolted out of their seats behind him.

And then another woman in black stood up in the back of the courtroom. "He has his mother." She walked forward to the gate. She pulled back her veil to reveal tears. She reached out.

Adam ran to her and took her into his arms over the gate.

His mother wrapped arms around him and nearly hugged the stuffings out of him. She wept and Adam wept.

The woman's butler stood behind her, silently. He was an elderly man in plain black suit.

Van der Kellen softened his appearance, removing his hands from his hips and standing politely.

"Mr. Hudson," the judge called. "Mr. Hudson!"

Adam stepped back and wiped his eyes. "I beg your pardon, your honor. May I present my mother, Mrs. Lena Rothschild. As she is in mourning, I ask that you do not call her to the witness stand. Please, your honor."

"I will speak. It is my right!" she called out in her Italian accent.

"Mrs. Rothschild, do you swear under oath that this is your son, the former Adam Theodore Rothschild III?" the judge asked.

"He is my son, and you know it, Gerard!" Lena said angrily, pointing at her brother-in-law. The butler moved in closer behind her.

"Please take a seat, Mrs. Rothschild. Thank you," the judge said. "Mr. Hudson, Mr. Van der Kellen, are you ready to finish this?"

"Yes, your honor." Adam quickly wiped his eyes and stood up properly.

"Please, your honor," Robin said. "Reasonable doubt."

"There is no need to remind me of the law, Mr. Van der Kellen, particularly when I have absolutely no doubt. I find that the name change in Amsterdam is legal. I find that the marriage certificate is legal. I find that the birth certificate is legal. Furthermore, I find that multiple people in this courtroom recognize this young man as the person he claims to be. You just don't like it that he ran away and changed his name! Mr. Hudson is the sole and rightful heir. Every cent, every property, belongs to him. This court is adjourned." The gavel rang in the courthouse. "I am fining Mr. Gerard Rothschild, and Mr. Bernard Rothschild, for perjury. I'm fining your legal team for bringing a frivolous case to court. Be glad that I overlook the documents from your wife and daughter."

"Adam ran away from home because he is a deviant caught in bed with another boy!" Gerard called out. "My brother wouldn't give a dime to him, and he can't claim inheritance now! He is not fit to manage such an estate. He should be committed."

The courtroom gasped.

Lena sobbed.

Robin gave a nod to Zoey.

Adam straightened his posture and put a fist on his hip. His wife stood up behind him.

Robin turned, holding up a finger but the judge cut him off before he could say the words 'here say'.

"Well, he has a wife now. I don't find any of your statements to be true here today, Mr. Gerard Rothschild. Frankly, I am shocked that a man of your standing would bring shame to your family. Extended family such as this, it is no wonder a 14-year-old boy ran away from home and took work as a valet in a household only down the street. You can thank God the boy found shelter at the Miller's. Mr. Hudson, good luck to you. Good day, sir."

As Adam walked out of the courtroom, holding hands with his wife and mother, his sisters and their husbands hurried along with them. Reporters begged Adam for a statement. "Adam Hudson, how does it feel to be rich? How is it to hire Mr. Van der Kellen? Will you ever speak to your uncle again? How rich are you, Mr. Hudson? Is it really $200,000?" Headlines would read, "Valet to Rich Man, Adam Hudson wins the Rothschild fortune". Of course, another headline read, "Famous Bank Robber Catcher Robin Van der Kellen Wins Rothschild Fortune for Valet."

And to Van der Kellen it was, "Won another case in New York, how does it feel? How is that shoulder? What was it like to be shot by a bank robber? How was Amsterdam? Will you stay in New York now? Give us a statement, will you?"

Robin stopped, allowing the reporters to gather around him as Adam escaped with his women into a carriage. His mother's butler went with them. The two brothers-in-law awaited at the curb with their carriage for Van der Kellen.

"What is your statement, Mr. Van der Kellen?"

"This is my statement. Are you ready? These are the words of Adam Hudson. If you maintain your dignity, you can hold your head up against any tide. Now, Adam Hudson can look after his mother and sisters properly. And that was all he could even think about after receiving word of his father's passing."

"You had two widows testify for your client today. Are you certain you do not take advantage of women?"

"Mrs. Miller and Mrs. Rothschild testified of their own free will. I did not even know they would be in the courtroom today. However, if it benefits my client, I am unlikely to turn them down," Robin said. "I meant no disrespect to women with my lighthearted comments. In fact, I am a great admirer of the strength of women."

"Mr. Van der Kellen, did you realize how many women were in the courtroom just to see you?"

Robin laughed. "And I thank them for beautifying the courtroom. If not for them, it's just a bunch of black suits. Now, if you will please, I have a wife and baby I must get home to."

Robin made his way through the crowd to the curb where he grabbed Elizabeth by the elbow and pushed her up into the carriage. Her butler, Jonas, climbed in as well. Robin and the brothers-in-law climbed in with her, and the carriage took off.

"Thank you, Elizabeth," Robin said.

She held onto her seat, beside Robin, as the carriage raced away. "I hope that I helped. This is all such a shock."

"Are you well?" Robin asked.

She nodded. "Well enough. Why didn't Marie come with you?"

"She needed to rest. We had to leave immediately and move quickly just to get here. We only arrived yesterday as it was, and read it in the papers," Robin said. "I spent all evening finding that doctor. I was afraid he was my only witness."

"Did I help?" She questioned.

"Immensely," Robin sighed. "I thank you so very much."

"Why didn't he call his sisters to the stand? They were ready," Elizabeth said.

"Chivalry. Last straw only. He did not want to make them confront the rest of their family," Robin said. "I suppose we are going to Adam's house?"

Adam and Zoey were taken to the mansion that now belonged to Adam, the home he grew up in, his father's house.

As they walked inside, Zoey looked up at the grand central stairway with the crystal chandelier. The stairs of polished oak wound around the entrance on both sides and scroll work on the banisters glimmered with gold leaf. Standing on the marble floor, she pressed closer to Adam.

Adam slid his arms, both of them, around his wife and he kissed her mouth in front of everyone.

The butler, Mr. Hobson, held out his hand for Adam's top hat. "Welcome to your home, Mr. Hudson. May I take your hat, sir? And from where do we bring your belongings?"

Adam removed the hat and handed it to him. "Here is my hotel room key. Also arrange for Robin Van der Kellen's things to be brought here. He's in the next room. He will have his key in his briefcase. He must be right behind us."

Lena asked, "What now will you do with this house, my son, now that it and everything in it, belongs to you?"

All of the staff began lining up in the hallway, looking at the family, looking at the young couple. All of them were older than their new master.

"Mother, this house will always be yours. You needn't worry about anything. You and my sisters will never want for anything. And my wife Zoey will never work again. And I will never go hungry again." Adam reached out to take his mother's hand.

Zoey turned to look at Lena.

Lena held her son's hand and took Zoey's hand into hers. "My son and his wife are home. Let us welcome them."

"Ahm. Everyone, my wife is Dutch. She is just learning to speak English so please be patient with her. I am hurrying to learn Dutch. We have only been married for two months. Ik hou van jou, Zoey." Adam made eye contact with each of the staff, finally resting his eyes and a warm smile on his wife.

"Adam, I love you," Zoey responded.

"Welcome to your home, Mr. and Mrs. Hudson." The butler, Mr. Hobson said. "May I introduce your staff."

Adam looked down the line of maids, cooks, bakers, drivers....

"They're here," a sister announced.

The other carriage was at the curb out front.

Zoey let Adam hurry to the door while she did not release her mother-in-law's hand.

Robin Van der Kellen stepped down from the carriage and looked up at a magnificent marble mansion. Down the road, he could see the Miller's corner mansion. He held up a hand for Elizabeth.

She took his hand, searching below for the step to slip her satin bootie into. She held up her skirt with the other hand, revealing white lace beneath the black fabric. Her tiny boot slipped a bit on the step, the heel catching. Robin quickly offered his other hand that caught her other arm. She landed steadily on both feet, not wanting to release Robin's firm hand. "Will I be welcome here?"

"Of course, you will. You nailed credibility to his runaway story." Robin looked up at three floors of stained-glass windows and balconies of glimmering bronze. He turned away from her. "Bit of a shack really. I don't know if it was worth it."

Elizabeth burst out laughing. She held up her skirts to begin climbing stairs to the front entrance. "Missed that sense of humor so much. I haven't laughed in months. You haven't changed a bit, Robin. I've become an old widow."

"Any comment I should make would be inappropriate."

The doors opened and Adam stepped out. He first pulled Robin into his arms. After a hard hug, Robin passed into the house and then Adam pulled Elizabeth into his arms. "Welcome Mrs. Miller. And I thank you for being so bold."

"I'm usually reprimanded for that," she admitted into his shoulder, surprised.

In the entryway, beneath the grand spiral stairway, there were introductions and handshakes.

The elegant barrister Van der Kellen gave a bow to everyone. "It has been my pleasure to be in the service of Mr. Hudson today. I return him to your care, in his lovely home."

The staff applauded. Elizabeth joined in the applause, then the sisters and their husbands.

All eyes went to Adam, the new young master. To them he was a youthful, elegant and mysterious young man.

Adam recognized that he must say something. He looked at Robin across the foyer. "I...owe my most sincere gratitude to Robin Van der Kellen, not just for his expertise in the courtroom today, but for a year of guidance, enlightenment, and friendship. You are the greatest lawyer I have ever known. You are a war hero. You are the finest gentleman I know. All these things, widely known. You are the best friend a man could have."

Robin nodded graciously to him. "A fine toast, Mr. Hudson. Should have saved it for dinner."

That broke everyone up laughing.

"I wish I had," Adam admitted. "I also owe a debt of gratitude to Mrs. Miller. I thank you for your brave testimony today."

"My pleasure, Mr. Hudson," she said.

"I guess you won't be expecting invitations from the Rothschilds' anymore," Adam said to Elizabeth with a smirk. "Neither will I."

"I couldn't care less. They threw a little boy out into the street," Elizabeth said. "I'm so sorry, Adam. Forgive me, I am speaking about your family."

"They are family no longer," Lena said. "Please stay for dinner, Mrs. Miller and Mr. Van der Kellen."

The two widows joined hands.

"I would be delighted. I do hope I am not imposing," Elizabeth said.

"You helped my son in court. Of course, you are not imposing. Is it not time to end your period of mourning? You have lost your husband almost a year now."

"It is hard to find a way to the end. I believe Mr. Van der Kellen did not end his period of mourning until he met Marie. I do miss her so," Elizabeth said. "Are they well? I do hope to go visit Marie soon."

"I know Marie would love it if I was to bring you home with me. Frida is starting to crawl," Robin told her. Then he smiled. "She's the most wonderful thing. It is the most wonderful thing to have a daughter."

"Yes, it is," Lena agreed. She moved on to grab hands with Van der Kellen. "But it is a son who may inherit, not a wife or daughter. Thank you for everything you have done for my son. I know it includes far more than what you have done today. He's written so much about you that I feel I know you. Though his description of how handsome you are hardly did you justice."

Robin blushed and smiled. "I see where Adam's blue eyes come from, and his charm."

"Do come and be seated." Lena directed them to the dining room.

"Just a moment." Elizabeth reached for Zoey's hand. "I have a wedding gift for you. It belonged to my husband's mother. I wish you to have it. Please."

Zoey looked down and Elizabeth removed a ruby and diamond ring from her own hand. Zoey tried to refuse it.

Mrs. Miller kindly closed Zoey's hand around it. "Please keep this, Zoey, as a token of my wishes for your marriage. I have come to learn how important kindness really is, now that I've had so little of it. Adam, your wife is a beautiful little Dutch girl. She adores you. I can see."

"It's all right, darling." Adam encouraged her. He stepped closer to her until her back was against his chest. He looked down at Zoey putting the ring on her right hand. "Zoey was the only kindness and affection I knew in seven years, except for the Van der Kellens," Adam said. "No offence. You did take me in, give me work and sent me to school. I am grateful for those. Do not misunderstand."

"Loss has opened my eyes," Elizabeth said. "I never had even a conversation with you, in all those years. It is I who have missed out. You were very brave today."

The household staff still lined the hallway between the entry to the dining room.

Lena turned to see all of them and took her son's hand. "Everyone, welcome back to his home, my son Adam and his wife Zoey."

They bowed and curtseyed to their new master. Lena re-introduced Adam to the same butler who was always there, Hobson. Then she introduced his new valet, a man twice his age. Then she moved him down the line to the chef, the cooks, the maids, and finally the drivers and horsemen.

Adam was a bit stunned, taking this all in.

"Let us show Mr. Van der Kellen and Mrs. Miller to the dining room," Lena said.

They took their places at the dining table. Four more place settings had been added, as Adam and his wife were just as unexpected as Elizabeth and Van der Kellen. For the first time, Adam sat at the head of the table. His wife and mother sat on either side of him. Robin was seated beside Lena and Elizabeth beside Zoey. Adam's sisters and their husbands rounded out the table.

"Will you be returning to Canterbury soon, Robin?" Elizabeth asked.

"Soon," Robin agreed. "As I have not been home except for a few hours in the past several months."

"You have no need to work anymore, Adam. Will you ever return to Canterbury with Robin?" Elizabeth said. "You can go anywhere in the world now."

"I have so much to settle here before I make any decisions. The factories need oversight as well," Adam said. "Mrs. Miller, you must be prepared if you do go to visit them in Canterbury, just how rustic his farm is. His mansion is only half built. The farmhouse is...well I don't believe you've ever seen a farmhouse such as his."

"If it is good enough for Robin Van der Kellen, it should suit me very well," Elizabeth said, looking at the handsome lawyer across from her.

"With winter coming, I should think you would stay here to look after your mother. I can get back to Marie myself," Robin said. "It's all right, Adam."

"If you say so," Adam said. "I never saw such a place until I was there at Robin's. He has the largest hay farm around, many cultivated acres and woods along a fine river. However, the countryside has no gas lights, no cobblestones, only the chorus of coyotes and crickets in the night."

"Yet you smile as you describe it. You long to return," Lena said. "You never saw the country before. The green must be wonderful, like the fields of Tuscany, your homeland."

"There is peace there in the country. Quiet. And a pace so slow that life has time to be savored," Adam said. "The butterflies on roses. The sound of the brook as it flows over the rocks. Dragonflies on the hay."

"You are a poet, indeed, Adam," Robin said.

"You were in Amsterdam. What was it like, Adam?" his sister asked.

"It was wonderful. A city of canals and windmills," Adam said. "The people are so kind to a stranger from abroad. They fill your hands with tulips, your stomach with herring. If you can stand herring, that is."

"I must say, I have not had such delicacies of Tuscany in fifteen years," Robin said. "The panzaella is excellent and the pomodoro the most amazing I have ever had. The crostini, I cannot describe. Is it truffles?"

"Ah, have you been to Italy, Mr. Van der Kellen? How are you so familiar with my favorite dishes?" Lena questioned.

"I have been to Italy but not in a domestic capacity," Robin said. "I was on foot, actually, leading my men from the Dutch cavalry up from Sicily. We were bound for Germany and made our way north by whatever humble means we found. And in our uniforms, we were taken into simple homes where we were doted on like royalty."

"Ti e piaciuto il pasto?" Len asked.

"Si molto," Robin said.

Adam's mouth fell open. "Is that five languages you speak?"

"No. No of course not. I only picked up a few words in Italian." Then Robin smiled. "Most that I learned got my face slapped by very lovely Italian young maidens."

The gathering laughed at his stories yet again.

"Did you know what you were saying to them?" One of the brothers-in-law asked.

Robin smirked with such deviltry, recalling his younger self. "Oh yes, indeed."

"And still you said this?" Elizabeth asked, riveted. "Do you remember what it was?"

Robin laughed. "Oh, I shall not repeat it tonight. I've been slapped enough for admiring particular feminine features. Better to admire and keep to myself."

"I'd imagine he's charming enough to get away with it. I question their sanity in that slapping," Lena remarked.

"Not if you knew what my younger self would say," Robin countered. "And all just to prove to my soldiers that I could get the attention of the ladies."

"A bag over your head and you'd still get their attention," Adam said to much laughter.

Adam walked Elizabeth to the door after dinner. "I'd imagine you were curious about me. Now you've seen what I inherited and where I came from, what I gave up for the sake of peace and my own identity you must wonder why I was able to walk away from this."

"I'll wonder about that later. Right now, I am just happy for you and your wife." Elizabeth looked up into Adam's blue eyes. "I'll be posting a letter to Marie. I miss her so. And I long to see Frida. You must ask Robin if I may use his escort to go visit them."

"That will please her. She misses you, I know," Adam said.

"I fear I would not be welcome in their home," Elizabeth said.

"Don't be so certain. I've never known anyone with bigger hearts than Robin and Marie," Adam said. "No one hates you, Elizabeth. Everyone finds Robin beautiful, all around the world. You can't help that you were one of us."

Beth smiled a little. "I envy the happiness Marie found with Robin, and the happiness you have with Zoey."

"You are free to seek your own happiness now," Adam told her. "Thank you for standing up for me today. I've been wrong about you."

"No, you haven't. I was cruel to you. I yelled at you endlessly. The truth is I was jealous of how well you got along with all the maids. I could hear you laughing in another room with them. All these girls and then you. And they hated me. I don't believe I ever thanked you for anything that you did. Ever. And you worked tirelessly, mending and ironing, and looking after my Edward. And here, all along, all you had to do was walk down the street and return to your status," Elizabeth said. "As a gentleman."

"And a father who beat me such that I had to crawl down these front steps, just because I loved a boy once. And don't get me wrong. I love Robin Van der Kellen. But I love Zoey like no one else in my life. Someone who is mine, just for me, and for me to look after."

Elizabeth patted him on the arm. "Goodbye, Adam. Please Ask Robin if he will be my escort, and only that. Wouldn't the world be a finer place if everyone loved as much as you?" Then she touched his cheek. "Congratulations, Mr. Hudson."

"Good night, Mrs. Miller. Hobson, my butler will walk you home."

Lena took Adam into her arms once again. "Adam, your father's room is yours. Everything has been removed from it. Your things have been brought in from the hotel and established into that room. It is not his mattress but a new one."

"Your room will always be yours. Are you sure you wouldn't rather I had my old room for now?" Adam said.

"Your room is my sewing room now."

Adam pulled back to look at her. And then he laughed. "I see where I get it from. Sewing. I'm pretty good at it except that stabbing myself in the finger is what brought me and Zoey together. She bandaged me."

"I've missed you so. And look at you now, such a handsome and tall young man. I was so proud of you in that courtroom. So proud of you." She looked up at him and touched his dark curls and his cheek.

"Get some rest now, Mother. This has been a terrible ordeal for you, and it is over now. I will take care of everything."

"Good night, darling." Lena kissed her son on the forehead when he leaned it down to her. "I love you so."

He kissed her on the cheek. "I love you, mother."

Adam returned to the parlor where he found Robin pouring himself another drink and enchanting the family with tales of India. The brothers-in-law were drinking and asking questions. Adam's sisters were blushing and entranced. Adam went straight to Robin.

Van der Kellen set a hand on Adam's shoulder. "And here he is, the finest legal assistant I ever had."

"The butler got our things from the hotel already," Adam said. "You're in the room beside mine upstairs."

"Oh? Hey, let me...." Robin reached for his pocketbook.

Adam stopped his hand. "I've got this. You don't have to do a thing. Except I am afraid to see you leaving soon."

"Adam. Adam. Adam." Robin held onto him. "Please forgive me. I need to get so very drunk tonight. I may oversleep in the morning."

Adam laughed. "You go right ahead. You're safe here. You saved me. You got all of us to America. You go right ahead. The butler and I will get you upstairs to bed."

Robin drank his aged Italian brandy. "To my lovely wife. May she never hear how exquisitely I sample the array of fine spirits on display in this household. Particularly the grappa invecchiata."

"You are speaking Italian now." Adam gestured toward the sofa for him and told the maid, "Keep him supplied, if you would please."

"Yes, sir."

"Gentlemen, drink with him, if you will. He's a war hero. He's a marksman so famous, the Dutch king asked to see a demonstration of his talent. Shall I tell you about that? Let's tell that story."

Adam entered what was his father's room in the home, the largest room on the upper floor, a corner room with two walls of windows and an enormous marble fireplace burning bright. Zoey got up from the sofa at the foot of the bed and took Adam into her arms.

"Can you sleep in here?" Zoey whispered. It was a room larger than the entire home she grew up in. The room had a seating area around the fireplace, a desk area, a window seat, a platform bed with canopy above it, and a balcony.

"I don't know." It was only then that he shuddered and wept.

Zoey spoke to him in Dutch, and he understood most of it, "You were so strong all day. And you were amazing in court. You won back your rightful life. And I would have you know, I loved you just as much when you were a valet. We made Robin's bed together. We ironed his sheets together before we put them on. You pricked your finger with your sewing of his buttons. And we touched hands for the first time. I do not understand everything that happened today. But I am yours."

She unbuckled his shoes and removed them. She removed his stockings. She stood up in her bed gown and held out a hand.

Adam took her hand and stood up. She helped him undress. And with the fireplace blazing, the room was warm.

Zoey folded back the bedding and Adam sat down on the bed in his underclothes. Zoey leaned to kiss his mouth.

"Are you home?" Zoey asked in English.

"This place frightens me," Adam said. "Ik ben ban hier. Home is Canterbury."

Zoey nodded. "But you love your mother and sisters."

"Yes."

"Then look after them. And I will look after you."

Adam wrote letters in the morning, one to Marie, and one to his cousin Erika, inviting her to visit soon.

Van der Kellen slept late, sleeping off quite a lot of brandy and Italian spirits.

The reading of the will followed breakfast. Adam inherited two hundred thousand dollars of his father's fortune, his mansion in New York, and ownership of factories Adam did not even know the family owned. They would promise continued income. He also had charge of ten employees there in the home, whom he assured would all continue to have employment.

Adam signed papers designating a trust for each of his sisters, and another to provide for his mother and to run the household.

Then he surprised everyone.

"I would see my factories. What do we make? Are the workers well compensated? Are they treated well?" Adam said. "Look after Zoey today and take me to see my factories."

The attorney who worked for his father rose from the table to walk around closer to Adam. "I will take you. Your father put managers in place who will carry on the work far into the future, the way your father wanted them run. Do not make sudden changes to what you know nothing about. With respect."

"With respect," Adam responded. "You do not know me. You know nothing of what I know about. Now, get my carriage and bring me to see my factories. And be sure to post my letters immediately."

Dearest Marie,

I long to visit you at your earliest convenience. Please send word that I may come. The city is quite lonely since you left and without my Edward. I long to see and hug your lovely baby Frida.

It was my honor to speak up for Mr. Hudson in a courtroom yesterday. I would have you be very proud of him. I met his lovely wife Zoey and dined with his family that evening. Robin was magnificent in court.

The trial itself was ugly. Adam's uncle called him an imposter, a deviant. Adam's aunt and cousins signed papers that this was not the heir. Adam presented his papers, even found the doctor who brought him into the world to verify his birth certificate. With incredible chivalry, Adam would not ask his sisters to stand up for him. And just when the trial was starting to turn against him, his mother walked in, took him into her arms, and yelled at the uncle that this was her son.

Adam's uncle Gerard was good friends with Edward. I am actually surprised he was not one of the bankers who came to dine with you that evening at my home. I knew Gerard and Sonya, his wife. I knew their son and daughter, Adam's cousins. I had even met Adam's sisters at a party once. They never mentioned a younger brother Adam. So, I had no idea who he was until I saw it in the papers. Please find the news clippings I have included.

"Rothschild Fortune Contested by Adam Hudson, Claiming to be Long Lost Heir."

"Adam Hudson Wins his Court Case and his Fortune."

"Van der Kellen, Famous Lawyer, Wins Fortune for Valet".

I dined with Adam and his family in their home. He seems to have grown up into a fine young man. Modeled after Robin, no doubt.

I am hoping Robin will not mind escorting me to visit you. Please trust me. Trust me to travel with your husband. I would never do anything to come between you. I only wish to see you and I fear traveling alone. Please advise me on what you wish me to do.

Your dearest friend in New York,

Love,

Elizabeth

Robin was not seen until lunchtime, and the only one home to dine with was Lena, who invited him to sit with her.

"Adam has gone to visit his factories. Zoey has been taken by my daughters for diversion to the theater for the afternoon. Everyone is due home for dinner, however. Please join me, Mr. Van der Kellen."

"Please do call me Robin, Mrs. Rothschild," Robin said.

"Then you must call me Lena. I cannot thank you enough for everything you have done for Adam. You have clearly inspired him and given him the means to become a fine young man. I would like to take credit for it, but as I have not seen him in seven years, it has hardly anything to do with me," Lena said.

"Adam is so intelligent. He can easily become anything he wants to be. He just needed the confidence, and he grew that over time," Robin said. "His upbringing as a young gentleman was there from the start."

"Was he very unhappy in the Miller's home, when you met him?" She asked.

"He had vastly outgrown their use for him in that home, I would say. He was a great valet, which is true. But in Amsterdam, his work as my legal assistant just blossomed out of nowhere," Robin said. "Suddenly he was able to find an address, get around on the canals, find someone who could speak English, and take on any task I gave him. He was the liaison between a detective and myself for the case."

"But something dark happened to him there. I sense this. He will not say what it was."

Robin nodded. "He will, in time. We were in quite a lot of danger toward the end of the case."

"It seems to me this is something he may not ever tell his mother. You must tell me." Lena gave lengthy eye contact to Robin across the table. "What happened that changed my son."

Robin set down his coffee. "The two men who had set my brother-in-law up for banking fraud, surprised us at my brother's house. Adam had to shoot one man and then fought over a pistol with another. He and I both shot that one. The bottom line is, Adam shot and killed two men, one of them a British Commander. It frightened Zoey away from him for a little while. But Adam's actions helped my brother to get upstairs to his wife having a baby. My wife had to deliver it by herself. Adam saved his own life and mine too. It haunts him at night sometimes."

"And the other change in my son? Surely you must know that one," Lena said. "The way he wrote about you, and seeing you now, he must have been... I understand why he followed you away. How is it that he married Zoey?"

"She can't take her eyes off of him." Robin smiled warmly. "She was a maid in my brother's house. She didn't speak a word of English. She was kind and affectionate to him. And he fell head over heels."

Lena smiled. "She is a lovely girl. Is she all right, being taken so far from her family?"

"Yes. She only has one married sister. Her parents had died. She really wasn't leaving many ties there. She wanted to come to America."

"You were certain of this marriage?" Lena asked.

"They had to be married," Robin said with a smirk.

"Oh? Oh." Lena finally laughed. "Well at least I don't have to worry they are only friends."

"No. I think you have to worry about grandchildren."

"Mr. Van der Kellen. Do please come in. Have you had lunch, sir?"

"Yes. I have. Thank you. Is Mrs. Miller at home?" Robin entered, removing his hat.

"Yes. Yes. Come right this way. You know the way to the parlor. I will send for her," Jonas, the butler at the Miller's said.

Robin entered the parlor where he'd once been helped to the sofa by Adam and Jonas following release from the hospital. He strolled to that very sofa, not feeling the pain of surgery or of being shot in the right upper chest. He held his silk top hat in his hands and strolled between the sofa and the table and he looked at the empty chair where Edward Miller had sat. The absence of his friend weighed heavily.

With light footsteps approaching, he turned to look.

Elizabeth paused there, dressed in plain black gown. Her blonde hair was up in a simple bun. "Robin, do please have a seat." She entered the room. "You have come in person to decline my request."

"Not at all. I have come to accept, actually. I did receive your letter this morning."

Elizabeth sat in that chair where Edward usually received guests.

Finally, Robin sat across from her on the sofa. He laid his hat on the cushion beside him. "I was hoping to persuade you not to travel with an entourage. I have a very simple home, but my maids can accommodate your needs, if you could travel independently."

"Oh? How kind of you to prepare me. Yes, I can travel independently. I do not wish to be an inconvenience in your home by bringing too many people with me," Elizabeth said.

Robin, mindful that Jonas was probably listening from the hall, said, "I apologize, Elizabeth. I have seem to have lost my valet and butler. I do have three maids and they also do the cooking. Oh, I should explain that the meals may be more simple in comparison to those you will find in the city. But you will be comfortable and cared for. I will see you safely there to visit with Marie and we will figure out a way to return you here."

"I am not dissuaded by the simplicity of your home, Robin," Elizabeth said. "Thank you for your suggestion to leave these mourning gowns at home. I am having a new country wardrobe prepared for me, more simple gowns." She smiled modestly. "Even I need a transition from this to gleaming yellow silk. And I was informed that to travel looking so wealthy could be dangerous for a woman alone."

"I...I will accompany you," Robin said. "You will be safe."

"There is the matter of the return trip. Once I learn my way there with you, I'm certain I can return on my own a few weeks later," Elizabeth said. "That is if a few weeks visit is acceptable."

"It would be delightful," Robin said.

"Well, then, Jonas will pay you for my train ticket so that you can purchase them together," Elizabeth said. "Just send word for when I should be packed and ready. I'm thinking only one trunk should be enough for me. I won't be needing a formal ball gown wardrobe."

"Elizabeth." Robin stood up.

She stood up before him.

"May I speak plainly?" Robin said very quietly.

"You have nothing to worry about, traveling with me," she whispered. "I can assure you. Marie is always beside you in my eyes."

Robin lowered his chin. He wet his lips. "I will have to explain to a number of people on the train, likely, that you are not my wife, but Edward's. There will be uncomfortable situations, if I do not."

"As it is the truth, our stories will match." Elizabeth forced a smile. "Jonas, are you there?"

Robin stepped back against the sofa.

"No. Ma'am. Of course not." Jonas appeared in the doorway.

That made Robin grin.

"Bring Robin a drink and the money for a train ticket, if you would?" Elizabeth said.

"Oh, I should be going. There is no need to pay me for your ticket. If you feel strongly about it, you may when I pick you up for the train station," Robin said.

"Perhaps it is best if we pick you up with one of our carriages?" Jonas offered. "No need to hire a coach."

"Oh, Adam's coach would have served us. Very well then. Wonderful," Robin said. "I will need to stay for a few days just to be sure Adam will not likely face an appeal. My thought would be to get tickets to leave on Friday morning. How would that be?"

"Wonderful," Elizabeth said.

"Very well then. I will send the travel details to you shortly." Robin picked up his hat. "I have business in town and will stop by the train station this afternoon."

"Can I offer you a carriage for your business then?" Jonas said.

"Thank you. I have one of Adam's. He had a Phaeton in his stables that I was dying to get my hands on," Robin said.

"Please express again to Adam how happy I am for him," Elizabeth said.

"I will. Thank you again for speaking on his behalf. Good day." Robin gave her a bit of a bow and exited toward the door before setting his hat on his brown locks.

Adam returned in a few hours and met Robin returning also with the Phaeton carriage.

"I wish I could think of some way to detain you, but I can't seem to come up with a thing. You will be leaving soon." Adam met him between the carriage house and the mansion. Adam's stablemen took care of Robin's horse and carriage.

"I will. Yes. I received a letter from Elizabeth already, and so went for train tickets. They are for Saturday morning," Robin admitted.

"Are you comfortable traveling alone with her?"

"I...don't think she would try anything now," Robin said. "Would Marie trust me?"

"Probably with anyone except Elizabeth, or Paula," Adam said. "She could bring a maid."

"Well, there's still the opportunity afforded by my cabin, even if there is a maid sharing hers," Robin said.

"Do you want to sleep with her?" Adam asked.

"No. She's Edward's wife," Robin shot back.

"Well, not anymore. She's perfectly free and available," Adam said.

"I wrote that she's not to bring any of those awful black gowns," Robin said. "Marie doesn't want to see her that way. She wants her to be happy again."

"A romp with you could certainly make her a new woman."

"No." Robin turned to look at him. "Wipe it from your mind."

"It's your mind traveling alone with a woman who once asked to have your child," Adam reminded. "She's desperately sad now, of course. But you're still a temptation to most creatures with a pulse."

"You're playing me," Robin said. "Tell me something, Adam. Something has been bothering me for some time. I'm putting a few things together that you have said. If you saw your father again you would kill him. When fighting with Collins, you pulled the trigger. When Jasper violated you, you beat him."

Adam turned to look at him. "What are you getting at? So I defend myself."

"I'm just fearing that Collins and the other man were not the first men you ever killed," Robin said.

Adam's mouth pursed and he shook his head. "Who do you mean?"

"What happened to Lucas?"

Adam dropped his hands and let out a gasp. "You think I killed someone I loved? No. I heard about it later. He was beaten to death by other boys, found dead behind his house. Lucas would not run away from home. He stayed when I left. He faced torment, derision. He became an outcast to society, all by the age of 16. He also faced my abandonment because I would not face it with him. It reaffirmed my decision to reinvent myself, into an identity where no one would ever look for me. An impoverished street urchin, all but invisible, and yet right beneath their eyes. But resilient."

Robin studied him. "And those night terrors were not because you killed Lucas first, in a heated break up?"

Adam bristled, staring at him furiously. He let out a breath and stepped back from Robin. "No. Of course not. How could you?"

Robin reached out to him. "Forgive me. Because of the war, I took that to the wrong turn. I'm sorry."

Adam withdrew from him. "Is this the way we will be parted?"

Robin looked at the gloves on his hands as he removed them. "No. I'm going to stay a few days to make sure nothing else is done to you here. I'm not sure if that's long enough. I think you're safe. I think you should spend the winter here. Look after your mother. Look after Zoey. If she should become with child, she's better off here."

Adam searched the cobblestones between them. "I feel like something has been spoiled. Friendship is just so hard."

Robin put a hand on his shoulder. "Adam, friendship is hard. That's what makes it good. And I am certain, our paths will cross again."

"My heart will break when you leave."

Robin glanced up at the windows of the mansion surrounding them. He kept Adam at arm's length. "You don't need me any longer."

Adam winced, looking him in the eyes. He folded his arms.

"I can't give you what you want, Adam. I am sorry," Robin said softly.

"I know."

Along with his laundry, Robin had found the suits he'd given to Adam folded on his bed. He picked them up and carried them down the hall to knock on Adam's door.

"Yes?" Adam opened the door. "Robin."

"You're returning these? I thought you let the trousers down a turn," Robin said. "You don't wish to keep them?"

"I...I do want to keep them, but I thought maybe you wanted them back. I bought so many new suits myself. You only meant to loan them to me for the palace," Adam said.

"I bought all new things in Amsterdam, and in London. I don't need them back," Robin said.

"Really?" Adam brightened. His fingertips landed on the suits in Robin's hands.

"Keep them." Robin held them out to him.

Adam's hands eagerly accepted the two suits. "I would love to. I wouldn't have made it through the trial without your vest. For luck, you know? Come in. I was hoping to talk to you before you go tomorrow."

Robin followed Adam into the bedroom, looking about at the seating area by the fireplace and the fine French furniture. "How did you feel moving into this room?"

"Awful. I'm getting rid of all this. I don't know what style of furniture I want but it won't be this. I remember these chairs and wardrobes all too well. So, Zoey and I will go shopping for all new things next week," Adam said. "How did you manage to move into your father's room?"

"Brought my own bed with me from Boston," Robin said.

"Good thinking." Adam took a seat by the fireplace and watched Robin sit down across from him. Adam crossed his legs and just looked at him for a moment, memorizing every detail.

Robin felt examined. "You still have money in the Norwich bank."

"I know. I will have to get it next time I'm out to visit you. You know how much I want to see your new horses." Adam forced a bit of a smirk.

Robin laughed. "Right. There is so much you can do now, with your fortune. You can do the grand tour. You can travel the world. You can buy for Zoey anything she wants. What do you think you will do?"

"If none of this had happened, I would have gone to law school. And I would have done well. But I would have done it to be a partner with you, not for the reasons one should become an advocate, to help people."

"Well, even I went to law school to earn a living," Robin said.

Adam nodded. "And to suit your vanity, at the time."

Robin smiled and nodded. "And now as well."

Adam smiled warmly. "I am planning to turn a room in this house into an art studio. I'm going to take painting lessons. I want to have my paintings in galleries, maybe here and Boston and in Europe."

Robin smiled. "Wonderful. I'm sure you will. If you can paint anything like the way you draw, you will have your work in galleries. You make sure I know when that will be, and I will be there."

"You'll tell Marie how much I will miss her?" Adam asked.

"Of course," Robin said. "You know, you are going to be all right. You'll have fun with Zoey and your house, your carriages, your new clothing."

"I'm going to give money to an orphanage and start up a home for the poor," Adam said.

"Wonderful plan, Mr. Hudson. Don't give it all away."

"You know, those factories bring me another fifty thousand a year. I couldn't possibly spend that much in a year," Adam said.

"Get a very good accountant and a financial attorney of your own. I know your father had people, but make certain nobody is stealing off the top from you. Get someone who is handling it for Elizabeth. I know Edward set her up with the right kind of people."

"That's a good idea. I will do that." Adam looked at Robin at length. "Are you certain you want a big home like this? I will always picture you with Marie in the kitchen of the farmhouse that brought you together. I'm glad I got to live there as one of you, if only for a short time."

"Adam, I was misleading about leaving tomorrow. I am leaving today. Elizabeth's carriage is coming for me in about an hour. I thought it would be easier for you if it was not prolonged," Robin said.

"Oh? Does Zoey know?" The color drained from Adam's face.

"Yes. That's why she went downstairs already," Robin said. "My bags are down at the door."

Adam's eyes welled and he lowered them down to Robin's boots. "Well, I...suppose I must thank you for coming to my rescue, again. You will have safe travels, I trust."

Robin reached forward and laid a hand on Adam's forearm. "You are going to be just fine here."

Adam looked down at that hand and nodded, biting his lower lip. "What is the going rate for an inheritance case?"

"Feed me and we'll call it even."

That made Adam smile painfully. "Of course. And you still owe me a dollar."

Robin pulled Adam up into an embrace like a brother and when they stepped back to separate, Robin kissed him on both cheeks. "There. Like a long-lost Dutch friend."

Adam brightened considerably.

"Hold it together in front of your staff," Robin told him.

"All those times you were telling me to build a cottage or buy the place next door, you were trying to prepare me for this moment. I wish I could read between the lines. Where my heart is concerned, I never could."

"Always the poet, Mr. Hudson."

"Always the Dutchman to me, Robin Van der Kellen."

Made in the USA
Middletown, DE
20 March 2024

51827824R00274